I0720975

RUNNING WITH THE ALPHA'S SON

Penny Jessup

Tiny Ghost Press

Copyright © 2025 Tiny Ghost Press

www.tinyghostpress.com

All rights reserved

The characters and events portrayed in this book are fictitious. Any similarity to real persons, living or dead, is coincidental and not intended by the author.

No part of this book may be reproduced, or stored in a retrieval system, or transmitted in any form or by any means, electronic, mechanical, photocopying, recording, or otherwise, without express written permission of the publisher.

ISBN:
E-book 978-1-915585-26-4
Paperback 978-1-915585-27-1
Hardcover 978-1-915585-28-8

Cover Art by: Kayleigh Fine
Title Font: Paula Painmar

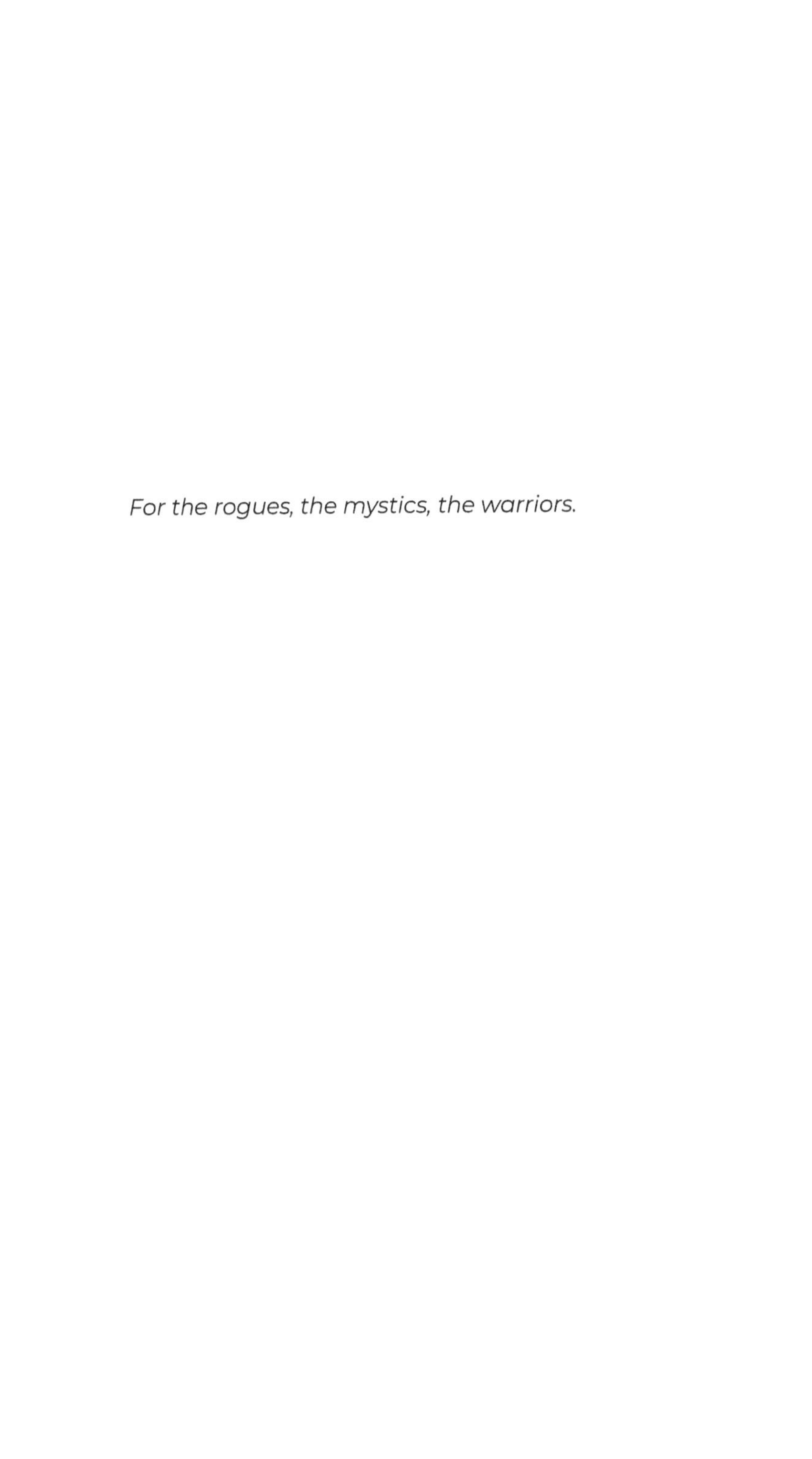

For the rogues, the mystics, the warriors.

A HOWL AT NIGHT

"Max, you okay?" Jasper asks.

"Huh?"

I pull my eyes from the dash and look around. We're in his car, idling by the curb out front of my house. I hadn't noticed we'd arrived. To be fair though, I've been pretty out of it since we left the packhouse.

"We're here already?" I ask.

Jasper narrows his eyes, leans a little over the central console. "Is everything okay?"

Let me think on that a minute... Jasper just announced in front of the who's who of the Elite Pack that we're mates. Even kissed me as the ball dropped welcoming in the new year to make his point. Sure, earlier in the evening, his former bestie Clayton tried to kill me—my back still scorches from the claw marks—and I tried walking away from Jasper for good. I'd just about given up on us being a couple, but with one gesture, albeit an impromptu one, everything has changed.

"I'm good," I say, the beginning of a smile creeping into my expression. "Great actually."

"Good."

He leans farther toward me, his eyes closing gently, his mouth open ever so slightly, and I lean in too to meet his kiss. One of Jasper's hands finds the back of my head and before I know it we're making out in his car. *Could this be more like a teen rom-com?! Is this for real?*

Jasper's free hand finds the side of my face and as it does a pain erupts in the front corner of my brain. Like an instant headache, only sharper, a targeted migraine attack. I wince and pull back.

"What's wrong? Are you hurt?" Jasper's eyes glisten with care.

I rub at my forehead as the sharp pain subsides to a dull throb.

"Headache," I say. "Probably just a little much for one night."

"You can say that again."

I glance at the house, to the dull light in the front window. "I should probably get going, my parents will be waiting up."

He places his hands on the steering wheel, like he's about to be pulled from the vehicle and needs something to hold on to.

"Y-you want to come in?"

He chews the inside of his cheek as his eyes roam the empty street. "Your parents are in there?"

"Yeah. They sort of live there."

Jasper's lips move like he's trying to form words but can't quite manage it. Is he...*scared?*

"It's okay," I say. "You don't have to."

"It's just, I think you're right about it being a lot for one night."

"Of course."

"Maybe another time?"

"For sure."

Jasper breathes a subtle sigh of relief but I catch it, just like I can spot the slight pinkish hue coloring his cheeks—

signs of intimidation that might be imperceptible to the average person but not to me, not to his mate. I can't believe stoic, princely, too-cool-for-wolf-school Jasper is nervous about meeting my unassuming folks. Now that's a surprise!

A totally endearing one.

To be fair I can imagine the deep-dive interrogation my parents have in store my mate, no matter who they are. And I wouldn't want to face that level of scrutiny. Maybe he's right to be frightened.

"When—when will I see you again?" I say, forcing myself to ask the tough questions.

"I go back to college in a week."

"Right and I go back to school next Monday."

"How about a date then, before school starts back up for both of us?"

"A date?"

Somehow the concept of going on an actual, real-life, bona fide dinner-and-a-movie date with Jasper is so foreign to me I can't quite imagine what it would be like. Where would we even go? Bowling? A concert? Would we hold hands in public? Get ice cream? Order one milkshake with two straws? I just can't picture Jasper wanting to do any of those things. As much as I've wanted this, somehow I have no idea what dating Jasper will be like. But I sure as hell want to find out.

"That sounds great."

"Are you free Saturday night?"

A niggling thought in the back of my brain tells me I had a vague plan to see Katie on Saturday, but with how she was acting at the New Year's party, I don't see why I need to be precious about keeping that date.

"I can be."

"Great. I'll pick you up around seven."

Oh, moon gods, he's making me breathless. "Okay."

"Okay."

My hand lingers on the door handle but for whatever reason I can't open the door.

"You sure you're okay?" Jasper asks.

"Mm-hmm."

"Good night."

"Good—" Jasper doesn't even let me finish before he plants another full-bodied kiss on my lips.

I can still taste cherry as I exit the car and head up the drive. Jasper waits until I'm at the door, making sure I get home safely, even though we are in the middle of suburbia and nothing bad ever happens here. I slip my keys in the door and give him an awkward little wave. He nods, satisfied that I managed the dangerous trek to my house without dying, and drives off.

Once inside, I lean back on the closed door, breathing deeply, one hand clutching my chest to stop it exploding from joy-fueled adrenaline. My smile is irrepressible.

It's been a stupidly mega evening, packed with stress and terror and so much drama. But for now the drama has ended, everything has turned out amazingly, because Jasper chose me. He chased me down and proved he wants to be with me. And now we're together. Jasper and I are officially—for all the world to see—a couple.

"Is that you, kiddo?" Mom calls from the living room.

Maybe not *all the world* just yet. I take one more breath, savoring this little moment of triumph, before heading through to see my parents.

"Hi," I say, hovering in the arched doorway, not wanting to get too close.

They're watching TV, bathed in dim lamplight and the cool glow of the screen. I remembered to collect my puffer jacket before I left this time, which means the slash marks on my back are well-enough hidden, but still I hover at the edge of the room. They're capable of scenting my trauma from a mile off. No reason to give Mom and Dad a reason to worry—at least, not tonight, not when I'm riding this Jasper-high.

"Good night?" Dad asks.

"It was pretty epic," I say.

"Looks like you had a nice time." Mom eyes my untucked shirt, my loose collar and absent bow tie, my messed-up hair. "No kidnapping this time?"

"No, no kidnapping. Bit of a rocky start but it turned out great."

"You hungry?" Dad asks.

"No, just tired. I might head to bed."

"Okay, kiddo," Mom says, clearly fighting the urge to pry for more information. "Sleep well."

"Night, Max." Dad is already unpausing the TV.

"Good night."

Once up in my room I pull off my shredded button-down and shove it into the back of my closet, reminding myself to take it out to the trash tomorrow before my parents can see it. I think about messaging Jasper but don't want to come off as too clingy or obsessed—*play it cool, Max*—so instead I head for the shower, wanting to make sure the already-healing wounds on my back are clean and any residual blood is gone.

When I'm washed and ready for bed, I slip my aching limbs under the covers, finally feeling the weight of the night's events settling into my bones and muscles, and glance at my phone to find a text from Jasper waiting.

Thank you for tonight. Have a good sleep. See you soon. Xxx

I begin crafting a reply but before I can hit Send my eyes are already closing. Exhaustion overcomes my body and I slip into sleep, dropping my phone on the comforter.

I'm standing on the roof of the packhouse, over a hundred stories in the air. Above me clouds roll and tumble, lightning splitting the sky and casting my attacker's face half in light, half in shadow.

Clayton has his paws on me, his claws digging into my chest, his jaws snapping, slick with glistening saliva, and crowded with razor-sharp teeth. My back is bending unnaturally over the balustrade as I fight to stay upright. Below, traffic whirs past in strips of gold and red light. The pedestrians are a crowd of black dots hustling to and fro—all unaware that I'm under attack.

I thrash and fight but it's no use against Clayton's immense strength. I have to do something or Clayton will surely kill me, push me over the edge and send me tumbling. As I stare into his black eyes I realize I do have strength, a power neither Clayton nor any other wolf has.

With my eyes closed, I relax my body and open my mind.

Like a spider's web the strands of my consciousness reach out, a net of squiggly and swirling red veins, curling and twisting in all directions. I search the strands for Clayton's, and find it in the darkness, rotten and deteriorating, falling apart like a diseased root. Just as I'm about to follow the thread into Clayton's consciousness I feel something, a gentle tug on my consciousness, pulling my attention elsewhere.

I glance about, searching for the source of the distraction, but it's gone. The blood strands flicker and pulse, they shiver and quake, they reposition themselves. They're alive.

Again I feel the pull, only it's stronger this time. I spin to catch it, and stare into the inky blackness. It comes again like a pulse. I move toward it. The pull tugs over and over, rushing past me like waves, drawing me nearer with each surge. And then I realize not only can I feel it, I can hear it. The pulse has sound, and that sound is a howl.

The second I hear it, I'm torn from the vision—pulled back onto the roof. Only Clayton is gone, the shape of his wolf replaced by a human form.

Jasper.

His hair is a mess, his shirt untucked and unbuttoned. He stares at me with dark, vengeful eyes. His teeth are clenched, his brow slick with sweat. His hands are on my neck and I can't breathe.

"Killer," he rasps between clenched teeth.

With a grunt and groan, he hoists me over the side of the building, and I'm powerless to stop him.

The ground rushes at me as I fall, and I'm about to hit the sidewalk when...

"Maximilian!" I'm woken the next morning by Mom bellowing my name from downstairs. "Maximilian Xavier Remus! Get your butt down here!"

I sit up in bed, wincing as the skin on my back is pulled taught, tugging at my injuries which have scarred over in the night. My head is throbbing like I drank a whole beer keg, even though I didn't touch a drop, and images from my dream are swirling in my mind. *What was that? A howl? Why did I feel like it was calling to me? And what was with Jasper calling me a...killer?*

"I'm not joking, kiddo!"

Mom doesn't sound like she's messing around, so as fast as I can I jump out of bed, slip on a T-shirt from the pile on my floor, and run downstairs. I'm still wiping my bleary eyes when I find Mom and Dad waiting for me in the hall.

"What is it? What's wrong?"

Mom looks flustered and Dad is wearing gardening gloves, like he was pulled away from planting his spring bulbs to address whatever emergency is happening.

"I just received a text from Katie's mom, who received a text from her friend Stacy, who was texted by Kaitlin Thompson."

"Okaaaaaay," I say, shaking my head. "You got a text. It happens. What's so important?"

"Kaitlin was at the packhouse last night," Mom says, her eyes wild.

Oh. Oh no.

"Care to explain this?!"

Mom turns her phone so I can see it, thrusting it at me like I've murdered someone and she's found a crucial piece of incriminating evidence.

Lit up on my mom's phone screen, however, is not a bloody murder weapon or some chart showing a perfect DNA match, but a photo of me and Jasper onstage at the New Year's party, fireworks exploding in a rainbow curtain behind us while we kiss.

"Anything you'd like to tell us?" Mom asks.

My face crinkles in on itself as I shrug meekly.

"Surprise..."

BURNT CAKE AND RAMEN

"Hello?" I lean through Aisha's open door and glance into her apartment.

"Come on in, dude," she calls from the kitchen, where she's leaning over the open oven door, waving steam away with a tea towel. Or maybe that's smoke? I didn't know Aisha baked.

As I step inside, Troy emerges from the bedroom wearing gym clothes, with a duffel bag strapped over his shoulder. "Is that Max?"

"Hey Troy."

"What's up, bro? Happy New Year."

He holds out his hand to give me one of those complicated handshakes I've never been able to figure out. I copy him as best I can but end up sort of smooshing my hand against his until the inevitable fist bump brings the operation to a close.

"Sounds like you had quite the party," he says. "Aisha told me all about it."

"Yeah, it was definitely one for the books." I rub the back of my neck and can feel the tip of a scratch mark. My wounds have mostly healed in the three days since New Year's, but they were deep enough that they will probably leave a scar.

"Don't make him relive his trauma," Aisha says, coming to join us, holding what looks like a loaf of something cakey on a platter, only it's so blackened it might as well have been baked on the surface of the sun. "I made banana bread!"

I force a smile. "Looks...great!"

"Damn, I wish I could hang for a bit," Troy says. "But I was just on my way out. Great seeing you, man."

I think he's about to go for another handshake but instead he takes my hand and pulls me in for a cute one-handed hug. "I'm glad you're okay."

"Thanks, Troy."

"Hey, save me a slice of that...what did you say it was?"

Aisha deadpans, "Banana bread."

Troy eyes the burnt loaf suspiciously. "Yeah. Save me a piece of that for when I get back." He kisses Aisha on the cheek and heads for the door, grabbing his coat on his way out. "Have fun you two."

After the door shuts, Aisha holds up her loaf and smiles. "Want a slice?"

"It's delicious!" I say, forking another bite into my mouth. It's not a complete lie: with enough butter spread on top, and if I avoid the corners where the loaf is the most charred, it does actually taste like banana bread.

"It's burnt." Aisha drops her plate on the coffee table and flops back on the sofa.

"No, it's...yeah, it is. What's up?" I ask, sliding my unfinished slice onto the table as well and pulling a leg up so I can face Aisha properly.

"I've just been feeling weird since New Year's," she says, fiddling with the hem of her jeans.

I wish I didn't have any idea why Aisha might be feeling off since the whole Clayton-attack thing, but annoyingly I have a greater insight than I would like.

"Hey, I"—I gulp-swallow and press on—"I need to tell you something."

"What is it?"

"I think maybe I have an idea why you might be feeling kind of shitty."

"Why's that?"

"When Clayton had me pinned to the railing up on the roof I was pretty sure he was going to kill me and I needed to do something to stop him. And I realized with this whole blood-wolf-wolf connection thing I have now, I could maybe use that to my advantage. So I sort of went looking for something I could use to, like, hurt him back."

"Hold up." She shuffles a little closer. "What do you mean you went looking?"

"It's hard to explain. It's like I could feel his emotions, and those were linked to events—memories—and if I concentrated hard enough I could see those memories, like visions."

She lifts her brow, impressed. "You're not escaping those Professor X rumors."

"True. A-anyway, I saw one of Clayton's memories. You were in it."

Aisha's amused expression drops, replaced by a wall of neutrality. She shrugs and looks away. "And?"

"I saw him trying to...and you when you rejected him. I know you were mates once."

With a huff and a shake of her head, Aisha purses her lips and continues not to meet my eye.

"It wasn't like I went looking for that memory specifically, it's just what I found. And I don't mean to be intrusive. I know it's weird. I know it's super uncomfortable. That's why I wanted you to know what I saw. So it wasn't a secret."

Finally, she turns and places a hand on my leg. "It's fine, I'm not mad at you. It's him, it's always him. That's why I'm burning cakes and acting all weird. Because I hate feeling this way. After all this time and after rejecting him he still makes me flinch, y'know?"

"I get it."

She looks at me now with tears springing to her eyes. "I told people he was an ass. I told them he was no good. But he's so rich and powerful, so entrenched in the pack and all that, no one cared what I had to say."

I place my hand on top of hers. "I'm so sorry that happened."

"Thank you." Swiftly, she wipes a single tear from her cheek and sniffs back the rest. "That's why I don't hang out with the pack as much as I can—I'm still part of it, but that's why I love dancing and that's how I found Troy, because it's separate from all that."

"Yeah but you shouldn't have to be separate. You're as much a part of the pack as anyone. You deserve to feel welcomed."

She shrugs. "I wish it were that way too. But that's just not how things are."

We sit quietly for a moment. There isn't much else to say. It's wrong that Clayton got to stay in the inner circle—got to hold on to his status and feel like he owned the whole damn world while Aisha had to look elsewhere to feel like she belonged. It's so wrong, it doesn't warrant stating. So instead we sit quietly, knowing we're aligned but that there's nothing much we can do.

"Man, this is terrible," Aisha says finally, pushing the unfinished plate of banana bread farther away with her foot. "You want to go out and get something decent to eat?"

"For sure."

"So your parents were cool with you and Jasper being mates?"

"Mmm, I wouldn't say that."

Aisha and I are sitting in the back of a cozy noodle joint in her neighborhood, enjoying a couple of steaming ramen bowls.

"After the initial shock had worn off they were happy for me, I guess. But then the floodgates sort of opened. They were suddenly suspicious of everything that had happened since the Blue Moon Festival. Wanted all the details."

"And what did you tell them?"

"Pretty much everything."

She sucks a noodle into her mouth with a slurp. "Whoa."

"I guess I figured since there was no reason to hide anything they might as well know everything that's gone on."

"And?"

"Now they're freaked. As much as they're happy for me and Jasper, they're worried about my safety and about what my future looks like. Like if I'm mated to the alpha does that mean I have to give up everything I want in life."

"Fair point," she says.

I shrug and stir my cloudy miso broth. "Maybe. But I don't know why they're being so dramatic about it all. And that's coming from me."

"I'm sure they'll adjust in time."

I raise a brow. "Yeah, but now they want to meet him."

Aisha drops her chopsticks and laughs. "Oh no."

"They said I wasn't allowed to go on a date with him until they'd spoken to him. It's so cringey."

"And how does Jasper feel about that?"

Now it's my turn to drop my utensils. "I haven't told him yet."

She shoots me a look that says *You in trouble, girl.*

"You don't understand. I don't want to tell him by text but he's been traveling a lot on pack business, I guess doing damage control after the whole coming-out-to-the-pack thing, and he hasn't had a chance to call me back."

"Mm-hmm." Aisha isn't convinced.

"You think he's being a shitty boyfriend?"

"I think he should be able to find time in his busy schedule to call you. He made a big gesture, which is great, but he wasn't the only one on that stage. What he did affects you as well. He should call."

I lean back in my chair, suddenly having had enough noodles. "Maybe you're right. As far as I know we're still on for our date tomorrow night. If he doesn't call me back before then, well...I hope he likes surprises."

"Jasper?" She rolls her eyes and grins at me. "Oh, yeah he loves surprises."

Saturday night rolls around and Jasper still hasn't responded to my texts asking him to call me. No, it's not a great start. But I'm willing to give him the benefit of the doubt, for now. Maybe he's not a caller—that tracks. Maybe he's been traveling and has been in and out of cell service, across time zones, maybe he ran out of battery?

He did manage to send a text this morning:

I'm excited for tonight. Be there at 7. Be hungry. xxx

I still have no idea what we're doing on our date, but at seven I'm sitting in the living room drumming my fingers on my knees. His car pulls up outside bang on the hour and I can't help the jittery mix of nerves and excitement playing havoc with my nervous system.

It takes all my willpower, but I force myself to stay seated until I hear the doorbell ring.

I open the door to find Jasper looking ridiculously dashing in an expensive-seeming white roll-neck sweater and a black suit jacket. He's dressed like he's going to the Oscars, meanwhile I'm in a hoodie and jeans. There is, however, a hint of rosiness to his cheeks and an easy, relieved smile on his face.

"Hey," he says, almost breathless.

"Hi. You look...amazing."

"Thanks. You too. Ready?"

"You don't think I should change? I didn't know what we were doing, so..."

"No you're great. You look perfect." He takes my hand. "Let's go."

"Wait..." Here comes the surprise. "We can't go."

He furrows his brow in confusion. "Is something wrong?"

My face is heating up, I'm doing this all wrong. "No. Well? No. It's just I didn't want to tell you by text. Maybe you should come in."

Jasper's expression remains confused as I usher him into the house and shut the door behind him.

"Max, you're starting to worry me. What's going on?"

"I wanted you to call me back so I could tell you."

"I'm sorry, I couldn't. I'll explain in a bit but first, tell me what? Do you not want to go on our date anymore?"

"No, it's not that, I...I do. I very much do." I place my shaking hands on his shoulders, then take his hands. "It's just...we can't go anywhere until..."

"Until?"

"Until you've met my parents."

Jasper's mouth topples open and his confused expression becomes one of utter dread.

MEET THE PARENTS

"Jasper? You all right?"

We've been standing in the hall for a solid minute and Jasper hasn't said a word since I told him he had to meet my folks before we went on our date.

"Are…are they here now?"

"They just popped out to pick up their order of Thai food. They'll be home in a bit. But they said we had to wait so they could meet you before I'm allowed to go anywhere."

Jasper's shoulders relax and he exhales. "Okay." He closes his eyes like he's meditating, and when he opens them his expression is uberserious. "I'll meet them."

I smile. *What a champ.* "Great." For a moment we hover awkwardly. "We probably have a bit of time before they're back. Do you…want to see my room?"

A light flicks on at the back of Jasper's eyes. "I'd love to."

Doing my best to seem casual and not at all freaked about having a boy in my house or showing that boy to my room for the first time, I take Jasper's hand and lead him upstairs.

Outside my room, I stop and gesture for Jasper to go in ahead. He shoots me a sideways grin that makes my stomach do a little flip and then wanders slowly inside. I watch him as he takes in the space. I did, of course, clean up a little bit. The dirty clothes are in the hamper, the bedsheets are pulled up neatly. Jasper wanders in a small circle, slowly, like he's in a museum, taking in each detail. He runs a hand across the surface of my desk, still sort of messy, his fingers coming to rest on the edge of the sketchbook.

"It's a good room," he says, nodding approvingly. "Smells like you."

"Oh god." My face heats up and I dart my eyes to the floor. An errant dirty sock I must have missed during my cleaning spree is sticking out from under the bed. I snatch it up and toss it in the hamper, shutting the lid, unwilling to turn back around. Jasper is suddenly behind me, wrapping one hand gently around my waist.

"I love it," he says, breath hot against my neck. His lips find the curve of my shoulder and I melt under his kiss. He spins me around to face him and pulls me in close.

Moon gods, is this really happening? I'm making out with Jasper Apollo in my little Stony Point bedroom. My raggedy childhood wolf plushie, Mr. Bitey, is watching us from his spot on my dresser, my old retainer is in its box on the desk, and my bed is right there.

Jasper's kisses intensify. His lips and tongue taste like cherries, his hands are firm on my back, our chests are pressed together. For the first time, we're alone in a room with no more bullshit keeping us apart. We're here and we're together. There's nothing in our way.

Awkwardly, I take a step in the direction of the bed, and Jasper mirrors my movement. Without breaking apart, we maneuver like two penguins glued together, across the room, unable to stop ourselves from kissing. My toes bump against Jasper's feet as we stumble a little and then, finding the edge of my bedframe, tumble onto the mattress.

"Ouch," Jasper says, pulling away. I open my eyes to see him rubbing his head where he must have bumped it against the wall.

"Are you okay?"

He eyes me hungrily, grinning like a wolf about to chomp down on a lamb. "I'm great."

In a flash he's whipped off his jacket and is suddenly on top of me and we're making out again. His body is warm and solid, and I like the weight of it. His hand is on my thigh, which sends a shiver running through me. I slide my hands up his back, firm and taught under my touch.

I don't seem to be able to catch my breath but I don't mind. I feel like I could do this for eternity. My whole body is zinging, my skin a mess of tingles, my heart and lungs and stomach filled with golden light. My fingers are lost in Jasper's hair, his hand cups the side of my face like a pillow. My tongue catches on his slightly elongated fang and I enjoy the prick of it. Jasper's hand comes to rest on the waistband of my jeans, his fingertips sliding under the hem of my hoodie and finding skin, making me gasp. This is euphoria, this is everything, I never want this to end.

"Ahem."

We shoot apart at the sound of someone clearing their throat, and I turn, breathless, to find Mom standing in my doorway, an unimpressed expression playing on her face.

"Am I interrupting something?"

Awkward doesn't begin to cut it.

Jasper and I are sitting on the sofa in the living room like a couple of dogs who have been told to sit and stay. Dad is sitting in the armchair across from us and Mom is standing, one hand on her hip, the other on the back of

Dad's chair—both of them staring us down like a firing squad.

Seriously, I have been kidnapped, held at gunpoint, almost thrown off a roof by a psycho werewolf, and I would rather be reliving those moments than sitting on this couch right now.

Jasper has his palms flat on his knees, his back straight, his hair still a little ruffled from our aborted romantic moment upstairs. He's supposed to be the next leader of our pack, an alpha in training, our superior in every way, but I've never seen him look more like a bashful kid, scared after having been caught doing something he knows he shouldn't have. If I weren't about to wet myself as well I'd find it ridiculously adorable.

"Jasper," Mom says, her mouth a tight line. "It's nice to have finally met you—although I would maybe have preferred if you weren't horizontal at the time. But it's a pleasure. Max has told us, well, not much about you."

"It's a pleasure to meet you too," Jasper says, struggling with eye contact.

"So…" Dad says, fiddling with the armrest. "You must have had quite the upbringing."

"Yes, uh, sir." Jasper's voice is low and quiet, like he's struggling to get the words out. "It has been quite different, I think."

"Having the alpha for a father must be, well…I suppose *inspiring* is the right word."

Jasper shifts uncomfortably.

"My father is a great man—a great, er, leader."

Mom tilts her head to the side, questioningly. "And how does he feel about you being mated to our son?"

"Mom!" I jump in.

"He is in favor of our pairing," Jasper says.

That's one way to put it.

"The alpha is fine with us being together—he encouraged it."

"Well, how would we know that, Max?" Mom asks, just a little exasperated.

Before I can clap back, Jasper begins speaking. "My father is quite strict. He's not always been the easiest person to have as a father, he wasn't around so much and when he was he…" Jasper trails off and my parents glance at each other, sharing a quick look of concern. "My father is complicated, but for all his…complexities…he is wise, and he only wants the best for the pack, for me."

"It must have been difficult for you all after—"

I shoot Mom a deathly stare and she thankfully stops before she really puts her foot in it.

"After my mother died?" Jasper finishes the thought for her. "Yes, it was the worst thing that could have possibly happened."

At this my parents' expressions soften. Mom leans a little more against the armchair and Dad crosses one leg over the other.

"I'm sorry," Mom says. "It was a great loss."

"Yes," Dad jumps in. "It was. We all felt it, though of course, not as keenly as you and your family."

"Thank you," Jasper says, lowering his head.

Desperate to move the subject away from Jasper's mom and dad, I rack my brain for anything to say. "Are we done here then or…"

"Hold on," Mom says, regaining her posture. "Before you go I think it's important we address a few of our concerns."

Dad clears his throat. "The thing is Max here has *finally*"—he eyes me pointedly—"told us what's been going on for the last six months or so, and we're just a little worried about safety."

There's that damn word again.

"Dad, I'm fine."

"Wait up," Mom says. "Just the other night you were telling us about rogue attacks, crazed wolves who wanted to kill you. It seems wherever you go, Jasper, trouble follows."

Why is she doing this? Just when Jasper and I have worked through all of this, Mom is bringing it back up again like it's hot tea ready for serving.

"We're just worried about our son," Mom says to Jasper. "As I'm sure you can understand. If we let you and Max see each other"—*Let us! Excuse me?*—"how do we know Max won't be caught up in more political drama? How do we know he's safe with you?"

"Mom, you're being crazy. You don't get to choose whether we see each other, just like you can't choose if we're mates or not."

"Max, don't speak to your mother like that," Dad says.

"We have a right to know," Mom drones on. "You're our child, we need to know you aren't in danger."

"I'm not!"

"And what about when Jasper becomes the alpha—what happens then?"

"How can you even ask that?"

"It's a valid question."

"But you're being ridi—"

"You're right," Jasper says, lifting his head for the first time in minutes and cutting me off. "My life is difficult and it's not always safe to be around me. That's why I called things off with Max in the past, why I tried to put so much distance between us. Even hurt him to push him away."

Jasper is making direct eye contact with Mom and Dad now. The three of them are locked in a staring contest, but somehow understanding is beginning to dawn on my parents' faces.

"But I've come to learn," Jasper continues, "nothing is as painful or as dangerous as not being with Max. He is my mate and being apart is not an option for us. So I have made it my goal to protect Max and do all I can to keep him safe. He is..." Pausing briefly, Jasper turns to look at me. "He is the most important thing in my life. And I will do everything in my power to make sure he is never hurt, or in pain, or put in any kind of danger again. I will protect him with my life."

I smile at Jasper and take his hand. When I glance back at my parents, they both have tears in their eyes. Dad has reached up to put his hand on Mom's.

"Well said." Dad wipes away a tear with the back of his sleeve.

I glare at Mom, who, despite her glassy eyes, hasn't backed all the way down just yet.

"Things aren't going to be easy for you two," she says.

"*Moooooom!*"

"But I think...I think together you have a pretty good chance."

Ugh. The conversation has turned from overzealous interrogation to embarrassingly sentimental and it's more than I can take.

"Great, so can we go?"

"Yes, you may," Mom says. "Just be home by eleven."

I roll my eyes but can't help the grin creeping across my lips. "Great, see you later."

I hop up, pulling Jasper with me. But before we can even make it to the hall he's let go of my hand and turned around.

"Thank you," he says, despairingly earnestly, to my parents. "I'm pleased to have met you."

"You too, son." Dad shakes Jasper's hand, and Mom, after a moment of hesitation, grabs him in a tight hug.

I can tell from the look of surprise on Jasper's face and the way his shoulders are up by his ears that he wasn't expecting it. But he quickly softens into the hug and they stay that way until I can't stand it any longer.

"Okay, bye!"

I take Jasper's hand and pull him into the hall, grabbing my coat on the way out the front door.

"Thank the moon gods that's over," I say, slipping into the passenger seat of Jasper's car. "I swear they're not normally so weird and intense."

He jumps in the driver's side, smiling. "You have great parents," he says. "They care about you, a lot."

"Too much," I say with a roll of my eyes. "But at least that's out of the way. So, where are we going on our date?"

"I was going to tell you ahead of time," he says, raising a cheeky eyebrow. "But after that jump scare I think it's my turn to surprise you."

"What? Come on, just tell me."

"Uh-uh, you'll just have to wait."

I sigh dramatically as Jasper puts the car into gear and takes off in the direction of who knows where.

FIRST DATE, LAST NIGHT

The car is way too quiet. We've been driving for nearly twenty minutes and we've barely said two sentences to each other. The only sounds accompanying us are the smooth whirr of the tires and the gentle hum of the engine. I clear my throat too loudly.

"Music?" Jasper says, and flicks on the stereo. "What sort of thing do you like?"

"Pretty much anything."

A screen in the center of the dash lights up with a selection of music, presumably connected to the music app on Jasper's phone. He flicks through until I spot an artist I like.

"This is good," I say.

He glances at me, then to the screen, then nods, as if he's cataloging some piece of information away for later, then he places both hands back on the wheel and focuses on the road.

Why is this so bizarre? We've been in his car before and things have never felt this strained. Then again, we've always been driving to or from some major calamity or big pack event. There's always been plenty to talk about. It occurs to me now that we've never just hung out, not really. We've always been consumed by the drama of our lives, the push and pull of our relationship. We've never just been cool with each other. It should be amazing, a weight off. So why is it so hard to think of anything to say?

"So, uh, what have you been up to since New Year's?" I ask, cringing internally.

Jasper's eye twitches almost imperceptibly. He flicks a thumb over the volume control on the wheel, turning the music down.

"Things were a little tense after the party," he says. "After, well, you know." He glances at me, blushing ever so slightly. He means since he kissed me in front of everyone. "My father and Alpha Morven have been in meetings all week. Morven wasn't too happy, he thinks we lied to him."

I'm not surprised Morven is pissed. Earlier that night Jasper and Jericho had given him the impression Jasper would be available to mate with Mia in the near future. It wasn't an outright lie but it wasn't the truth either. It was almost the last straw for Jasper and me. I wonder how many straws are left before Morven turns his back on the alliance between our packs completely.

"Is he still allied with your dad?"

"After four days of meetings he returned to the Rocky Pack to consult with his advisers. The last I heard he'd said he needed time to consider his position."

"And Mia?"

Jasper's throat bobs as he swallows. "He made her go back with him."

My chest aches. "Is Olivia okay?"

"Hard to say. She's not the most emotive. I think they're just relieved Mia hasn't been forced into an arranged mating, yet. I spoke with my father, implored him to help them. He said he would do what he could but things are tense. Morven is one of our strongest allies and without his support we're vulnerable to attack along our northern and western borders."

"Aren't we allied with any of the packs between us and Colorado? We must have some friends."

"A couple. But there are twelve packs between us and the Rocky Pack. Father sent me to speak with our current allies to firm up those connections while he's been visiting alphas from the other packs. That's why I didn't call you back, I was a little occupied. I'm sorry."

I shuffle around in my seat. "It's okay. Sounds like there's a lot going on."

"Still, I don't want my duties to get in the way of this..." He reaches out a free hand and places it on my knee. *There are those tingles again.* "Let's change the subject."

"Okay."

I lean back in my seat, watch the streetlights swish by, and try to think of something, anything, not pack related to say. After what feels like a lifetime I manage to eke out, "What's uh, what's Harvard like?"

"Fine," Jasper says, not offering more detail.

"Cool."

A song comes on that I like and I nod along ever so subtly, but Jasper notices and, I think, desperate to relieve some of the awkwardness from the car, turns up the volume. We drive the rest of the way into the city just listening to music and vibing.

Once we're in the city I'm able to relax a scooch. Something about the hubbub, the busy streets outside the windows, the noise and motion, relieves a bit of the pressure.

"You going to tell me where we're going yet?" I ask as we cruise downtown toward the financial district.

"Nope."

Eventually, we pull up outside an art deco high-rise. Jasper casually slides to the curb and switches off the engine.

"Uh, I don't think you can park here," I say.

"It's fine," he says with a grin. "Wait there."

I glance around in confusion as he jumps out of his door and dashes behind the car. In a moment he appears at my window to open my door and help me out. *What a gentleman, amiright?!*

"Sir." A lady in a red vest appears with her hand open to accept the keys. Jasper hands them over with a twenty-dollar bill and I stare open-mouthed as she slides into the car and takes off.

"You just let her drive off like that?" I ask.

"Of course." Jasper shrugs like this is the most natural thing in the world, then gestures to the door before heading inside.

We're whisked up something like sixty floors in a gold-plated elevator, stopping with a ping when we reach our destination. The doors open to reveal a sleek, modern restaurant. Circular tables of black marble are surrounded by designer chairs with deep-mahogany armrests and cushions upholstered in rich ochre-colored velvet. Floor-to-ceiling windows run around the perimeter of the room, which looks as if it could seat a hundred dinner guests but is currently conspicuously empty.

"Are they open yet?" I ask, eyeing the smartly dressed waitstaff idling in the background, the bartender wiping the empty onyx bar, and the maître d' in a tuxedo coming toward us.

"Master Apollo," the man—slicked-back silver hair, an impressive mustache, a bend in his back not unlike a banana—says, smiling to greet us. "Welcome, welcome. It's our pleasure to host you this evening."

"Thank you, Giovanni," Jasper says, like he's greeting an old friend.

"Right this way, sir."

Giovanni spins on his heel and escorts us to a table right by a north-facing window. Manhattan is a glittering painting stretching out before us.

"Your dinner will be served shortly," Giovanni says, helping us into our seats. "May I fetch you something to drink?"

"Just a seltzer for me," Jasper says. "With a slice of lime." He glances at me and I somehow have forgotten all of the drinks. Do I ask for something sophisticated like wine? I don't even like wine.

"Uh, a Coke?" I ask, lifting my hands so Giovanni can whip my napkin open and drape it across my lap. "Also with lime."

"Very good, young sir."

Once Giovanni is gone, Jasper smiles across the table at me. "They do an amazing tasting menu here. Best vegetarian food in the city. I hear the venison is excellent as well."

I rack my brain trying to remember if venison is deer or lamb. "Jasper, where, um, is everyone?"

On all sides the remaining tables are set, ready for guests, with silver cutlery placed at exact lengths on either side of a folded napkin, water and wineglasses standing at the ready, bouquets of real flowers—lilies I think—sprouting from designer vases in the center. But the chairs are all empty. Has there been a zombie apocalypse and no one told me?

"I wanted us to have some privacy," Jasper says, "so I booked out the whole place."

"You...?" I glance around again. This place is seriously fancy—like next-level-rich fancy. "But that must have cost a fortune."

"It's fine."

Our drinks arrive and with them our first course. I stare down at the small plate with an indistinguishable mound of ingredients in the center; orange balls and brown specks, tiny herbs, and a creamy-looking sauce oozing outward. I'm pretty sure the food is staring back at me.

"Enjoy," Jasper says, taking up his cutlery and diving in.

I prod at the mound with my fork. "It looks...great."

Tentatively, I fork a little of the mound into my mouth and I can't believe the explosion of flavor that erupts on my palate. "Whoa."

"Pretty good right?" Jasper asks.

"I've never tasted anything like it, it's so small but so intense."

What follows is a series of fine-dining courses, each small and delicate, a strange medley of ingredients, some I've never heard of, compiled into artlike dishes, all of them completely tasty. It turns out I actually enjoy fancy-person food. And I suppose I don't feel so conspicuous in my hoodie and jeans considering we're the only diners in the entire restaurant, but there's also something a little off. For whatever reason, conversation just isn't flowing the way I thought it would. Maybe it's the sound of my cutlery scraping on the plate, the fact we can hear the chefs in the kitchen, every movement of the waitstaff. Maybe being the only customers is actually more conspicuous than if we were surrounded by other people.

"Is everything okay?" Jasper asks over our entrées. Mine is duck served in a hot pot with sauce and vegetables, Jasper's is some sort of vegetable parfait.

"Mmm, yeh everything is great."

Jasper eyes me quizzically. He drops his cutlery. "You hate it."

"No! No, it's not that. Everything is amazing. This food is insane. It's just…"

"What is it?"

"It's just, everything is so amazing and fancy, it's just a little hard to, I dunno, relax."

Jasper wipes the corner of his mouth on his napkin then drops it on the table next to his dish. He looks around, perhaps taking in the expensive light fixtures, the grand view, the waitstaff who outnumber their customers. "It's too much, isn't it?"

"Maybe a little. Not that I don't appreciate the effort and, you know, the cost. I just thought seeing as we won't get to hang out for a while maybe we could do something a little more fun."

"Fun?" He raises a brow.

"Yeah, fun. Heard of it?"

"What did you have in mind?"

"Strike!"

The pins tumble every which way and I pump my fist, turning to find Jasper staring open-mouthed.

"What? I have secret talents, okay?"

"I wouldn't have agreed to bowling if I knew I was gonna get sharked."

I shrug, pleased to have the upper hand for once. "Your turn."

We're halfway through our first game and my score is already nearing a hundred while Jasper has only just surpassed fifty. His first few turns he kept rolling gutter balls, much to my surprise. He stands over the balls, a stern expression on his face, as he takes his time choosing the perfect one. In his fancy outfit he looks delightfully out of place, like a prince descending to mingle with the commoners.

The bowling alley is wonderfully busy. Kids and families are everywhere, people on dates are laughing and cheering when they score big. Cheesy old-school pop music is blaring from the sound system, and the thud of balls and the clatter of falling pins is so loud we almost need to shout to be heard over it all.

Finally, Jasper chooses a ball, which he slides his fingers into, then takes a moment to line up the shot. He hurls it down the lane and I jump as it connects with the pins, wincing as it knocks over all but two.

"Ooh, a seven-ten split," I say. "Bad luck."

Jasper growls lowly, grabs a new ball and throws it a little more gently this time toward the right pin. Before his ball can connect it topples sideways into the gutter. Defeated, Jasper returns.

"That's too bad."

"Don't get cocky," he teases. "You're up."

As I make my way to the ball-dispenser-machine thing I take a second to revel in this moment. A couple of weeks ago I thought things between Jasper and me were over for good, but here we are at a bowling alley on a date, laughing and teasing each other. It's like some bizarro-fantasy I never thought would actually happen.

Before I can choose a ball I notice a kid and his dad a couple of lanes over staring at Jasper. The boy is pointing and saying something to his dad, who nods and encourages him forward. The boy skip-runs to Jasper and I step back from the balls so I can hear their interaction.

"Excuse me," the boy says. "Are you Jasper Apollo?"

A quick whiff of his scent tells me this kid is a werewolf. I glance over at his father, who gives me a nod hello.

"I am," Jasper says, kneeling so he's eye to eye with the boy. "What's your name?"

"Tommy," the kid says.

"It's a pleasure to meet you, Tommy."

"Who's that?" Tommy asks, turning to scowl at me.

"That's my friend, Max. Do you want to say hi?"

"Not really."

Jasper glances at me and I can't help but laugh. *I wouldn't want to meet me either, kid.*

"Tommy, that's enough," the boy's father says, coming to collect his son. "Leave the future alpha alone." Tommy runs back to his dad, who reaches out a hand to shake Jasper's. "It's a pleasure."

"Same," Jasper says.

It's strange watching him while he interacts with them. They know so much about him, probably feel like they know him, but to him they're complete strangers, and yet he's perfectly at ease, his decorum and willingness to engage perfected with years of practice.

"Didn't think I'd ever see you in a place like this," the dad jokes.

"I'm here with my mate." Jasper gestures to me. The dad takes another look at me, like he's really paying attention this time.

"Hi." I manage an awkward wave.

"Right." The dad sounds a little hesitant. "I heard something about that. Wasn't sure if it was true."

"It's true," I say.

"Nice to meet you too," the dad says to me, only I'm not certain he means it. "Come on, Tommy. Let's leave them to their game. You want a hot dog?"

Without saying goodbye Tommy is led away from us back to his lane.

For the rest of our game I can't help but notice the dad glancing over every so often. Does he not approve of Jasper being mated to me? To a guy? Or is he just confused as to why the alpha's son is bad at bowling? Either way I do my best not to let his strange looks distract me. I'm determined to whoop Jasper's ass.

But Jasper notices too and for whatever reason, he's unable to ignore the dad's suspicious glances. His game suffers, even more so, and ball after ball lands in the gutter. His heart just isn't in it.

"Let's go," Jasper says, having bowled his last bowl. The dad's eyes bore into us as we leave the lanes and pass through the doors of the bowling alley.

The ride back is tense. Jasper is clearly not in a great mood. His foot is heavy on the gas and, while I fear for my life on a couple of the bends, we make it back to my place in record time.

"Thanks for tonight," I say tentatively when we're back at the curb outside my folks' house.

Jasper grinds his teeth. "I'm sorry."

"Why are you sorry? I had a nice time."

"Those people. That father, the way he was looking at us."

I shrug. "Hey, not everyone is going to be cool with you being mated to me right away."

"Then why did they interrupt us?" Jasper bangs the steering wheel with the ball of his palm. "Couldn't they see we were on a date?"

"That's what you're angry about? He was a kid, he probably didn't know any better. I assumed you were used to people approaching you in public."

Jasper takes a few slow breaths to calm down. "I am, just not when you're there too. I realize now that being with me might mean people approaching you too. And I'm worried they won't all be as subtle about how they feel as that guy."

"You think that was subtle?" I joke, but Jasper is too upset to laugh. "Look, I'm not gonna lie, it was a bit weird to have the guy staring at us the whole time. But it's okay. It's a small price to pay if we get to hang out."

"We only had one night before we have to go back to school. I wanted it to be perfect."

Okay, so Jasper is being overserious and a little too sensitive, but that's part of who he is and so I can't help finding his reaction pretty damn adorable. But I also hate that he thinks he's failed on some level.

"So it wasn't exactly perfect," I say. "You can't control everything and it was still pretty great. I had a good time."

"I don't know when I'll see you next," he says.

"Look at me." He turns so that our eyes can finally meet. "You're seeing me now." Suddenly, an idea pops into my head. "I want to show you something."

"What is it—"

I don't answer Jasper's question because I'm already slipping out of the car and making my way toward the side of the house.

"Come on!"

MIND - LINKING

Once we're past the house, the gold light from the windows disappearing behind the trees, I take Jasper's hand and lead him farther into the woods. The air is icy but his hand is warm in mine.

"Where are we going?" he asks.

"Trust me."

We reach my spot by the lake, where I like to sit and draw, and I point out the small path that leads up the bank on the opposite side. With a leap we cross the frozen lake and make our way up the sloping forest trail. Eventually, we come to a rise. An opening appears between the bare trees and as we reach the summit of this small hill the moon pops out from behind a cloud. Beneath us the forest drops away, the descent on the other side of the hill is much steeper and deeper than the one we just climbed. The tree line is a jagged black carpet leading to the horizon. Moonlight shines down, casting the tops of the trees in an uneven silver glow.

"You said you wanted tonight to be perfect," I say, staring out across the forest, taking a deep breath, and letting my soul fill with energy from the moon. "It doesn't get much more perfect than this."

"Maybe we should have skipped dinner and bowling and come right here," Jasper says dryly.

"Maybe. But then I wouldn't have gotten to kick your ass."

"Why *are* you such a good bowler?"

"My dad used to be in a league. I'd hang out at the alley when he had games. He taught me everything he knows."

Jasper turns to me and takes my free hand. "You're full of surprises, you know that?"

I want to say something funny, make some clever retort, tease him or be all pretend smug, but I can't because Jasper is looking in my eyes, moonlight reflecting in his. His lips are moist and puckered and right there.

Kissing under moonlight is just better. Every subtle movement, every place our bodies connect, every feeling is heightened. By the time we break apart I'm completely breathless. Jasper pulls me into him and I return his embrace.

"It's going to be hard to be away from you," I say. "We only just figured things out. Now we have to be apart."

"It's just for a couple of months at most then I'll be back."

"Too long." I sigh and nestle into his chest, loving the way his arms feel around my back and the way he feels wrapped up in mine.

"We can call regularly. I'll be better at texting, I promise."

I glance up at him, deathly serious. "You better be."

"I was also thinking..." Jasper leans away a little so we can see each other's faces again. "Have you heard of mind-linking?"

"Yeah, sort of. It's like when wolves can talk with their minds."

"It's extremely rare. It requires an intense connection. Some alphas have been able to do it in the past to communicate with their soldiers. But mostly it's only mates who can manage to mind-link with one another."

"You think we could...?"

"If we could then we wouldn't need to worry about phones, or school, or distance. We could talk anytime we wanted."

"I guess you are the alpha's son and you do your meditation thing all the time."

"Right, and you're the blood wolf. You already have a mental link to other wolves."

"So if anyone can figure out how to freaking mind-link it should be us."

He grins. "You read my mind."

I can't even with how stupidly handsome he looks right now.

"What do you think? Does that sound okay?" he asks. "Shall we try it?"

"Sounds perfect."

We kiss under the moon once more, until it's finally time to say goodbye.

I wake on Sunday morning wiped after what turned out to be a pretty major first date and also a little depressed. Jasper is heading back to Cambridge in a few days and I have the latter half of junior year to worry about.

I check my phone to find a good-morning text from Jasper—he meant it when he said he'd be better at texting—and a string of texts from Katie.

Max! I'm sorry I've been awol.

I really want to talk

How have you been since New Year's?

I'm sorry

Maybe I should be more angry about how she acted at the party, but part of me is still scared that she meant what she said—*Maybe we're drifting apart.* Now that things with Jasper are in a good place, and especially with him heading back to college, I want to make sure that Katie and I don't drift too far. I dial her number.

"Thanks for coming to meet me," Katie says.

Above us the Brooklyn Bridge is a solid mass, blocking out the sun. We wander a little farther in the direction of Jane's Carousel, tubs of ice cream in hand, looking for a spot in the park to sit. The weather is still decidedly wintry, but warm enough where the light hits.

"Of course, I wanted to see you."

Katie glances sideways in my direction, a look of worry etched on her brow, but also a questioning tilt to her head. Does she think I'm lying?

"I wouldn't blame you if you didn't," she says with a sigh, her breath puffing in front of her face in a little cloud.

I stop walking. "Katie, I always want to see you."

She sniffs. "I know, I suppose lately it's just started to feel like maybe that's not the case."

"It's been sort of a wild six months."

She nods and huffs in agreement.

"But no matter what's happening in my life," I say, "I never want you to think there isn't room for you too."

We step out from under the bridge and the sun is delightfully warm. It's so bright I'm forced to squint.

"I think..." She begins to speak but trails off, her eyes traveling across the river to the Manhattan skyline. "I think maybe there was part of me that was jealous."

"You? Jealous of me? Does not compute."

"Even though things with Jasper have been hard, it's also been sort of epic—like a classic love story full of drama and excitement. It's the sort of romance I always wanted."

"Believe me, all that drama is not the one. It's not like it's been fun."

"I know." She gestures with a nod toward the steps by the carousel and we make our way over, passing the fiberglass horses, spinning aimlessly inside the large glass cube structure. "I know I shouldn't covet your trauma. I think I just saw your life and then looked at mine and wondered why things had shaken out the way they did."

We sit on the cold steps and I shiver into my jacket but continue to spoon the delicious cookie-dough ice cream into my frozen lips.

"I thought things with the bro-twins were better than ever. It's not like you've been drama-free this whole time."

She laughs a little and bumps her shoulder against mine. "Tell me about it. I had no idea dating two guys would be so admin heavy."

"Can you expand on that?"

"It's part of why I haven't been in touch sooner. There's just so much work figuring out when to see each of them individually, when we're going to spend time together as a group, making sure everyone feels equally valued, squashing any jealous thoughts. Being poly takes work.

Today is the first day since New Year's I haven't had plans with one of my mates."

"I'm flattered you'd choose to spend it with me." I offer Katie my tub and she offers hers in return. Hers is choc mint and it's super refreshing. "Actually I think I can relate. With Jasper going back to college my life is about to get super adminny too. It's going to be all schedules and booking dates in advance and finding times to FaceTime."

"Who would have thought romance would be so much like working a reception desk?" she asks with a laugh.

"Not me. And I totally wouldn't have signed up for it if I knew it came with homework."

We share a laugh and it feels so good. Katie hands me back my tub of ice cream and I scoop the remains from the bottom before watching her polish off hers as well. She smudges some on her lip and I hand her a napkin.

"Jasper and I are going to try and mind-link," I say. "To combat the rising tide of paperwork."

"Wow," she says. "I've heard about mind-linking. It's supposed to be really difficult."

"We're going to start practicing."

"Good luck. But I suppose if anyone can do it it'll be you two. What with your new powers and all."

At this I sense her mood shift. The sun dips behind a cloud and I'm suddenly reminded of the season once more.

"What about my new abilities?" I ask. "You seemed weirded out by them, when you first heard about them and at the party."

She places her empty cup down and studies the rocking river. "I can't lie to you, Max. It is sort of strange. Like you get this insight into me that I don't get into you. It's like you get the upper hand."

"But we're not in competition?"

"No but—I'm not explaining it right. It's like you get to know me in this new and intense way and I don't get that with you."

To our right, the carousel has stopped moving. Kids are jumping off while others stream on, picking their horses, their faces excited about the ride they're about to embark on.

"Remember when we used to ride on that carousel when we were kids?" I say.

"Totally. Remember that time you ate too much popcorn and nearly vomited all over Thunder?"

"Who's Thunder?"

"That was the name of your horse. We named him that because he had a black mane and gold stirrups."

"See! I don't even remember my horse's name, but you do."

Katie shakes her head like she's not understanding.

"My point is we know each other better than anyone else on the planet. And no mates or blood-wolf powers are going to change that. And it's not like I can just read minds anyway—it doesn't work like that—plus I wouldn't if I could, but you think if I did there'd be something about you I wouldn't already know?"

She chews her bottom lip, perhaps thinking about all the little thoughts she does want to keep secret, because the truth is there are things we keep from each other, that *are* secret—that's going to be true about anyone. But if they're secrets, we need to respect that. Eventually her face softens and, as if coming to the same conclusion, she turns to smile at me. "No."

"Right, because we're soulmates. Not in the same way you have Todd and Simon or I have Jasper. In a whole other way that's just ours."

At this she begins to tear up.

"We don't need to read each other's minds," I continue, "because we already can."

She laughs and it's music to my ears, a trill that swoops in to harmonize with the honky melody pumping from the carousel.

"I didn't mean it when I said we were drifting apart," Katie says, wiping a tear from her eye. "I mean, maybe we are a little, because we're growing up and whatever, but I don't want to."

"Katie, we could never." I wrap an arm around her shoulders and she leans into me. To our left the carousel is spinning once again and I catch a glimpse of a horse with a black mane.

"Are you looking forward to going back to school?" Katie asks, and in unison we turn to face one another and shake our heads.

"Nah!"

The first week of classes simultaneously drags and whizzes by. Every second I wish I was with Jasper, or calling him or texting him. I struggle to concentrate in my lessons, thankful most of the teachers have decided to take it easy on us during the first week back. My mind is so adrift wondering what Jasper is up to, waiting for his next message that I hardly notice time passing.

I glance at my phone under my desk during Calc on Friday and can't help the smile spreading on my face. Jasper has kept his promise to be better at texting since he left for Cambridge on Tuesday.

Mind-link practice tonight?

I type back "**YES**" in all caps then struggle to regain my focus. *Seriously, when will I EVER need to use calculus in real life?*

"Ready?" Jasper asks, his face bright on the screen of my phone, which is propped up on a pillow at the foot of my bed.

I pull my legs under me. Maybe sitting like a yogi will help me access my cosmic wolf connection.

"Ready," I say.

Jasper closes his eyes first. His college dorm makes an impressive backdrop behind him. It looks more like he's calling from some historic library than a bedroom. Dark wooden shelves are filled with wide-spined books featuring academic-sounding titles. His face is lit in lamplight, accentuating his chiseled jaw and bringing out his freckles.

He's already slipping into a deep state of concentration, his breathing has slowed, his muscles relaxed. I need to stop gawking at my hot boyfriend and do the same.

I close my eyes, take three deep breaths, and try to open my mind.

In the darkness of my mind I let the walls I've held in place for protection dissipate. The noise of the world creeps into my consciousness like a fuzzy murmur, a woolen blanket of sound on all sides. I do my best to block it out and return to the calm, blank, nothingness. Whenever I've reached out before I've always visualized the presence of other wolves as squiggly red lines, like veins or electricity. I do my best to search the darkness for them, trying to hunt out the one with Jasper's energy, his life force.

They start to come into view, small and distant at first, but growing larger, flickering and vibrating. They race toward me until I'm standing in the midst of them, a sea of pulsing veins, each the strand of a life, a spark of consciousness. There are too many to count. Their red light extends and floods the void around me a dark crimson. I squeeze my eyes tighter, trying to find Jasper among them, reaching out with my energy and my consciousness.

Suddenly, a howl tears through the silence, erupting from nowhere and everywhere, and a blinding pain slices through my brain. My eyes shoot open and I clutch my head, crying out in agony.

"Max!" Jasper shouts, eyes open as well, peering into the phone with terror in his expression. "What's wrong?"

The pain lessens more slowly than it arrived, but fast enough that within a few seconds all that's left is a pounding headache.

"I'm okay," I say, despite the fact I can't quite catch my breath and sweat has broken out across my forehead. "I'm fine."

"No you're not. What happened?"

"I...I don't know. I heard something—a howl."

Jasper tilts his head like he doesn't understand. Probably because I'm talking gibberish.

"What do you mean?" he asks. "What howl?"

"I think..." I say, trying to string together the thoughts swirling in my aching mind, "I think it was calling to me."

"I don't understand."

"Someone is calling me," I say. "And whoever they are, they're in pain."

MAXIE IN THE BATHROOM

As the weeks pass by my headache remains—a constant reminder that somewhere out there is a wolf in pain. But how am I supposed to help them if I can't focus in on their life force without my head feeling like it's being torn in two, like there's a drill whirring away at my gray matter?

If only I had a better grasp of my blood-wolf abilities, if only I understood my connection to wolfkind better, how it works, what I'm capable of, maybe I could sort out where this distressed cry is coming from. But right now it's taking all of my energy just to keep the wall of sound at bay. Each night I arrive home from school exhausted and ready for a nap.

Jasper put a pin in our mind-link practice until we can be sure it won't send me into an agony spiral. We return to texts and FaceTimes as our main means of communication. But as winter turns to spring, tensions between our and the neighboring packs rise and I hear less and less from him.

"Jericho has him traveling pretty much anytime he doesn't have classes or exams," I whisper into my phone.

"That's tough," Mason says, his voice staticky on the other end of the line.

I'm crammed into a stall in the boy's bathroom on the third floor of my school. No one really comes in here unless they're on their way to the art rooms, so it's a great spot to take private calls during my lunch period. On the door of the bathroom stall in front of me someone has scrawled *Brad sucks cox.*

I roll my eyes. *Super original.*

"I know he's trying to stay in touch as much as possible but it's tough when he's between time zones and keeping weird hours."

"And the mind-link thing didn't work."

"Nope."

"Will you keep trying?"

"Not unless I want my brain to explode out of my ears."

"Gross."

"Anyway, how are things with you?"

School has been weirdly lonely since the semester started back up. I have a couple of friends, Becky and Peter, who I sit with at lunch, and a cool lab partner in Biology, a girl named Norma, who always has a different-colored streak in her hair. But I can't exactly tell them about everything that's going on in my life. Wolf and human culture aren't supposed to mix. They'd probably report me to the school counselor and petition for me to be hospitalized if I did try to tell them the truth.

With so much going on it sucks not to be able to talk it all through. Scheduling time to see Katie has been difficult—school and her mates are keeping her busy— and Aisha's dance company has just started rehearsal for a new show, which is taking up the brunt of her time. With Jasper stretched thin between his studies and pack duties, Mason is the only other person I can talk to. And he's stuck in the mountains, in a pack that may or may not be harboring hostilities toward ours.

"I've got to say," Mason says, sounding sort of tired, "things have been pretty weird since Morven came back from New York. This whole year has had a strange vibe."

"What's going on?"

"All pack dinners have been canceled. Morven and my dad have been in meetings with the other officers pretty much day and night."

"What do you think they're meeting about?"

"I dunno. Strategy? In case things fall through between our two packs."

"Has your dad said anything?" Not that I'm trying to spy on the Rocky Pack, but getting a little bit of inside information from our rival pack's beta, their second in command, could be useful.

"He said Morven is pissed."

"Because of what Jasper did at New Year's?"

"Sort of. I think it had more to do with the promises that had been made and broken. He feels humiliated. Morven is quite proud."

"Do you think he's going to turn on Jericho and the Elite Pack?"

There's a pause and a muffled sound. Mason takes a long breath. "I don't know."

The sound of footsteps echo off the walls and I sit frozen for a moment, prepared to pull my feet up onto the toilet seat if whoever it is finds their way into the bathroom. But they pass by, the sound dwindling as the person moves away from the door.

"Sorry, thought my solitude was about to be interrupted."

"It's okay." Another pause. "Look I shouldn't tell you this but..."

My heart rate accelerates at the sound of Mason's conspiratorial tone; I clutch my backpack tighter to my chest.

"Morven knows Jericho and Jasper have been visiting other packs. My dad said he's worried your alpha is courting allies so he can turn on the Rocky Pack."

"That's nonsense," I reply. "Jericho is just making sure we're safe."

"Maybe." Mason doesn't sound as convinced as I am. "Or maybe he's trying to amass a contingent of packs so he has the advantage if things were to get...violent."

A shiver passes through me from head to toe. My headache flares up just a little.

"You think things could get violent?"

Mason doesn't respond but I picture him shrugging. "We're wolves. Natural predators. Coveting territory is second nature to us. Violence is always a possibility."

My head is swimming and not just because of the approaching migraine or the smell of toilet cleaner. Could the fracture between the Rocky and Elite Packs turn into something worse—something a lot worse? Could it turn into *war*?

It's too much for me to consider right now. Jericho is a proud alpha, he's strong, he's known for his stature, his power. He wouldn't shy away from brutality. But would he instigate it?

"Max, you still there?"

"Huh?" I shake myself free of my dread-filled thoughts. "Yeah, I'm here. How is Mia doing in all this?" I haven't heard from Mia since she went back to the mountains with Morven.

Mason gives another sigh in response. "She's...not great. She misses Olivia obviously. Truth is I haven't seen all that much of her. Morven's had her on a pretty tight leash."

Anger flares in me bright and hot. How can he keep his daughter from her mate? It's diabolical.

"I'm sorry," I say. "Will you tell her I was asking after her? And that she can call me if she likes."

"Of course."

"And you?" I ask. "How are you holding up?"

"It's hard not to feel pretty hopeless sometimes," he says, breaking my heart.

A small spike of pain pricks at my brain. I can't stand my friends feeling this lost and alone. Suddenly I feel majorly whiney for complaining about not having enough people to talk to, when in actuality I think maybe I'm one of the lucky ones. If only I could pass on a little of my luck.

"I wish I could be there," I say. "The next time I talk to Jasper I'll see if there's anything we can do."

"Sure." I can practically hear Mason rolling his eyes.

"Why do you sound like that?"

"It's nothing."

"Come on, you can tell me."

"It's just...you think Jasper is going to do anything if it's not what his dad wants?"

What is he implying? Yes, Jericho's approval means a lot to Jasper. He cares way too much about what the pack needs. But he's not a mindless drone.

"He's not like that—I mean, not all the way like that."

"I'm sorry. I know he's your mate, but you have to be realistic. When it boils down, Jasper is a tool for his father to control."

I want to hang up, flush my phone down the toilet, but I know Mason is probably acting out of some dark emotional place and not a place of truth. "That's not fair."

Mason takes a couple of breaths and when he speaks again his tone is noticeably lighter, like he's trying his best to sound chipper. "I'm sorry. You're right. That wasn't fair to Jasper."

I rub my neck, trying to adjust to the emotional whiplash. "Thanks."

"Hey, listen, I've got to go," Mason says, suddenly in a hurry to get off the call. "I'll call you soon."

"Yeah, okay—"

"See ya."

Before I can say goodbye, Mason has hung up and I'm left in a daze. I sit in the cubicle, by myself in the quiet of the empty bathroom, until the bell rings and I need to head to class.

As I make my way to English I can't help but wonder if Mason really does think Jasper is a simp for his dad. Does he really believe Jasper is just a mindless tool, an instrument his dad can use to manipulate situations? And if I'm with him, if I'm defending him, what does that make me? Does Mason think I'm a tool as well?

These thoughts plague me all the way through the rest of the day. I'm so preoccupied I hardly even notice the final bell ringing to release us.

On my way from the bus stop to my house I try calling Jasper, hoping he's free and not in the middle of afternoon tea with some random wolf dignitary or cramming for an exam on human history.

"Hey!" he says, his voice like a balm, instantly calming me. "How are you?"

"I've had a bit of a day."

"I'm sorry. I wish I could chat but I'm about to run into a class. Can I call you later?"

I sigh, but understand. It's not Jasper's fault the world goes on spinning when I'm in desperate need of some affection.

"Of course."

"Whatever it is," Jasper says, "we'll figure it out."

And just like that I'm satisfied. Jasper cares about his father and about our pack but he isn't a mindless drone, a hapless tool, he's a person who cares and wants to make things better. And I'm not a simp for believing that. I've seen him in action.

"Thanks."

"I'm excited for spring break. I'll be coming back to the city. We can have our second date."

"Really?"

"Yeah. I can't wait." My heart does a little leap, sticking the landing and saluting the judges with a flourish. "I can hear birds. Where are you?"

"I thought you had class."

"I can be a minute late. Answer my question."

"I'm just walking down my street, about to—"

My feet come to a standstill as my house comes into view.

"Max?"

I can't quite believe what I'm seeing. Someone has graffitied our house, scrawled a word in red spray paint across the garage door.

"Max you there?"

I can't answer, I'm too busy staring at the message left in large, aggressively angular letters:

TRAITOR

TRAITOR

A team of five gamma wolves, security officers from Alpha Jericho's forces, are outside my house. Big people dressed in black suits and wool trench coats, wearing the same sunglasses—must be standard issue—poking around in bushes, wandering the perimeter of our property, and talking into their earpieces. I feel like the president or some big pop star with private bodyguards. Like Whitney Houston or something.

"Seriously, Jasper, I think this might be overkill."

"Until we know who did this I'm not taking any chances," he says through the phone.

"My neighbors are going to think there's a bomb threat or something."

Jasper twists his lips together and doesn't say anything.

"You think there could be a bomb?!"

"We don't know yet," he says. "Clearly we've upset some people. I'm..." He stumbles and pauses. "I'm sorry it's affecting you. I should be there."

I roll my eyes and smile. "It's just a bit of paint. Sure, it's not ideal, but I don't think I'm in imminent danger."

"Still, I said I would keep you safe."

Oy, this again. "We have a SWAT team combing the area for suspects," I say. "We're going to be safe."

"Are your parents home yet?"

Speak of the wolf-devil. My mom's car is slowly pulling up the drive. She and Dad carpool to the train and I usually beat them home after school. They pull to a stop as one of the security guards approaches. Mom rolls down her window, looking from the guard to the garage and to the house, possibly scanning for further damage. Dad jumps out his side and approaches the garage door. Begrudgingly, Mom puts the car in park, rolls up her window, and exits the car as well. Why aren't they letting them park in the garage? Maybe something to do with contaminating a crime scene.

The beefy security guards shepherd my parents toward the door.

"They've just arrived," I say, turning my attention back to Jasper, who's still waiting for my reply. "I should go talk to them."

"Okay."

"And you should get to class. Don't flunk out of Harvard because of me."

"I'll call you later," he says and hangs up.

"Max!" Mom is calling for me before they've even made it halfway inside.

"In here!"

Mom and Dad arrive in the living room with wide, concerned eyes. Dad is scratching the back of his head and Mom has her arms out, coming straight for me.

"Are you okay?" She grabs me into a tight hug.

"I won't be if you break my ribs," I squeak out.

"Who did this?" she asks. I can only shrug in return.

"What does it mean? *Traitor*?" Dad asks, not to anyone in particular.

I sigh and run a hand over my face. "We think it's for me. Because I've...I dunno, corrupted the alpha's son, disrupted the family line or something."

"That's nonsense," Mom says, turning to Dad for support.

"Absolute horse manure," Dad says.

My folks are the best, always trying to be supportive, if not a little naive. I shake my head and shrug again, in a way that says *This is just how the world works*. The wolf world especially.

Mom stops looking at Dad and holds me in front of her, studying my face like she's looking for obvious signs of distress, or physical injuries. Then before I know it she's hugging me again, holding my head to her chest and stroking my hair.

"I'm so sorry, kiddo. It isn't fair."

She's right, it isn't fair. For most kids, having their first boyfriend is fun and exciting. For most wolves, finding your mate is something to celebrate, a wonderful gift for the community, the continuation of the species.

For me and Jasper, it's a political statement—one not everyone is on board with, apparently.

"Thanks," I mumble.

One of the security dudes pokes his head around the entrance to the living room, disrupting our semi-cozy moment. "We've searched the perimeter. You're all clear. Whoever did this didn't stick around. They must have just wanted to send a message."

Message received. Hooray for them!

"Thanks," Dad says.

"The alpha has requested two wolves be positioned outside for the next forty-eight hours. You'll be safe."

"Great," Mom says, though she doesn't sound so enthusiastic. I'm with her. I just want to be left alone.

"People are jerks," Katie says, glancing at me from her lawn chair then turning back toward the garage door and calling out to Todd and Simon, who are in the middle of painting over the graffiti. "Keep up the good work boys!"

The bro-twins look over their shoulders and wave. Katie waves back and I nod my head from my seat. I felt a little weird about dragging these chairs from the back patio to the front lawn just to watch someone else paint over the graffiti that was meant for me, but now that we're here it's sort of fun—plus, from the way Todd and Simon are splattering each other with paint and chasing each other around like a couple of regular pups, they seem to be enjoying themselves.

"Thanks for coming," I say. "And bringing reinforcements."

"Of course. It's really shitty of whoever did this. I hope Jericho finds them and excommunicates them."

"Whoa, extreme much?"

Katie blushes. "Sorry, it just makes me really angry."

Todd swipes his brush across the top of the *T*, the red disappearing behind the olive green my parents chose to repaint the door.

"Me too," I say.

"I bet Jasper was steamed. I'm surprised he didn't race back when he heard."

"I had to convince him not to."

"That's sweet." She glares at the garage and leans forward. "You missed the dot above the *i*!"

Simon looks from the door to Katie, shoots her a little salute with his paintbrush, and reaches up to green-out the dot.

"I'll be seeing him soon anyway. He's coming back for his birthday and spring break."

"Oooh, boyfriend's first birthday. Do you know what you're going to get him?"

"No clue. Seriously, I'm more worried about that than whoever did this."

"Really?" Katie says, skeptically chewing her bottom lip.

I laugh. "Mmm, I guess not. I am concerned about the party."

"That's right!" Katie says, eyes lighting up. "Jasper's annual birthday ball. I can't believe we're both going this year!"

My shoulders slump forward. "Yeah."

Jasper's birthday isn't just a familial affair. The whole pack celebrates the birth of the alpha's son and every year a big event is held in his honor. It's basically like a national holiday, only for werewolves.

"You're not excited?"

"It's just, since Jasper and I have been together properly we've barely seen each other, and he's only in town for a week. A lot of that time is already booked up with meetings his father wants him to attend. We only have so much time, and the one night it would have been nice to do something just the two of us, we have to spend it with the crusty upper class of the Elite Pack. It's not exactly romantic."

"It's nice though that he wants you there. It'll be your first official appearance in front of the pack. It's a big deal."

"I suppose." I take a long, deep breath and watch as the final strokes of paint cover up the red lettering. The word is gone. But I can't help repeating it over and over again in my mind. *Traitor.* It's scrawled on the back of my eyelids just like it was on the door. Is that what people think of me? Is that what the pack thinks of me? "I'll tell you who is excited about being invited to their first big pack event."

Katie leans over the arm of her chair excitedly. "Who?"

"Them." I point in the direction of Mom and Dad, who have just appeared in the open doorway of the house, coming out to appraise the boys' handiwork.

Katie squeals a little. "Cute!"

"Attending my first official event as the mate of the alpha's son and my parents are coming...I can't wait."

Spring break rolls around, thankfully without another incident like Graffitigate, as I've taken to calling it. The last few weeks Jasper has been especially hard to reach, torn between exams, finishing up papers, and traveling to meet with more pack dignitaries—lately he's been focusing on the five small packs along our southern border.

Even though Jasper hasn't wanted to out of fear it'll induce another migraine attack, I've tried a few times to access the mind-link. With no success. Each time I close my eyes to focus on my blood-wolf connection, exploring the endless sea of consciousness, I wind up clutching my head and groaning into my pillow. The dull headache that follows has become a constant companion. I might be holding up the aspirin market single-handedly.

As I wait for the elevator to arrive on the sixty-eighth story of the packhouse, where Jericho—and therefore Jasper's—city apartment is located, I rub my temple and close my eyes, hoping my last hit of painkillers will kick in any minute.

The doors ping open and I wander out into a large living area. The floors are black marble, which reflects the view of Manhattan shining in through the wall of floor-to-ceiling windows.

By the elevator is a black grand piano with an oversized vase and an explosive bouquet of tropical flowers erupting from it in a plume of bright colors. In front of me, a set of perfectly white sofas are arranged around a large stone coffee table and white rug. This place looks like a display home, like no one actually lives here. Beyond the sofas is a long dining table, a slab of white marble long enough to sit twelve or thirteen guests at least. Artwork hangs on the walls opposite the windows. One looks like a bona fide Monet and one I think is a Pollock, the abstract squiggly lines reminding me of the red tendrils that represent each wolf in my mind.

"Max!" Jodie comes bounding from a doorway between the two paintings, dressed like a princess. She wraps her little arms around my waist and I hug her back.

"Hey Jodie, it's nice to see you."

"You too. You know you don't have to wait for Jasper to come home to visit."

"I know. I'm sorry. You excited for the party?"

She steps back, scrunching up her face. "Not really. It'll probably be boring like all the others. I'd rather you and Jasper just hung out with me here."

"You don't have any friends coming?"

"Just Jessica and Mandy from school, but they'll probably want to talk about boys the whole time." On the word *boys* she rolls her eyes like she couldn't think of anything less interesting.

"Ugh, that sounds lame," I say, very aware of just how boy obsessed I've been for the last nine months.

"It's very lame," she says.

"What's lame?" I glance up to find Jasper, leaning ever so casually next to the Pollock, looking crazy handsome in a sleek new suit, his hair slicked back, his arms crossed over his chest.

"Boys," I shoot straight back at him.

"Uh, yes," he nods, grinning at me. "Boys. The lamest."

I can't help grinning back at him. After three months of not seeing him in person, taking in the sight of him feels like coming up for air. My teeth vibrate with giddy excitement, my legs are immediately a couple of gelatinous poles, wobbling all over the place, my chest swings open like a cuckoo clock, my heart pounds.

Jodie is eyeing us, glancing back and forth with a suspicious glare. "You two are being gross, aren't you?"

"Why don't you go finish getting ready, Stink Face?" Jasper asks, stepping toward me.

"I am ready," she protests.

"I think you could be more ready."

She rolls her eyes. "Okay I get it, you want to be alone with your *booooyfriend*. You could have just said."

"Thanks, Stinky," Jasper says.

Jodie stomps past him. We wait until she's gone, then our eyes meet and we collide. Jasper pulls me into his arms and plants a passionate kiss on my lips.

"I've missed you," he says when we finally come up for air.

"I've missed you too." Reluctantly I let go of Jasper with one arm and pull the rolled-up present from the inside pocket of my white suit jacket. "Happy birthday."

"You didn't need to—"

"Shut up," I say. "Of course I did. Though it's not much..."

Eagerly I eye Jasper, studying his face, every micro-expression and twitch of muscle, as he unwraps his gift. He drops the wrapping paper on the floor and unfurls the piece of paper. For a long time he stares at the drawing I made for him, his brow furrowed, and for a painful moment I'm worried he hates it. He has everything in the world. Why would he want a dumb drawing of us onstage at New Year's?

"It's—"

I don't let him finish his thought. "I based it off a photo someone took at the party. It's okay, I could have done more shading, especially on the arm there"—I point at the picture—"see?"

"Max, it's perfect. Thank you."

With a firm hand he pulls me toward him and kisses me again. And he keeps kissing me, until I think my feet might leave the floor. The dull ache in my mind drifts away and I lean into his embrace. Then before I know it he's pulling away.

"I—I have some bad news," he says, his thumb running over my cheek.

"What is it?"

"There's something we have to do before we can leave for the party."

"What's that?"

"Actually, it's more of a *someone*."

I shoot him a confused look. Why is he talking in riddles? What could be so bad he's scared of telling me?

"Someone?"

"My dad. He wants to speak with you before we go."

Oh. The last time I spoke to Alpha Jericho was at the New Year's party, when I was giving him a piece of my mind, telling him to step up his parenting game. He didn't look pleased then and I can't imagine he's anymore pleased now that Jasper and I have messed up relations with Morven and the other packs.

"I'm sorry," Jasper says. "Hopefully, it'll only take a second."

A second? Is that how long it'll take for Jericho to hand me my ass?

"Uh, sure," I say.

And as Jasper takes my hand and leads me to a corridor, I have a distinct feeling I'm being led to my death.

SPRING BREAKERS

Jericho is reading a book in a leather chair, the back of which rises above even his immense height, bathed in warm light from an antique lamp nearby. He's surrounded on all sides by bookshelves, intricately carved out of rich mahogany. The shelves are stacked with leatherbound volumes, artifacts, and sculptural curiosities that sit somewhere between crazy science gizmo and art piece. Under his feet is a large rug with geometric patterns. I feel like I've just wandered into the Library of Alexandria.

"Max," he says, standing to greet me, placing the paperback novel, diminutive in his massive hands, on the table beside him and reaching out to shake my hand. His grip is firmer than firm, like steel wrapping around my poor fingers. "It's a pleasure to see you"—he lowers his gaze, pinning me to the spot—"as always."

Gulpity gulp.

Jasper is a warm presence beside me and I wish I could reach for his hand. But I also don't want to show weakness in front of the alpha. Even if he chews me out for having a go at him on New Year's it's important I stand my ground. *Right?*

Or maybe I should fall on my sword, drop to my knees and beg forgiveness, anything to make him stop glowering at me like that.

"It's...nice to see you too," I croak.

"Come in."

I take a step but Jasper doesn't accompany me, instead nodding to encourage me forward. With my palms raised I shake my head at him. *What are you doing?* To which he smiles and ushers me onward. I shoot him my best death stare then turn back to the alpha.

"That'll be all, Jasper," Jericho says. "I'll send Max out when I'm done with him."

Gulpity gulpity gulp gulp.

Jericho flashes me a toothy grin, like he's hungry and looking for a snack to take a bite out of.

"Yes, sir."

Jasper gives me one last encouraging nod then leaves the room, shutting the large and probably quite heavy door behind him.

"Take a look around," Jericho says, when Jasper is gone. "You like to read?"

"Uh-huh," I say, casting another exploratory glance across the shelves. "When I have the time."

"Of course." Jericho gestures to his collection of books. "The entire history of our pack is contained within these volumes. Decades of power struggles, political uprisings. And through it all the Apollo family has ruled the Elite Pack with an iron jaw."

He comes to stand next to his chair, placing a threateningly large hand on the leather back.

"What you and Jasper are doing has never been done in the entire history of our pack."

"I see." *I don't see, I'm completely in the dark. What's he getting at?*

"To do what you've done...takes guts—the guts I thought you had."

Whoa, wait a lunar minute? Was that a compliment?

"Sorry?" I stammer.

"The resilience and fortitude it takes to stand proudly as you and my son have done is no small feat." Again he grins like he wants to gobble me up. "I'm proud."

Holy smokes!

"I...uh, thanks?"

Jericho laughs, the sound reverberating in his expansive barrel chest. "I expect you thought I might be less hospitable after our last interaction."

I rub the back of my neck. "Yeah, uh, sorry about that."

"The truth is you were right, Max. And you weren't afraid to tell me exactly where to stick it. I appreciate that sort of forthcomingness. That's how I know you are the right wolf to stand by my side now during this time of uncertainty."

"Uncertainty?"

"Yes." He sighs and rubs his eyes, and for the first time in my life the alpha seems to shrink before me, to appear—just a little—like a normal wolf. Suddenly he looks his fifty-something years. "Not every pack is as understanding or welcoming of change as ours. You and Jasper have made quite a splash, one our rivals are willing to take advantage of."

"Riiiiight."

"And sadly there is also discord within our own ranks. A division in the pack. I believe you've already had a taste of the divisive attitudes of our pack members."

Does he mean the graffiti?

"I'm truly sorry you and your family have had to bear the consequences of our pack's ambivalence."

"That's okay," I say, rubbing my neck raw. "The garage needed a new coat of paint anyway."

Jericho lowers his brow, and his fingers clench the chair a little tighter. "I'm afraid that could be just the tip of the iceberg. Changing long-held opinions and uprooting ancient traditions is an uphill climb."

"Yes," I say, well aware of just how tricky it can be to make a stubborn-ass wolf come around to logic. "It takes time."

"Time and strong leadership." His gaze focuses and he takes a breath. "A lot will be asked of you in the coming months and years, Max. But you've proven to me that you're up to the task."

"M-me?"

"Yes. You and Jasper. The two of you will be instrumental in showing our society that we are still a strong, united pack, with capable and unwavering leadership. Tonight's event is just the first step. In the coming days it will be imperative that you are able to show up and prove to our pack members that we are still the pinnacle of power and the very example of prowess amongst wolves. We must accomplish this if we are to face the external forces who would wish us and you harm."

Jericho's words are a big swampy mess in my mind. Jasper and I are going to be instrumental to the pack, to keep everyone's shit together in case we're attacked by outside forces. Right. But what does that mean? How on earth am I supposed to do that? The responsibility feels too large and the actual task too vague. "That all sounds, um...sorry, what do you mean exactly?"

"The first step is introducing you to the pack. At the party tonight we start with the inner circle, the most influential of wolves. They will be the most discerning and the ones you'll need to charm if we're going to convince the rest of our people that you and Jasper are the right fit for future leadership. Win over the crowd tonight and you'll have won the hearts of every Elite Pack wolf."

Okay, so no pressure then.

"I'm counting on you, Max."

"Of course," I say, and nod obediently. "I'll do my best."

Another sinister grin. "I know you won't disappoint."

As I leave Jericho's office, wandering slowly through the halls of the apartment, dazed and adrift, I can't quite piece together what's just happened and what's been asked of me. Somehow it's my job to prove to the crusty Elite Pack elite that I'm worth putting their support behind—that my and Jasper's relationship is strong enough to raise the sprits of the entire pack. We've only been on one proper date, for moon gods' sake!

And what if we fail? What if we can't convince the pack to get behind us? Does the pack crumble? Will some sort of civil war break out? And what does that mean for our relationship? Will Jericho decide to find a new mate for Jasper and order him to reject me?

"You okay?" Jasper says, eyeing me as I meander back into the living room. He's standing by the elevator, ready to go. "You're white as a sheet."

"Fine," I say. "I think."

He reaches out and takes my hand and a cool, reassuring wave crashes over me. Instantly, I feel better, less confused, less unsure.

"What did he say?"

"That the fate of the pack is on our shoulders."

Jasper laughs. "He didn't...did he?"

I try my best smile but I know it turns out all crooked and forced.

Jasper, furrowing his brow, takes my other hand and steps closer. "Don't worry about him. He's just got a lot going on. All you have to do is be yourself, everyone is going to love you."

My lips are dry, my stomach is gurgling like I haven't eaten in days, my knees are knocking against each other.

"If you say so."

Jasper's birthday bash is taking place at a trendy, upmarket bar and restaurant in Williamsburg—the sort of place up-and-coming pop stars would hang out to be seen in, and young tech entrepreneurs would spend too much on cocktails in for their staff. Just one drink at the place would pretty much wipe out my savings.

As we pull up outside, the dull, fuzzy feeling of encroaching voices presses in on all sides of my mind like storm clouds. I haven't been around this many wolves since New Year's and I guess I'd gotten used to lowering my guard. We're still in the car and already I'm squinting and twitching trying to keep the noise at bay.

"You okay?" Jasper asks, carefully placing a hand on my knee.

I nod and force a smile.

"I know it's a lot, but you get used to it."

I'm not sure I'll ever get used to this, I want to say, but I don't want to come off as too negative. Jasper has been dealing with this sort of thing his entire life, going to big events, hobnobbing, putting on a brave and charming front. I can manage to act like a normal, well-adjusted wolf for all of four hours. *Can't I?* Plus, it's Jasper's birthday. I'm sure he isn't exactly thrilled to be spending it with his dad's colleagues and the wealthy blob. I'm sure he'd rather be hanging out with me and Aisha and Jodie at home. But he's here, looking debonair in his suit, and trying to be encouraging to me, when I should be the one making sure he has a good night.

"It'll be fun," I squeak, and he slips out of the car. Before he can zip around to my side to open the door for me I check my messages. I'd texted Aisha on the way over to see what time she'd be arriving and all she said was "Be there in a bit." I was hoping for something more concrete so I knew exactly when backup would arrive to rescue me. My door clicks and swings open and suddenly there is Jasper reaching out his hand for mine, to help me from the car.

Music is pumping from inside and a trickle of smartly dressed wolves are lingering by the entrance—girls in sleek satin dresses with spaghetti straps and guys in suits who stop laughing and turn to greet us as we step toward the door.

Shoulders back, head high, I take a breath, and as Jasper slips his hand into mine, we make our way inside.

Walking into the party feels distinctly different than the handful of other times I've arrived at pack events. Usually I wander into these completely unnoticed, like a shadow or the invisible man. This time, all eyes turn to Jasper and me. Jasper, while not entirely comfortable—his back is unnaturally straight, his chin raised, an easy but performative smile has appeared on his face—is clearly used to this. He nods in greeting as we pass partygoers standing along the concrete bar, grins at the guests on the other side of the room in the velvet banquettes beneath the large warehouse-style windows, seemingly unfazed by just how many people are staring at him, waving as if they're close friends, leaning in as if he might stop and talk to them.

Meanwhile the noise of this many wolves is making it hard to keep my expression neutral. I grit my teeth and press my lips together, trying not to screw up my face like I've been stabbed and someone is twisting the knife. I must let out a small groan because Jasper squeezes my hand and glances in my direction. He shoots me a look of concern and I do my best to shake off the darkening clouds compressing my brain and smile.

We're about halfway into the large room, crowds of polished, well-dressed wolves surrounding us on all sides, when a couple approaches us. The woman looks to be in her twenties, blond hair, a black cocktail dress that hugs all of her ample curves, and the man has to be somewhere in the region of fifty, his salt-and-pepper hair gelled smartly to one side, his wide shoulders filling out his suit, the crinkles around his eyes betraying him.

"Jasper," the man croons. "It's good to see you."

"You too, Cyrus. And you as well Jessica." Jasper shakes Cyrus's hand and goes full European as he air-kisses the sides of Jessica's face. "Allow me to introduce my mate—"

"Max!" Cyrus erupts before Jasper can get my name out. "Yes, we've been so eager to meet you since that little show at New Year's."

I can't tell if this guy means to patronize or if he just talks like a game-show host. Either way, his smarmy, amused tone is setting me on edge.

"It's nice to meet you too," I say.

"Cyrus is my father's head of PR," Jasper says.

"Oh, cool."

"Yes and I've been trying to nail the two of you down for a while now," Cyrus says.

He has? I shoot a questioning glance at Jasper. Has he been dodging Cyrus all this time on my behalf?

"I'd love to set up some interviews with the both of you so the pack can get to know you better." He literally runs his gaze up and down the length of my body, as if appraising me. "I'm sure there are some fascinating stories about how you met and I'd love to know about your upbringing, Max. Where on earth did you come from?"

I fight with every fiber of my being not to rub the back of my neck and give away how awkward I feel. "My upbringing?" I ask. "It was pretty normal."

Cyrus shakes his head like I've just made the most beguiling statement. "I can't begin to imagine."

"We'd love to help," Jasper says, maybe coming to my rescue, maybe jumping in before I explode. "Let's set something up. I'll give your people a call in the morning."

"Perfect," Cyrus basically purrs.

"If you'll excuse us," Jasper says, placing a hand on the small of my back and leading me away.

"Does she not get to speak?" I whisper once we're out of earshot.

"Cyrus loves the sound of his own voice," Jasper whispers back.

We make our way through the party and I search the crowded room for familiar faces but come up short. Where is everyone? Jasper stops to say hello to a few more people, shaking hands and introducing me. Everyone shakes my hand and smiles welcomingly but I can't help noticing the curious glint in people's eyes, like I'm some strange amusement. The smirk playing at the corner of people's lips. It's like they can smell how out of place I am, and I can't help feeling a little judged. Although, of course, that's what this night is all about, right? Letting the pack judge me and me proving to them I'm worthy of being Jasper's mate.

Before I know it we're approached by another couple. This time both the guy and the woman look like they're in their sixties. Her silver hair is piled in an intricate updo, while he's red in the face and almost bald.

"This is Stefan and Maria Lykos," Jasper says. "They belong to one of the oldest families in the pack."

I actually think I've heard of the Lykos family. They're descended from a high-ranking gamma wolf who was instrumental in the formation of the Elite Pack. His battalion won a key victory in the Wolf Wars, which assured our then alpha, Jericho's great-great(-great?) grandfather, success in claiming what's now our territory.

"It's nice to meet you," I say, trying to keep my voice steady.

"A pleasure," Maria says, holding her gloved hand out as if I'm supposed to kiss it. Gingerly, I take her hand and shake it. "How charming," she says, with a lifted brow and a smug pout.

"How are things with the allied outreach program?" Stefan asks Jasper, not even acknowledging me.

"Progressing nicely," Jasper says, all business. "I've recently met with Alphas Matteo, Carmine, and Meyers along the southern border and they've assured me we have their allegiance. As long as our pledge to provide military support should they be threatened by the southeastern contingent remains, they're happy to stay aligned. In fact I wanted to ask your opinion on a matter..."

Jasper continues talking shop but I lose the thread, confounded by how complex and dense it all sounds. There are so many packs I never even think about, each with their own alphas and hierarchies, each wanting something different from us, so many names and complicated relationships to keep track of. I'm amazed watching how adept Jasper is at all this, how easily he is able to slip into his role of noble diplomat. I had no idea just how well versed he was in military strategy, trade, foreign affairs. It's all over my head and while I'm no longer listening to a single word, as his mouth moves, I can't help but puff out my chest with pride that this is my mate.

"And what about you, Max?" Maria asks, pulling me back into the room.

"Ex-excuse me?"

"Where do you stand on the issue of water supply between us and the Eastern Riverside Pack?"

Eastern Riverside Pack? I've never even heard of them. My mind races, trying to think of something not completely dumb or ignorant to say. If they're based on a riverside then surely they have plenty of water, I assume. So I say the first thing that comes to mind: "It's very generous of them to share their water supply and I think—"

The woman stifles a little laugh and Stefan makes a confused grunting sound.

Jasper leans into my ear. "The Eastern Riverside Pack has a contaminated water supply. We provide them with clean drinking water in return for their allegiance."

"Oh, I see." My face is a hot plate. "Then I think...if we have enough clean water we should share it with packs who need it."

Stefan and Maria lean back and eye me cautiously.

"Interesting," Stefan says. "And what should we expect in return?"

"Nothing," I say, shrugging. "Isn't the point of having all these resources so we can use them to help people?"

Stefan chortles like a bulldog. "Next you'll be suggesting we share our resources with the local rogue contingents."

"If they could use our help I don't see why we wouldn't give it," I say, feeling less sure than ever but also gaining a little momentum. "Jasper and I have actually visited a rogue encampment and I think they could really use our assistance. With just a tiny portion of what we have—"

"They'd overrun us!" Stefan interjects.

Jasper's cheeks have turned a rosy shade of pink and the muscles in his jaw are working overtime. *Jeez, was it something I said?*

"Give the rogues an inch and they'll take a mile," Stefan continues. "You best school your mate on the ways of the wolf world, Jasper. Before we become a hot spot for rogue incursions."

"Yes, can you imagine?" Maria joins in, laughing like I've said something outrageous. "We'd all be frothing at the mouth!"

"I didn't mean...we'd—"

"When is your father arriving?" Stefan says, turning to Jasper, done with me and my lofty ideals.

"He should be here shortly," Jasper says, sounding a little choked. "I'll tell him to look out for you."

"Please do, my boy. And best of luck with your delegations. With any luck we won't be dining with rogues in the next year."

"Yes, very good," Jasper says, a little too accommodatingly.

When the Lykoses have finally wandered off I'm practically steaming in my shoes.

"That was fun," I say, too snarkily.

Jasper shoots me a sideways glance and for a minute I'm scared he's about to take a bite out of me. His calm demeanor slips and I can tell how stressed he is by the tightness around his eyes, the way he swoops his hair back trying to smooth it into place.

"I'm sorry. Guess I'm not doing a great job convincing people to like me."

He eyes me again then quickly his expression softens. "You don't need to convince people to like you," he says. "I want you to be yourself."

"You sure about that? They didn't seem to enjoy me being myself."

"Stefan flunked out of the military academy when he was eighteen and has been dining out on his family's fortune ever since. The man has no idea what he's talking about when it comes to strategy or interpack politics."

"Then why did you ask his opinion like he was some fountain of knowledge?"

"He still considers himself an expert, and while his politics may be stuck in the Stone Age he's a big supporter of my father and he runs in some influential circles. I'm just humoring him, making him feel relevant."

I have a feeling Jasper is pretty good at humoring annoying and ignorant people, me being the captain of the team.

"You were just being nice to him," I say.

He shrugs. "You didn't know the whole story. I should have briefed you on who would be here."

"I'll try to keep my crazy super modern beliefs to myself from now on," I say.

He smiles and takes both my hands. "Please, don't."

Jasper grins at me in a knowing and adorable way that makes me drop my guard almost completely and, as the sound of the surrounding wolves rushes in, a stab of pain makes me wince.

"What's wrong?" he asks.

"It's just...taking a lot to keep everything in check up here."

"You want to go somewhere quiet?"

"Just for a minute," I say.

He nods. "Of course."

He leads me by the hand in the direction of a set of stairs. "It would be nice if any of the people I actually know were here."

"When did Aisha say she'd be here?"

"She didn't. Not really."

Just then a hush settles over the room. We're about three steps up and as we turn to look back across the floor we're able to see over the sea of heads. A couple of newcomers have just entered the bar and are lingering by the entrance. It's still daylight outside and the light is casting the pair in silhouette, but as the doors close behind them I realize one-half of the couple is Aisha. She's finally here, in a green dress with her hair in braids, and standing next to her, looking petrified in a loose suit jacket, the reason everyone has stopped midconversation to stare in silence, is Troy.

Aisha has brought a human to a wolf party, and from the way people are starting to growl, the crowd looks ready to prove just how inhuman they are.

INTERLOPERS

"What is she thinking?" Jasper whispers to himself, barely audibly.

I take one step back down the stairs but he grabs my arm. I glance up at him and his expression is all concern.

"Shouldn't we go say hi?" I ask.

"Wait," he says.

Back over at the door, two security wolves have approached Aisha and are talking to her while subtly blocking her way into the party. She grows agitated as the conversation continues, gesturing to the party, shaking her head, looking at the unhelpful and unmoving faces watching this interaction unfold. Beside her Troy remains a step behind. He isn't looking at the guards, he's surveying the crowd, his eyes wide with fear, hands shoved in his pants pockets. He knows he's stepped into a wolves' den.

Brazenly, Aisha moves to step between the guards but they block her path, one putting his hand on her shoulder to coerce her backward. She shrugs him off, staring up at him with flared nostrils and furious eyes. Her mouth moves and I think she's saying, "Get your hands off me."

"We should do something," I say. But Jasper isn't moving. He's watching the interaction with a clenched jaw.

"We can't," he says.

"Why not?"

"Humans are forbidden from attending pack events. Aisha knows that."

The guards are walking Aisha back toward the door, their hands raised slightly to create a wall. Troy is saying something, half turned to leave. Maybe he's telling Aisha it isn't worth it, that they should go before something bad happens. But Aisha is still arguing her point.

Finally, when they've been backed up all the way to the entrance, Aisha looks up and over the guard's meaty, padded shoulder, searching the crowd, looking for a friendly face, anyone to fight in her corner. No one steps forward.

I shake off Jasper's arm and jump down the steps but I'm met by a thick wall of partygoers all turned to face the commotion. Between heads I catch a glimpse of Aisha throwing up her hands in frustration and defeat. With a huff she turns to go.

Elbows out, I push my way through the crowd, wanting to get to her before she's back out on the street, before it's too late. But I reach the doorway and it's empty, the guards already repositioning themselves on either side. I lunge through the entrance, squinting as I hit the pavement, glancing in either direction. A few yards away, Aisha is sliding into the back of an Uber, closing the door, and before I can reach her, the car pulls away. I don't even think she sees me as she's driven past the restaurant.

I run a hand through my hair as I watch the car turn a corner and disappear. What just happened? Why didn't I move sooner? How could I let those douchey guards treat Aisha that way? How could Jasper?

"Max?"

Behind me, Jasper is standing in the open door.

"She's gone," I say.

Jasper comes to stand at my back, placing a hand on my shoulder. "It's for the best," he says. "Troy wouldn't have been welcome. If they'd stayed, things would have gotten uglier and I couldn't have protected them. It's better they left, for their own sake."

I shake my head and bite my lip. "I don't see how things could get any uglier."

"Will you come inside?" Jasper asks.

I turn to face him. His eyes are shining with regret, deep with resolute sadness. Is this what being a figurehead for the pack means? Abandoning your real friends to save face. I know Jasper is only doing what he thinks is right for everyone involved. But how could he just stand by and let Aisha be treated that way?

"I need a minute," I say. "I'll meet you inside."

Jasper swallows, nods, and leaves.

The sun is getting low and golden hour is casting Brooklyn in a copper glow. It should be beautiful—the air is warm for this time of year, the sky is clear, I should be excited to spend time with my mate. But after a whole forty minutes at this party, I'm ready to leave.

Behind me the music is thumping through the open door. And the alpha's words are repeating in my head in time to the beat. It's integral for the pack that I show up for them, to prove I have what it takes to lead, so the pack can come together and face the external forces who want to destroy our way of life. I can't run away. But I'm also not sure what sort of leader lets their friends be ejected and does nothing to stop it from happening.

Thinking I'll take a short walk, clear my head, I wander a little ways down the footpath. Beside the restaurant is a narrow alley, and standing in the alley, leaning against a brick wall in a pearl-colored dress, is Olivia.

She glances up and spots me. "You had enough of the party too?"

As I head into the alley the air becomes a little more chill. I shove my hands in my pockets and take a spot leaning on the wall opposite Olivia.

"It's been a second," I say. "How…how are things?"

Olivia's head hangs low, a strand of brown hair falling over her eyes. "Not great," she says.

"Mason says Morven's been keeping Mia pretty busy."

She huffs a bitter laugh. "More like imprisoned. You know he won't even let her have her phone anymore? Says she needs to distance herself from negative influences. Meaning me."

I shake my head. "That's such bull."

"You're telling me. I've just about had it with all this old-school *shit*." Olivia spits that last word. "That whole farce in there. Everyone pretending everything is all right. Drinking their little drinks and eating their tiny little canapés. I only came because my dad made me."

"How is he about everything…Mia and you?"

"He's fine mostly. My mom's the one who's been looking at me weird. Dad's probably the only person who thinks it could be good for our packs—sort of like how they were going to mate Jasper off to strengthen the alliance or whatever."

"He's got a point."

"It's Morven though. Man, he's such a dick."

"I hear you."

"I just wish I could see her, y'know? It's like a chunk of me went with her. It's mad painful. I guess you'd know something about what that's like."

"Yeah." I rub my neck. "Maybe."

She lifts her head and shifts her weight. "Must be all right now though. I saw you and Jasper in there shaking hands, doing your little dance. You're one of them now."

My turn to scoff. "I think I could go to about a million finishing schools and still not know the right thing to say."

"Good," she says, with a capital letter and a period at the end. "You gotta stay you. Hell, we've all gotta do what we gotta do, you know?"

Her lip twitches like she's thinking hard about something.

"What *are* you gonna do?"

She narrows her eyes. "Dunno yet. Something."

A slight breeze picks up, whirling a couple of leaves and a candy bar wrapper around.

When I look back Olivia is pushing off the wall. "I'm gonna get a drink. Can't avoid the circus forever." She makes toward the street. "You coming?"

"Yeah."

As we walk back to the street, she glances down at my feet. "You got your dancing shoes on?"

I laugh. "Never leave home without them."

A car is pulling up as we emerge from the alley and I'm shocked when the back doors open and my parents, glammed up to the nines, hop out. Mom is wearing a shimmering black dress embroidered with glistening beads, and I don't think I've ever seen her wearing so much makeup. Dad is in a fitted charcoal suit, his top button undone, hair combed neatly into place.

"Whoa," I say, and my parents turn, surprised to find their son gawking at them. "You guys look...amazing."

Mom lifts her shoulder casually, as if to say *I know.* "Don't look so surprised, kiddo. We were people once too."

"How come you're not inside enjoying the party?" Dad asks, wrapping a hand around Mom's waist. *Mom has a waist!*

"I, uh, just needed a break."

Olivia adjusts the straps of her dress beside me.

"Oh this is Olivia Castillo, Beta Salazar's daughter."

"It's a pleasure," Mom says.

"We were just getting some air," Olivia says, smiling at my folks. "It's a pleasure to meet you. See you all inside?"

I nod and she heads in by herself, her shoulders back, her head high.

"You having a good time?" Mom asks once we're alone. There's concern in her eyes but also hope. This is the first major pack event they've been invited to and I don't want to disappoint them.

"Yeah, of course," I say. "You wanna go in?"

"Lead the way, son," Dad says.

I head inside with my parents close behind me. The party has continued on as if nothing has happened. Music is blaring, lights are flashing, drinks are flowing. The crowd is dancing and laughing like they're having the time of their lives. We're barely over the threshold when Jasper appears.

"There you are," he says.

"My parents are here." I gesture to where Mom and Dad are standing, barely a foot inside the doorway, glancing around like kids in a candy store.

"I see." Jasper steps toward them, hand outstretched, ready for shaking. "Mr. and Mrs. Remus. I'm so glad you could make it."

Mom blushes beneath her foundation. "Thanks for the invite."

"Swell party," Dad says and even he cringes at his use of the word *swell*. "That is…I mean…happy birthday!"

"Yes happy birthday," Mom echoes.

"Thank you," Jasper says, a polite nod of the head. "Please help yourselves to drinks and food. I hope you enjoy your night."

Jasper is in his element. He's so polite and polished—the perfect host, modest and welcoming, and not overeffusive like I probably would be.

"Come on," I say to Mom and Dad. "Let's get you a miniquiche and a cocktail." I turn to Jasper. "Go mingle. I'll get them settled in then come find you."

"Okay," Jasper says, then leaning closer so only I can hear, adds, "is everything fine?"

I push out a smile. "Perfect."

Doing my best to ignore the occasional sideways glance and the waves I receive from complete strangers who must recognize me—that's new!—I lead my parents over to the bar. Dad orders a beer and Mom some unnaturally blue-colored cocktail. I shoot her an unconvinced look and she shrugs.

"What? I never get to have cocktails. Let me live."

My eyes roll back in my head but I can't help smiling. She's living her best life and honestly I'm here for it.

"Max! There you are." Katie pushes her way through the crowd. "Mrs. Remus you look stunning!"

Mom performs a little twirl, ending with a flourish of her hand. "Thank you, Katie."

Dad makes a strange coughing sound.

"You too, Mr. Remus," Katie says accommodatingly.

"Well, thank you," Dad says, bending at the waist in a little bow.

"And you too, Katie," Mom says. "That dress is gorgeous."

Katie is wearing a pastel-green dress that hugs the curves of her torso then flows in a straight line to the ground. She does look great.

"Where are the twins?" I ask.

"Can I speak with you?" Katie doesn't wait for an answer before she grabs my elbow and pulls me away.

"What's up?" I say once we're out of my parents' earshot. Back at the bar they stand awkwardly, like they've forgotten how to behave in public, watching the party and sipping their drinks too quickly. "I probably shouldn't leave them alone for too long."

"It's Todd and Simon," Katie says, suddenly distraught.

"What's wrong?"

"They...they're dancing with other girls."

"Where? I haven't seen them all evening."

"There's more party upstairs, you haven't been up yet?"

"No, I haven't made it that far."

"Well they're up there and they're..." Tears spring to her eyes.

"Hey." I take her by the shoulders and turn her so she's facing away from the throng. "I'm sure it's just dancing."

She crosses her arms with a huff and sticks out her bottom lip. "I wouldn't be so sure."

"Why? Did—did something happen?"

Before a tear can ruin her mascara Katie holds a finger up to her eyelid to wipe the errant betrayer away. "Todd told me he—he kissed some girl from his school."

"Oh."

"He said he thought he was allowed to because of the whole polyam thing." Poor Katie. It seems her pups might need a little more training. "I told him that's not how it works, that it's not some free-for-all buffet, and he said I was being unreasonable."

"I see."

"And now they're both up there dancing with different girls."

I glance at the stairs, imagining the scene happening on the second floor. "They're still your mates, that has to count for something."

"Maybe." Her anger turns to sulking.

I wish I knew how to help but her situation is more complicated than I have the bandwidth to comprehend. "You probably just need to talk to them and set some boundaries, no?"

She sniffs back her tears and shakes the pout from her face. "Ugh, you're probably right. Would you come up with me?"

Over at the bar my parents have found another couple to talk to and they look happily engaged, chatting away like they're with old friends. Socializing is just like riding a bike, I guess. "Sure," I say.

On the second floor the party continues much the same, only a smaller bar is on the opposite side of the room, and tables have been pushed back against the exposed brick walls to make space for the crowd of dancing wolves. Glass doors lead onto a terrace with a view of the East River and Manhattan.

"See?" Katie says, death-staring at her mates, who are both manhandling a couple of wolfgirls. "Come on."

Before I know what's happening, Katie has taken me by the hand and led me into the middle of the dance floor. She wraps one arm around my neck and places her free hand on my waist and moves to the music, swaying her hips and spinning while I do my best to keep up with her. But I'm not much of a dancer, especially not when I know so many people are watching me, trying to get a sense of who Jasper's mate is.

Her plan seems to be working, however, because very slowly her mates start to notice us. A glance over a shoulder at first. Then Simon is spinning his partner so he can face Katie for a better look. She leans her back against my chest, moving against me, and I play along as best I can.

Todd is the first to break away, abandoning his partner and coming to take Katie's hand. Simon is quick to react—the second Todd moves on Katie he's there as well. I quickly feel like the meat in a Max-and-Katie sandwich of which Todd and Simon are the bread, so I slip away, wondering how red in the face I am. Katie's plan seems to have worked: her mates have forgotten all about the girls they were dancing with and instead have closed ranks on either side of her. It feels like a Band-Aid over a larger issue but I suppose it'll do for now, and I'm glad I could be of service.

I search for any sign of Jasper but don't see him so decide to head back downstairs. The fuzz surrounding my brain has started to feel firmer, the storm clouds full and ready to burst. Strikes of lightning erupt, causing sharp pricks of pain. With an inhale I try my best to hoist my mental guards back in place.

Back on the ground floor, I immediately run into Mom and Dad, who are dancing up a storm, looking like they're having the time of their lives. They wave at me like a couple of teenagers as I approach, and I can't help thinking it's kind of adorable.

"Have you seen Jasper?" I ask and they both shake their heads.

"You tried upstairs?" Dad asks.

"Yeah, I thought he'd be down here."

"I'm sure he's somewhere," Mom says, super helpful.

Just then both my parents stop dancing and the smiles drop from their faces. Even though we're inside I feel as if a cloud has just blocked out the sun, and the noise in my head is overcome by one singular presence. I turn and come face-to-chest with Jericho.

"Alpha," I say, bowing my head slightly.

"Hello, Max." Jericho shifts his gaze to behind me. "These must be your parents."

I spin back to find my parents standing completely still, arms pressed at their sides. They're freaking.

"Alpha, sir, your honor," Dad stammers and bows. "It's such a pleasure." He nudges Mom, who has yet to bow and is instead staring wide-eyed up at the alpha, gently in the ribs and she immediately curtsies.

"Yes," Mom says to the ground. "We're delighted to be invited."

"Please," Jericho booms, his voice cutting through the music. "There is no need for such formalities."

Mom and Dad return to their upright positions and Jericho slaps a hand on my shoulder, knocking the wind out of me.

"After all," he continues, "we're family now."

"So gracious," Mom says in awe, then slaps Dad's chest with the back of her hand. "Isn't he gracious?"

"Uh, yes, very," Dad says, about as bemused as I am at how Mom is staring at the alpha.

"I must apologize for the vandalism done to your property," Jericho says, unbothered, clearly used to being stared at.

"It needed a new paint job anyway," Mom says, giggling.

"We are working on finding the culprit and mending the cracks within our pack that would allow such distasteful actions to occur." Jericho's grip on my shoulder tightens. "Max will be very important to the future of the pack. I'm glad he has parents like you to guide him. We're all very lucky."

"Well, we're very proud," Mom says. "And Jasper seems like a lovely boy."

"Yes," Dad agrees. "A little high-strung maybe."

This time it's Mom who elbows Dad in the ribs, only she's not as gentle.

"Oof, I mean—that is to say"—Dad stumbles over his words—"he takes his role very seriously."

Jericho waits a beat, nodding ever so subtly. "He does. Now my daughter is around here somewhere. If you'll excuse me I need to make sure she hasn't gotten to the cake before it's been cut."

"Yes of course," Mom says, almost curtsying again but stopping herself and instead shooting the alpha her most winning smile.

Once Jericho is gone they both breathe a huge sigh of relief.

"He's very impressive," Mom says, fanning herself, while Dad rubs the back of his neck the same way I do. Guess that's where that comes from.

"He cuts quite the figure," Dad says. Is he a little red in the face as well?

Now that that minute of torture is done I really need to find Jasper. "Are you guys fine if I go?"

They nod and encourage me to enjoy the party. "We're fine," Mom says, in a way that makes me think *I'm* the one cramping *their* style. *Okay you two, have fun, don't get into too much trouble.*

As I search the party for Jasper the noise presses in harder and more aggressively than before. My head swims and my legs are unsteady. I climb the stairs, assuming Jasper must have slipped onto the next floor while I was talking with my folks. By the time I reach the top I'm out of breath and dizzy. I grit my teeth and swallow back a wave of nausea. Then my eye catches on a familiar face—a long, slender nose, a wide forehead, an impressive swoop of formerly blond hair now turned gray—and the pain hits me like an ice pick.

Walter Bridgers is standing across the room talking to Stefan and Maria Lykos, one hand tucked into the pocket of his suit trousers, the other clasped between two buttons of his waistcoat. He has a snide upturn in the corners of his mouth, a smug, entitled grin that looks too much like his son's.

Why is he here? I assumed after what Clayton did his whole family would have been demoted or excommunicated.

Why is the father of my attacker at Jasper's birthday party?

LET THEM EAT CAKE

Walter Bridgers throws his head back and laughs. *At least someone is enjoying the party.*

My hands clench into fists and for a moment I think I'm going to storm across the dance floor, interrupt his conversation, and tell the smarmy douche exactly what I think, but just then the doors to the patio slide open and Tobias Volk enters the room.

"Excuse me, Ladies and Gentlewolves," he proclaims, his handlebar mustache wriggling like a caterpillar and his nasal voice piercing through the hubbub. "If you would please join me outside, we would like to celebrate the birth of our future alpha with you."

With a grand gesture he steps aside and ushers people outside. The crowd begins to flood through the doors. Already people are streaming up the stairs.

"Max!" Jodie is among the stream of wolves ascending from the ground floor, her two friends, also in dresses that would fit in at a human quinceañera, on either side of her. "What are doing just standing there?"

"I—uh—"

"Come on, they're cutting the cake." Confidently, she slips her hand into mine and together we make our way outside.

Jodie pulls me through the crowd, unbashful about simply moving people out of her way, and before I know it we've emerged through the front line, met by a three-tiered cake, with royal-blue icing and gold details, so tall it might as well be a wedding cake. Jasper and Jericho are already there, framing the towering confection.

Jasper smiles apologetically.

"Hey," I say, moving to stand next to him, while Jodie moves to stand with her father, who welcomes her in with a hand on her arm.

"Hi," Jasper says. "Sorry about all this, it'll be over quickly."

"It's fine."

I glance up for the first time at the wall of faces looking back at me. Katie is there, looking less than happy, with her arms crossed and her mates on either side of her looking like they've been going at it on the dance floor, their shirts untucked, their top buttons undone, Simon's tie askew. My parents shuffle sideways until they come into view, Mom raising her eyebrows at me and Dad giving me a proud little wave. Olivia is off to the side looking unimpressed. The Lykoses are smiling like they're celebrating their own child's birthday, and a step behind them is Walter. His head is lowered, casting a shadow over his eyes, which are leveled squarely at me. I clear my throat and look away as Jericho clears his throat.

"Tonight we are here to celebrate the birth of my son," Jericho booms. "And while each year is an auspicious occasion, tonight is an especially important milestone in Jasper's life. For the first time Jasper's mate is with us to join the celebration."

Excuse me?

Every eye turns to me, and the noise of their thoughts is a freight train coming at me. I squint, placing one foot slightly behind the other to brace myself against the impact.

"Maximilian is a courageous and determined young man. His spirit and vitality will be a welcome addition to the leadership of this pack." Jasper slides an arm behind my back, maybe to show how proud he is as well, or maybe because he can sense my urgent need to retreat and is holding me in place. "So tonight let's raise a glass to Jasper and his new mate. A welcome addition to my family!"

The crowd before me lift their drinks—everyone except Walter—and hold them there as Jericho reaches his crescendo. "Happy birthday, Jasper. Here's to you and your mate!"

A cry of "Cheers!" erupts and I take the opportunity to wipe a bead of sweat from my forehead. In the third row Mom is wiping away a tear and Dad's eyes have gone all red and sore looking. Olivia tips her glass in my direction with a raised brow. Katie applauds wholeheartedly, like she's trying to prove a point.

"And now," Tobias says, slipping through a gap in the front row, "cake!"

Jasper takes up a large knife and slices into the mammoth tower. The crowd applauds and a pair of servers emerge with plates. Jasper hands off the knife and they go to work carving up the frosted beast.

When the mass of wolves finally disperses I inhale like I've been holding my breath for hours and let my torso fall forward.

"Max?" Jasper rubs my back and leans closer so I can see him.

"I'm fine," I say. "It was just like all the thoughts were concentrated for a moment."

"You need to sit." Jasper is looking around for a chair, but I have something more pressing to address.

"Why is Walter here?" I ask.

Jasper exhales, pouting like a model, and rubs his eyes. "I wish he wasn't."

"So? It's your party. Don't you get to choose who's invited?"

"It doesn't really work like that. This"—he swings his hand in a semicircle toward the party—"is more for the pack than for me."

"I don't understand. After what his son did, why does Walter still have a seat at the table?"

Jasper takes my elbow and leads me a little farther toward the railing.

"Walter holds the keys to the Elite Pack's treasury. He controls the purse strings. That makes him incredibly influential. If my father has any hope of bringing the pack back together he needs Walter's support. As much as I wish his whole family were sent to live with the rogues, it's not an option. He has too much power."

I scoff and look out across the water at Manhattan, at the shimmering towers lit up against the increasingly dark sky, twinkling like jewels. "I wouldn't wish that upon the rogues."

A tiny growl rolls in Jasper's throat. "Rogues are still rogues."

"You still believe that? After what we've seen? The people we've met?"

"Rogues are still the ones who kidnapped Aisha, who invaded my father's house, who..."

Jasper trails off, his eyes drifting to the floor, but I know what he was going to say.

Who murdered my mother.

I soften. Tonight has already been too much without getting into a debate about whether or not rogues are good or bad or all the same even. I'm tired and, judging by the blank expression on Jasper's face, so is he. All that schmoozing really takes it out of a wolf.

"I'm sorry," I say. "I get it. It's not ideal, but I get it." I slip my hand into Jasper's and smile. "So, are you having a good birthday?"

He glances up, a smirk blooming in the corner of his lips. "It's okay." He steps closer, taking my other hand. "It could be better?" His lips hover less than an inch from mine.

"Oh yeah, what would make it better?"

"This." He kisses me and all the noise in the world falls away. For a moment, as our lips connect and we can taste each other, it's like there's no one else here, my mind is clear. This is all that matters.

When we pull apart, Jasper holds my face, his thumbs soft on my cheeks. "I'm sorry tonight has been so hectic."

"It's not your fault. Like you said, this is a pack event. I just wish you were able to celebrate your birthday properly and..."

"What?"

"Well, it's hard after being apart for so long. All I want is this." I wrap my arms around him a little tighter. "But there's so much small talk and noise, and politics. I keep thinking about Aisha and—"

"I know. I'm sorry that happened. I'll speak to her tomorrow."

We lean our foreheads together and his breath is a warm comfort on my lips.

"I just wish it could be us. Without all the rest."

"Me too."

We kiss again, a little more slowly this time, a little less playful, as if we're trying to kiss away our problems.

"Is this a bad time?"

Jasper's lips leave mine and I turn to find Melissa, a smug grin plastered on her otherwise welcoming face.

"Sorry," she says. "I know you were having a moment. It's just Mr. and Mrs. Fastolf wanted to wish you a happy birthday in person before they had to leave."

I look to Jasper.

"Annette Fastolf is our foreign secretary and grand emissary in the north. She and Mr. Fastolf live in Rochester."

"They need to get going if they're going to get home before dawn," Melissa finishes the thought. "Jasper?"

She gestures to the door but Jasper waits a beat, hesitant to leave me.

"Will you be okay?"

"Yes, go."

I shove him gently and he takes my hand, holding on as long as he can until we're standing with our arms outstretched, our fingers unable to keep their grip, and we break apart. He glances back one more time before slipping through the door and vanishing back into the party.

I can't quite bear to go back in. Now that the cake has been served and night has settled in, onyx and endless over New York, the guests have gone inside for the most part. Only a couple of stragglers remain on the terrace and finally it feels quiet. The fuzz and the clouds have receded, and despite the dull throb that remains, I can stop focusing so much energy on keeping the noise at bay. I take a few deep breaths right down into the pit of my stomach.

Why does everything have to be so complicated? Maybe I should have expected this. After chasing Jasper for so long—so long I nearly gave up and turned back—I almost can't believe how little thought I've given to what our future might hold. Someday, Jasper will be the alpha and I will be at his side, a figurehead, responsible for the pack, for our people. How am I supposed to lead when I can barely get through one night as Jasper's officially recognized mate? Am I just not cut out for this life?

I never really wanted a boyfriend or a relationship until I met Jasper, and when I did I went all in. But there are so many strings, I'm like reverse-Pinocchio. You *can* hold me down.

The metal railing is cold under my hands as I lean against it. In the distance cars speed along FDR Drive, their head and taillights stretching into streaks of color. Manhattan looks kind of small from here, but I know it isn't. There are over a million people on that island. How many of them are wolves? And how many more wolves are out there—in our pack, the packs at our borders, and beyond? How many rogues?

The moon is a big ball of cheese above me. I wonder if the gods are sitting in their palace looking down on me too. For some reason they've seen fit to gift me this power, this connection to all of wolfkind. And for what? So I can be responsible for even more wolves. But how can I do that when I don't feel up to leading a single pack? And how do I start when my powers feel like more of a burden than anything else, a persistent migraine. Unwieldy, uncontrollable, unbearable.

With a heavy sigh I let my head drop. There are too many thoughts and too many doubts. Even without the noise my head aches.

All I want is to spend time with Jasper and figure out who we are when we're together. None of the rest of it matters. Not when it's this hard.

"It's a beautiful night," a smooth, male-sounding voice says. I spin to find Walter Bridgers standing a foot away. "Don't you think?"

"Uh, yeah. I guess."

"You don't seem particularly joyful."

Without asking if I'm in the mood for company Walter steps to my side, placing one calm hand on the railing.

"It's a nice night," I concede, wishing he'd leave me alone.

"It's funny. For someone of your...*stature*, I would have thought all this would be a little more appealing."

My stature? What the actual? "Excuse me?"

He shrugs and continues facing out to the water. "You've worked hard to get here, Maximilian. After everything you've done to reach these lofty heights, I expected you'd be a little more...grateful."

What is this dude on?

"This *is* what you wanted, isn't it?" He turns to face me, grinning like the devil. "Hmm?" He leans closer. "All of this. The parties, the connections. The alpha's ear?"

I shake my damn head. "You don't know anything about me."

"I know you're good at what you do." He actually bumps his shoulders into mine, as if we're old friends, as if we're anywhere near being on the same page. "Somehow you've managed to claw your way from the soil and the sod into the alpha's house. You've bent his ear. Turned his attention away from what really matters. Swayed him to all your modern, progressive ideals."

My whole body is quivering—from anger or fear, I'm not sure. "You have no idea what you're talking about."

His smile drops, his face suddenly grave. "But I think I do, boy."

"I need to go. If Jasper finds out you're—"

Before I can step away his clawed hand grabs my upper arm in a viselike grip. I grunt but am powerless to extricate myself.

"Not so fast," he says, a violent whisper. "I've been at the helm of this pack for a long time, boy. A long time. And I've dealt with more than my fair share of weeds like you. You sprout through the gaps in the concrete hoping to weasel your way to notoriety, to prove you're somebody. But the truth is you're nothing. You were born nothing and you will remain nothing."

I tug harder, trying to free myself. "Get your hand off me."

"You think you can do what you did to my son and get away with it?" he says, his fangs long and lashing. "I'll stomp you out like I've stomped out every upstart who came before you. I'll take everything you hold dear and destroy it."

"If the alpha knew you were talking to me like this—"

"The alpha?" he says, almost laughing. "You think the alpha can save you. You have no idea where the real power lies."

"Max?" Jasper's voice is music to my ears. In a flash, Walter has released me and is smiling, acting cordially, as if nothing untoward had ever happened. Jasper steps toward us, confused but not the right level of worry considering what Walter just said. He mustn't've caught much of our conversation. "Everything okay?"

"Wonderful," Walter says with a flick of his hand. "A perfect evening. I was just acquainting myself with your astute young mate." Jasper glances between us while I rub my arm. Walter has definitely left a bruise. "A wonderful addition to the pack's royal family."

"Thank you," Jasper says curiously, as if he isn't quite buying Walter's act. *Good.*

"The two of you will have a bright, history-making future ahead of you, I'm sure."

Why did that sound like a threat?

"You're very kind," Jasper says, bowing ever so slightly, then turning to me. "Max, your parents were asking after you. Shall we?"

"Yeah, okay."

I slip past Walter and join Jasper as he makes his way to the door, but turn back one last time to find Walter still staring absolute daggers in my direction, grinning maniacally, and I'm pretty sure his fangs have elongated once more.

I expected him to be angry about what happened to Clayton but I never thought he would be outrightly hostile—and in a public setting. He mustn't be afraid of much.

As we make our way back into the party, nodding at Jasper's guests and smiling like good figureheads, I can't help remembering what Walter said. *You have no idea where the real power lies.*

All of my life I thought Jericho was the ultimate power, the end of the line, top of the heap. If I was wrong…who is?

THE HIGH ROAD

"You have to go already?" I ask.

Jasper leans his back on the window of his car. We're out front of my house the day after his birthday party.

"I didn't know you had to go so soon."

Jasper runs a hand through his hair. "I thought I had a few more days but Alpha Jackson of the South Ridge Pack suddenly became available and my father wants me to ensure our southern border is secured before the semester starts back up."

"Right." More pack business. Of course.

Jasper and I have been officially together for around three months and in that time we've seen each other, what, four times in person? With all the commotion and pack duties, last night hardly counts.

He reaches for my hand, slipping his fingers between mine. "I'm sorry. I know it's not ideal."

"It's not your fault," I say. "There's a lot going on. I just wish…"

With his free hand he lifts my chin. "I know. I want that too."

"You have to go right away?"

"If I want to hit the southern border in time for dinner with Alpha Jackson."

With a huff, I roll my shoulders back and stare up at the fluffy clouds dotting the otherwise perfect sky. "We haven't even debriefed about the party. Jasper, I need to tell you what Walter Bridgers said to me."

Jasper's eyes narrow, his lips pucker. "What did he say?"

"He said the alpha wasn't the true power in the pack."

A muscle twitches in Jasper's forehead. "He said that?"

"Or—I guess, that's what he implied."

"He said or he implied?"

"Does it matter? It was a threat against your father. Believe me, he's not happy about what happened with Clayton and he's not happy about me being—you know, with you."

Jasper glances sideways, staring at the spot where the grass meets the curb, his cogs spinning. "Tell me what he said exactly."

"I don't know—"

"Max." He takes my other hand and stares into my eyes. "It's important. Walter is too powerful, too entrenched in every aspect of pack life, too influential to accuse without enough evidence to take him out. If he threatened you, I'll kill him myself. But we need to be a hundred percent sure, otherwise..."

"Otherwise, it could only tear us apart even more."

He nods. "Exactly."

I tell Jasper what Walter said as best as I can remember. That whole moment is a bit of a panicked blur. Adrenaline was thumping through me, not to mention the noise in my head and how distracted I was by what happened with Aisha.

When I'm done, Jasper leans forward so our foreheads are pressed together. "I'm sorry, Max. I'm sorry he said that to you."

"Is it enough?" I ask. "To do something?"

He sighs, big and heavy, like the world on his shoulders is starting to wear him down. "Maybe. I—I don't know. I'll speak to my father."

"Okay. And what about—" I'm hesitant to ask. If this is the last time I'll see Jasper until the summer break I don't want to taint it with awkward conversations, but sadly that's all we seem capable of. "What about Aisha? Have you spoken to her?"

Jasper leans back onto the car once more. "I called her this morning before I left the city."

"Is everything—okay?"

He scoffs. "She's not so happy with me."

I chew my bottom lip, wanting to console Jasper but also feeling like Aisha is completely in the right here.

"But I think—I know she'll come around. Aisha knows how things work and she knows my hands are tied in a lot of ways."

The thought of Jasper with his hands tied flashes into my mind and my cheeks heat up instantly. I need to force that thought out before I can refocus on the conversation.

"Sometimes, I wish—" Jasper starts saying something and then stops. I step a little closer and wrap my arms around him. "I wish I had more freedom to be the—the sort of friend, the sort of partner I want to be."

It's obvious from his clipped, forced way of speaking that this is a hard thing for him to talk about. To admit that he, even sometimes, wishes not to be burdened with the responsibility of being the future alpha is antithetical to everything he's been taught and believed his entire life. To him it's a betrayal. Something tells me that he wouldn't say this sort of thing to anyone else on the planet, and my cheeks warm again as I focus on that thought instead.

"I know—we know you're trying," I say, holding his face in one palm. He leans his head into me and I run a finger over his ear.

"It's only two more months then I'll be back for the summer," Jasper says.

"Manageable," I say with a laugh. "I want to...try the mind-link again."

"Max, no. It hurts you."

"That's just because I haven't figured out how to control my abilities yet. If I work on it I can—figure it out. I know it."

He exhales, blowing air through his lips, and I want so badly to kiss him, but I need his answer first.

"Okay," he says. "We can try. But I want you to make sure it's not too much."

"Scout's honor," I say, making the appropriate hand signal.

He laughs a little, the tension that had built up during our conversation expelled, then he turns to look at the road. "I should get going."

"You sure? My dad's making steak sandwiches. First time he's cracked out the barbecue since winter."

Jasper eyes me like I'm the steak sandwich. "That does sound delicious." Then his shoulders droop. "But I told Alpha Jackson I'd be there by midafternoon."

"Baah, okay. I know you have to go."

"We'll speak soon." Jasper rests his forehead on mine once more.

"Speak soon."

He kisses me hard and long, imbuing his lips with all the words he can't say, as if he's trying to fill me up with enough passion to last until we see each other again.

When we break apart, Jasper moves swiftly to the driver's side and ducks into the car, like he won't be able to leave if he says one more word, if he doesn't go this second.

I wave and wait until the car is gone.

I meet Aisha on Monday evening after school. She's just come from rehearsal, so we grab a bubble tea and hit the High Line. We wander along the raised boardwalk, enjoying the lush gardens reaching for us on either side, passing the slatted recliner seats, and heading under the Standard Hotel. Our conversation remains casual, until we emerge on the other side, back into the evening light. We haven't mentioned the party yet and I was worried Aisha would be cold off the bat, but she left the studios in a surprisingly good mood. Still, I know I need to get this off my chest.

"Hey," I say, not really knowing how to begin but also knowing exactly where to start. "I need to apologize."

She glances at me and sips her drink, the tapioca balls moving up her giant straw.

"For what happened at the party. That was—horrible. I did try to get through the crowd to you but I wasn't fast enough. I can't believe they did that."

Surprisingly, Aisha grins, just a little, then sighs. "I can. But don't worry, dude. That's not on you."

"But it is. And I should have been faster. The second I knew what was happening I should have stepped in or forced Jasper to."

A laugh. "I think you know about as well as anyone that there's no forcing Jasper to do anything."

"Maybe." I rub the back of my neck, unable to tell exactly how well this is going. "I'm still so, so sorry, Aisha. What happened...it's—not okay."

Tourists slip by us taking pictures, and a couple of kids nearly barge right into us. I feel like I'm constantly sidestepping and ducking so I don't run into anyone. Aisha, on the other hand, glides through it all unbothered.

"The truth is," she says, "I knew it was a big move. I'm actually sort of impressed we made it through the doors."

"If you knew it was a long shot, why did you…?"

"Actually, it was because of you."

I stop walking, nearly choking on a tapioca ball. "Me?"

"You and Jasper. What you did at New Year's. I kept thinking it was so brave of the two of you to take a stand like that—to show everyone who you are without fear."

"Trust me, there was a lot of fear."

She shrugs. "That just makes you more brave."

We start walking again, heading uptown with the buildings of Manhattan slipping by on our right and the Chelsea Piers on our left.

"For the longest time I've felt pulled in two directions: the wolf side of me and the human side of me, the pack and my life with Troy. I'm starting to feel, I don't know, like whichever part of me I'm inhabiting is a lie."

"I think I get it," I say. "Like whatever you do you're ignoring a whole chunk of who you are, so neither feels right."

"Pretty much. And I'm tired of it—of feeling like I'm not myself anywhere I go. So I thought, *If those boys can be brave, I can too.*"

"I'm sorry it didn't work out."

We curve away from where we're heading and come to rest against the metal balustrade, looking out toward the Hudson, where boats zip by.

"What happened at the party made one thing clear," Aisha says, her voice level and self-assured. "The pack will never accept me for all that I am. Troy will never be welcome. He doesn't belong." She leans over the barrier, her elbows resting on the steel. "So neither do I."

Aisha isn't talking to me so much anymore as to herself. It's as if she's putting these thoughts she's been sitting on into words for the first time, and as if by speaking them into reality she's confirming something she's known but hasn't been able to accept…until now.

"What do you mean?" I ask.

"I'm done," she says. "With the pack, with playing by their rules. It's a losing game. And I'm not playing, not anymore."

It's hard to figure out what she means exactly. Is she going to reject the pack? Will she leave New York? Become a rogue?

"What will you do?" I ask.

She's squeezing her hands together, rubbing one palm with the opposite thumb. "I haven't decided yet. I'm not going anywhere." She turns and leans her back against the balustrade, facing back toward Manhattan. "This is my home. But I'm not attending any more pack events. Or abiding by the alpha's rules if I don't want to."

"Did you tell Jasper this?"

"No," she says. "When he called to apologize I was still sort of cut up and hadn't been able to make sense of what I wanted. Or maybe I had but I'm not ready to tell Jasper yet. He wouldn't—I don't think he'd get it."

"You'd be surprised," I say, remembering what he said to me yesterday, about wanting more freedom.

"All Jasper's life he's known what his future holds. He's never really had to think about what that means for his life and his ability to choose his own path. Until you showed up."

"Hey-o."

"You really shook his tree, I hope you know that," she says, making my mind race with questions.

What was she privy to during the last six months that I wasn't? What insight does she have into Jasper and his struggle coming to terms with our connection? Even though everything has worked out for the best, I'm still curious to know.

"So I don't begrudge him," she continues. "Because he doesn't know any better. I just hope one day he'll understand." She side-eyes me knowingly. "I think you'll help him on that front."

I turn around so we're shoulder to shoulder. "Yeah, maybe."

We stand like that for a good minute, not saying anything. It occurs to me that as my destiny seems to be pulling me further into the pack and the pack's business, Aisha is moving away. Does being with Jasper mean accepting the distance growing between me and the people I care about? Does it mean compromising what I believe?

If that is that case, I don't want it to. And I decide then and there that I won't let it. Whatever my future with Jasper looks like, I won't accept sacrificing the things and the people that mean the most to me—not in service of a pack who accepts people like Clayton and turns away people like Aisha and Troy. I just hope Jasper can understand that.

"You want Froyo?" Aisha says all of a sudden, pushing off the barrier and continuing to walk north.

"Um, always."

Jasper calls me the Sunday after he's gone back to college and I've gone back to school. The first week crawled at a painfully glacial pace. My teachers struggled to hold my attention. And while I had hoped we'd talk a little more often, Jasper has been weighed down with a backlog of essays and assignments, ones he's been neglecting because of the situation with the bordering packs.

I happen to be on my way to my spot in the woods when he calls.

"Hey," he says, his face large and gorgeous on my phone screen. "I've missed you."

"Ohhrr, I've missed you too," I say, a teasing hint in my voice.

"So I was thinking—"

"Uh-oh!"

"Shut up, I was thinking we could try mind-linking, if you feel up for it?"

I reach my spot and plonk down on the rock where I usually sit, dropping my sketchbook beside me on a mossy patch of ground. The stream is full and rushing by at a speedy pace, the spring air is fresh but warm, the afternoon sun is midway toward the horizon and shining warmly on my skin. Much like the trees and flowers coming back into bloom, I feel like I'm being reborn, my leaves sprouting, energy replenished.

"Yeah," I say. "Definitely up for it."

"Okay," Jasper says. "You ready?"

"Ready."

Jasper places his phone farther in front of him, probably leaning it on a pile of textbooks or the edge of his desk, and I notice he's already sitting on the floor, a plump cushion beneath him. He's ready to go. He closes his eyes first, palms facing upward on either knee, so I pull my feet up under me and try to get comfortable on my rock. I close my eyes, relax the walls of my mind, and reach out with my consciousness.

Part of me is scared of another stabbing pain, so I take things slowly this time, hoping I can head off any unwanted howling before it becomes too much to take.

I swim in a dark void as fizzing red streams of consciousness take shape around me. I pull them toward me in my mind and from all directions they come, looming closer, growing larger and more vivacious.

Up ahead I notice one that's brighter than the others. Could that be? *Jasper.* I feel his essence like I know his scent. I lock onto the light of his life strand and move toward it.

His presence is like warmth, a hot bath, or my favorite sweater, enveloping me as I move toward it. It expands and spreads until I'm surrounded, bathing in his heat and light.

Jasper? I call out with my mind. *Can you hear me?*

Could this be it? Are we on the precipice of mind-linking?

Are you there?

In a flash I'm pulled downward. The light disappears and I'm sucked into darkness—free-falling. Then suddenly the light is back, only it's white and blinding and I'm still falling. With a splash I land in a shallow body of water, then thrash my way to the surface and gasp for air. Once I've shaken the water from my eyes, I squint into the light.

I'm standing at the edge of a waterfall, forest on three sides and mist rising from the sheer edge over which the sky, a perfect blue, stretches on for eternity. The sun is a blazing ball of light. Across the water something catches my eye—a dark shape floats on the surface. A body.

Dread seizes my gut like a ravenous wolf and I sprint, lifting my knees and splashing my way across the basin.

I dive for the body, slipping an arm under Jasper's back and cradling his limp head in the other. His face is blue and puffy, one eye swollen shut, his bare chest covered in angry cuts and livid bruises. His mouth is open ever so slightly and, no matter how much I shake him, he doesn't move.

Madness flares in my abdomen, rage expands in my chest. I wipe the hair from his face, touch his battered skin. Still, he doesn't respond. He's gone. *Dead.*

With a guttural urgency I open my elongating jaws as fur sprouts all over my body and claws and fangs spear outward. With one mighty breath, I look to the moonless sky and release a bloodcurdling howl.

HAPPY BIRTHDAY

When I wake up it's dark. I lift my bleary head, my mind still swirling in a fog, and something pointy sticks into my back. Leaves crunch under me as I shift my weight and try to sit up. I'm lying on the ground among the moss and fallen branches. One leg is still draped over the rock where I sit and draw.

I must have passed out after...

The vision I experienced comes back to me in a flash. At the waterfall. Jasper's limp body in my arms, his broken face, his lifeless eyes. My breaths become short, and I grope around in the brush for my phone.

"Max!" In the distance I hear my name. Someone is calling for me, shouting my name over and over: "Maaaaaaaaax!" It's Mom.

"Over here," I mutter as loudly as I can, my chest aching with the effort.

It's a struggle but I manage to haul myself back up onto the rock. My phone is on the ground a couple of feet away, where I must have dropped it. Looks like it slid a little ways down the riverbank.

"Max?" Mom and Dad explode from the nearby trees, Mom coming straight for me. "Are you okay?"

"Yeah, I'm fine. I think I must have passed out. I was on the phone to Jasper."

"We know," Dad says. "He called us. Said you stopped responding. But we didn't know where you were. What happened?"

I stare at my parents' faces, concern, worry, confusion etched into their features, and I don't know how to respond. What did happen? I've only ever been able to see memories before: Jasper in the car with his mom the day she…and Clayton when Aisha rejected him. But this—this couldn't be a memory, because Jasper was—he was—I can't even think it.

A bewildered shake of the head is all my parents need to know that now's not the right time to get into it. Mom grabs my phone while Dad helps me up, and together we make our way back to the house.

"So, kiddo," Mom says, handing me a steaming cup of chamomile tea with organic honey, then moving to sit on the armrest of the chair where Dad is situated. "You want to tell us what's going on?"

I pull my feet a little farther under me on the sofa, hold my favorite cozy blanket tighter around myself. A plate of chocolate chip cookies is balanced on the armrest.

"Jasper and I have been trying to mind-link," I say.

They glance at each other, communicating something I can't comprehend. I wonder if they've ever tried it, ever been able to speak without words. Could they be doing it now?

"Mind-linking is a pretty tough thing to accomplish," Dad says. "Your mother and I have never been able to."

"Not that we've tried all that hard," Mom says, nudging Dad semiplayfully.

"We know," I continue. "But we figured since Jasper has all that alpha training and I'm the blood wolf or whatever…"

Another unreadable look is shared between them.

"Max, we don't know much about your—I can't believe I'm about to use these words—blood-wolf powers." She shakes her head like she just said the most fanciful thing imaginable. "Maybe it's best not to push yourself. Until we know more."

"But how am I supposed to learn more?" I set my tea down on the side table and edge forward on the sofa. "No one seems to know much of anything about it and I'm so tired from keeping everyone's brain noise at bay, even if I wanted to experiment, I'm not sure I could figure out how before something like today happens."

Mom leans forward, her hand inching out from her body like she wants to reach for mine.

"And I just thought if I could mind-link with Jasper it would make this whole long-distance thing easier."

"You haven't had a lot of time together, have you?" Mom asks.

I shake my head. "And there's also…" I trail off. I don't know how to tell them I had a vision, if that's what that was.

"What is it?" Dad leans forward so both my folks are bent awkwardly toward me.

"A few times now when we've tried to mind-link I've heard this howl and I dunno, it's hard to explain. I feel like I'm being called, like someone's trying to tell me something. Then today I saw—" I can't say it out loud, the words catch in my throat. "I saw something awful and I feel like I need to figure out what's going on. But with all the stuff with the pack and with school and everything else going on I…"

I can't explain why but suddenly I'm tearing up. My eyes sting and my head wants to flop all the way back. Mom jumps up and comes to join me on the sofa.

"You must be exhausted," she says.

I rest my head on her shoulder and realize she's right. I am so, so freaking tired. Keeping everyone's voices out of my mind is a twenty-four-seven job. I've become so used to it I don't really register how much energy I'm expending keeping my walls up. That, coupled with my regular teenager duties—homework, school, friend drama—and my directive to be a good leader for the pack, *AND* missing my boyfriend, is a lot for this little wolf.

"School will be done for the year soon," Dad says, doing his best to be comforting. "And we can look into finding someone to help with the whole blood-wolf thing. How does that sound?"

I nod as Mom brushes my hair back from my forehead. "Your birthday is coming up too," she says. "Have you given any thought to what you might like to do?"

"Probably just something small," I say. Planning a birthday party is the least of my worries. "I dunno."

"Don't think about it now then," Mom says. "And maybe it's best not to try and mind-link for now."

"Yeah," Dad joins in. "And you can forget about the pack for a while. There are plenty of people whose job it is to take care of that stuff. You just concentrate on getting through the school year."

"Okay," I say, sniffing.

"You want to go to bed?" Mom asks.

"Uh-huh."

I shuffle off to my room thinking they're right. Screw worrying about the fate of our pack. I'm a sixteen- (nearly seventeen-) year-old kid, not a diplomat with a degree in international relations. And Jasper and I have plenty of time to figure out this mind-link thing. Maybe we're just putting too much pressure on it. Maybe it would be easier to back off for a while.

Once I'm tucked under my covers, I give Jasper a quick call.

"Max!" He answers on the second ring.

"I'm fine," I say before he can ask. "Just a bit of a headache. Pretty standard."

"I didn't see what happened, I had my eyes closed."

"Hard to say, really. Think I blacked out."

"Was it the same as last time? That wolf call?"

I take a beat before responding. Should I tell him the truth? Tell him what I saw? Or is that a little preemptive? Would it be just another thing to worry about? I don't want to place any more pressure on Jasper, so I decide not to tell him about the vision.

"Yeah, just the same thing."

"You've never lost consciousness before," he says. "I was worried."

"I know. I appreciate that." I snuggle back into my pillow. "What were you doing before I called?"

"Packing," he says.

"Where you off to this time?"

"Philadelphia."

That must be the farthest he's gone on these diplomatic trips. Jericho really has him shipping out all over the country at this point.

"I wish we could go somewhere," I say. "Just run off for a bit."

"That would be nice."

"Somewhere quiet," I say, noticing my eyelids getting heavy.

"Perfect," Jasper says quietly.

A yawn erupts from my mouth, breaking our peaceful moment. "I should go," I say. "So sleepy."

"Okay, Max. Sleep well. I'll—I'll speak to you tomorrow if I can."

"Good night."

"Night."

My eyes are shut before Jasper has time to hang up the phone.

"Happy birthday, Max!" Katie screams, dropping her two bags overladen with picnic supplies and balancing a sheet cake in a plastic container as she leaps into my arms.

My birthday always lands in the last week of school—a fact that has plagued me my entire life. It's almost impossible to plan a birthday party when everyone is already planning their summer vacations, their end-of-year parties, distracted thinking about ice cream and beaches and leaving school behind. This year is no different. But for the first time I'm actually happy about it.

After my little tumble off the rock in the woods, I decided to take my parents' advice and chill out on the whole future-leader-of-the-pack front. Jasper and I have put a temporary hold on trying to mind-link. And luckily Katie and her mates seem to have come to something of a stalemate, so there hasn't been too much extracurricular drama. I was able to finish my junior year, get through my exams, without too many distractions.

Jasper has been busy as well, wrapping up his freshman year at Harvard (for Selene's sake!) and continuing to extend his father's advocacy program to farther reaches. I swear he's covered almost the entire northeast corner of the country at this point. If the Elite Pack was looking for friends, we must have found them by now. We've still managed to speak every other day or so—although that still doesn't feel like enough.

So instead of planning a big blowout birthday bash, I've invited a small group of close friends to Central Park for a picnic with a view to finding some place to sing karaoke later if we're still in the mood and haven't maxed ourselves out on sausages, burgers, and cupcakes. Katie agreed to meet me a little early at a cozy spot near Bethesda Fountain to string ribbons between trees and set up the picnic. My parents are also buzzing around somewhere, getting the barbecue going (Dad's job) and scoping out the nearest public toilet (Mom's job).

"Oh my god," Katie says, finally releasing me from her death hug. "We're so old!"

Katie's birthday was a couple of weeks ago and she's obviously still adjusting.

"Absolutely decrepit," I say.

She surveys the area. "This is a cute spot."

We've planted ourselves between a number of trees—aspen or oak, I'm not sure. Through a copse it's possible to see the lake, and there's enough shade without blocking out the fresh summer sun altogether. The grass is green and lush and dotted with daisies.

"Who's coming again?"

I smile at her and start unpacking one of her bags—piling bags of potato chips, queso dip, doughnuts, plastic cups, and paper plates onto the rug I previously laid down.

"You, Todd, Simon," I say. "Aisha and Troy. My parents. Your mom."

"She's on her way," Katie says.

"And that's it."

"No Jasper?"

I take a breath. "He said he'd try and make it but he's coming back from visiting a pack in Atlantic City."

"Oh," she says, glancing up from where she's peeling the foil off a platter of chicken wings. "I'm sorry. I'm sure he's called though."

My face screws itself up into a weird formation.

"What's that face about?"

"Jasper's been really great at communication this last month—all year, even. But the last week or so...he's been sorta hard to get in touch with. He hasn't even messaged me today."

"Not even to wish you happy birthday?"

"Nope."

Katie shuffles over on her knees and gives me a best-friend hug. "I'm sorry. I'm sure he's just been busy."

"Yeah," I say with a quick sigh. "You're probably right."

"What's up, party people?" Katie and I look up to where Troy, in loud Bermuda shorts and an open shirt with a bucket hat and large sunglasses, is heading across the grass, waving. Aisha is beside him looking super freaking chic in a tank top and denim shorts, also with massive sunglasses and a very wide-brimmed sun hat.

I wave back and run to meet them. Troy gives me one of his signature confusing handshakes and I hug Aisha. We haven't spoken much since the day we hung out on the High Line.

"How are you?" I ask.

"Right as rain," she says, a touch of steel in her voice. "Happy birthday, dude."

"Yeah, happy birthday, man." Troy slaps me on the back, making me splutter. His eyes lift over my shoulder to where Katie has ripped the Saran Wrap off a large plastic bowl. "No way. Is that potato salad? This picnic is about to be lit!"

Troy heads over to, I guess, ogle the potato salad, and Katie enlists his assistance hanging paper ribbons.

"How is everything?" I ask when Aisha and I are alone.

She lowers her sunglasses just enough so I can see her eyes. "Things are great, Max. I'm hella focused on my dancing, things with Troy are great. Forgetting about the pack was the best decision I ever made."

"I'm glad. Hey, um, have you...?"

"Heard from Jasper?" she asks, finishing my question.

"Yeah."

"No, sorry." She brushes past me before I can ask any follow-ups, which I think is sort of cold, but I try not to dwell on it.

I follow her back to where Katie and Troy have started blowing up balloons.

"I love this song," Troy says, jumping up from the rug to dance along to the music blaring from Simon's portable speaker.

Evening is settling in, the sky turning pale, orange and pink at the edges. Other people are packing up, leaving the park, but my party is still in full swing. My parents are sitting on a separate rug from the rest of us, Katie's mom having come and gone already to a previous engagement, leaving Mom and Dad as the sole adults present. From the way they're canoodling I don't think they mind. *Happy birthday to me!*

Aisha jumps up to join Troy, and Katie, Todd, Simon, and I watch on, laughing and picking at the remaining corn chips and gummy bears.

My phone buzzes on the rug nearby and I snatch it up. I hate that I'm just a little disappointed.

Mason: Hey birthday boy! Don't have too much fun without me.

Mason: But actually have the BEST day you sexy beast!

Mason: xxx

I fire back a couple of super witty thank-you texts and finish up with "Wish you were here!"

Then I click through to my thread with Jasper. His last message was sent yesterday. Nothing at all today.

"We might have to make a move soon," Katie says, leaning in so only I can hear her. She glances up through the trees to where the sun has pretty much all the way set. The sky is darkening, the stars popping into existence like faraway lights being switched on one at a time. "Still up for karaoke?"

With a sigh I drop my phone, which lands dangerously close to the almost-scraped-clean potato salad bowl.

"He hasn't said anything yet?" she asks.

"Nope."

"I'm sorry."

I lift my head. Aisha smiles at me as she and Troy continue dancing, Todd and Simon are fighting over the last Cheeto, my parents are laughing at some private joke, and Katie is here, and it feels like things between us are back on level ground. This would be the perfect birthday, except for one glaring absence.

"Okay," I say, rising to my knees. "Better warm up those vocal cords."

Todd loses the Cheeto battle and looks over.

"What's that?"

"Time to go," Katie says, slapping his shoulder.

"Sick," he says. "Time to show off my amazing voice."

Simon cracks up. "Time for us to invest in earplugs."

Todd shoves him in response and the two of them topple over, wrestling on the rug.

"Are we heading off?" Aisha asks.

I glance across the grass one more time, then with a breath I say, "Yep, let's go."

As I say those words, however, a warm familiar presence emerges from the deepening shadows, and I spin hopefully, not quite believing my eyes as they find Jasper, wandering across the grass, waving, looking fresh as hell in black jeans and a white tee. He smiles and waves, and the grin stretching across my face is so wide it might break my face.

Instantly I'm on my feet running toward him.

"Oomf!" He grunts as I crash into him, but his strong arms hold me as we kiss hello.

"Where have you been?"

He grins mischievously. "I wanted to surprise you." He lifts his eyebrows. "Surprise."

I press my lips together trying to act unimpressed but too happy to stop the grin.

"You bonehead," I say.

He licks his lips and says, "Happy birthday," then plants a serious kiss on mine.

When he's done wishing me happy birthday in a physical sense, I take his hand and make to head over to the group. "Come on, we were just about to pack up and head downtown."

"Wait up." He pulls me back to him with one hand while the other retrieves an envelope from his back pocket. "This is for you."

He hands me the blank envelope. I glance up at him questioningly, then pull out two airline tickets.

"What is this?" I ask, studying the destination. Jasper has given me two tickets for a flight departing from JFK and landing at LAX. "California?"

"My family has a house out in Joshua Tree. The nearest neighbor is miles away. I thought we could take a couple of weeks to hang out there, just us—away from everything else, like you said. We could go camping, hike, sleep out under the stars."

"That sounds..." I'm too bewildered to finish my sentence.

"What?" he asks, looking suddenly worried. "Is it okay? If you don't like it we can go somewhere else. This is just the most peaceful place I know."

"No," I say. "I—I love it. This is perfect."

"It is?" When did he get so adorably unsure?

"It is," I say. "Let's run away."

THE TALK

"Absolutely not," Mom says, looking up at Jasper and me from where she and Dad are still sitting on their picnic rug.

"What do you mean?" I ask, face flushing with embarrassment.

"You're not running to the other side of the country unsupervised."

"Are you being serious right now?" I ask.

"Deadly," Mom says.

I groan performatively, doing my best to communicate how freaking annoying they're being. "Dad?"

"I'm with your mother on this," he says, completely useless.

"Mr. and Mrs. Remus," Jasper says, his voice a little shaky. "I promise we'll be safe. I won't let anything happen to—"

"You didn't find him passed out in the woods a month ago," Mom snaps back.

Seriously, why are they being so ridiculous?

"Is it really that big of a deal?" I ask. "You were more than happy for me to go camping without you around last summer."

"At the Blue Moon Festival?" Mom asks. "There were hundreds of other wolves there."

"So? It's not like we haven't been away before."

"When you went running into a den of dangerous rogues?"

Aisha shifts uncomfortably in my periphery. Our little argument has put a dampener on the picnic party vibes. Katie and the others are all sitting quietly, pretending not to listen. I don't get it. After everything I told my parents about needing some peace and rest, why are they blocking this?

"It won't be like that," I say. "Come on, this is what we talked about. It's what I need—some time and space to, I dunno, clear my head?" I don't know why it comes out like a question. But the upward slope of my intonation has Mom raising a brow, as if she's just as uncertain.

"If it helps," Jasper interjects once more, "I can have a couple of pack security guards positioned nearby. If anything does happen they'll be there to intervene."

Mom and Dad share a look. Has the promise of additional wolf-muscle convinced them?

"The thing is," Dad starts unsteadily, as if he's searching for the exact right phrasing, "we're not just concerned about the danger of you two running off together, it's…"

Is he? Is my dad blushing? Oh…oh no. Oh my freaking moon gods, no.

"It's that going away with someone that you're"—he clears his throat painfully—"that you're *with* is—is a big step."

I run a hand over my steaming-hot face.

"And your mother and I are concerned about—uh—about…"

I can't believe this. Are my parents trying to have *the talk* with me now, at my birthday party, in front of my boyfriend and all my friends?

Mom slaps a hand on Dad's knee and takes over. "We just don't want you rushing into any decisions before you're ready."

"Moon gods!" I say, clutching my face.

"And we also want to make sure that you're prepared."

This is not happening. This can't be happening. Jasper is motionless at my side, most likely as devastated as I am.

"It's important to know—what you're doing and how to do it safely," Mom continues. "And it's not something we've spoken about before, so your father and I think it would be better if we all took a minute and talked about—"

I've heard enough. I let out a huff, throw my hands up, and storm away. I don't even know which direction I'm walking in, I just need to get away from the abject torture of hearing my parents discussing my possible future sex life. All I want is to spend some time with my mate without the burden of thinking about how it affects the pack, without being scared my head is going to explode. I haven't even thought about if we'd...

My feet stop moving of their own accord. Somehow I've made it halfway across the bridge that crosses the lake.

Have I been naive? Should I have been thinking about sleeping with Jasper? Should I have assumed that's what would happen if we went away together? Things have changed a hell of a lot since the first time Jasper and I shared a bed at that dingy motel, back when Jasper was still trying to pretend he hated me. And the time we stayed in the tent in the mountains, neither of us were in a particularly sexy mood. Will this trip be different? Are we different? Am I? And is that something I'm ready for? I place a steadying hand on the railing as footsteps approach behind me.

"Hey," Jasper says, arriving on the bridge. "You okay?"

I turn and face him, my cheeks still warm, and find him looking strangely bashful, his head bowed, his eyes darting from mine to the ground.

"I didn't mean to suggest that we'd—I don't want to pressure you into—we don't have to—"

With a single step I come to stand an inch in front of him and slip my hands into his.

"Honestly, it hadn't even crossed my mind until my insane parents brought it up. I mean—I don't mean it *never* crossed my mind. Believe me *that* has definitely crossed my mind." Where am I going with this? "What I mean is I didn't think that's what you were suggesting. Not that I wouldn't—not that I wouldn't like to, at some point."

Finally, his gaze settles on mine and I force myself to hold his stare.

"You would?" he asks, his voice low, with just enough gravel to it.

I bite my lip. "Yeah, I mean, yeah. I would. Would you?"

His smile reaches the corners of his eyes and he nods. "Yes."

For a moment we're locked in a never-ending expanse of time. The stars reflected in the calm surface of the water twinkle and rise like fireflies all around us. The wind rustling in the branches of the willows is a gentle whisper, a hum, singing some romantic tune. If this was a rom-com the camera would be circling us as we drift closer together, closer and closer, until we kiss.

When the rom-com moment ends I pull back, stifling a laugh.

"What is it?" Jasper asks, his forehead grazing my bangs.

"I can't believe how awkward that was," I say. "I'm sorry."

"They're just being good parents."

I sigh. Jasper is right and in a way that's sort of comforting. In a sea of wild emotions and dramatic events, my parents wanting to awkwardly discuss sex with me is a wonderful island of normalcy.

"How are we going to convince them to let us go?" I ask.

"We could...make it a group thing? See if Aisha and Troy want to tag along? Katie too?"

"Sort of betrays the point of getting away, no?"

Jasper's shoulders slump forward. "I guess."

As much as I want to get away without anyone else, to spend some serious one-on-one time with Jasper, his idea has merit. Maybe making our solo trip into a group hang is the only way to convince my folks to let us go.

"It's worth a shot," I say.

"It won't be too disappointing?"

I shrug. "It'll be fun."

We head back to the picnic site hand in hand. The sun has fully set and the park has grown dark. The rugs have been packed away, the food and cups stashed in bags and a cooler. Everyone is standing in a line, waiting for us, ready to leave.

"Hey," I say to my parents, letting go of Jasper's hand and stepping forward. "About the trip. We were thinking maybe if everyone is free it would be okay if—"

"Max," Mom says, stepping forward. Dad follows closely behind. "Your dad and I have had a little chat and..."

Mom pauses. I glance across the faces of everyone present. Aisha has a cheeky grin and Katie is swaying from side to side with a knowing smirk.

"Well, you are seventeen now and in some wolf cultures that makes you an adult. Your father and I met when we were fifteen and sixteen."

Dad joins in. "And we certainly didn't wait to—" Mom coughs, stopping him before he says *way* too much. "What I mean is," Dad says, course correcting, "you've been through a lot and we know we can trust you—"

"So, we would be happy for you and Jasper to go on this trip"—oh my moon gods, what? This is too good, this can't be happening—"on one condition."

Oh. My stomach drops. Of course there's some random condition. We can't just have a good time.

"You need to check in with us every day," Mom says, issuing her decree. "Let us know immediately if anything goes wrong. We need to be in the loop. No radio silence like the last time you ran off."

I rub the back of my neck. So far so good. "Okay, I can do that."

"And Jasper, you mentioned a couple of security guards," she continues.

Jasper nods. "Yes, I'll have my father arrange it."

"Good," she says. "But double that number. I think four guards is reasonable after the trouble you two have been in."

Jasper's blushing but also smiling. "I'll need to confirm with the alpha, but I think that can be arranged."

I look between Jasper and my parents. "So, is that it? Can we go?"

Mom and Dad glance at each other. I can tell they're unsure, but they know how much this chance means to me and I know they don't want to deprive me of a second of happiness.

"Yes," Mom says, and I'm just about to jump for joy when she spits out, "and one more thing!"

"You said one condition," I say, knowing how whiny I sound.

My parents share another awkward glance. Both of them are hesitant to say whatever they have planned next.

"What is it?"

Dad raises his eyebrows at Mom as if to say *Go on then.* She stares at him with a tight mouth for a moment before sighing, rolling her eyes, and huffing.

"Fine." She pauses, shakes her head as if she can't quite believe what she's about to say, which does not bode well. "Your father will take you shopping for"—she clears her throat—"supplies."

I squish up my face. "What sort of supplies?"

"The kind that you might need…in…order…to…have…safe—"

"Condoms!" Dad says, announcing it to the entire park.

Katie and Aisha can't help giggling. Todd and Simon pretend to stare at the ground. Troy hides his embarrassed grimace behind a hand. Even in the dark I can tell Jasper has turned raspberry red. My face is devoid of blood, my hands cold and clammy, my mouth hangs open in stunned silence.

Dad coughs and adjusts his posture, realizing just how loud he shouted *condoms* in front of a bunch of teenagers and the stragglers making their way out of the park.

"That is, we want you to take—"

"Don't say it again!" I shout, holding out a hand in a stop sign. "Fine, you can buy us those, just please, don't say it again."

For a moment it seems no one out of the nine of us lingering in the dark knows what to say next, until eventually Katie clears her throat.

"Anyone up for karaoke?"

An hour later Katie and I are belting out the lyrics to "Cruel Summer," pretending we're center stage on our very own *Eras* tour. The karaoke room we booked is in the basement of a building in Greenwich. Down here it's just us. Blue lights cast everyone in an otherworldly glow.

In a way we have moved into a new era. We're still besties but now we both have relationships, our friendship group has expanded from just the two of us, into a mixed and fun group. I know Katie was worried we were growing apart—and we are, sort of—but as I take her hand for the final chorus I know there's no one In the world who gets me quite like she does.

After their embarrassing attempt at sexual education my parents headed home, telling us to be safe and to have fun. So far we've covered everything from Olivia Rodrigo to *Wicked* the musical. Troy performed an Usher song with surprising vocal dexterity. The bro-twins gave a stunning duet performance of "Total Eclipse of the Heart."

Jasper refuses to sing. But as I howl into the mic I lock eyes with him and neither of us can help smiling.

Finally, after all this time we're going to be together, without school or college getting in the way, without pack relations, friend drama…no kidnappings, mystical powers, or psycho wolves to distract us.

This just might have been the best birthday ever, and this summer is going to be one I'll remember for the rest of my life.

CALIFORNIA HERE WE COME

"You're so lucky," Katie says, spinning in a circle on my desk chair. I drop a sweater in my duffel bag and shoot her a smile. "I wish one of my mates had a holiday house in California."

I laugh a little and consider the pile of clothes I pulled from my wardrobe, wondering what else I should pack.

"Do you think I need to take more than one pair of pants or just shorts? Does it get cold at night?"

"I don't know," Katie says, stopping her spin to face me, a devilish grin slapped across her face. "Do you think you'll be wearing clothes at all?"

I toss a pair of balled-up socks in her direction. "*Staaaaahp.*"

"What?" She shrugs, acting all innocent. "It's romantic. You and Jasper alone in the desert. No one around but coyotes and cacti."

My face is burning up so I turn away from Katie, grab a handful of T-shirts and shove them into my duffel

"What's up?" she asks. "Are you nervous?"

I take a large breath. "I dunno. Maybe. I haven't—I've never—what if I'm...?"

"What, Max?"

"What if I'm bad at it?" Once the first question is out the rest seem to follow of their own accord. "What if he doesn't want to? What if we're not a good fit? Like incompatible or something? What if he's done it a bunch of times with other people and they're, I dunno, better? What if I don't like it? What if he doesn't?"

"Max, Max, Max," Katie says, jumping up and coming to stand at my shoulder. "Stop. It's okay. It's natural to be nervous."

Something about the way she says that last part, as if she knows what she's talking about, clues me into something I'd been wondering about. "Wait, have you...?"

Katie shoves the pile of unpacked clothes across my bed and sits. She glances up at me through her eyelashes, her cheeks turning pink.

"You have!"

She covers her face with her hands.

"Katie!" I take her hands, pull them away from her face, and hold them. "You didn't tell me. When? With...with which one?"

"After my birthday," she says. "With both."

My mouth drops open and my eyes shoot wide. Katie sees my expression and matches it.

"Not at the same time!" she shouts, toppling backward in an embarrassed pile.

I move my bag and flop down next to her. "Katie, that's so...I mean...how was it? Tell me everything."

We both turn onto our sides. "I was really scared. Simon came to my house the day after my party while my mom was out and one thing just sort of turned into another and he was really careful, he kept making sure I felt okay and wanted to...you know"—she blushes a deeper shade—"keep going."

"Sounds nice."

"It was. He was. It was all really nice. I mean it sort of hurt at first but after a while it was…" Her smile spreads and her eyes sort of glaze over as if she's lost in the memory of it.

"And Todd, how did that happen?"

"The day after," she says. "I went over to his house and he'd made this whole sort of setup in his room with fairy lights and music."

"Mmm, romantic."

"It really was," she says.

"And was it the same? Better?" She doesn't answer right away. "Worse?"

Eventually she exhales. "It was different. Still good. The thing is it just felt so right with both of them. Because they're my mates and we love each other I stopped being nervous and it just felt good, like it was meant to happen."

"That's really sweet." I slip my hand between hers. "I'm proud of you."

She looks deeply into my eyes and I realize we haven't hung out like this in a while.

"It'll be like that with you and Jasper too," she says. "I just know it."

I blow air out between my puckered lips, my heart rate picking up speed. "You think?"

"I know."

"And has anything changed? Since you…?"

"Yes," she says, her smile softening. "It's better between us—all three of us. It's like we've figured out that we're the only people for each other. There's less jealousy between them, less fighting. They haven't been flirting with other girls either."

"Good," I say with a snort.

"I was scared of how I would feel after, how things could change for the worse. But now that we've done it

I—I never felt closer to them. I hope that's how you feel as well."

She squeezes my hand and I squeeze back.

"I'm glad you told me," I say.

"MAAAAAAAX!" Mom calls up the stairs, breaking the quiet of our best-friend moment. "Are you ready? Jasper will be here soon!"

"I should probably finish packing," I say to Katie, then plant a soft little kiss on her forehead.

"He's here," Mom says as I lug my overstuffed duffel bag down the stairs, Katie following behind me.

"Stop peering through the blinds like some creepy stalker," I say when I spot Mom kneeling on the sofa so she can lean over the headrest to spy through the window.

She jumps up and smooths out her shirt. "He's here," she repeats. "You all set?"

I take a little breath and try to pull my shoulders back. The truth is…I'm a little nervous—not just about sleeping in the same bed as Jasper, but about leaving my life, my friends, and my parents behind for two whole weeks, about flying across the country. Suddenly this whole escape plan feels too big, the destination too unknown. And I can't help wondering whether it's too late to turn back.

"Uh…" I say. "I think so."

Mom comes over and puts her hands on my shoulders, instantly making me feel more settled. "You'll have a great time," she says. She places one hand on the side of my face. "You deserve this. Your dad and I are really proud of you, kiddo."

"Thanks, Mom," I mumble back.

"Now have you got enough underwear? Bug spray?"

My head falls backward as I groan. "Yeeeees."

"Okay," she says, grinning at me. "Have an amazing time." Mom kisses my forehead then pulls me in for a hug. "Dad said to squeeze you extra hard since he couldn't be here to see you off."

Her arms are wrapped so tightly around me I'm worried she'll break a rib. "Did he say to crush your only child?"

I take in a deep gulp of air when she lets me go and turn as Katie opens the front door. The sun is bright and warm and floods through the door, blinding me, but I know out there Jasper's car is parked at the end of our drive, and he's waiting for me. I step to Katie and she gives me another too-firm hug.

"I'm really happy for you," she whispers in my ear. "Enjoy it."

I'm not sure whether she's talking about the trip or…something else. But either way I say, "Thanks. You too. Don't get too experienced while I'm gone."

I lean back, smiling smugly with a suggestive raised brow. She grins back. *Since when did we get so adult?*

I shield my eyes from the light and step outside. As my sight adjusts, Jasper comes into focus. He's leaning against his car, looking too cool and carefree in a pair of sunglasses, a fitted black tee, and a pair of cargo pants. When he sees me his face lights up and I almost have to shield my eyes again.

"You ready?" he asks, taking a few steps toward me.

I glance back at the doorway where Mom and Katie are waiting. Katie shoots me a wave and Mom—is she wiping away a tear? It's not like I'm leaving for good.

"You take good care of him," Mom shouts to Jasper.

He salutes her with two fingers. "You have my word."

"Don't have too much fun," Katie says.

Jasper reaches out to take my bag, his fingers grazing mine as they linger on the handle.

"Hey," he says, smiling.

I bite my lip. "Hi."

"All set?"

One more breath to settle my racing heart, then I say, "Yep. Let's go."

He takes my bag and moves to the back of the car, opening the trunk and placing it inside, before continuing to the driver's side. At the car I pull the door handle and take one last look back at the house. Mom and Katie both wave this time, and I wave back before opening the door and jumping in.

On our way to the airport I watch the traffic around us and can't help noticing a pair of black SUVs that seem to be heading the same way as us.

"Is that...?" I ask, nodding toward what looks like an armored car in front of us.

"Security," Jasper says. "They've been with me since before I arrived at yours. They'll be tailing us until we arrive at the house." He reaches over and places a hand on my knee. "We'll be safe."

I shoot him a reassuring smile, grateful that he cares so much and a little thankful to have the extra protection. But part of me is also a little put off. This is supposed to be our first big trip away by ourselves. Are we going to be sharing our holiday with a fist of beefy security guards? What are they going to do? Come hiking with us? Swim in the pool? (I'm assuming there's a pool.) Sit one table away if we go out to eat?

A small but sharp pain slices behind my eyes, making me rub my temple.

"Still hurts?" Jasper asks.

I grimace and nod.

"Not long and we'll be the only wolves for miles."

Except them, I think, glaring at the SUV up ahead.

As we pull up outside the terminal at JFK I notice a woman in a business suit waiting by the doors. Jasper stops the car and jumps out without even switching off the engine.

"Madeline!" he says, his tone rich with familiarity.

"A pleasure as always, Jasper," the lady in the expensive-looking blazer says, tipping her head to greet us. "You've nearly racked up enough frequent-flier miles to buy the airline."

"Almost," Jasper croons. He shakes Madeline's hand and she glances over her shoulder. "And this must be Max."

"Yeah, hi!" I step forward to shake her hand also.

"A pleasure," she says. "And welcome, it's an honor to have you flying with us today."

"Uh, pleasure's all mine," I stammer.

A guy in a red vest appears from inside. "Sup, Jasp."

"Hey Antonio," Jasper says. Does he know everyone who works at the airport? As casually as anything, Jasper tosses his car keys at Antonio, who catches them like this is some well-rehearsed routine.

"How was traffic today?" Antonio asks, pulling open the driver's side door of Jasper's car.

"Not so bad," Jasper says.

"Ay, you royal wolves have all the luck. Catch you round."

With that Antonio ducks into the car and zooms away. I guess Jasper has been traveling a lot. I just assumed he was flying private this whole time. Maybe not.

"Would you like to follow me?" Madeline asks, gesturing to the doors.

"Uh, sure," I say.

We're whisked through the airport, slipping through a door into a private section and avoiding the usual queues at security, barely pausing as they pass our bags through an X-ray machine, and then we're led to a private lounge. Gentle music plays from unseen speakers, elegant yet comfortable-looking sofas warm the space, crystal light fixtures glint overhead. So this is how the other half lives.

"Whoa," I say as my gaze lands on the free buffet.

Before us is an open-salad-bar-style spread. Piles of cantaloupe and watermelon catch my eye first, but also pastries, bagels, lox, bacon, eggs. I already ate breakfast but that doesn't matter because right next door is another spread, this time sandwich meats, crusty-looking bread, salads, cheeses, and next to that a full-on dinner selection with pastas, roast meats and potatoes, grilled veggies, and then...then I spot the dessert cart. My mouth is salivating so bad.

"Can we just stay here for two weeks?"

Jasper laughs. "You hungry?"

I grin and shrug. "I could eat."

Once we've piled a couple of plates high with free food we find a spot to sit and dig in. Not only is the spread extensive, it's also freaking delicious. I don't think I've ever tasted lamb so moist and tender, a Caesar salad popping with salty anchovy goodness, peaches and apricots so ripe and juicy, soft serve as smooth as silk.

"This is so good," I say, mouth full, head down. When Jasper doesn't reply I look up and he's barely touched his plate. "You don't like it?"

"Huh?" He glances up, looking distracted, which, considering my extreme level of gluttony right now, is maybe not the worst thing. But I can tell something is up.

"Everything all right?"

He actively twists his lips into a smile. "Yes, everything's fine," he says, a wistful lilt to his voice. "I just—haven't been back to the house for a while."

"When was the last time?"

He pauses for a long time, his eyes not moving from a Tater Tot that's fallen off my plate and onto the table. "Since my mother…"

Jasper trails off but he doesn't need to say anything else.

"Oh." He hasn't been back to the house in Joshua Tree since before his mom died. It must have taken a lot for him to decide he wanted to go there, to take me there. "You're sure you want to—?"

"Yes." His eyes shoot up to meet mine and he nods. "I'm sure. I want to see it."

"I'll be there…" *Obviously.* I shake my head. "I mean if you want to talk about it or her at any point…"

He smiles, genuinely this time. "Thank you."

When it's time to board, Madeline appears again to escort us to our seats. I could get used to this level of service, for sure. We're sitting in first class and Jasper has booked a pair of seats in the middle of the plane. I say *seats*, but actually they're more like pods—whole rooms even, complete with a chair that converts into a bed, a TV screen bigger than the one back at my parents' house, a table, and a minibar. The whole thing is sleek and clean, with marble-effect surfaces, polished wood detailing, and gold trim. They've converted our two separate pods into one large suite. Already laid out on my chair are pajamas, slippers, and a toiletry bag full of products I couldn't afford samples of.

"Mamma mia," I say, motionless in the aisle staring at this ridiculous setup.

"What did you say?" Jasper asks, storing his small suitcase in the overhead compartment and tossing his black backpack into his side of the joint pod.

"I said...holy freaking smokes."

Jasper is staring at me with an amused smirk, but he turns from me to scan the pods with his hands on his hips. "It's pretty nice, right?"

"Yeah, I mean...I get that you're used to it, but I never thought I'd be flying first class."

"I get it. We flew coach once when I was about seven and there is no denying this is pretty special."

"You flew coach once?" I ask indignantly, verbally rolling my eyes. "That must have really sucked."

"It did—oh, you're making fun of me."

I feign shock. "Me? Never!"

We settle in and it isn't long before we're taxiing out to the runway.

As the plane speeds up, the tarmac slipping beneath us as we surge forward, I reach over and take Jasper's hand.

"Thanks," I say. "For planning this."

He holds my hand up to his face and kisses my knuckles. "I can't wait to show you the house."

An hour into the flight, we've eaten more amazing food and had our seats converted into the equivalent of a double bed. Jasper, the consummate traveler, is out in a second, breathing lightly. He must be exhausted.

I watch him sleep for a while, distracted from some rom-com I've got playing on my TV. And as my eyes begin to close as well I realize for the first time in months, my head isn't aching. The dull throb is gone, left behind with the wolves back on the ground, the troubles of our pack and the thoughts of our kind forgotten, unable to reach me up here.

I just hope when we land my mind stays as clear.

THE HOUSE IN THE DESERT

A painful howl tears through my mind as I'm wrenched from sleep, springing upright, my hips pressing against my fastened seat belt.

What was that? Was I dreaming or was that the same howl I've heard before in my visions—only magnified? I thought I was escaping the noise, yet somehow it's traveled with us. Maybe it was just a dream, a fluke, the last death rattle of a fading life force. It has to be, right?

"Sorry," the flight attendant, a petite blond woman who has been super-duper friendly the whole flight, says. "I didn't want to wake you but"—she glances up and down the plane as if to say *You're the last ones on board*—"we're here."

"California?" I ask like a doofus.

"Uh-huh, welcome to the Golden State."

Jasper is beside me, only just stirring awake. He opens a squinty eye. "Are we here?"

"Yeah," I say. "I think they want us to leave."

Jasper sits up, having spotted the flight attendant. "Right. The car should be waiting."

He's adorably sleepy, his hair sticking up at a strange angle on one side, his eyes a little puffy. We both must have slept all the way through landing. I would've thought someone would have woken us, made us put our chairs in the upright position. Things really are different in first class.

"You sure you're okay to drive?"

"Will be...with coffee."

"I'll have some waiting for you as you disembark," the flight attendant says, still friendly, but obviously wanting the sleeping passengers to get out of her hair so she can begin cleaning up after us.

It's dark out when we exit the airport. There's a car waiting for us just outside the sliding doors of the arrivals terminal. It might as well be Jasper's car's identical sibling; it's so similar. The valet driver hands off the keys and we slide in.

"Ready?" Jasper says. "It's about a two-and-a-half-hour drive."

"Perfect." I nestle into my seat and try my best to stay awake as we drive off into the night—though of course, it's all of three minutes before I'm drifting off again.

When I wake we're still driving. I glance over at Jasper, who looks content behind the wheel, his eyes focused on the road, his finger tapping along to some slow song on the stereo. Outside I can't see much. We're on a long, thin road with no streetlights. I can just make out the dusty edge of the road and a bit of the natural surroundings: rocks and dry-looking plants, the occasional cactus.

"Almost there," Jasper says.

"Sorry," I say, smacking my dry lips. "I didn't mean to drift off."

"It's okay. You must be tired. And we're on holiday now so you can sleep as much as you like."

"Music to my ears."

Jasper leans forward as if trying to make out something in the distance. "The turnoff is ahead. Just a few more minutes."

We finish the drive in silence. Jasper takes it slow as we leave what I guess was a highway and travel up a winding dusty path, the tires jumping on the bumpy road surface as we go. Eventually we come across some sort of oasis. Palms and large-leafed succulents are lit by moonlight, a rainforest seemingly sprung up in the middle of this desert. Jasper slows to a stop and parks the car. The headlights stream through the layer of foliage to shine on the caramel beams of a fence, the boundary of the property.

Stepping out, I feel the crunch of sand beneath my feet and warm, dry air on my face—a welcome relief after the hours of air-conditioning. The air out here smells and feels different from the air back home, sweeter almost: aloe and sand, pure, clean, uncomplicated. I throw my head back and breathe in deeply, then I spot the stars.

"Whoa." I turn in a small circle as the Milky Way rotates over me. I've never seen a sky quite like this: so clear, the darkness deep and unending, but dotted by the most brilliant stars—so many they seem to twist and meld until they're a river of light, swirling through the cosmos. For a moment I feel like I've closed my eyes and am reaching out with my blood-wolf senses, the sky and the stars the void of my mind and the souls of all of wolfkind.

"Pretty spectacular, isn't it?" Jasper says, hoisting open the trunk and grabbing out the bags.

"It's...ridiculous."

Stretching out toward the inky darkness in every direction is a moonlit desert. There's not another house or town or even a light source whichever way I turn. The horizon is dotted by the spiked limbs of desert plant life, the curved shoulders of large rock formations, and the jagged silhouettes of the smaller rocks that pepper the landscape.

Jasper sidles up next to me, watching me as I explore our new environment.

"The next house is over sixteen miles away. Out here it's just us."

"We're really alone," I say, closing my eyes and enjoying the quiet. The humming sensation at the back of my mind is gone, the pressure of wolf noise vanished and in its place stillness, calm, a cool balm on my tired consciousness. Then a pinprick pierces that calm.

I glance behind us to see the headlights of two other cars, wobbling their way along the rocky path. Our entourage of security guards. They stop about two hundred meters from us, flip their lights off, and switch off their engines. The purr of car motors dies away, leaving only the quiet of the night. I rub the side of my head where their presence made itself known.

Jasper must notice because he says, "I've asked them to keep their distance. Hopefully they won't bug you too much."

I shoot him a smile. "It's fine. Better safe, right?"

"Sure. You want to see the house?"

"Can't wait."

Crunching footsteps in the dirt, I follow Jasper through a narrow gate, flanked on either side by large cacti with tear-shaped arms. Inside, a paved pathway lined by monstrously large aloe veras curves toward the house, an adobe cottage with smooth dusty-red walls, light wood finishings, and a low-corrugated-iron-roofed veranda with a rustic fence.

I stop on the path and take it in. Jasper stops as well.

"You like it?"

"It's—not what I expected. It's sort of quaint."

"You were expecting one of those sleek, modern *Architectural Digest* mansions?"

"Pretty much."

"Are you disappointed?"

"No, this is perfect."

Jasper was right, I had been expecting a wall of concrete, some complex feat of engineering, burnished metal, treated timber—a smooth, hard, modern piece of design that stood out amongst the landscape. This is a cottage, a humble casita: it blends in with the vistas surrounding it, like it belongs, like it's been here forever.

"My mother found this place," Jasper says. "Dad would probably have bought the first concrete slab house he saw but she..." He fades off wistfully, his eyes traveling over the wonky roof, the plants growing up the sides of the walls, the lopsided windows and natural finishings. "She wanted this place to feel homely—less like we were imposing on the land and more like we were being welcomed into it."

I step to meet Jasper and slide my hand into his.

"I love it."

He takes one last little breath. "Come on."

It takes some rattling but Jasper is finally able to get the heavy iron key to turn in the lock. He steps inside and flicks on the overhead light. The house blinks to life. A warm glow from the dusty bulbs is cast over the terracotta tiles and patterned rugs. Immediately before me sit a few burnt-orange leather sofas, with woven rugs draped over the seats and armrests, and cushions all along them. A mirror hangs on one wall over a thick wooden shelf dotted with handmade-looking ceramics and old magazines. Beyond the living space is a kitchen with bottle-green tiles, a deep farm-style sink, light natural wood cupboards, and an island topped with more hefty natural timber. Doors lead off on either side of the living space.

"Through there is the meditation room," Jasper says, pointing in one direction. "And the bedrooms are this way." He makes in the direction of the bedrooms, ducking through the low doorway.

I follow him into a small hallway. An alcove at one end with a window looking out onto the back patio is furnished with a hanging chair and a stump of wood that serves as a table, and three doors punctuate the opposite wall. Jasper stops midway to nod at an open doorway.

"Bathroom," he says, then moves on.

I stop to appreciate the geometric pattern on the tiles, the tub by the window, the large waterfall-style shower, then follow Jasper, who is turning into one of the bedrooms.

He tosses his bag onto a chair at one side of the large bed, already made up with white linen sheets, rich-yellow pillows, and a woolen throw, while I linger in the doorway.

"Is this..." he says stiltedly, glancing from me to the bed. "Are you...I'm usually on the left."

I shake myself back into the room. "That's okay. I usually sprawl, so..."

"There's another room if you'd prefer. I can—"

"No," I say before I know I'm speaking. "This is good."

Finally, I enter the room, with a nervous smile, dropping my bag on the opposite side of the bed. I don't know why I'm acting all bashful but there's something about the quiet and the distance from the rest of the world that makes the fact Jasper and I are here together without supervision, without anyone to interrupt, all the more apparent, and all the more real.

We turn to face each other, the mattress an ocean between us. Jasper wipes his hands on the sides of his legs, his shoulders lifting and his lips pressed together. I chew my lip and rub my neck.

"Shall I..." Jasper begins, a little unsure, "show you the rest?"

"Yeah! That'd be great."

Relieved to be leaving the bedroom, but also a little disappointed we didn't christen the bed right there and then, I follow Jasper to the other end of the house. The meditation room is furnished with cane chairs, rugs and pillows with geometric patterns, candles, a small gong, and a few ferns in pots leaning their fronds against the wall, reaching for the window. It occurs to me that everything looks a little too clean, a little too ready for visitors for a place that hasn't been used in years.

"Was someone here before us?" I ask.

"We have a property manager, someone who comes out here regularly to clean, water the plants, and fix anything that's broken."

I run my hands over the strands of string hanging from a dream catcher that's hung on the wall. "Someone comes here to take care of this place even if no one comes here."

"Yeah," Jasper says, clearly feeling a little awkward about this admission. "It was actually my idea. A few years ago Dad wanted to sell the place. I convinced him to keep it and to hire someone to watch over it." His eye catches on something sitting on the windowsill. "Oh, look at this." He picks up a small glass figurine from the sill and I move to his side. Made from a dark-burgundy shade of glass is a horse figure, its mane flying furiously in an unseen breeze behind it. Jasper holds the delicate object up so I can take a closer look. "This was my mother's. I remember she bought it at a local market. My father told me not to play with it because it was too fragile, but Mom—she showed me how to hold it so it wouldn't break."

"It's beautiful," I say. "She must have cared about this place a great deal."

"She did. She loved it here almost as much as I did." Jasper lifts his gaze from the object and surveys the room. "I can feel her. Her energy is all over this place."

His eyes become glassy as he goes completely still, lost in thought or memory, I'm not sure which.

"Are you okay?"

He lowers his chin and smiles at me. "Yes. I like feeling her presence. I—I've missed it."

Gently, he places the horse figurine back in its spot on the windowsill and glances out through the glass. "There's more," he says. "Come on."

The back door seems to be stuck, but with a kick and a shoulder Jasper manages to dislodge it from its frame. For a moment he fumbles with the light switches next to the door, declaring "Uh-huh!" when he's found the right one and flicking it on. A web of string lights illuminates the back porch, hanging from the slatted wooden veranda that stretches along the entire back of the house. Cool tiles rest under our feet, and a large wooden table sits with eight hefty chairs around it waiting for guests. Large planters line the edges of the veranda, encasing us with verdant plant life. Cacti, cacti, and more cacti! Beyond the veranda sits a glistening blue pool, also lit up and casting refracted swirling light onto the ceiling. Beyond that is nothing but desert, drifting off toward a mountainous horizon until the light can't reach and everything becomes shadow.

"It's so huge," I say, stepping off the tiles, onto the dusty ground toward the pool and the expansive, arid world beyond. "It looks like it goes on forever."

"It sort of does," Jasper says, arriving at my side.

"And it's just us," I say, then remember the guards camped out in their SUVs on the other side of the property, "well, almost."

"We can go exploring tomorrow," he says, although if he'd offered me his hand and said, "Let's go, right now," I would have taken it and run off with him to the mountains this very second.

"Thank you for bringing me here," I say, taking a long inhale of desert air. "I think this place is exactly what I—we needed."

Somewhere far off I make out the distant call of a coyote. My mouth falls open half in shock, half amazement. I turn to Jasper and his eyebrow is arched as if to say, *I know.*

"Pretty wild, right?"

I nod and turn back to the view. The next couple of weeks are going to be perfect.

THE FIRST NIGHT

"What the fudge is that?!" I shriek, dropping the bedsheets and leaping backward.

Right smack bang in the middle of the bed is a scorpion, sitting with its tail raised, its black limbs all sharp and dangerous pressing into the mattress, two orbs on its head looking like demonic eyes.

"What is it?" Jasper says, appearing in the doorway in a tank top and boxers, his toothbrush shoved in his mouth.

I point an accusing finger at the intruder. "How did that get in here?" As if sharing a bed with Jasper for the first time since we officially became a thing wasn't nerve-racking enough...now we're contending with venomous critters?

"Oh, that little guy?" Jasper is nowhere near the right level of freaked the frick out.

"Yeah, that treacherous little bed-devil with the poison stinger."

Jasper shoots me a look before disappearing back into the hall. I listen as he spits and runs the faucet, then he's back, wiping his mouth with a facecloth. Much to my dismay he moves straight to the bed, reaching out both hands and scooping the scorpion up in them.

"This breed doesn't have enough poison to do much damage to a werewolf—not with how quickly our healing ability counteracts the venom."

He heads from the bedroom back to the living room and I follow, terrified he's about to be stung and fall over dead before we're one night into our vacation.

"Plus, they react to fear. If you're stressed they get stressed," he says, very unstressedly. "Do you mind?" He gestures from me to the door with his head.

"Huh? Oh sure." I trot to the door, running through it as Jasper passes a little too closely with the scorpion in hand.

Crouching down, he gently shakes the death-bug off his hands and into the soil, then claps his hands together at a job well done.

"See?" he says, turning to grin at me all smuglike. "Nothing to worry about."

I gulp, because now that the scorpion is dealt with, there's no escaping that Jasper and I are about to share a bed.

"Ready for sleep?" he asks.

"Uh, yeah."

I slip into the bathroom on the way back to the bedroom and shut the door behind me. The person staring back at me in the mirror looks different than I remember him. His hair is a little messier, his face a little more defined, his shoulders a little more square. He's not unattractive, not by a long stretch, but still, his smile is sort of lopsided, his front two teeth are a little too large compared to the rest of his chompers. I run my hands down my chest and onto my stomach. It's not *not* flat but it's not a rock-solid wall of muscle either, like I expect Jasper's to be. Cringing, even at myself, I lift the bottom of my T-shirt and survey the state of my abdomen.

"You all right?" Jasper calls from the bedroom.

I sigh and drop my shirt. Guess I'll have to do.

Back in our room, Jasper is sitting up in bed, leaning on the rattan headboard, holding a book. He's lit by a single dim lamp, which accentuates his sharp jaw, his muscled arms. I gulp, suddenly aware of how incredibly quiet it is out here.

"What are you waiting for?" he asks, and I realize I'm lingering in the doorway like some weirdo.

"What are you reading?" I ask as I move to my side of the bed, lifting the sheets and slipping under.

Jasper glances at the cover of his book. "It's uh..."

"Is it for school?"

"Actually, no." Okay, blushing. Why is Jasper being coy about his book? "It's a romance book. Well, a fantasy actually—a fantasy with romance in it."

"A romantasy?" I ask.

"Yeah, I guess. But with lots of battles and swords and dragons," he says, increasingly flummoxed. "It's pretty lame." He quickly deposits the book on his nightstand.

"Sounds fun."

My shoulder blades press against the headboard and we both sit quietly for a minute, like we're waiting for something to happen, or for the other to make the first move. Should I kiss him? Hold his hand? Ask him about the plot of his novel? The silence is suddenly deafening and I long for the buzz of cicadas, the chirp of crickets, a damn coyote howl, anything to break this awkward silence.

Suddenly we both erupt at the same time:

"We don't have to—"

"Is it okay if we don't—"

We turn to face each other, laughing a little at how awkward we're being. I can't help but sigh with just a smidge of relief. Jasper runs a hand through his hair. I guess he's feeling the pressure as well.

"It's not that I don't want to…" he begins, struggling with eye contact but forcing himself to meet my gaze. "I do." He places his hand on mine. "I really do."

"Same," I interject swiftly. "I definitely want to." We both huff a little laugh. "It's just our first night out here and…"

"Let's not rush," he says, lifting his free hand to cup my face. "We have forever."

His lips find mine and he kisses me slowly, tenderly. "Is this okay?" he asks, pulling back for just a moment.

"Very," I say, and go back in for more.

We slip down the headboard and roll onto our sides, kissing all the while. His body is super firm under my touch. My hand slips over his waist onto his back, pulling him a little closer. He slips one hand up under my T-shirt, making me gasp gently. My body is telling me not to wait, screw patience, but my mind is telling me this is enough, more than enough. I'm out in the desert, alone with Jasper Apollo, and we're making out under the covers. Through the ceiling the stars are shining down like the souls of every wolf who's ever existed. And we're together, connected like never before. I don't need anything more––for now, this is absolute freaking bliss.

After a while, Jasper pulls back. His eyes remain closed and his tongue slips along his bottom lip, as if he's savoring the taste of me.

"I could do that all night," he says, his eyes fluttering open ever so slightly.

"Me too."

"*Buuuut* we should get some sleep."

"Yeah."

"Big day tomorrow."

"Is it?" I ask. I didn't know we had plans beyond more of this.

"Mm-hmm," he purrs. "Tomorrow we run."

I don't know what Jasper means but before I have time to ask he's kissing me again, his thumb playing with my earlobe, his feet tangled up in mine.

"Good night, Max," he says, pulling back with a sharp inhale.

"Good night."

He wipes the hair from my brow as if he needs a clearer view to study my face, then he kisses my forehead. I spin around so that his arm is draped around me, pulling my back against his chest, and drift off almost immediately.

Rested is an understatement. I wake up the next morning feeling fresher than a newly sprouted spring flower. Sure, it takes a moment or two for me to open my eyes—the bed covers, pillows, and mattress are so soft and warm, and they envelop me in such an amazing way I could probably lie here forever—but eventually the smell of brewing coffee rouses me. I sit up, stretching my arms over my head and yawning. Jasper's side of the bed is empty but an indentation in the pillow sits where his head would have rested last night, and the sheets are still warm.

Content and reaching an acceptable level of alertness, I fling back the covers and swing my feet over the edge of the bed, glancing back one more time at the ruffled sheets. I can't believe we get to stay here. I can't believe I got to sleep in Jasper's arms, and I can't wait to do it again. For now though I want to know where he is, so I stand and move lazily through the house.

Jasper is in the kitchen, wearing only his boxers—to be fair it is warm already—poking at a frying pan with a spatula. He's so busy cooking, grabbing a pinch of salt, adding what look like chili flakes and scallions to the pan, and continuing to stir its contents, that he doesn't notice me in the doorway. I lean on the doorframe and watch him for a moment. He moves from the pan to one of those hourglass-shaped glass pour-over coffee contraptions and tips some of the freshly brewed brown liquid into a stout ceramic mug, adding a dash of cream and sipping slowly. The toaster pops and he snatches out the piping-hot slices of thick, crusty bread, tossing them from hand to hand in the most adorable way, and goes about buttering them. The muscles in his back pop and move with each swipe of the butter knife.

As he turns back to the pan he must catch sight of me in his periphery, because without looking over he grins and says, "Enjoying yourself?"

"Just appreciating the view," I say with a laugh and move from my spot in the doorway, crossing the living room to join him in the kitchen. "This smells amazing."

"Hungry?"

My stomach rumbles on cue. "Totally."

"Help yourself to coffee," he says, switching off the gas burner and arranging the toast and what I can now see are the most perfectly fluffy, yellow scrambled eggs on two plates. Lastly, he grabs a large, deep-green avocado from a well-stocked fruit bowl and slices it in half.

"When did all this food get here?" I ask, pouring myself a mug of coffee.

"This morning. We had it delivered. You slept through the whole thing."

"I was wiped." The scent of the coffee wafts into my nose and I take a long, deep whiff. "Heaven."

"What was that?" Jasper asks, spinning with two stacked plates of breakfast in his hands.

"Oh." I blush. "Nothing."

We head to the table outside, because as if we're about to eat indoors when the weather is this nice. The sun is already hot and bright, and in the shade of the veranda the air is the perfect temperature. Jasper places my plate in front of me and sets his own down at the spot next to me.

"Nearly forgot," he says, dashing back inside and swiftly reappearing with a bottle of hot sauce. "This stuff will blow your socks off."

"If only I was wearing socks."

He hands me the bottle and our fingers graze each other's, sending sparks of electricity through me.

"Maybe it'll blow something else off," he says, making me nearly choke before I've even touched my food.

Jasper seems unfazed as he sits and goes about carving the flesh of his avocado half and mushing it into a cream on his toast. I do the same, although nowhere near as coolly.

Delightedly, I shovel the first fork of eggs and avocado toast into my mouth. "Thanks for cooking," I say with my mouth full.

"No problem. I take it you slept well?"

"Like a baby."

Jasper smiles and eats and I can't help thinking something seems sort of different about him. His movements are more fluid, his posture looser, his rigidity gone, his hair more unkempt. He chews his food slowly, relishing each bite, as he stares out at the desert with big, open eyes. He seems...relaxed. And it occurs to me how strange it is that I've never seen him properly relaxed before.

"No wonder," he says, then takes a large inhale. "It's the air out here. It's just different."

So are you.

Beyond the shade of the patio sits the pool, looking perfectly blue and stupidly refreshing against the dusty-yellow backdrop. It's the first time I've taken in the view in the daylight and it's even more stunning. The pale, sandy-colored earth is dotted with green tufts of desert grass, spiky cacti rise like lizards leaning into the sun, and in the distance sit these amazing stone structures, like pebbles made smooth by rushing water—only on a much larger scale and in the most arid of climates. Farther off mountains, mauve-colored in the haze, line the horizon, and all of this rests beneath a vast, cloudless sky.

"I could stare at this forever," I say, suddenly itching to grab my sketchbook and document this ridiculous landscape.

"Just wait," Jasper says, "it only gets better."

"Oh yeah?"

"Yeah, after breakfast we'll go explore. How is it?"

"I don't know what you put in these eggs but they taste like crack," I joke. "Honestly so good."

"It's cheddar," Jasper says. "You grate it in before you whisk the eggs, makes them extra flavorful. My mom taught me that."

"Delicious."

After breakfast, we wash our dishes and I'm about to grab my sketchbook when Jasper moves to the back door. "Ready to explore?" he asks, a devilish glint in his eye.

Why do I somehow think he's got more than exploring on his mind?

"Do we need to plan a little before we go hiking?"

"We're not going hiking," he says, raising a brow like he's challenging me

"Then what are we—"

Before I finish he's slipped out the door. What is he up to?

"Jasper?" I ask, following him outside.

He steps from the tiled patio onto the dusty ground. The sun hits his tanned shoulders, making them shimmer like gold. He glances over a shoulder and eyes me eyeing him.

"Time to run," he says.

I step forward, unsure and completely confused. "It's kind of hot for running, isn't it? And you're not wearing shoes."

"We don't need shoes."

He's sort of scaring me, the way he's talking in riddles, his voice eerily calm, like he's in some sort of trance. I move to the edge of the patio area and Jasper walks farther toward the open expanse of desert.

"Come on," he says, then to my complete dismay he drops his boxers.

I try not to but can't help staring at his pert ass, enjoying the way the sun hits the curve of his hip, the muscles as they move. Surely he's not about to go running naked into the desert. Maybe that scorpion did sting him and he's having some sort of poison-induced psychosis. Maybe the heat is melting his brain.

"What are you doing?"

He turns back one last time, grinning from ear to ear.

"Time to let the animals out."

With that his whole body convulses, his shoulder blades poke agonizingly toward the sky, nearly tearing through his skin. Fur sprouts at his feet and rises up his legs until it's growing all over his body. His hands crunch and curl in on themselves as razor-sharp claws push from his nail beds. Jasper drops to all fours as his wolf emerges. Onyx-black fur covers his body, his limbs crack and twist as they reconfigure within his muscles. His face is the last to change, his nose lengthening into a muzzle, his teeth dropping and sharpening into dangerous fangs. His eyes remain as emerald green and piercing as ever. Finally, when the transformation is complete, Jasper—or Jasper's wolf self—stands before me, majestic and so at home in the wild countryside.

He snaps his jaws at me, twisting his head as if encouraging me to do the same, to shift into my wolf form and join him.

But I haven't let my wolf out since the blood moon, since I shifted involuntarily and almost maimed a bunch of my friends and Rocky Pack wolves. I've been worried about what would happen—that like the last time, I wouldn't be able to control myself, that my new wolf powers might be amplified to the point I can no longer stand it.

And yet my skin is tingling, my fingers twitching. Clearly, my wolf wants to burst out, to be free, to run wild and carelessly with his mate.

Jasper growls and lifts his muzzle toward the desert.

I pull my T-shirt over my head and step forward into the sand.

RUNNING WITH THE WOLVES

I let the beast inside me rise to the surface, my animal instincts kick in, and before I've even dropped my underwear on the ground, I'm shifting, morphing from teenage boy to wolf. In an instant my muscles have rearranged, my bones cracked and forged back into place, and I've bent forward to all fours. Letting my wolf out feels like breathing in after months of holding my breath. It feels like the release of a deep tissue massage. My body feels powerful, relaxed, lithe, and ready.

I shake my muzzle, letting go of the last shreds of human tension, and eye Jasper ahead of me. In wolf form the world takes on a multicolored hue, scents rise like clouds of phosphorescent light—and the strongest, most blindingly beautiful belongs to Jasper. He's watching me carefully, eyeing me with a mix of pride and sly enjoyment, his citrusy, mint-fresh scent emanating off him in waves, drawing me in. I scratch at the dirt a little, testing the ground for grip and temperature, then make my way to Jasper.

Instinctively, I press my head against his flank, nestling into his neck to let him know I'm here, and he leans into my touch. We circle each other, snapping our jaws playfully, huffing barks of acknowledgment. Luckily, it seems being in my wolf form hasn't sent me into a blood-wolf manic state. In fact, the world seems quieter—the presence of other wolves is still there, but it's less cloudy, like a sound that had been distorted but is now clear, piercing with clarity, but not painful. It's as if I could reach into the ether and pick out a single wolf as easily as picking a ripe cherry from a tree. It's sort of wild, actually, how much calmer it is in my wolf form, as if I'm closer to the source, maybe. Or does that sound too intense, too woo-woo? Maybe the desert air is playing tricks on my mind.

But it's easier to ignore the press of noise and, as Jasper lifts his muzzle toward the horizon, I do just that. He leaps into motion and in a second is off, running away from me. My feet know what they're doing before I do, and without thinking I take off as well.

The muscles in my legs pump as I quickly catch up to Jasper, my wolf speed in full effect. The burn and stretch of using my wolf limbs feels so stupidly good. Breathing large gulps of air into my wolf lungs is like breathing clean air for the first time. I come level with Jasper, snapping at him as if to say, *This all you got*? Wolves can't really grin but I swear he does as he tilts his head, accepting my challenge, and accelerates.

Desert landscape swooshes past us as we dodge cacti and leap over rocks, flowing like water, finding the route of least resistance. Our claws dig into the sand, flinging it up in a yellow cloud. A quick glance behind and already the cabin is barely a speck in my rearview. We dart and race, constantly aware of our proximity. Jasper, his scent, his presence are connected to mine like radio waves. If he swerves right I can feel the distance between us increasing and if he twists left I know he's getting closer without having to look.

Up ahead the level terrain begins to dip and undulate, and a large, smooth rock formation rises before us. Eager to explore, I pick up my pace, making Jasper push to keep up. We crest a small rise, coming to the base of the towering boulders, digging in to turn at speed and navigating to one side as we glide around them. Jasper darts in front of me, forcing me closer to the rocks, and then suddenly he leaps into the air, over my head, and lands on my other side, kicking up dust, before ducking into a passage. I hadn't seen it before, but where two boulders meet is a narrow tunnel—a glorified crack, really, which Jasper slips through as though he's done it a million times. Huffing to keep up, I skid to control myself and follow him into the cool, shady space.

We emerge on the other side of the rocks to a rolling vista dotted with more large rock sculptures, the desert rising and falling like waves, each punctuated with boulders and spurts of grass. Jasper ducks and weaves, dives from the peaks of hills, and I follow in his wake. It's like his wolf is testing me, the canine version of playing hard to get, wanting to see if I'll keep up. But I can do better than simply keep up.

Jasper nods toward a copse of yucca trees and makes for it. Knowing our goal means the race is on. I push harder, flinging my hind legs out behind me, digging deeper into the ground, and hoisting myself forward at ever-greater speeds. Jasper does the same. And soon we're racing, jumping from boulder to boulder, skirting spiky plants and ragged rocks. We enter the copse of trees, winding through them, always keeping each other in our sights. Our paths diverge, leading us farther apart, and for a moment I feel like these trees, this obstacle course, represents everything we've been through, all the fights and bullshit, the dangers and threats, the emotional land mines. I keep one eye trained on Jasper and as we press on, our paths come together once more.

Bursting from the tree line, we arrive at a water hole, a small oasis surrounded on three sides by bulging and uneven rocks, a pebbly shore leading to the water. We've emerged from the copse at the same time, perfectly matched, and Jasper skids to a stop. I press the pads of my feet into the stony ground and slide to the water's edge. My chest is heaving, sucking in great, panting breaths. Jasper is the same. I can't imagine the effect of the hot desert sun on his pitch-black coat. I'm warm enough and my caramel-colored fur is pretty good at reflecting heat. He must be hot because before I realize it, Jasper has pounced on me, knocking me sideways, straight into the water. We tumble over each other as the cool water refreshes us, breaking apart when we come to a stop. I lift my dripping muzzle from the water and eye Jasper as he shakes out his fur. But I don't let him regain his composure before tackling him back.

My paws wrap around his thick neck as my weight barrages into him and we fall sideways. We wrestle for a moment, splashing crystal clear water into the air. Jasper tackles me again and I go right back in for payback. We tussle and roll over each other until we're both panting and need to catch our breath. We heave our heavy, soaked wolf bodies onto the shore and flop down next to each other.

The sun beats down hot on our backs, drying our fur as we lie in the pebbles. Jasper's green eye surveys me for a moment, then he shuffles closer and licks the side of my face, like he's wolf-kissing my cheek.

I really ought to let my wolf out more frequently. That felt so good. To use my body, to embrace my power and spend some of that pent-up wolf energy, has had the revitalizing effect of caffeine or a cold shower. My soul feels lighter, I'm physically tired but not exhausted, mentally I'm switched on. My skin tingles as blood pumps through my system.

Jasper flops back onto his front and I nestle into his neck once more to say thank you for bringing me here, for running with me, sharing this place and this moment. It's all so perfect.

For a while we lie next to each other, letting our wolf selves enjoy the dry breeze and hot sun, and the proximity to our mate. Then a presence suddenly makes itself known. I lift my muzzle, propping a paw under me, ready to stand and pounce.

Jasper looks over his shoulder and I follow his eyeline. A large, dark-gray wolf appears at the top of a boulder, its shadow a dark blob stretching down the side of the rock and onto the water. Jasper sighs and lets his head fall back onto his outstretched paws, clearly unbothered—or maybe a little bothered, but not worried. I sniff the air and realize I know the scent of this wolf. It belongs to a member of our security detail. It's been with us since we arrived, distant but recognizable.

We're not in danger from this wolf, it's here to check up on us. Still something about it being here has lifted the hazy spell of the morning. Our private oasis is no longer private.

I huff and gesture back the way we came. Jasper takes a second and then nods. He lifts his body up and shakes his muzzle. I stand too and we make our way back to the house.

"I'm starving!" I whine, arriving in the kitchen freshly showered and pulling on a tank top.

Jasper turns from where he's slicing bread and eyes me up and down. "Is that my top?"

"Um, yeah. Is that okay? I can take it off."

"Keep it," he says, turning back around. "It looks good."

Jasper makes us a pair of towering sandwiches—roasted chicken breast with lettuce, cheese, mayonnaise, and paprika—which we eat outside.

"That was fun," I say, mouth full as usual. "I need to let my wolf out more often."

"Same," Jasper says with a nod.

Off in the distance I notice a dark spot moving about in the desert. It's the security wolf who found us earlier.

"Shame about those guys," I say. "Think my wolf was enjoying spending time with you...alone."

"Mine too," Jasper says, eyes on his half-eaten sandwich.

"Do they need to follow us everywhere?"

He places his sandwich back on the plate, toying with the crust between two fingers. "They have orders to keep eyes on us at all times, straight from my father."

"Man." I sigh and lean back in my chair. "So we can't have any privacy?"

"Only when we're inside. Out there"—he nods to the horizon—"they'll be watching."

I press my lips together while my leg bounces impatiently up and down. "Are they coming hiking with us too?"

"Yes. They'll keep their distance though."

I roll my eyes. "I guess that's fine. It's just...I really enjoyed spending time out there with you. And...the whole point of coming out here was to get away from all the extra wolf noise."

"Is it bad?" he asks, taking his sandwich back up.

"It's not bad. It's definitely better. I'd…I'd just like to know how good it could be if they were elsewhere."

Jasper glances at me with narrow, contemplative eyes, then chomps down the last couple bites of his lunch. "I'll see what I can do."

"Really?"

"There aren't any packs for miles, I don't think one hike could hurt."

"That would be amazing."

After lunch Jasper goes to speak with his security team while I sit under the veranda with my sketchbook and try to capture the landscape as best I can. I want to remember this view for its rugged wildness, the contrast between smooth stone, ragged rock, and spiky plants.

When Jasper comes back he's wearing black swim shorts and has a towel draped over his shoulder. He's carrying what looks like an oversized cell phone, which he places on the table.

"What's that?" I ask.

"Satellite phone," Jasper says. "I convinced the guards to let us camp without supervision as long as we take this with us."

I sit up and lean over the armrest, beyond excited. "You mean…?"

"Privacy," Jasper says.

"When can we go?"

"Tomorrow if you like? We'll need to pop into town for some supplies this afternoon but I'm game."

"Yes! Great. Let's do it."

After our brief morning run, all I want is to explore this stupidly beautiful piece of land with my mate, without the buzzing presence of other wolves in my head distracting me. I want the calm and quiet, and I want to use this as an opportunity to get to know Jasper better.

"I'm going for a swim," Jasper says. "Be ready to head off in about an hour?"

"Perfect."

Jasper heads to the pool, drops his towel on the tiled edge, and dives into the clear water. I quickly add a few lines to my drawing, wanting to include Jasper. He swims a few lengths of the pool, gliding like a pro freestyler, before stopping in the middle and bobbing up and down with his hair slicked back, watching me.

"What?" I ask.

"The water's really nice," he replies, treading water and grinning.

"Aaaaaand...?"

"Why don't you join me?"

I roll my eyes and huff jokingly, but I can't resist his smile. I slap my sketchbook on the table—I'll have to finish my drawing later—pull off Jasper's tank, and run to the pool. I dive in, making sure to splash water in his face.

The drive to town takes roughly an hour. Desert stretches out on either side of us as we drive, like that's all there is in the world. For a moment I stare out the window and wonder what it would be like if Jasper and I were the only people left—like some apocalyptic event wiped everyone out and we were trekking across this barren wasteland on a mission to find a shred of hope that all was not lost. Would we make a good team? Or would we bicker and get sick of each other? Not that we've been bickering, or disagreeing or arguing at all since New Year's. So maybe we would make a good team then? Maybe our postapocalyptic mission isn't doomed. Maybe our relationship has legs.

Dusty road turns to tarmac the same time we enter the town. None of the buildings are over a story tall, making them blend in with the expansive desert plain the town sits in the center of. We pass a souvenir shop that could be straight off the set of an old Western, the curving sign and old-log-cabin aesthetic lending it something of a theme park vibe. The main drag of the town follows suit. Old-school buildings line the wide street, and I keep expecting to see cowboys chewing tobacco or tying up their horses outside.

Jasper pulls into a small parking lot belonging to a three-store strip mall. First we visit a grocer and stock up on camping supplies. Jasper pulls fresh produce, cans, and bottled water off the shelves and into the trolley while I take responsibility for adding marshmallows, chocolate, and graham crackers. Next we pop into a camping store where Jasper talks to the sales assistant and we leave with a new tent, sleeping bags, large water canisters, and a battery-powered lantern. We drop all of that off at the car then head over to the Joshua Tree Visitor Center, its metal and concrete exterior standing out amongst the old-timey vibes, where we grab a map and speak to a lady who gives us advice about which trails to take, the prime times of day to head off, strategies so we don't disturb the natural habitat, and safety tips such as what to do in an emergency or if one of us is bitten by a rattlesnake—all of which goes over my head and which I pray Jasper was paying closer attention to.

Finally we head back to the car, but when I stop to open my door, Jasper continues on.

"There's one more place we need to visit," he says.

Okay, mysterious. What else could we need?

A block or two down the road we turn into a U-shaped bank of quaint-looking shops. Unlike some of the other buildings, these aren't made to look like relics of the Wild West, or like modern concrete slabs like the visitor center. These look more like cabins, with wooden posts holding up the porch-roofs, wind chimes and stained glass hanging from strings. One of them is a gallery showcasing paintings and ceramics by local artists, the other sells jewelry and homewares, again made by locals, and the final shop is hard to describe. I guess I'd call it the one-stop shop for yoga-practicing hippies. I stop in shock when that's the store Jasper heads to, pressing through the door and leaving me in the literal dust with my mouth hanging open.

A moment later I follow Jasper inside and find him talking to a frail-looking old man at the counter. His ponytail is gray, thin strands of hair pulled back from the sides but not the top of his balding head. His wrists are so slim it's a wonder they haven't snapped right in two, his shoulders are curved forward, and he's about a foot shorter than Jasper. But he has kind eyes, big bushy brows, and a gentle smile. He and Jasper communicate quietly, their voices lowered as if in respect to some unseen spirits. Finally, the man nods and disappears through a beaded curtain into the back room.

"He'll just be a minute," Jasper says.

"What do we need from here?" I ask, looking around, somewhat bewildered.

The shelves are stocked with all manner of crystals. Dream catchers and wind chimes hang from the ceiling. An antique shelving unit to one side is laden with candles, soaps, and incense in a vast array of scents. Pillows and rugs in bright colors with intricate designs sit in wicker baskets in the corners.

"You'll see," Jasper says with a wink.

While we wait for the man I wander through the store, trailing my fingers over a series of small figurines made from all sorts of materials: stone, smooth and cool, crystal, glistening and unforgiving, driftwood, clay, and finally glass. I stop and survey the glass objects. These look a little like the one in Jasper's house, the one his mother owned.

With a trickle of cascading beads the man arrives back on the shop floor with a small burlap bag. He hands it to Jasper with a courteous nod and Jasper offers his credit card. The man moves behind his antique, glass-topped counter and puts the payment through his system. I move to join Jasper, and as the man returns with Jasper's card our eyes meet.

For a moment he freezes, the credit card held in front of him like he's about to slip it into an ATM. His nostrils flare ever so slightly and his eyes crinkle in the corners.

A waft of something breaking through the overwhelming stink of incense fogging up the shop and I smile nervously.

"There you go," he says to Jasper, turning his attention from me to him and handing him the bag. "You should have everything you need."

"Thank you," Jasper says.

"May the spirits guide your hand."

No idea what that's supposed to mean, but there's something off-putting about this guy. He seems nice, but he's giving off this strange energy—like he's an alien in disguise or like he knows more than he's letting on.

Jasper turns to leave but I don't join him. I'm too busy watching the man, who shoots me one more furtive glance then shuffles back behind the counter, to his stool and the book on astrophysics I assume he was reading before we interrupted.

"You coming?" Jasper asks, and I shake myself back into the room.

"Yeah, uh, coming. Thanks," I say to the man, who looks up from his reading, one eyebrow cocked.

Outside it hits me, the scent I couldn't quite make out because of the incense.

"Jasp," I say, taking his arm to stop him. "I think that guy was a wolf."

Jasper glances back at the shop, squinting in thought. "Nah, that's not possible. The nearest pack is over a hundred miles away."

"What if he isn't part of a pack?"

Jasper lifts his nose like he's trying to scent the dude out.

"He didn't smell like a wolf to me."

"He could have been hiding behind all that stinky incense—using it as a decoy."

Jasper purses his lips. "Maybe. But I didn't sense his energy the way I usually would. You're connected to non-Elite Pack wolves better than I am. Did you feel any wolf energy?"

I pause. Is it possible I've gotten so used to keeping my barriers up I missed the shop guy's energy? Or am I imagining things? Because Jasper's right: there was no werewolf energy coming from that guy.

"Max, are you okay?"

"Weird," I say. "My nose must have been tricking me."

"Come on," Jasper says, turning to leave once more. "It'll be getting dark by the time we get back."

"Okay."

He heads off to the car, but I linger for a moment longer, staring back at the crystal shop, wondering if I missed something.

There aren't supposed to be wolves around here, just like Jasper said.

But what if he's wrong?

JOSHUA TREE

We head out early, just as the sun is peeking above the horizon. The morning air is dry and cool, but the day is already warming up—in no time it'll be sweltering. I shrug my heavy backpack over my shoulder and wait for Jasper to finish locking up the house. Before bed last night we made snacks and sandwiches to take, and packed our camping gear, a small gas burner, a few changes of clothes, our sleeping bags, our new pop-up tent, the lantern, and the satellite phone.

Even though it was still dark when I dressed, I'm pretty impressed with my camping outfit: a blue tee, cargo shorts, hiking boots, and a red neckerchief that adds a little flair and will—I hope—catch the sweat that's sure to be pouring down the back of my neck in no time.

"You ready?" Jasper asks, reaching for my hand. I take it and we leave the house behind, heading off into the desert.

"I thought we'd have to drive somewhere," I say, stepping over a rock that could be a camouflaged lizard.

"This property backs onto the national park," Jasper says. "I know the way."

"How come we still got a map?"

"In case I forget. I used to know the trails like the back of my paw. But I haven't been here in a long time."

Jasper's eyes glaze over and he picks up the pace a little. I drop the subject.

As we approach the first large boulder formation I glance back at the way we came. The house is already a dot on the horizon; two more black dots just beside it must be the SUVs belonging to our security team. We're leaving them behind, along with the rest of civilization and all of wolfkind. Maybe I should be more apprehensive or worried, but the satellite phone is strapped to the side of Jasper's bag. And it's not as if we're doing anything too crazy or out of the ordinary. People camp around here all the time. I take a deep breath. Already my head feels clearer. We're finally going to be alone, away from wolves and stress and distractions.

I take a second to let the walls I've built up around my mind drop slowly, bracing for the impact of some pinlike presence stabbing at my brain, but nothing comes. I exhale and let my guard down completely. My shoulders drop. In fact, my whole body feels like it lets go of some tension it's been holding. My limbs feel light as I swing my free arm—the one Jasper isn't holding the hand of—back and forth, my legs feel springy, my stomach is unclenched, and my lungs are full.

"Excited?" Jasper asks, potentially sensing my whole-body exhalation.

"I am."

For the next three hours we hike and hike and hike. As the sun rises and the heat increases, I wipe the constant beads of sweat from my brow. My springy legs are starting to feel the burn as we navigate our way down dusty trails, and into the rocky hills. But I don't hate it. Traversing the large rock formations feels like walking along the back of some giant dinosaur skeleton. It's exciting and feels good.

My blood is pumping, the toxins are leaving my system, my muscles are earning their keep. And the landscape is ridiculous. I've never seen rocks like these, so smooth and undulating, sticking up out of the ground like fingers. Between rock formations the earth is littered with grassy shrubs, sharp and lopsided Joshua trees, and a whole host of cactus varieties. It's dry and hot, but it's such a nice change from the city and the lush greenery of the woods near where I live. I could be on an alien planet for how different it all seems. And I like that idea—the idea of being as far away from real life as possible.

Jasper stops at the top of a rise and pulls out his water bottle. "Here," he says, offering it to me first.

I take it and gulp down the refreshing liquid, letting it water my insides like a desert rain.

"Thanks," I say, handing it back.

"We should stop for lunch soon." Jasper surveys the surroundings like he's trying to get his bearings. "I think I know a good spot."

For almost another hour we continue our trek, heading into more mountainous territory. Climbing an ascent after this much walking is hard, and I'm huffing by the time we reach a plateau. Jasper stops and turns to take in the view.

"This is perfect," he says.

I turn as well and my breath catches in my throat. Before us the desert rolls out as if it goes on forever. The sky is a clear, deep blue overhead, the cool tone contrasting with the warm yellows of the earth.

"It's gorgeous," I say.

Jasper leaps up a couple of boulders until he's reached the highest spot and sits, his legs dangling over the edge.

He dips into his pack and pulls out our premade lunch. I follow him up, although less gracefully, and pull out my sketchbook.

"Do you mind if I draw this?" I ask.

"Take your time," he says, handing me a sandwich then leaning back to chomp on his.

I sip water and take a hunking bite out of my sandwich and put pencil to paper. Quickly I mark out a few of the defining features of the landscape, cutting the page in half where the sky and land meet, then I go about adding details. We eat quietly while I draw, until drops of sweat are falling from my nose onto the page, in an extremely gross fashion. I glance beside me to find Jasper in his meditation pose, legs crossed, eyes closed, hands on his knees with his palms facing up. For what feels like a solid hour I sketch, adding shading where the trees and boulders cast shadows across the desert.

"Can I see?" Jasper says finally, peering over with one eye.

"Sure." I hold up the book so he can look.

He shakes his head, laughing a little to himself. "It's beautiful. You're stupidly talented, you know that?"

I didn't think it would be possible for my face to get any hotter out here but somehow it does. Suddenly feeling shy, I flip the book closed. "Should we keep going?"

"If you want." Jasper goes about getting his things together, standing and slipping on his backpack.

"Actually," I say, looking over the landscape once more. "Where are we going? Do you have, like, a spot in mind?"

"Oh yeah," he says, grinning smugly.

"Holy moly."

I can't believe my eyes. After walking for another few hours, until my feet feel about ready to fall off, my shoulders are aching from carrying my pack, and all the moisture in my body has evacuated through my pores, we've arrived at the most stunning lake.

"How is this even possible? I didn't think there were lakes in the desert."

Jasper simply shrugs, then smiles like he's pleased with himself. "Pretty special isn't it."

"Uh, yah-huh."

The trail winds down a hill toward the body of glistening water. Boulders rise like mountains on the far side and dot the water like lily pads. On the shore, green vegetation sprouts in bursts of emerald. The whole place is alive and magical and so freaking serene.

"Is this where we're camping?"

Jasper doesn't answer right away. He takes in the scenery with a wistful expression, then finally turns to me. "This is the spot."

We make our way down to the water, dropping our packs by some rocks and heading straight for the edge. Immediately I drop to my knees and splash the cooling liquid on my face and my neck.

"We should set up camp, then we can explore," Jasper says a few steps behind me.

After investigating the shore we find a spot to pitch our tent at the base of a boulder, near a patch of trees. We set up the tent and unload our sleeping gear and some of our supplies. I'm halfway through rolling out a sleeping bag when I notice Jasper pulling off his tank top.

His body glistens like the water in the sunlight, his muscles seeming even more defined than normal. He kicks off his shoes and pulls off his socks, draping them over a low-hanging branch of a nearby yucca tree, and catches me looking. He grins mischievously.

"Fancy a swim?"

Before I know it he's dropped his shorts and is running to the water, throwing up splashes as he enters, then diving under. He stays underwater long enough for the surface to return to its placid state, then emerging like a dolphin a moment later. Only it isn't Jasper who's emerged—well, it is, just not in his human form. His wolf dog-paddles its way back toward the shore until he's standing ankle-deep, then shakes his fur, releasing a firework of water. With a yelp in my direction, Jasper takes off around the edge of the lake, and as swiftly as I can I leap up, undress, and shift.

I chase him around the edge of the lake, hopping from boulder to boulder, splashing in the shallows, until we begin to ascend one of the more mountainous rocks on the far side. Jasper wastes no time when he reaches the top, turning sharply, leaping into the air, and plunging toward the water below. His wolf body breaks the surface in a graceful, streamlined dive. I hesitate, pawing at the edge of the rock. It's farther down than I thought. Jasper is already swimming in little circles, barking up at me.

I huff and growl—*Come on, Max, you've faced worse than this*—then propel myself from the ledge. Much less gracefully than Jasper, I flail about in the air as the water nears, and I do my absolute best to enter in a way that doesn't shatter all my bones. Cool water envelops me as I break the surface.

For a moment I linger underwater, suspended somewhere between the bed of the lake and the air above. Jasper dives under to meet me and paddles until we're face-to-face. Two wolves maybe shouldn't be hanging out underwater like this, but there's something so calm about the silence, the cool tones, the refracted light squiggling on the sand below. We hover like this for a moment, until my lungs start to burn.

Breaking the surface, I rise gulping for breath, kicking all four of my legs to stay afloat. Jasper pops up beside me and swims around me like he doesn't have a care in the world. He nips at me and barks, then dives back under like a seal, and I follow. We spend the next half hour or so diving and seeing how far down we can go. The lake is surprisingly deep—I guess it'd want to be in this heat, otherwise it would evaporate away.

When my legs are tired I paddle myself back toward our campsite, wandering out onto the sand and shaking my fur. For a second my ears perk up at a distant sound...a coyote maybe. But it's so faint it must be miles and miles away. It's amazing what wolf ears are able to pick up. Jasper follows me out of the water, shaking out his fur and spraying me in the face. I growl playfully and tackle him back into the water.

Later that night, as the sun sets, we build a ring of stones and a fire inside it. It's totally *Survivor* vibes as we sit and eat burgers with the firelight bouncing off the rocks and bathing our campsite in a warm glow.

"The stars are ridiculous," I say, wiping ketchup from the corner of my mouth.

"They are," Jasper says, turning his attention skyward. "You want to take a walk?"

"Uh, sure. You finished?"

Jasper still has a couple of decent bites left of his burger. He smiles and shoves the whole thing in his mouth. "Finished," he says, although with his mouth full the sound is muffled.

"Classy."

We head out from the campsite in a straight line away from the lake so that we can keep an eye on the fire. Wouldn't want to be responsible for starting a wildfire. Jasper's hands are shoved deep in his pockets, his head tilted back as he stargazes.

"This place means a lot to you," I say.

"It does."

"How come you haven't been back in so long?"

Jasper stops walking but keeps his eyes on the heavens. "After my mother was killed things changed in my family. We used to come here every year. My father would always complain about coming—too hot and dry for him. But my mother loved it and even though I was so young, I could tell he didn't mind coming, not actually, as long as she was happy. He was different around her. When she died it was like part of him died too. He shut off, focused all his energy on the pack and being the alpha. Nothing else seemed to matter, not even his kids. He stopped being the father we knew and became something else...an army general or the boss of some big corporation, and we were his interns. I remember the year after she left us I asked him if we could come here."

"He said no?" I ask, my voice catching.

"He threw a chair through a glass door."

"For the longest time I thought, *This is the real him. With Mom gone there's no one to stop him from treating us this way, acting like this.* I'm starting to realize that maybe wasn't the case. His behavior didn't change because she wasn't there to hold him back. He changed because he was hurting, because despite their mating being arranged, he loved her."

"I'm sorry," I say because I don't know what else to do.

He shrugs and faces me. "It's okay. I just—being out here makes me wonder if there was more I could have done to help him. If I'd been more aware, maybe I could have stopped him from losing that part of himself."

"Jasper, you were only a kid. You can't blame yourself for his actions." I step to him and take his hands. "You blame yourself for everything. But..." I trail off, not sure if I'm about to say the right thing or start a different kind of wildfire. "But you shouldn't. Do you remember the vision I had, back in the mountains? Where I saw the crash that took your mother and how I knew you were there?"

His head quirks to one side. "Yes?"

"It wasn't just like seeing a memory it was more like living it, like I was you, I could see what you saw and—feel what you felt."

He takes a step back, letting my hand fall to my side. His narrow eyes are boring into mine and I can't tell if he's furious that I kept this from him, that I saw this in the first place, or if he's just trying to understand what's going on.

"You were just a kid, really, so young and you were terrified. But when you looked at your mother, and saw how much she wanted to protect you, how much she loved you, you felt it. You felt her protection and it calmed you. She did what she had to do, by swerving to protect you. And that doesn't make what happened your fault. It makes her your parent, who loves you and wants to take care of you."

Jasper's expression softens. "It's funny, I can't actually remember much from the crash."

"That makes sense, it must have been extremely traumatic. Maybe I was able to tap into your subconscious in a way you won't let yourself," I suggest. "Because, you know, blood wolf and all that."

"Maybe." He sits quietly for a moment. "Maybe part of me wanted you to see that."

I shrug gently. "Yeah, maybe."

"What did she...what did she look like, at the end?"

"She was beautiful and determined and fearless. And she loved you. She did what she needed to. I don't think she would want you to blame yourself. She sacrificed herself so you could live. You should."

Tentatively, I slip my index finger around his and thankfully he doesn't pull away.

"And you shouldn't blame yourself for your father's actions either. He was the adult, the parent, he should have stepped up and taken care of you and Jodie, not shut himself off. I'm sorry that happened."

He drops his head backward and exhales all the air in his chest.

"Are you okay?"

With one hand he touches my cheek, running a thumb over my skin. "I think perhaps I've acted too much like my father with you."

"You Apollo men, you're all kinds of messed up."

"I'm serious, Max. I treated you poorly and for that I am responsible, there's no way around it."

I cup the hand that's holding my face and kiss his palm. "You're making it right. That's all that matters."

"Thank you for telling me about the vision. Maybe we can talk more about her. I would like to—I would like to remember more of her."

"I'd love that. To be honest I was a little terrified just now." We both laugh a little, then he pulls me closer and rests his forehead against mine.

"I never want you to be terrified of me."

"But I'm terrified of everything." I'm only half joking, but either way he makes a face like I've said something really dumb.

"No you're not. You're one of the bravest wolves I know."

He kisses me under the stars. When we pull back he looks up at the blanket of twinkling lights once more. "It's funny," he says. "I can feel her. I feel more connected to her here than anywhere else. I wish I hadn't stayed away so long."

"We can come back," I say. "Every year."

"Yeah?"

"Yes, this place is freaking paradise. Of course we can come back."

"I'd like that."

I wrap my arms around his and hug him tightly, resting my head on his shoulder.

"Max, do you want to try the mind-link again?"

THE DISTANCE BETWEEN US

We sit by the fire facing each other. Jasper pulls his pack to him and rummages around in it before grabbing out the hessian bag full of whatever he bought at the crystal and incense shop in town. He tosses his pack aside and opens the bag.

"Whatcha got there?" I ask, rubbing my knees a little nervously.

"Just some things that are supposed to help with the mind-link."

Almost ceremoniously he pulls items from the bag, one by one, and starts placing them around us. The first is a large crystal, the pastel-pink color of Turkish delight, which he sits between us.

"This is rose quartz," he says. "It's good for removing emotional blockages and balancing chakras."

"Blockages and what? You think we're blocked?"

He smiles at me, the fire dancing in his eyes. "No. It's just an aid, to help open the channels of emotional connection."

I quirk an eyebrow at him and he tilts his head, his expression softening.

"Don't read too much into it."

"Okay, what else you got in there Mary Poppins?"

He pulls out another crystal, this one a little smaller and a deep, stunning purple. In the darkness of the night the surface reflects the fire and the stars like oil.

"This is amethyst. It's supposed to help us communicate on a spiritual level."

He places the amethyst to his right and goes back to the bag. The next crystal is blue and semitransparent.

"Chrysocolla."

"Gesundheit."

He shakes his head gently. "This is supposed to amplify our ability to empathize, giving us a greater chance at hearing each other." He pulls one last crystal from the sack. "And finally, citrine."

"Let me guess, for citrusy freshness?"

"No," he says, scolding playfully. "For positivity."

"Oh, right. What's left?"

The last few items he pulls out at once: a stick of incense, which he lights on the fire and places between two rocks so it stands upright, and a bouquet of dried herbs. "Calamus to amplify our voices, blue vervain to clear our minds, and thyme—"

"For the roast chicken?"

He rolls his eyes. "Thyme to attract loyalty, love, and to increase our psychic powers."

With a gentle wave he wafts the herb bouquet in the air around us then places it next to the rose quartz.

"You really went to town," I say.

"I wanted to give us the best shot at linking."

My stupid cynical heart melts. He's done all this so that we can get closer. I should be less teasing and more focused.

"I'm sorry, I'm just not used to all this sort of stuff."

"I know it's a little out there," he replies. "But if it helps, there's some science to it—especially for us. The energy of the moon interacts with the crystals, which interacts with our brain waves and our connection to other wolves through pheromones, bloodlines, and our senses. The herbs are medicinal, just like the ones Agatha made that tea from that helped soothe your headaches."

"The incense?"

Jasper shrugs. "That's mostly just for atmosphere."

"Thank you," I say. "For going to all this trouble."

"Max." Jasper takes both my hands. "I want to make this work."

I chew the inside of my lip for a moment, feeling just a little overwhelmed. Under the blanket of stars I feel small, like a speck of dust in an eternal desert. The fire is hot and bright and I'm surrounded by crystals and herbs. But in front of me is the most stupidly handsome guy, asking me to try and connect with him, to shorten the distance between us, and after everything we've been through I owe it to us to try.

"Me too," I say. "Shall we?"

"Close your eyes."

I do as Jasper says.

"Breathe."

I fill my lungs and exhale slowly.

"Focus."

I let my consciousness expand into the inky blackness, darker than the night sky.

"Reach out."

Like a homing pigeon I plunge through the darkness, traversing it at neckbreaking speed, looking for a connection, for those red veins that represent the wolves of the world. Jasper's presence looms like a warm haze before me, but for whatever reason I can't find him in the void. Maybe it's because we're farther away from our pack or from wolves in general, but the darkness of my mind, usually crowded with veins, branching and crossing like an overgrown tree, is especially empty. There are no signs of red, just darkness.

Why can't I find him? He's sitting right in front of me. Shouldn't I be able to find the thread of his consciousness and latch on to it? Shouldn't I simply be able to reach out and speak to him? Why can't I seem to connect to the person who means the most to me?

I grit my teeth and squeeze my eyes together, concentrating harder, trying to push through the dense, dark fog. And I realize something isn't right. How can there be no signs of wolf life at all? Yes we're far away, but that shouldn't matter. Back in New York I could sense wolves from across the country, even other countries—there was so much noise it was a constant battle to block it out—and now nothing, silence, not even the voice of my mate.

Something must be blocking me. I remember the positions of the crystals Jasper laid out and think about what he said, that they were channels through which we could access lunar energy. I focus on pulling that energy toward myself, let it flood into my body, and almost instantaneously, the fog begins to lift. My muscles are enlivened. My skin tingles. The veins of life fade in like lights on a dimmer switch slowly rising. The familiar fizzle and crack of energy arrives. And there before me is Jasper. He's not just a warm blob, he's a glowing light. At this close proximity his thread is no longer red, but a burning yellow, like the sun. I'm about to speak to him, to link our minds, when I feel a tug from behind me, and as I turn to see what it is, the familiar ear-piercing howl breaks through, and the feeling of something slamming into the side of my skull knocks me sideways.

I topple over, knocking the crystals out of formation as I sprawl on the desert floor clutching my head.

"Max!" Jasper is instantly next to me, his hands holding me, supporting my head so I don't smash it against a nearby rock. "What happened?"

I glance up at him, grimacing through the pain. "It didn't work."

"You feeling all right?" Jasper asks, crouching in the entrance of the tent. I'm already wrapped in my sleeping bag, facing the fabric wall.

"Uh-huh," I mumble.

Jasper crawls in, placing his toothbrush and toothpaste in a small wash bag by the entrance, then positioning himself behind me, draping his unzipped sleeping bag over himself.

"I'm sorry you got hurt," he says, gingerly placing a hand on my shoulder.

"Not your fault."

"I'm sure it'll work, we just have to figure out what's going on. Maybe the blood-wolf thing is messing up your thoughts."

I grunt. "Maybe."

Jasper lingers a moment longer, before lying his head on the pillow beside mine. He moves his hand from my shoulder to my waist, slipping it under my arm.

"We'll keep trying," he says. I don't respond, instead pressing my lips together. "Max, is something else wrong?"

With a sharp exhale I voice the fear that's been gnawing at me since we tried linking for the first time. "What if we can't do it? What if—what if we aren't meant to?"

"Lots of wolf couples can't mind-link. It's not an easy thing to do. But I'm sure—"

"*We* should be able to. You said yourself, you have your heightened alpha abilities and I'm the freaking blood wolf. If we can't mind-link then what if..."

"What if what, Max?"

"What if it's a sign—that we aren't—that we don't—?"

"Max?"

"What if this isn't going to work?"

Jasper's sleeping bag rustles as he sits up, leaning over me slightly so I can just make out his face in my periphery.

"Is that what's really bothering you?"

I roll onto my back so I can face him. The corners of his eyes are pinched with a quiet desperation.

"We were paired together by fate or hormones or whatever you want to call it. And not that I'm complaining but who's to say that's enough. If we can't connect like other couples then something must be wrong, mustn't it?"

"Are you..." Jasper pauses, licks his lips, and presses on. "Are you having second thoughts about us?"

"No!" I rise onto my elbows, trying to decrease the amount of space between us to show him I'm not the one backing out. "No, I'm not having second thoughts." I reach up and touch his face. "But so much of our lives are governed by the moon and our wolf selves. I'm just scared that if we can't mind-link, there must be a bunch of other things we can't connect over. And what if that means we—we aren't—"

Jasper brushes a curl out of my face and stares down at me with intense feeling in his expression.

"Max, you're right it was fate that brought us together." My chest tightens. "But fate has nothing to do with us being together now. Yes, lunar energy might have had a hand in making sure we ran into each other—"

"Literally," I add.

"But I wouldn't be here if I didn't want to be, if I didn't choose this. Fate may have been the catalyst but it can't force a person to stay. I want to stay. I want to be with you. Even if fate had told me to date someone else I would still want to be with you."

I take a breath as my chest relaxes and our eyes stay connected.

"I know I haven't made that as abundantly clear as I should have...I know I haven't been the best mate...but I...I love you, Max. I love *you*. Fate has nothing to do with that."

All of a sudden my head is spinning and my breaths are coming short and fast.

"I...love you too," I say.

There's nothing left to say, so we kiss inside our tent. Outside the stars must still be shining, a glittery blanket cocooning us, the wind still blowing warm and dry, and the moon—somewhere between half and full—glowing as it looks down on us. But none of that matters. The world outside, the rest of wolfkind, the moon gods themselves can't reach us in here. We've run to the desert, the ends of the world, as far as we can go, away from prying eyes, responsibilities, and civilization, to find peace and connection and somehow, despite not being able to mind-link, it's worked. We've reached a deeper understanding of each other, I feel closer to Jasper than ever before.

He unzips the side of my sleeping bag so we can get even closer.

"Is this okay?" Jasper asks as his hand slides up the back of my T-shirt.

"Yes," I say, completely breathless.

"Do you want to...?"

Again, I say, "Yes."

I dream of Jasper.

He stands before me wearing a tuxedo. His hair is slicked back, his lips quirked into a smile, his green eyes shining brilliantly in the sun. We're standing on the roof of a building—the packhouse, only it isn't. In my dream version this rooftop has a garden: neat topiaries line the balustrade, grass as green as Jasper's eyes rolls out before us, cherry trees dance in the breeze, letting their petals fall and drift like confetti.

To my left a crowd is seated on white foldout chairs on either side of an aisle. Everyone is here—my parents, Katie, Aisha, Jericho, Mason—wearing formal wear and watching us as we stand before them.

"I'm so happy," Jasper says, rubbing the back of my hands with his thumbs.

Glancing down, I notice I'm also wearing a suit—a white jacket with a red cummerbund, a black bow tie and pants, shiny patent leather shoes.

I glance between him and the crowd of expectant, happy faces.

"What's—what's happening?" I whisper.

He smiles and shakes his head. "What do you mean?"

"I mean why is everyone staring at us?"

"It's our mating ceremony, Bonehead."

"Our—what?"

"The happiest day of our lives," he says and clasps my face.

"You mean we're..." I look to Katie for answers but she only dabs her eyes with a handkerchief. My mom squeezes Dad's arm, he's crying too. Jericho nods at me proudly. And Jasper...Jasper is smiling, staring into me like he doesn't have a care in the world. "We're...in front of everyone?"

"Do you accept me as your mate, Maximilian?"

I'm flummoxed. A melon-sized lump forms in my throat as I choke out a response. "Of course I do, but Jasper, can't we—?"

"Will you accept my mark?"

"Your what?"

Jasper opens his mouth wide enough that I can see his fangs elongating. The crowd leans toward us, edging forward in their seats. To my right is a steep drop, over a hundred stories to the unforgiving pavement below.

"Do you accept my mark?" Jasper repeats, his lip curling back ever so slightly.

The sunny sky is suddenly cloudy, the wind is picking up, tearing blossoms and leaves from the cherry trees until their branches are bare. The crowd runs as rain pelts the roof, toppling over chairs and leaving chaos in their wake.

"Jasper, can we...can we talk...I'm not sure I'm ready."

Jasper reels back, snapping his slightly lengthened jaws, huffing and growling.

"Stop, Jasper!" I cry out, but I can hardly hear myself over the thunder.

"You reject me?!" Jasper roars.

"No, no, no! Let me explain!"

Lightning crashes close enough I can feel the shock wave as it strikes. When I turn back Jasper is clutching his chest. A bloom of red is spreading from beneath his hands, turning the white fabric of his shirt crimson.

"Jasper?" I step forward but he retreats, his face twisted in pain and disbelief.

"Killer," he says.

Another flash of lightning and Jasper howls to the sky, his jaws tearing open as he shifts into his wolf form, the clothes exploding off his back as his muscles expand, and he falls onto all fours, scratching at the rain-soaked grass, readying to strike.

"Jasper, I'm sorry!" I cry. "I'm sorry!"

Thunder claps as Jasper leaps, lunging for me with his teeth bared, about to tear me apart when...

I start up in bed, gasping and rising to my elbows.

Jasper is beside me in his wolf form, his shoulders hunched, the hairs along his spine standing upright, growling through the tent's gaping doorway.

"Jasper?" I ask, wiping the sleep from my eyes. "What's going on?"

Jasper glances back, his one visible eye large with concern.

The flap of the tent is fluttering in the wind as I crawl forward to see what's caused Jasper to take this defensive stance.

Blinking in the morning light, I lean through the opening and find myself greeted by over twenty wolves surrounding the entrance to the tent, each growling and showing their teeth.

WE'VE GOT COMPANY

This is bad. Standing on the lakeshore in a crescent shape are twenty, thirty...a whole bunch of wolves, leering, snapping their jaws, growling at Jasper and me.

Where did they come from? They couldn't have been far from us last night. How come I couldn't sense them? How come I couldn't sense any wolves whatsoever? And what do they want?

Judging from their dripping jowls, their snarling, curled-back lips, their raised noses, their narrowed, accusatory stares, their sharp teeth glinting in the light, they aren't happy to see us.

Jasper's wolf is by my side, his breaths coming out ragged and thick. His jaws are clenched together, his rear legs tense like coiled springs, ready to pounce. He paws at the dirt with a front foot, growling at the wolf crowd who must have roused him from his sleep.

Last night was stupidly amazing. Jasper and I...well...we *really* connected. The last thing I thought I'd wake up to was this! It's a pretty sharp left turn.

I place a steadying hand on Jasper's side. His black fur is warm and soft, his chest expands into my palm.

"Hey," I say to the crowd of wolves. One snaps in my direction and a few edge forward in response. "Let's not do anything too crazy." I lift a hand like they're the cops and I'm trying to show them I'm unarmed. "We're wolves too. And we don't mean any harm—"

"Max?" a familiar voice cuts me off. The snarling wolves glance between each other as a human face appears amongst their ranks, rising in the second row.

"Omar?"

His skin is more tanned than the last time I saw him, and his hair is a ruffled mess, probably because he, like the rest of our uninvited guests, was in his wolf form. He's also wearing a whole lot less clothes than when we said goodbye in the snowy valley near the Rocky Pack. But I'd recognize his bushy eyebrows and pouty grin anywhere.

"What are you doing here?" he asks, shaking his head in a bewildered way.

"Camping?"

Jasper glances back at me, unwilling to let his guard drop just yet, and I don't blame him. Omar's companions are still growling back at him, at us.

"Tell your attack dog to back down," Omar says. "Then we can talk."

Jasper snaps his jaws in Omar's direction.

"Ooh, feisty," he says.

But I'm actually with Jasper on this one. "Why don't you tell your...friends to back off first?"

"No can do. You're on our land."

"But...I didn't think there were any packs around here for miles."

"We might not be a pack. But you're still on our land."

Not a pack? *Oh!* I finally figure out why there isn't a distinctive unifying scent about this group. They're rogues. No wonder Jasper is especially snappy.

"We didn't mean to intrude," I say. "And we don't mean any harm."

"Doesn't matter, I'm afraid." Omar shrugs half-apologetically. "Our charter is clear."

"Charter?"

"Any foreign wolves found encamping on our land must be taken to the central committee."

"The central…what are you talking about? We aren't going anywhere."

"I'm afraid you don't have a choice." Omar doesn't sound like he's particularly sorry. In fact, I think he's sort of enjoying this. "Orders are orders. We've got to take you in. Grab your stuff, you're coming with us."

"Where?" I ask, more than incredulous.

"Where else?" Omar cocks an eyebrow. "Rogue Sanctuary."

"You found it then?" I ask as we're marched through the desert.

Jasper, Omar, and I are three humans in a herd of wolves, flanked on either side by ten or more rogues. They were nice enough to let Jasper and me get dressed appropriately for hiking, and Jasper reluctantly offered Omar a set of his gym shorts, although I notice they're the pair he wore yesterday and are probably quite sweaty still.

"I did," Omar says, chin held proudly and a wistful look of contentment in his eyes.

"You've come a long way. Did you travel here by yourself?" When I met Omar he was living with the rogue healer Agatha at the base of a very snowy mountain in Colorado. We're far from Colorado.

"For the most part," he says. "I met up with some other traveler wolves near Seattle and we headed south together for a bit. Left them back in San Francisco."

"You weren't tempted to stay with them?"

"No way, cuz. I had a feeling if I kept heading where it was warmer, more isolated, I'd find the Rogue Sanctuary and, hey, that's just what I did."

Jasper grunts beside me. He was reluctant to go with the rogues and was especially unhappy to hand over the satellite phone before we were escorted from our campsite. I totally get it. Apart from Omar, the rest of the rogues seem a lot less friendly. They snap or growl if we veer out of their tight formation. It's interesting seeing these rogues working together so well. Not at all something we were taught they could do.

"You're looking better than the last time I saw you," Omar says, his cheeks a little flushed—although that might just be the desert heat—and an approving smirk on his face.

Jasper shoots him a sharp look.

"Yeah, I was a mess." I rub at the sweat dripping down the back of my neck. "But I've gotten a lot better at blocking out the noise."

Omar eyes me curiously. "Is that so?"

"I can still feel it but most of the time it's like a haze pressing in on me, not painful at all."

"You just blocked it all out then," he says, more a statement than a question.

"Uh-huh." I glance around at the wolves, their shoulders rolling as they walk, the way they seem to communicate with a subtle lift of the head, a glance. "Actually, it's weird. I should have felt your presence, but I didn't. How did you manage to sneak up on us?"

"We have to be careful," Omar says casually, glancing at his rogue comrades, "even out here. The rogues who first established the Sanc—that's what we call Rogue Sanctuary—wanted to find a place so remote they wouldn't be bothered by pack wolves. But even in the middle of this desert they still fear trespassers and wannabe colonizers." He lifts his head back in Jasper's direction; Jasper clenches his jaw and stares straight ahead. "So they learned to quiet their presence, to hide themselves. Every wolf who joins the Sanc has to learn to do this or risk revealing the location to every alpha in America."

"Whoa." I survey our escort once more. "Everyone here has that much control over their wolf energy?"

"Hell yeah," he says, kicking a pebble along the ground playfully. "We can teach you. Then maybe you wouldn't have to block everyone out, y'know."

I smile and shrug. "That would be kind of cool. But aren't we sort of...your prisoners?"

Omar stops walking to give me a dirty look like I insulted his mother.

"Prisoners? Who said anything about prisoners? It's not like that—I mean, we're a peaceful bunch, the council just wants to talk with you to see whether you mean us any harm."

"If we mean *you* any harm?" Jasper says, his voice rough, indignant. He's stopped walking as well, the rogue wolves meander around us. "If we're not prisoners then let us go."

"No can do, my man," Omar says, clapping his hands together and continuing walking once again. "Council's orders."

"Max," Jasper whispers roughly in my ear. "This is bad. If I cause a distraction, you can shift and make a run for it.

Run back to the house and let the guards know what's happened."

"Don't be silly," I say. "I'm not leaving you. Besides, I don't think we're in danger, just because they're rogues."

"They've kidnapped us and are taking us only the moon gods know where. I don't see how this ends well."

"Let's just talk to them, then I'm sure they'll let us go."

Jasper doesn't look convinced.

"What?"

"Why do you think no one has found this place before? You think they just let their prisoners go?"

"If they wanted to hurt us wouldn't they have ripped out our jugulars while we were sleeping? They're rogues, not murderers. They're probably just making sure they're safe from us."

Jasper clicks his tongue and rolls his eyes.

"You boys coming?" Omar calls over his shoulder, and a large chocolate-colored wolf knocks into me with her shoulder, nudging me forward.

"Honestly, I don't think I'd make it back anyway," I say as Jasper and I begin trekking along with the wolves again. "We know Omar," I venture a moment later, "that has to count for something."

"Barely."

"Still, try reading his energy. He doesn't want to hurt us. Let's just go with them and explain that we were camping out for a night and we don't want to intrude, then I'm sure they'll let us go."

I can hear myself and even I'm surprised at the slight hint of excitement in my voice. Here we are being potentially kidnapped but I'm more intrigued than frightened. These wolves have some wild control over their energy, and if they're willing to show me how they do it, maybe I could learn a little more about my blood-wolf abilities, maybe I could stop living in fear of migraines, and maybe Jasper and I could finally mind-link.

"Let's give them the benefit of the doubt," I say, low enough not to be heard by the rogues. "Don't you want to see what a real rogue settlement looks like?"

"Not especially."

"Come on, give them a shot."

Jasper stares into my eyes as if trying to ascertain something—maybe whether I've lost my mind completely, or maybe some other unspoken concern I can't quite read. But finally he relents, shaking his head. "Fine. But the second things get out of hand I want you to promise you'll run."

"I promise." I take his hand in an attempt to be comforting. "And, hey, seeing as I didn't get to say it yet, last night was…pretty freaking great."

He squeezes my hand back, staring straight ahead. "Agreed."

We walk for a few hours before Rogue Sanctuary comes into view. I don't know what I was expecting but it sure wasn't this.

The whole thing has the look of a music festival—like Burning Man, only with less drugged-out influencers and more of a hippie vibe. Tents ranging in size from circus big top to glamping yurt have been erected as far as I can see, with flags and banners between them waving in the breeze. For the most part they blend in with the beigy, camel-toned environs, although some of them have been painted in mismatching, colorful patterns.

"It's the size of a city," I say from where I've stopped to take it in.

The sun is overhead and heat waves rise from the hot sand, making the sky extra pale and hazy, creating a miragelike effect. Rock formations sit to one side of the expansive encampment, and plant life springs up between the tents lining the paths—or really they're more like roads—linking everything together. Gardens with colorful desert flowers have been planted at the base of the tents. Even from a distance it's easy to tell how alive the sanctuary is: the silhouettes of kids running between tents flit like dragonflies, wolves go about their days, some in human form and others in their wolf form, smoke rises in a number of spots, and a distinctly savory and delicious smell is drifting toward us.

"Is that...barbecue?" I say, drooling.

"It's pretty amazing isn't it," Omar says, turning back to join Jasper and me. "Bet you didn't think it would be this big."

"It's so cool," I say, open-mouthed and wide-eyed.

"Oh yeah," Omar says, then turns to Jasper, who is also staring at Rogue Sanctuary, although with less awe and more confusion. "What about you? What do you think?"

"It's cute," Jasper says, intentionally patronizingly.

The rest of the wolves have already gone on ahead.

"Come on, the council will be waiting."

We make our way to the edge of the sanctuary and all I can think is how this is nothing like the ramshackle, abandoned warehouses of Rogue City in Pittsburgh. As we wander between tents and I'm overwhelmed by all the different scents: food, floral and sweet, wafting from yurts and fenced-off patio-type areas, nearly eclipsed by a cacophony of wolves—the scents of wolves from all across the country clashing, mingling, in this mind-tingling but thrilling way. I've only just been able to fully comprehend the scent of a wolf from somewhere in the southeast, Florida maybe, before another scent—is that Texas? Milwaukee?—emerges to overtake it.

I glance at Jasper to see what he thinks, and from his scrunched-up face and turned-up nose, I don't think he's having the same olfactory response as me. For someone so attuned to the scent of his own pack, maybe all these conflicting scents are hard to stomach.

Our escort leads us deeper yet as we catch stares from all around. Wolves lie in the shade cast by the tents that I assume are their homes, careless and unbothered about remaining in their animal form, their dark eyes watching us as they yawn or kick out a back leg.

"I've never seen so many wolves just existing like this," I whisper to Jasper. "It's like they aren't worried one bit about humans. Can you imagine?"

"It's wild," Jasper says, only he sounds like he means it in a literal sense, like these are wild animals and not the civilized company he's used to.

Finally, we reach a large tent at a spot where six or seven paths converge. Two flags stand proudly on either side of a shaded doorway, painted in bright colors with a mix of patterns and symbols clashing all over them, flapping ever so slightly.

Omar stands at the door with a host of the wolves who brought us here. "This is the tent of the rogue council. They oversee the sanctity and protection of our city."

"I thought you were supposed to be a democratic society," Jasper says snidely.

"We are. All rogues are eligible and the council members are elected by vote every leap year."

"How big is the council?" I ask.

"There are five members, each one a representative of one of the five moon gods."

A rotund wolf emerges slowly from the shadowy entrance of the tent. From here it looks like he's missing an eye, but maybe he still has one eye closed from the nap he apparently just woke up from. Omar speaks to this wolf in a voice low enough that I can't make out what's being said and when he's done he bounces upright, smiling. "They'd like to speak with you both."

He gestures for us to follow and slips through the doorway.

In the shade of the tent the air is instantly cooler. We're led through a narrow canvas-lined passage that finally opens out onto a large circular room. A small fire burns in a pit in the center of the room, the smoke escaping through a hole in the tent's roof. The dirt floor is covered in mismatching rugs, rolled out in all different directions, and around the perimeter of the room large cushions are laid out for larger gatherings, or kumbaya circles I guess. Opposite us are five shadowy figures—all are seated on stools except one, who has shown up in their wolf form and is resting on a cushion one spot to the right of center.

"Come forward," the central figure says. Her long, gray hair is tied back in two plaits, her face is weathered, with deep wrinkles cut into her dark-brown skin, and her eyes are round and thoughtful.

Omar gestures for us to approach the fire, and together Jasper and I edge forward hesitantly.

"My name is Malamar. You may call me Mal. I am the representative of Nannar, the oldest of the moon gods. Welcome to our sanctuary. This is Buck." She gestures to the bulky white man sitting to her left. He looks to be in his forties, with cropped hair, a heavily muscled chest, and arms the size of logs sticking out of his sleeveless shirt. He salutes us with two fingers and a clenched jaw. "Buck sits as representative of Mani."

I hazard an awkward wave but Buck doesn't look like the type to return the gesture, or smile even.

"I believe you've met Tomas," Mal continues, looking to the man sitting farthest from her on the left.

Their faces are lit only by the flickering firelight and I hadn't realized until now that I do, in fact, recognize one of them. Tomas is the guy who sold Jasper all the crystals and things in town, with the ponytail, thin limbs, and round shoulders.

"A pleasure to see you both once more," Tomas says, nodding gently. A low growl rolls in Jasper's throat. This guy must have been the one to alert the rogues to our presence, and Jasper isn't happy about being tricked. "I sit as the representative of Igaluk. I trust your connection ceremony went as planned."

It's hard to tell if he's serious or making fun of us, like he knew all those crystals and incense wouldn't help. Jasper clenches and unclenches a fist.

"This is Akari," Mal continues, gesturing to the young woman on her far right. Her posture is ridiculous, her hair straight and black as Jasper's—in fact she bears a striking resemblance to Jasper's mother. "Akari is Tsukuyomi's representative."

Akari bows her head slightly by way of greeting.

"And finally, on my right is Kairos." Mal gestures toward the wolf sitting between her and Akari. Now that we're closer I can make out the graying fur around his muzzle. Kairos must be getting on. "Kairos represents Selene."

"How can he represent anything if he can't speak?" Jasper mutters.

Mal pauses at the interruption but doesn't look upset. She sits back with a patient smile.

"Kairos chose long ago to remain in the form in which he feels the most connected to wolfkind. He has remained in his wolf form for the last forty-odd years. We do not begrudge him this choice—in fact, we aren't even sure if he is still able to shift back into his human state. He speaks through me."

I quirk my head sideways. What does she mean?

Mal must catch our confused expressions.

"Kairos and I are mates, we communicate via mind-link. Thus I am able to speak for him."

They can mind-link! Whoa!

Kairos lifts his head to sniff the breeze, perhaps scenting us out, or perhaps using his wolf senses to ascertain whether we're worth his time. Promptly he flops back onto his cushion, where he remains docile for the rest of the meeting. Maybe we aren't worthy?

"You are very welcome here in Rogue Sanctuary," Mal says, before lowering her eyes and her voice. "Now please tell me how the son of an alpha came to be on rogue territory and what your intentions are while you're here."

I try to swallow so that I can introduce myself but before I've had the chance Jasper takes a small step forward and speaks in his most alpha-sounding tone.

"I am Jasper Apollo, son of Alpha Jericho Apollo of the Elite Pack."

Mal watches with an amused grin, while Tomas lifts an unimpressed brow, Buck leans forward onto an elbow, and Akira's face doesn't move.

"My family owns land a few miles west of here. We were simply camping on that land when your soldiers apprehended us unlawfully. I must demand that we are released at once and allowed to return peacefully to my family's home."

In such a large space you'd almost expect the sound to echo, but instead Jasper's words leave his mouth and seem to die instantly, fizzing to nothing. The council waits a beat, a growl coming from Buck's direction, then Mal smiles.

"Are you finished, Child Alpha?"

Buck laughs a little at this epithet and Tomas grins wryly, but Jasper is only angered further—I can practically hear his teeth grinding.

"First of all," Mal continues, "the laws which govern you and your pack hold no bearing here. We have neither acted unlawfully or outside the realms of our jurisdiction. Secondly, the land which you claim to *own* sits squarely within the boundaries of the territory of the sanctuary. What freedoms your family have enjoyed upon our land were gifted by this council many years ago."

"Lies," Jasper says. "My father would never do business with rogues."

Buck slams a fist on his knee. "How dare you?" he roars, poised to stand and tackle Jasper to the ground.

"There's no need for violence," Mal says, holding a hand in Buck's path. He settles uncomfortably back in his chair and she returns her attention to Jasper. "The use of our land wasn't gifted to your father."

Jasper's eyes narrow like he's trying to figure out exactly what Mal is saying.

"The house, the land...was given to your mother."

"What...what are you saying?" Jasper chokes out.

Mal places her hands gently in her lap. "What I'm saying, Child Alpha, is that your mother was no stranger to us here at Rogue Sanctuary. In fact she played a vital role in creating the safe and thriving community we have today."

Jasper is flummoxed, a bead of sweat is rolling down his temple.

"You...you knew my mother?"

THE ROGUE COUNCIL

Jasper's face has turned so red I'm worried his head is about to explode.

"Answer me," he rasps. "You knew my mother?"

"Yes," Mal says, nodding. "We were good friends."

Jasper's eyes are darting between council members, as if he's looking for any sign of deception, a lie betrayed by a knowing smirk or a quirked eyebrow. He mustn't find any because he grips his hands into fists and squeezes his eyes shut. "I—I don't believe you."

Mal waves a dismissive hand in front of her face. "Whether you believe me or not is of little consequence. Your mother was important to us and to this settlement, and because of that we are willing to offer you hospitality."

"You *offer* us?" Jasper's tone is incendiary, he's insulted and not afraid to show it.

"Watch yourself, Child Alpha," Mal warns. "We are a peaceful tribe, unlike your militaristic packs, we do not rely on our bite to assert our dominance. But we are also proud and we are not without fangs of our own."

This must be tough for Jasper. Clearly he had no idea his mother was so involved with the rogues. Yes, we knew she reached out to them in her time as luna, but not to this extent. He's learning things about her he couldn't possibly have known. I reach out and take Jasper's wrist in my hand, trying to send him calming energy. He takes two deep breaths and opens his eyes.

"There we are," Mal says, her tone bordering on friendly. "Tomas here was especially close with your mother." The ponytailed wolf nods in consensus. "If you would like, Child Alpha, you can stay awhile, get to know her better. I'm sure he would enjoy reminiscing with you."

"It would be my pleasure," Tomas chimes in. "Mitsuha was an inspirational woman and a great friend."

Jasper's back straightens and his chest muscles tense. "I don't need you to tell me who my mother was."

"Am I correct in thinking you were unaware of just how involved your mother was in the business of rogues?" Mal asks, leaning forward.

Jasper doesn't respond.

"Why do you think that is?" she asks. "Why do you think your father has kept that side of her hidden from you?"

"Leave my father out of this."

"Your alpha father has kept the truth from you," Mal says, her voice level and strong. "Don't you want to know her for who she really was?"

"I've heard enough," Jasper snaps. "If we are not prisoners, as you say, then you will not prevent us from leaving. Come on, Max." Jasper turns, not waiting for me, and stomps to the exit.

I glance between him and the council. "I—I'm sorry."

As Jasper disappears I make for the door as well but freeze when Mal's voice booms from behind me.

"Blood Wolf!"

A ripple runs down my spine. How does she know about that? Jasper is gone and now I stand alone, slowly turning to face the council.

"Oh yes," she says, a knowing smile crossing her face. "We have sensed your presence."

"How—how did you—?"

"Tell me something, Blood Wolf. Have you heard the call?"

An echo of the distant howl that's plagued my dreams since the beginning of the year ricochets through my head and I can't help but rub the back of my neck.

Mal leans back with the fire reflected in her widening eyes. "I see. You have heard it then. And I suppose you've been told to ignore it. To pretend you hear nothing. To remain in the dark like your packmates."

"I—I—"

What is she talking about? Does she know who's been calling to me? Interrupting every time I've tried to link with Jasper?

"Would you ignore the call of the moon gods?" she asks.

"No but..." My head is swimming. The *moon gods*? Is that who's calling to me? "How did you know about that?"

"The powers you have are great," Mal says. "But they are not unique. Every wolf is capable of accessing the greater consciousness of wolfkind. But it is a skill that takes discipline and practice. Back in your pack system those skills have been all but bred out of existence, kept from you by leaders who wish to control and subjugate their people. But here in this sanctuary we encourage every wolf to develop their ability to connect to their neighbors, to access the great connection shared between all wolves."

"If..." I try to speak but have to stop to clear my throat. "If these abilities have been suppressed in me then why do I have them?"

"The blood moon awoke something inside you, something latent and powerful. It must have sensed a desire in you."

"A desire?" What, like a wish?

"Yes." Mal nods sagely. "An unspoken yearning for something more. So now your ability to connect is unmatched. And it is a skill that could be used to improve the lives of wolves the world over. You have been given a gift, Max, an amazing gift."

I huff. "Some gift. If I wanted a constant migraine I'd have asked someone to drop an anvil on my head."

"You are closed off," she continues. "That is the source of your discomfort."

"Discomfort?" She has no idea. "Discomfort is sitting for too long without a cushion. Discomfort is not knowing what to say when you're being forced to speak with some old noblewolf. Discomfort is...is your mate ignoring you. Try brain-melting agony. Try an electric drill piercing my skull. You have no idea about discomfort!"

Okay, I didn't mean to rant, but she's got me all worked up. As if I could have avoided all the headaches and the pain by simply being more open to the connection. All those voices, all those wolves, that's why blood wolves have a bad reputation, that's why they go insane. I had to close myself off to protect myself.

"Maybe not," Mal says gently now, kindly. "But Max, we can help you."

"How?" I say, a little too bluntly.

Her face looks less stern now, and she extends an open palm, as if she's offering to help me up after a fall.

"Every rogue who passes through our community is given the chance to explore their inner wolf. Our spiritual practices are designed to help wolves who feel disconnected from their own kind find a way back. We can help you too—help you to open up, relieve your pain, and help you to connect."

Connect?

Isn't that what Jasper and I have been trying to do? Isn't that what I've wanted since I figured out there was more to being a wolf than the confines of a pack? Connection to something bigger. When I discovered just how many queer wolves were out there I began to see the truth of our kind. That we're all valid and connected. One pack under the moon. Is Mal offering to help me find that?

"We can help you harness your power, help you open your mind. If you stay with us a short while we can show you all that you are capable of."

Stay here awhile? How long is a while? Does it even matter? There's no way Jasper will go for this. But what if she's right? Every wolf that arrived at our camp this morning was able to block me from sensing their presence. If that's what the rogues' spiritual guidance can accomplish in a wolf without my blood-moon abilities, what could I do with my enhanced skills? Maybe I could stop these headaches, figure out who is calling me, figure out what I'm supposed to do with this strange gift, and maybe even mind-link with Jasper.

For a moment I chew my thumbnail and think over this proposition. The council waits and watches me, patient and silent. Finally, I let out a sigh.

"What will it be, Blood Wolf?" Mal asks.

"I want to learn from you," I say without thinking. "There's just one problem…"

"The child alpha."

"Yes," I say. "Jasper. He's my mate, I can't force him to stay here if he doesn't want to."

"If he truly cares for you he will do what's best."

I look up at her from under my bangs. She may have got my number, but she doesn't know Jasper at all.

"Hey," I say, squinting in the sunlight with a hand held over my eyes. After I left the council's tent I found Jasper outside kicking the dirt with his hands shoved firmly in his pockets. There's no sign of Omar or the wolves who brought us here.

"Hey," he says. "Ready to go?"

"I, uh...I..."

"What is it?" he stops kicking dust up and comes to me with a look of concern etched on his face. "What happened in there?"

"They said...they said they could help me control my blood-wolf powers. They want us to stay."

"You aren't honestly considering staying here?" he asks, incredulous.

"I am," I say, a little more determined. "Jasper, if they can help me stop using all my energy to keep people out of my head, if they can stop me from keeling over every time I try to reach out with my powers, then maybe...maybe I can use this gift for good."

"They're lying, Max," he says through clenched teeth.

"You don't know that."

"They're rogues, we can't trust them. Did you hear what they said about my mother?"

"Yes, but what if it's true? Don't you want to learn more about her? Don't you want to find out what she was like when she wasn't around your dad? What she believed in? Who she was...really?"

"I know who she was!"

He's red-faced and a drop of saliva is hanging from his curled lip. But I get why he's angry. The very people he thinks are responsible for his mother's death are now telling him they knew her better than he ever did. I take his hands and try to keep my voice calm, mostly so he'll chill out as well.

"I know you do," I say, rubbing the backs of his hands with my thumbs. "You know who she was to you. But, Jasp, you were twelve when she was...when she died. You can't possibly have known everything there was to know about her. I know you don't trust them but why don't you give them a chance. It might be a good thing. Who knows, maybe you'll be surprised?"

He turns his face away and stares at a tent peg, chewing his lip.

"We don't have to stay long—a couple nights, that's all. Just long enough for me to see what they can offer, if they can actually help me."

"It's dangerous," he mutters.

I lean sideways so that he has to look at me.

"If I can get my abilities under control," I say, locking eyes with him, "then maybe we'll be able to mind-link, like we wanted. I think it's worth a shot."

The muscles in his cheeks move as he grinds his teeth, thinking things over, then finally he turns to face me once more.

"You really want to stay?"

"Just a couple of nights, that's it."

"You promise?"

"Swear to the moon gods."

He exhales roughly. "Fine. But the second things turn bad we're getting out of here."

"They won't—"

"The second they turn bad," he echoes.

"Okay." We stand for a moment holding hands and letting the dust settle. "So, we'll stay?"

He rolls his eyes but he's backing down. "You'll be the death of me one day."

I laugh because he's joking, but I don't find it all that funny.

"You two stopped squabbling?" Omar asks, coming around the side of the council's tent.

"We weren't squabbling," Jasper growls.

"Sure you were. Like an old married couple." Omar joins us, one hand under his shirt scratching his chest and displaying his toned abs. "Mal tells me you're going to stay awhile?"

"How did she...?"

He shrugs. "She's pretty well connected." He winks at me. "Anyway she asked me to show you to one of the guest tents."

"Great," I say.

"We've already dropped off your belongings," Omar says, then glances at the sun. "Come on, it's almost lunchtime. You won't want to miss Miss Sammy's barbecue ribs."

He turns on his heel and takes off down a path. I glance at my reluctant mate one last time and follow Omar, pulling Jasper along behind me.

ROGUE SANCTUARY

Omar leads us through the tent city, nodding and greeting rogues as he does. From the way that people smile when they see him, waving and winking, it's clear he's ingratiated himself within this community.

"You seem popular," I say.

He shrugs. "It's easy to get along when everyone is this friendly. Here we are."

We arrive at an expansive shaded area. A tent ceiling is held aloft by thick wooden poles, and underneath are at least a hundred collapsible picnic tables. The place is already crowded by wolves eating and chatting with the others at their tables. My nostrils widen as a stupidly delicious scent wafts by.

"What is that smell?"

Omar grins. "Told you. Miss Sammy's ribs are the best in the country."

I glance at Jasper and his eyes are wide as well. "Smells good, huh?" I ask and nudge him gently.

He shakes his head a little and resets his face. "Not especially," he says.

I turn to Omar, desperate not to have offended him. "Jasper...uh...doesn't eat meat."

"Don't worry, Alpha Boy," Omar says. "There's plenty of veggie-loving wolves here too. You'll be well fed."

Jasper can't even hide his shock at learning there are other vegetarian wolves, as much as he'd like to.

We wander through the tables, Omar slapping his pals on the back. At one table three men are sitting not touching their food while they glare at us. They don't look as happy as everyone else that we're here.

By the far end of the shade cloth, four tables have been set up and food laid out buffet style, with wolves dishing out all manner of delicious-smelling food to the patrons lining up with their dinner trays. Behind them in the sun sit three industrial-size barbecues that wouldn't be out of place in some steampunk fantasy. We make our way to the end of the line and take our trays.

"Miss Sammy!" Omar says with an open-mouthed smile, throwing his hands wide and nearly taking Jasper out with his tray.

"Omar, baby," Miss Sammy says from behind a mountain of glistening, succulent-looking ribs. "You better be hungry today."

"Always," he replies.

Miss Sammy has big, rosy cheeks, her curly red hair is held back by a bandana, and her apron is covered in barbecue sauce smudges.

"Who are your friends?" she says, pointing at Jasper and me with a pair of saucy tongs.

"This is Max. He's the blood wolf and a super cool dude. And this is his mate, Jasper Apollo, he's..." We stare at Omar, waiting to see how he plans to finish that thought. "He's here too."

Jasper rolls his eyes but Miss Sammy leans over the table, her belly nearly coming into contact with the pile of ribs, to squint at Jasper.

"You have her eyes," Miss Sammy says.

Jasper pulls his head back like he's smelled something rotten.

"You boys are a long way from home. You must be hungry. Load up, there's plenty to go around."

I let Miss Sammy stack way too many ribs on my plate then move down the buffet, doing as told and loading up corn, potato salad, sausages, a succulent-looking burger, some other salad with chickpeas and broccoli. Behind me Jasper is being much pickier but he accepts a large spoon of both salads, plus some grilled eggplant and halloumi and a seasoned mushroom head the size of my face. Both satisfied, we find an empty table and sit.

"Looks good," I say, taking a whiff of the spicy, sweet scent of barbecue sauce and salivating up a storm.

Jasper doesn't say anything. Omar joins us swiftly, dropping his tray on the table with a loud thunk.

"Tuck in, boys," Omar says, already pulling pork from the bone with his teeth.

I sink my teeth into the steaming meat and the juices explode across my palate. I've never had ribs this meaty, this tender and delicious. "Oh my moon gods!" I mumble with a mouth full, knowing I must have sauce all over my face.

"I know, right?" Omar says, nodding. "And yours?" he asks Jasper.

With a knife and fork Jasper cuts a neat triangle of his mushroom, stares at it briefly as if it could be poisoned, then finally slips it between his lips. Instantly his eyes pop open and he chews with an amazed look on his face.

"Pretty good?" Omar is staring at Jasper with very high eyebrows.

Jasper stares at his plate. "It's fine, I guess," he mumbles, but Omar and I can both tell that's the best damn mushroom he's ever eaten.

"So after lunch I thought I could show you around a little," Omar says. "Then Max, I want to introduce you to Yoki."

"Yoki?" I ask.

"Yoki is our spiritual leader, they'll be the one working with you on the blood-wolf front. They're amazing, they'll be able to help you out, no trouble."

"And what about Jasper, what will he do?"

Omar smiles mischievously at Jasper. "Earn his keep."

Jasper and I stare questioningly at Omar.

"You'll see," he says, then goes back to his lunch.

"That's the healer's tent over there," Omar says, pointing to a large tent with a thin plume of pale smoke rising from the center. "And over there is one of our communal vegetable gardens." Between two rows of tents I spot an out-of-place patch of green dotted with bright colors—yellow corn and red bell peppers all growing in abundance.

"It must take a lot of work to cultivate all that produce," I say.

"The biggest issue is sourcing enough water," Omar explains. "But we all chip in with the garden work and there's no shortage of sunlight."

"And you grow everything you eat yourselves?"

"Pretty much." Omar glances at me looking suitably smug.

"That's so cool." I nudge Jasper. "Isn't that cool? Living completely off the land?"

Jasper grunts.

"We have a water reservoir just a short distance from here in the shadiest part of the valley," Omar continues, turning right down a slightly narrower path. The tent walls on either side of us ripple in the warm breeze. "Down here is our meditation center where we go to hone our wolf senses."

"Is that where Yoki is?" I ask, eager to meet the spiritual practitioner who might be able to help me.

Omar grins knowingly. "No. Yoki has their own space."

We stop at an intersection with five paths leading off in different directions. Omar points down a trail to the left. "If you head this way you'll find our library. We have an amazing collection of books. There's volumes and volumes about the history of werewolf culture, a great section on horticulture and germination. But there's also some wicked fiction, some romance, mystery, the classics. A big selection of young adult."

"Awesome," I say.

"That way"—Omar turns and points down another pathway—"leads you to the music tent. And down there"—he turns and points down yet another—"is our gym."

"You have everything you could ever need," I say.

Jasper remains stoically silent.

"Almost," Omar replies. "Your mate doesn't seem so impressed."

"Jasper?" I say, hoping he'll muster the strength to say something nice.

"It's impressive," he says finally, surveying the encampment with one eyebrow raised like he isn't so sure. "Especially considering the lack of consistent leadership."

Omar bristles a little at Jasper's obviously underhanded compliment, but he shrugs it off. "That's what's so great about this place. Everyone has a voice. There isn't one dictator controlling everything."

Jasper locks eyes with Omar and steps toward him. "An alpha isn't a dictator."

"Fascism by any other name, right?" Omar says, not backing down—in fact, squaring his shoulders and stepping to face off with Jasper.

"What did you say?" Jasper growls.

"Heyheyhey," I say, stepping between them, putting a hand on Jasper's chest to ease him off. "Put the claws away. This is a peaceful place, right Omar?"

"Yeah," he scoffs. "It is." He steps back and turns away, his cheeks flushing with embarrassment.

Jasper withdraws as well.

"From what I've heard," Omar begins, and I pray he isn't about to provoke Jasper further, "your mother was pretty instrumental in helping this place get off the ground."

Jasper doesn't say anything. He glares sideways at Omar, studying him to see if this is some kind of goading or if he's sincere.

"People around here, they talk about her like she was some kind of saint."

Still, Jasper doesn't say anything.

"She must have believed the rogues needed a place like this, where they could be safe."

"She..." Jasper falters. "She cared about all people. No matter who or—*what* they are."

Omar rakes his eyes over Jasper's face carefully. "Shame the acorn fell so far from the tree."

Jasper lifts his head once more, his chin a proud blade slicing the air.

"Come on," Omar says. "Tomas will be waiting."

Jasper hangs back a little but follows Omar and me as we make our way down one of the five paths until we emerge at what appears to be a construction site. Bare wooden poles are being dug into the ground, crossbeams nailed into them, and the tent roof, which is only halfway erected, is being strung up between them.

"What's this?" I ask.

"It will be a school," Omar says, "when it's finished. We sort of outgrew the last one." He gestures to a wide patch of dirt off to the side where fifty or sixty kids of all ages are sitting in groups listening to a handful of teachers. "Our numbers have been swelling lately. Tension in the packs is forcing more and more people to go rogue, and well, a lot of them end up here. Since the weather is nice we're holding classes outside until the new school tent can be completed."

"How long will it take?"

"Should have only been a couple of weeks," Omar says. "But with more and more wolves flocking to us, the council decided to divert some of our wolfpower to the security teams, to ensure the new arrivals don't attract any unwanted attention from the packs."

"Why? What would the packs do if they found out about this place?"

"Why don't you ask your boyfriend?"

I turn to Jasper, who has just caught up, but before I can say anything Tomas approaches us, pulling off a pair of gloves and lifting a pair of protective glasses onto the top of his head.

"Ah, there you are," Tomas says. "Just in time. We can use all the help we can get."

Jasper leans into me and whispers. "What is he talking about?"

Omar answers for me. "We thought while Max was learning from Yoki, that you, Jasper, could help out with our wolfpower-shortage problem and lend a hand to our builders."

"I—excuse me?" Jasper asks, so low even I can hardly make him out.

"Yeah, you know, put those alpha muscles to some use," Omar teases. "Since Tomas here is in charge of the project and knows a lot about your mother, we thought it was a great win-win."

"We'll be glad of the assistance," Tomas says. "This school is exactly the type of project your mother would have shepherded when she was still with us."

"You want me to help build a school?" Jasper asks, still incredulous.

At that moment a handful of kids come running by, screaming and laughing and almost knocking Jasper right off his feet. Jasper watches them like bugs he'd rather squish.

"Jasper is actually great with kids," I say, catching the concerned expression on Tomas's face. "He and his little sister get on like nobody's business."

"Max," Jasper says through gritted teeth.

"What? It's true!"

"Of course, if hard labor isn't your thing we're also short of a teacher or two. You could help out with the children's lessons?"

Jasper looks over at the mass of kids, their hands shooting eagerly into the air to answer a question, shouting for attention, getting into scuffles, pulling hair, picking noses. Eventually he sighs.

"Pass me a hammer."

"Wonderful," Tomas says, gesturing for Jasper to follow. "Let's get you all set up."

"See ya," Omar says in the most patronizing tone. "I'll take care of Max."

Jasper is hesitant to move.

"I'll see you later," I say, rubbing his shoulder. "I'll be fine."

Eventually, he follows Tomas toward the half-built school tent, but not without looking back, all worried and uncomfortable, to give me a reluctant wave.

"He'll fit right in with the other builders," Omar says. "They hate unnecessary conversation."

I roll my eyes but smile a little. It's sort of fun the way he makes Jasper squirm. I just hope Jasper can learn a little bit about his mom while also hammering away.

"Okay," Omar continues. "You ready to meet Yoki?"

"Is this it?" I ask.

Omar has taken me to the very edge of the settlement. All the other tents sit behind us, and in front is a lopsided shelter that looks about ready to topple over. The fabric walls are aged and dusty and look as though they're almost wearing through in places. Some weed or shrublike bush grows around the base of the poles and climbs up one side of the structure. The doorway is a tattered flap, being frisked about by the breeze. It looks small and dirty, but at the same time homely. It's like the desert equivalent of a witch's cottage you'd find in the woods in some fairy tale. Beyond Yoki's tent the desert seems to stretch on forever.

"This is it," Omar says and moves to the shelter, lifting aside the flapping door and entering without announcing himself.

Tremulously, I follow.

The entrance is so low I have to duck but inside things open up in a weird *Doctor Who*–type way. The tent is long and narrow, with two large sheets of fabric pulled back at the far end to reveal the view—or more like the walls have been peeled away so that the inside and the outside are one and the same. The floor is dusty but covered in rugs that seem to move under my feet. Ferns and succulents grow in pots and in baskets hanging from the vaulted ceiling. Antique-looking cabinets and stools are dotted around the perimeter of the room, along with old wooden shelves housing jars of powders, herbs, and strangely colored liquids. In the middle of the room, floor cushions surround a circular table with rocks and—are those...? Yep, bones in a pile in the center.

"Yoki?" Omar calls out to the seemingly absent guru.

He turns and gestures for me to come farther in. It's cool and dry in the tent, and a pleasant, faintly floral aroma fills the air. I join Omar by the central table.

"Right on time," Yoki—or who I assume is Yoki—says as they appear at the opening on the far end, draped in flowing white fabrics, their silver hair long and held back from their face with a braided leather headband.

They're younger than I imagined. For some reason I was picturing some hunched-over nanna type. But Yoki can't be much older than Omar. Their skin is flawless, russet but freckled slightly. Their eyes are startling gray.

Omar heads to greet Yoki, taking their hands in his and bowing his head. "Lunar greetings."

"Moon gods' blessings," Yoki says in return, their voice smooth and dulcet, as though they possess wisdom well beyond their years.

Omar and Yoki nod to each other before Yoki looks up at me and smiles. My breath catches in my throat. Who is this strange ethereal person? Where did they come from? I've never met anyone like them before.

"And moon gods' blessings to you, Blood Wolf," they say, only their lips didn't seem to move, or did they?

"And, uh, the same to you," I stammer, more aware of how un-ethereal I am than ever.

"Come, sit," they say, for sure with their mouth this time, and gesture to the cushions. "Tea?"

"Um, sure. Tea would be great."

"Omar, would you mind?"

"Certainly." Omar bows not unlike a butler and then moves over to an electric stove I hadn't noticed before where a steel kettle is already heating.

For some reason I assumed Omar would leave me here and head off to help, I dunno, patrol the borders or build something like Jasper is doing, but instead he goes about making tea as if he lives here as well.

When I sit and turn to Yoki, I find them watching me with an amused expression and a gentle smile. "Omar has become an attentive acolyte these past months," they say, answering the questions I had only thought.

"Oh." I didn't realize Omar was so interested in the spiritual realm.

"After spending all that time with Agatha up north," he says, carrying a tray of cups and a teapot to the circle, "I started to see the benefits of communicating with the spirits. Yoki has been training me since I arrived at the Sanc."

He places the tray by our feet and pours tea into three ceramic cups before passing one to Yoki, then one to me.

"So you'll be staying?" I ask.

"If you don't mind," he answers.

My cheeks are warm and I don't think it's from the hot tea. "I—I don't mind."

"Omar will be a steadying presence as we explore the great consciousness," Yoki says, blowing gently then sipping their tea. They have this melodic way of speaking and this slight grin that makes them seem amused by everything, as if the ways of us earth dwellers are adorably novel to them.

For a moment we sip our tea quietly. Yoki and Omar seem content to sit in silence, but my mind is racing and I want to know what's going to happen next.

"So uh, I was sort of hoping you might be able to help me figure out this whole blood-wolf thing…Omar says you're amazing at all this wolf-energy spiritual stuff, and I really need some help to quiet down the noise in my head. You wouldn't believe the headaches I've been having. It's been majorly bad, like uberpainful, and I've been a mess, a complete zonker!"

Yoki waits patiently while I ramble, then finally looks up, smiles generously at me, and laughs ever so quietly.

"The lupine chorus is not a noise to silence but a blessing to embrace," they say. "Like a river, you cannot fight it. You must let the current direct you and enjoy the flow."

Are they going to speak in riddles the whole time?

"Uh, yeah, you're right. Sorry. I know it's not noise to block out, at least that's what Omar told me. It's just—"

Yoki raises a delicate hand to stop me from blathering any further.

"You have no need to be nervous," they say. "I know why you have come."

Unless Mal and the council sent a quick email or text, I don't know how Yoki could know exactly why I've come, but I guess that's just how in tune they are.

"So you can help me?" I ask.

Again they smile and laugh into their teacup. "You do not need my help. But I am happy to serve as your guide through the lunar planes."

I take a breath and let my shoulders relax. "Phew, okay. Great. A guide. That would be—that's perfect."

Yoki places their cup down on the tray gently, then presses their palms together lightly. "You are unsure. Afraid that your path is not your own. Afraid to be lost among the multitude of voices that sing within the lupine chorus. But you need not be afraid. The path you tread can only be forged by the wolf within."

Oy, again with the riddles.

"I would like, if I may, to begin with a ritual." Yoki doesn't move but Omar stands all of a sudden, as if he knows what they need without them asking.

"What sort of ritual?"

"It is one of calming and cleansing. It will help you to focus and open your mind."

"Okay," I say, as Omar moves to the wonky shelves, picks up a basket, places a wooden bowl in it, and begins picking bottles from the shelf.

Yoki moves onto their knees by the table and gestures at a spot on the floor. "I would ask you to lie flat on your back."

Trying to be as not-awkward as possible, I maneuver myself onto the spot on the rugs Yoki suggested and lie back with a cushion under my head. Omar comes to kneel nearby and I shoot him a questioning glance. He nods subtly to reassure me and places the tray on the table. Immediately Yoki takes out the bowl, mixes some fragrant herbs with what appear to be spices, dried leaves, and seeds. They take up a blunt stirrer and mix the contents of the bowl, crushing them together before finally lighting the contents on fire. The bowl erupts with a purple flame that immediately goes out but leaves behind a bowl of smoking herbs and spices. Why do I feel like I'm about to experience the wildest contact high since that time a guy lit up on the L train?

"Close your eyes," Yoki says, gently wafting the scented smoke from the bowl in my direction. I do as I'm told. "Inhale deeply. Let the smoke envelope you. Feel your rib cage expand as you breathe, feel your stomach muscles widening. Once you have taken in as much air as you can, hold that breath."

My body expands as I breathe in, the smoke fills my nostrils, sweet and tangy and purely natural. As I hold my breath, it's hard to explain, but it's almost like I can feel the smoke moving through my cells, seeping into my veins and filling my body. My skin tingles, my fingers twitch, my muscles relax, and my limbs become heavy.

"Now release that breath and let the walls that protect your mind fall."

I'm scared that this is going to hurt, scared that by letting in all the noise I'm going to be overwhelmed, damaged somehow, and yes…lost, like Yoki said. But I'm here to try and figure this out and I won't be able to do that if I don't give this a go, if I don't put my trust in Yoki and Omar. As I let go of the breath I've been holding, I picture the walls around my mind falling outward.

Immediately my consciousness expands. I'm floating at the center of an infinitesimal void: weightless, buoyant, vibrating, eternal.

"Good," Yoki says, as if they're with me, as if they can feel the same thing I'm feeling. "You have left the physical world. And now you exist on the lunar plane. Just like the moon you are a reflection of the light that surrounds you. The noise you fear is not sound but light. Embrace light, search for it, and let it shine upon you."

As they say this a speck of something glitters far, far off in the distance, then like the sun rising over the horizon, it grows, ethereal beams of yellow and gold spike out in all directions as the light grows bigger and hotter. For a moment I'm afraid, scared that it will burn or blind, but then like a wave the light passes over me. I inhale sharply as I embrace the warmth and the light.

It's not unpleasant, but it's intense, my muscles seize and my, my—everything disappears, evaporating and becoming nothing but light.

My eyes shoot open and I sit upright. The tent feels darker than before, the smells more intense and unpleasantly pungent. Everything is swirling around me, but even though I very well may topple over...I smile.

"What did you glimpse, Blood Wolf?"

"I saw it," I say, breathless. "I saw us."

THE LIGHT OF THE MOON

"You wouldn't believe how good it felt," I say, pacing, almost bouncing around Jasper and my tent.

Outside the night air is cool and the choir of insects is buzzing a soaring ballad.

"It was like a warm bath only it was all light, moonlight, and I didn't have a body but it wasn't scary—it was like being a tiny part of something so big and wonderful and if I can just learn how to tap into that intentionally who knows what I could..."

Jasper is sitting on the edge of our bed, a dumpy mattress on the canvas floor, not responding.

"Are you listening?"

He turns his head slowly, squinting at me, then shakes his head as if he's waking himself up.

"I'm sorry. Tomas had me hammering poles into the ground all afternoon. I'm wiped."

He runs a hand over his face and through his hair and I join him on the bed.

"Did you at least get to ask about your mother?"

"No. Tomas palmed me off onto one of his team then disappeared. I didn't see him for the rest of the day."

"That's so strange. I'm sorry." I rub his back and shoulders.

"I doubt he even knew my mother well enough to tell me anything about her."

Jasper's muscles are crazy tense.

"Maybe he got distracted or pulled away. I'm sure he'll tell you about her at some point."

"I'd be surprised. My best guess is tomorrow they have me drilling holes or erecting the tarp roof and by the time our two nights are up we'll leave and Tomas won't have shown his face again."

"Two nights?" I ask, leaning back a little, my hand stilling on Jasper's shoulder.

"Yes. That's what we agreed."

"I didn't think we necessarily agreed on two nights exactly."

"We said a couple of nights. That's two. A couple is two, Max."

"I know but I just thought..."

Jasper looks at me questioningly.

"How long do you think we're staying here?"

"I thought it was more vague, sort of like depending on how things go with Yoki."

"Max, we can't stay here. The longer we're here the less likely they'll let us go."

"We're not their prisoners, they said as much."

Jasper stands but doesn't move from the side of the bed. He takes one large breath. "You heard what Omar said, right? About how they're diverting their wolfpower to their border patrols. They're scared, Max—of nearby packs, maybe, or...either way, while I'm here they have bartering power. They could use me as a hostage."

I roll my eyes. "I'm sorry, I forgot you were so valuable."

He turns and the anguish is clear on his face. "This isn't an ego thing. We left our security back at the house. No one knows where we are. And like it or not I'm—we're not inconsequential. We are high-ranking pack wolves and that makes us valuable to people like the rogues. We have to think about this sort of thing."

I stand, too, and step to face Jasper, putting my hand on his forearm in the hopes it'll calm him down.

"I know, okay? I know this isn't comfortable for you and I know why you're worried. But you're also making assumptions about the rogues that I don't think are true. They're peaceful. They've welcomed us as guests, not hostages. They built this whole place just so they could get away from the packs, not so they could be in a war with them. They said we could leave whenever we wanted and I believe them."

He lowers his head, making the bags under his eyes more pronounced.

"They may not start the war," Jasper says, his voice catching. "But when war comes to them, believe me, they'll behave just like any pack wolf."

I take his face in my free hand and rub his cheek with my thumb. "You don't know that."

He leans into my touch and I rise onto my toes to kiss him. When I pull away he's staring at me intently, familiar concern creasing his brow.

"You're too trusting," he says.

"And you're tired. Why don't we sleep and we talk more in the morning."

"Fine."

We don't say anything else as we get ready for bed. Our belongings were left in the tent as promised, so I grab my toothbrush from my pack and head to the communal bathrooms a little distance from our tent. Once I've brushed my teeth and washed my face I head back. Along the way I stop and turn to look at the moon, almost full and shining silver. For a second I bask in the light, feeling a fraction of the warmth and connection I experienced earlier during Yoki's ritual. I know I need to stay as long as it takes to figure out how to access my powers. I just don't know how to convince Jasper the rogues are good people.

Back at the tent, I arrive to find Jasper already under the covers, lying on his side, staring at the wall.

I flip off the battery-powered lantern and slide in behind him, slipping an arm around his waist. He shuffles so that his back is pressed against my chest.

"We can stay," he mumbles lowly. "For as long as you need."

When I don't say anything right away, he turns awkwardly, straining as he tries to look over his shoulder.

"You're sure?" I ask, lifting onto my elbow to ease his twisting neck.

He rolls over so that we can look at each other properly.

"If it's what you want," he whispers. "Nothing else matters."

"Thank you," I whisper back. "I'm sure it'll just take a few days. I promise it'll be worth it."

I kiss him quickly, trying to say thank you without words, and he returns the kiss but pulls away faster than I'd like.

"Good night," he says, before rolling back over, so I can't see his face any longer.

"Night."

Sweat drips down the side of my face.

"Concentrate," Yoki commands. "Find your center."

I squeeze my eyes together even tighter than before, grit my teeth, and attempt to focus. A low, strained growl rolls in my throat.

"Don't force it," Yoki says, cool as a goddam cucumber. "You're forcing it."

I risk a sneak peek through one eye and find Yoki already smiling at me like they knew I was about to cheat.

"Take a breather," they command, and I exhale, opening my eyes and letting the tension flood from my muscles.

"I don't understand," I say, frustration heating my cheeks. "It's been two days and I'm nowhere nearer to finding that light again."

Yoki tilts their head to the side, appraising me with gentle eyes. They're sitting on a cushion opposite me in the open doorway at the back of their tent. The scent of palo santo wood and burning sage drift from the shaded interior. The desert sun is high in the sky. I wipe the sweat from my forehead.

"You are attempting to commune with all of wolfkind, it takes patience, discipline, and above all else, concentration."

"But I was concentrating."

"Max," Omar says, chiding me for whining. I glance into the tent where he's sitting at the central table, organizing herbs or making bouquets of dried flowers for some lucky wolf's wedding, I don't know. "It'll happen. Just relax."

Omar has been a comforting presence the last couple of days, but even his sturdy and lighthearted ways aren't much help right now.

"That's easy for you to say," I huff. "I've been meditating and chanting and inhaling burnt herbs and I've barely stopped the headaches from attacking me every time I try to connect with the lupine chorus or whatever."

"It's only been two days. Take your time."

"I don't know how much time I have. Jasper is—he's worried we've been away too long already. I don't know how long I can stay, and I need to figure this out before I go."

"Connection to the chorus cannot be rushed," Yoki says with sudden urgency. "You have innate power, that is certain. But to wield it takes practice. You must learn to focus. If you are unable to control your abilities, to funnel the voices, the results could be disastrous."

I rub the back of my neck and sigh. "I know. You're right. Shall we try again?"

"No, enough for today," Yoki says, already standing and straightening out the skirt of their robes.

"But it's only just after noon. Should I come back in a couple of hours or..."

Yoki rubs their chin like an old wizard, only they look like a child playacting. "Something is blocking you from truly connecting. I must think and commune with the moon gods to come up with a solution. Come back tomorrow."

With that Yoki turns, their robes flung out like the petals of a flower, and leaves the tent for the desert.

I slump forward on my cushion, my shoulders rolling and head dropping. "Maybe it's no use. Maybe I just don't have what it takes to be the blood wolf."

"Hey," Omar says, suddenly standing right next to me. "You were chosen for a reason. The moon gods don't make mistakes like that. Besides, you've barely started. It took me two weeks to even figure out how to sit still during morning meditation, let alone control my wolf presence."

"Really?"

"Yeah, you're already leaps and bounds ahead of me."

"Thanks," I say, and Omar places a hand on my shoulder.

"You'll get it."

For a moment his eyes are full of this strange intensity, like he's trying to tell me something, but I can't figure out what. Then he laughs and smiles that crooked smile.

"You must be hungry. Wanna get some lunch?"

Just the mention of the word *lunch* and my stomach rumbles like there's a thunderstorm brewing in my belly.

"Totally."

"I just don't understand what I'm doing wrong," I say as we make our way to the lunch tent. "Why was it so easy that first day?"

Omar chews the inside of his cheek and thinks for a moment before answering.

"I think it probably caught you off guard," he says. "That was the first time you'd truly let your guard down, right?"

He's not wrong. On that first day I felt safe, with Yoki and with Omar. I knew they were trying to help me. And while that hasn't changed, for some reason, whenever I've tried to truly let my guard down over the last couple of days I've hesitated. I have no idea why.

"I suppose."

"Yoki said something was blocking you. You just need to figure out what that is."

What could be blocking me?

Back home there's a whole bunch of reasons why I might not want to open myself up completely. There are prying wolves who want to know too much about what I'm thinking. Wolves who'd like to use that information against me. Then there are the wolves I'm closest to. But why would I be worried about letting my guard down around the wolves I care about the most? And then it hits me…is it Jasper?

The last couple of days he's been pretty quiet. He's been working to help build the school and getting nowhere with Tomas. I know he wants to leave, that he's only staying for my benefit. Is that why I'm having trouble connecting? And is this blockage the same thing that's preventing us from mind-linking?

"Earth to Max," Omar says, waving a hand in front of my face. I hadn't even realized I'd stopped walking. We're standing a few paces from the entrance to the lunch tent. "You okay in there?"

"Huh? Oh yeah. Sorry. Just thinking. Ow."

Something pinches in the back of my mind and suddenly I'm aware of a presence behind me. I spin to see who's there but all I see is a shadow cast on the ground as whoever it was darts away behind a tent.

Weird.

"Something wrong, cuz?"

"I'm—I'm fine."

I turn back to the tent and cast a glance across the tables. Jasper is sitting alone in the far corner, watching us.

"Oh, he's here." Omar has clearly spotted Jasper as well. "Listen, you know that full moon ritual I was telling you about?"

"The drum circle thing? It's tonight, right?"

"Yeah, I should go help the gang get ready. Make sure all the drums are—drumming. But I'll catch you round."

"Will I see you there?"

Omar is already backing away, eager to make his exit. "Yeah, I'll be there, I'll be the one banging on the offbeat."

"Great, you'll stick out then," I say.

"See you," he says, then turns and jogs away.

I head inside the tent, signaling to Jasper that I'll grab some food then join him. Once again I load my plate with the most ridiculously delicious-smelling food—today it's pork chops, coleslaw, green beans, and mash—then plonk myself down across from Jasp.

"Hey," I say when he doesn't greet me but instead stares at me like there's something on my face.

"Hey," he grunts.

"Still no info about your mom?" I ask, assuming that's the reason he's in a sulky mood.

"Tomas wasn't even at the school today. Good news is the roof is up. Should just be a day or two more until the whole thing is finished."

"At least you can say you've accomplished something while you've been here."

His expression softens a little. "Still no luck accessing your blood-wolf powers?"

"Nada."

"That sucks."

For a moment we sit quietly, neither of us touching the piles of food in front of us.

"Maybe they overestimated—"

"I don't want to leave yet," I interject before he can finish his sentence. "Yoki is going to figure out what's blocking me and then—"

"What if nothing is blocking you?" he asks, sounding more irritated than I'd like. "What if they're just saying that to keep us here."

"Jasper, do you really think that's what they're up to? If they wanted to hold us prisoner they would just lock us up. They're trying to help."

"And Omar? Is he just trying to help?"

I reel back, pressing my shoulder blades into the chair behind me. He can't be serious.

"Omar is Yoki's apprentice. He's learning how to be in touch with his spiritual self. What's your problem with him?"

Jasper doesn't say anything. He shoots me a glare then picks up his fork and moves the unwanted salad around on his plate.

"Jasper, don't you trust me?" I ask, keeping my voice low so the tables around us can't hear. "After all this time. Everything we've been through. Don't you...?"

He drops his fork and sighs. "Of course I trust you, Max. It's not that. It's..." He looks around and I realize what the issue is.

"It's them. You don't trust them."

"I don't trust him," Jasper says, all too petulantly.

"Omar is helping me." I reach out and place my hand on top of Jasper's. "That's all."

"We'll see."

I pull my hand back and stare at Jasper, who's biting his lip and scowling.

"You know what? I'm not hungry anymore."

Before he can say anything else, I'm shoving my chair back and stomping from the lunch tent.

A couple of hours later I'm sitting on the rug in our tent, legs crossed beneath me, trying to meditate. My hands are resting on my knees, palms open to the pointed ceiling, my eyes squeezed shut. I keep trying to accept the intrusive thoughts darting into my mind, to acknowledge them and let them pass the way Yoki showed me. But I can't. They keep coming in an angry swirl and I find myself only getting more riled up.

Why is Jasper so incapable of trusting? Why is he determined to hate the rogues when they've done nothing to hurt him? Why can't he let go of the past and accept the moment he's in? Why can't I?

"Hey," Jasper says, his voice piercing through and breaking the negative spiral. "You mind if I come in?"

"I'm trying to concentrate."

"You look like you're in pain."

I open one eye and find Jasper leaning sheepishly through the door, half in, half out. With a sigh I let my posture collapse and quit meditating.

"You can come in," I say.

He slips through the flap but hovers anxiously at the edge of the rug.

"About earlier," he says, "I want to apologize."

"Oh yeah?" I crab-walk on my hands and feet backward to the bed, hoisting myself onto the lumpy mattress.

"Yeah," he says, and comes to sit at my side. "I'm sorry, Max. I didn't mean to—I don't not trust you. It's just hard for me to be around the people who..."

"Who you think murdered your mother."

He looks up, a little shocked at my candor.

"Jasper." I squeeze his knee with one hand and clutch his arm with the other. "I'm sorry. I know how much losing her has hurt you. But these aren't the same people, the same wolves who did that. This place is proof that rogues are just as civilized as any pack wolf—more than some of the ones we've met. You can't blame them for something they didn't do."

To my surprise he leans into me, resting his head on my shoulder and burying his face in the crook of my neck.

He stays there for a moment, just breathing, then he kisses my neck and sits up to look at me.

"I know. You're right. And I'm sorry."

"It's okay. I know I'm sort of forcing you to stay here. That can't be comfortable for you. I appreciate it."

"I appreciate you." He kisses me softly then leans back, smiling. "Did we just have an adult conversation?"

I laugh. "I think so."

We both smile and Jasper pulls me in for a hug.

"Sooooo, it's a full moon tonight," I say. "There's this drum circle thing happening out in the desert. You want to go with me?"

He takes a moment, swallows. "Sure. Yes. I'd—love to."

The night is warm and the lamplight golden as Jasper and I walk hand in hand along the path that leads to the edge of the Sanc. Around us rogues are emerging from their tents to join the trail, everyone dressed in their nicest clothes—light, flowing fabrics dyed natural colors. Kids are running excitedly up and down the path and there's a sense of occasion in the air, like something special is about to happen.

Once we reach the edge of the settlement, the desert stretches out into eternity under a deep, dark, star-dotted night sky. Rogues drift toward the horizon, all heading in the same direction but finding their own paths. Jasper and I follow.

We walk for the better part of an hour until the Sanc is just a light haze on the horizon at our backs and a bonfire comes into view up ahead, lighting up the yucca trees and the bulbous rocks. In a circle around the bonfire are wolves wearing hooded robes of the darkest crimson.

Before them sit tall drums, with real hides stretched over the top of the wooden barrels. Sparks fly up from the fire and get lost among the stars. The moon is already a quarter of the way across the sky, full, silver, and welcoming. The crowd of rogues meanders at the edge of the drum circle. Some groups form, others stand holding hands with their loved ones, watching and waiting. Jasper and I find a spot between a family of five, their youngest kid swinging from Mom and Dad's arms like an excited monkey, and an older couple, the woman leaning her silver-haired head on the shoulder of the man.

For a second I catch a glimpse of a face across the circle, half in shadow but weirdly familiar, and a ping pinches at the front of my brain, just like the one I felt earlier. I squint to relieve the pain and when I look up the face is gone as quickly as the sensation.

Who was that?

"I think they're starting," Jasper says, stepping forward ever so slightly.

From the edge of the circle Yoki emerges in a matching robe, carrying a long stick with a bulbous globe at one end. Omar trails behind them, also sporting a blood-red robe but unlike Yoki and the others, his is sleeveless, revealing his muscled arms and his rogue tattoo. He has a drum strapped to his chest.

He and Yoki stand at the edge of the bonfire and the crowd settles, silence stretches across the desert. Slowly, Yoki raises their staff to the sky and shakes it. The bulbous head must be filled with beans or rice because it makes a sound like a maraca. Yoki's shaking grows in intensity as they raise their free arm to the sky and let out an animalistic yelp. In response Omar raises his right hand complete with drumstick, the other drummers in the circle follow Omar, and then in unison they bring their drumsticks down onto the skin of their drums.

The beat is deep, resonant, and echoes across the desert. Together the drummers beat a steady rhythm, with Omar leading and keeping the pace. Yoki yelps again and the drummers in the circle turn in unison to the right so they're each now facing the back of the drummer in front of them. Another yelp and they begin to walk, their steps uniform and in time with the beat. They march and drum, kicking up dust and gaining momentum. Omar beats faster and the circle responds in kind.

Each beat of the drums sends a vibration through my body, as if the sound waves are rippling through my muscles. I shiver and squeeze Jasper's hand tighter. He squeezes back. I wonder if he's feeling it too.

As the circle continues to move the wind picks up, seemingly whipping the dust in a whirlpool along with the drummers. The edges of their robes catch and flutter about as if caught in a magic cyclone. The fire spirals. I turn my gaze skyward and it feels like the stars above are rotating as well. Or maybe the stars remain where they are and it's me and the earth that are spinning.

Jasper leans a little closer and I catch a glimpse of him staring up at the moon, a serious revelry in his eyes. I follow his eyeline and there she is, a still beacon in the center of the swirl, the calm at the eye of the storm. The moon's light is all-encompassing, flaring in all directions, and I feel it again: the warmth I felt the first day here when Yoki performed their ritual—the sense that we are all connected, one pack under the moon. In this moment I believe I could reach out with my mind and speak to any wolf on the planet.

The moment is interrupted by a growl. I pull my attention from the moon to find Jasper, no longer caught up in the moment, staring across the drumming circle. His top lip is curled back, exposing an elongated fang.

Again I follow his eyeline across the circle, just to the left of the blazing fire, and my gaze lands on the same face from earlier, only this time the pieces click into place in my mind. I know who that face belongs to.

A sharp pain stabs at the corner of my mind but doesn't hurry away. I bite down through the pain as I stare at the man on the other side of the fire, the man staring back at us.

A FAMILIAR FACE

"Mr. Peng," Jasper says, and before I can stop him, he's pulling me around the circle.

"What is Eleanor's dad doing here?" I ask, panting and struggling to keep up.

Mr. Peng, the man who convinced his daughter to kidnap Jasper, his dad, and me, who nearly killed Jericho and forced Jasper to be Eleanor's mate, who fled that night, is here, his gaze fixed on Jasper's from the opposite side of the bonfire. We maneuver through the crowd, distracted by the drumming and the hypnotic swirling movement of the drummers and the fire.

"I don't care. I'll kill him," Jasper rasps.

Rogue faces turn to look at us as we barge through their ranks, shocked and appalled that we would disturb this sacred moment. But Jasper is too enraged, too focused to care.

When we finally reach the far side of the bonfire, Mr. Peng, who until now has kept his calm gaze locked on Jasper's, flinches and darts. He runs. And we follow.

Jasper releases his grip on my hand as he pursues the shadowy figure fleeing the light of the fire and making toward the desert. The man is quick but not as quick as Jasper. His older limbs aren't nimble enough to navigate the uneven desert floor. Swiftly, before we're even ten or so yards from the crowd, Jasper is on him, spinning him around, grabbing him by the collar, and hoisting him into the air.

"What are you doing here?!" Jasper growls, shaking Mr. Peng. "You dare show your face?"

"Release him," a strong, stern voice commands from behind us before Mr. Peng can answer.

I turn to find Mal, the bonfire at her back casting an ethereal orange glow around her silhouette, watching us with a grave expression. Behind her more rogue wolves are gathered, their fists clenched, their faces tense. They're ready to take us on if need be. And I don't like our chances.

"He tried to kill my father," Jasper says, unwilling to look away from his captive.

"George came to us looking for sanctuary. He is under our protection. Let. Him. Go," Mal commands again.

"He should be locked up!" Jasper shakes him again, and George—who knew his name was George!?—remains silent, his limbs flopping like a lifeless puppet's.

"Let him go," Mal says one more time, slowly and calmly, with the authority of someone who knows the odds are in her favor. "Or we will restrain you, Mr. Apollo."

Jasper glances over his shoulder, the realization dawning that we're outnumbered and no one is backing him up. Carefully, I place a hand on his shoulder.

"Jasp, put him down. Let's talk about this."

He hisses through his teeth, but finally lets go of Mr. Peng's collar. The older man flops to the floor. Two of Mal's companions swoop in to help Mr. Peng up and carry him off. He looks weak as he struggles to walk and I wonder if perhaps life hasn't been so kind to him since he fled the pack.

Jasper is breathing heavily, his anger directed squarely at Mal, but she doesn't seem concerned.

"Not now, not here," she says. "Tomorrow morning, my tent." She then turns on her heel and returns to the crowd.

When she and her rogue cohort have left us, Jasper runs his hands over his face, growling, then kicks the dirt.

"Hey." I pull him to me and put my hands on the sides of his face. "I'm here. It's okay."

He tries to steady his breath and rests his forehead on mine.

Somewhere off to the side, the drumming continues.

"He should return to the Elite Pack to stand trial for his crimes," Jasper says.

"Mr. Peng is a member of this community," Mal counters. "He will not be going anywhere."

"He is a traitor and should be held accountable."

"He is protected by the governing laws of the Sanc."

"I thought your society had no governance."

"You are more than two and a half thousand miles from your pack, Child Alpha. You have no jurisdiction here."

"He tried to kill my father!"

I twist my toe into the dusty floor of Mal's tent. Jasper and Mal have been going at it like this for almost fifteen minutes now and neither seems willing to back down. Mal sits on a wicker chair, the kind with a high, rounded back, which makes it look like a tropical-themed throne. To her side Kairos sits on a large cushion, uninterested, literally dozing off during this wolfy squabble.

After last night's surprise guest appearance, Jasper and I made our way back to our tent and I know he didn't sleep from the way he was tossing and turning. Meaning I didn't sleep either. I rub my eyes as I let them go at it, hoping they'll wear each other out eventually.

"Rogue life is about redemption and forgiveness. George is committed to rehabilitating himself."

"He's a murderer and a traitor," Jasper spits. "He should be locked up."

"Just because you and your pack system do not believe in second chances—"

"We believe in second chances, just not for traitorous murderers."

"One less alpha in the world doesn't seem like such a bad thing to me," Mal says, leveling her gaze.

Jasper's mouth hangs open, his brow tight. "You support his crimes?"

"I do not support violence. But I am not about to be railroaded in my own sanctuary."

"You're a fool."

"And you are out of line." On this Mal rises from her wicker chair, Kairos stirs and lifts his head but remains placidly on his stomach. "You are a guest in this community. Invited to attend a sacred ritual, during which you incited violence and disturbed the peace. I have every reason to expel you from this land."

"Then why don't you?!" Jasper asks, his hands out wide.

Mal's eyes flick to mine, so swiftly it's hard to notice, but Jasper does. He turns to look at me, red-faced and incredulous.

I shake my head because I do not want to be dragged into this. And I definitely don't want to try and convince Jasper that he shouldn't care about the man who almost had his dad and me killed.

Mal takes a breath and settles back into her chair. She rests her head in her palm briefly, her exhaustion poking through for just a moment, then she glances at Kairos, who's beady black eyes stare back at his mate. I wonder if they're communicating without being heard, if they're speaking across the mind-link. Finally, Mal straightens her back once more and turns her attention back to us.

"I should," Mal says finally. "I should kick you out on your gilded ass. But for reasons I'm not willing to share, I think it best that Max stays until Yoki is able to help him commune with the lupine chorus." Jasper glances at me once more and I shrug in return. "So until I'm informed that Max has a grasp of his powers, I'm obliged to let you stay."

Jasper grunts.

"Believe me, if I didn't know you two came as a package things would be different. You've long spent the currency which your mother afforded you here."

"And Mr. Peng?" Jasper asks, his voice gruff.

"I have asked George to stay within the confines of his tent for the duration of your stay. He will give you space, I hope you can at least offer him the same in return. Now, I believe you have a school to finish building. But be warned, Child Alpha, one more incident like last night and you will understand the full might of this community."

Jasper snarls one last time before spinning and exiting the tent. He doesn't look back or wait to see if I'm following.

I shoot Mal an apologetic smile then turn to follow, but I stop when she speaks again.

"Max," she says. "I meant what I said. If you can tap into the great consciousness, you could do amazing things for all of wolfkind."

I turn back to find Mal watching me intently, and for a moment I have the distinct feeling she's trying to tell me something without words, though what it is I haven't got a clue. Kairos has laid his head on his front paws, but he's watching me too.

"Do you understand?" Mal asks.

"I—I'm not sure."

"You will." She nods slowly, ending the conversation, or so I think as I turn to leave once more.

"Oh and..." I stop when she speaks again, but stay facing the exit. "You might want to keep an eye on that mate of yours. I know your love runs deep. But we never know what or who might be standing in the way of our own greatness."

I bristle at this last comment. Because who is she to suggest Jasper is preventing me from accomplishing anything. She barely knows him, has only seen the prideful, alpha-bred side of him. She doesn't know how much he cares, how much responsibility he takes on. And yet...something has been blocking me. Could it be...?

I shake the thought away and leave her tent.

Jasper is waiting outside, leaning on a wooden signpost.

"Hey, you okay?" I ask.

"Fine," he says, kicking off the post. "What does she know?"

Yeah, what does *she know?*

He nods in the direction of the construction site. "Walk me to the school?"

"What are they thinking?" Jasper asks while we're still a few minutes from the site. "Harboring criminals. If the packs found out they—"

"Jasper," I say, stopping in my tracks, realization smacking me in the face. "The packs can't know about this place."

He stops as well, turning to look at me with confusion on his face.

"They can't know," I continue. "If the packs knew where Rogue Sanctuary was they'd want to take it over, invade it or control it, police the borders. Rogues need somewhere they can go that's safe, where they'll be looked after. If the alphas knew...they'd destroy this place."

He rubs his chin like he's thinking it over.

"Jasper, you can't tell anyone about this place. Not even your father."

Jasper's eyes shoot from the dirt to my face.

"Max, I—"

"No." I step closer to him. "Promise me, you won't tell anyone."

He slips his hands into mine. "If you'd let me finish. I was going to say...of course. If the packs knew about this place it would be a disaster. I don't have to love how they do things and I don't have to trust them implicitly. But I also won't be responsible for ruining the lives of these people."

I can't help grinning a little smugly, just a smidge.

"What?" he asks.

"You called them people."

He rolls his eyes and lets his head fall back. "Well, they're not *not* people. Come on."

He leaves one hand in mine as he leads me on. Just as we reach the almost fully erected school tent, Omar appears looking ready for a six-month hike. Seriously, he's got walking boots on, a khaki baseball cap made of some waterproof fabric on top of his head, and a pack that looks stuffed with enough clothing and provisions to last a long winter.

"Whoa," I say, "you going somewhere?"

"Not just me," he says in return, smiling.

"Wait, what?"

"I was just coming to find you actually. Yoki thinks you're ready to take things up a notch."

I glance at Jasper, who is eyeing Omar skeptically.

"What does 'up a notch' entail?"

"We're going on a little trip," Omar says, vaguely.

"Might need a little more info."

"Okay cuz, don't get too excited. We're trekking out to this rock circle. It's wicked cool. Super sacred. Takes a few hours to get there. Yoki's already on their way to get everything set up. I'm here to escort you."

Jasper steps forward. "You're escorting him where exactly?"

Omar tilts his head, looking confused that his message isn't quite coming across, then points to the desert. "Out there!"

"No way," Jasper says, pulling on my hand ever so slightly, making me step backward.

"Don't worry, muchacho. Max will be completely safe. Yoki will be there. I'll be there."

"Exactly what I'm concerned about," Jasper mumbles so only I can hear.

"Look, it's sort of a big deal. Not everyone gets to visit this sacred site or participate in this ritual."

"Ritual?" I ask.

"Yeah, it's called a moonwalk."

"Like the...like the dance?"

Omar laughs. "Not exactly. We head out to a spot where the lunar energy is vibing and Yoki performs a ritual and you go on a little journey."

"Where?" Jasper asks, almost growling.

"The lunar plane," Omar says, throwing his hands up like we're the ones being super annoying.

But suddenly I understand what he's saying. "Whoa. You mean Yoki is going to help me access the lunar plane?"

"Yes, and while you're there you'll go on a journey and learn all about yourself and hopefully get to know your blood-wolf self at the same time. Figure out what's got you blocked and all that. At least, that's the plan."

"How long does this take?" Jasper asks.

"I'll have him back by tomorrow morning."

"You're camping out overnight?!" Jasper's face is beginning to turn red.

"We just need a moment," I call over my shoulder to Omar as I pull Jasper aside.

"You can't be seriously thinking of going out into the desert with that guy," Jasper says.

"Jasper." I use my most clipped tone so he knows I'm not messing around. "I need to do this. Something has been blocking me and this might be the best way to figure out how to stop it." He crosses his arms and looks petulantly anywhere except my face. "It's a once-in-a-lifetime opportunity." He rolls his eyes. "Not many wolves get to experience this." He twists his foot in the sand. "I'm going to visit the lunar plane! I need to do this!"

Finally, he huffs and stops avoiding eye contact.

"It's a bad idea."

"What is? Me going into the desert with Omar or leaving you here alone with the rogues?"

"Both," he says, full-on pouting.

"Remember what we said about trust."

"I trust you," he says. "Just not him."

"Well...I trust him. So you need to trust my judgment."

"I should come too."

"I don't need a chaperone. And you're needed here." I gesture to the construction zone. "The school is nearly finished. You should be there to see it through."

I cup the side of his face and give him my best puppy dog eyes.

"Everything will be fine."

Eventually, he inhales, his shoulders rising next to his ears, then lets the air out in one big huff. "Fine."

The second we turn back to Omar, Jasper chewing his bottom lip and me unable to suppress my massive grin, Tomas emerges from between two tents.

"Ah, there you are!" he says to Jasper. "Listen I know there's still a little more construction work to be done, but one of our teachers has called out sick for the day and we need someone to watch over the preschoolers."

Jasper's face is blank. His gaze flicks from Tomas to me to the unfinished school in a circuit he repeats three of four times.

"What?"

"I heard you were great with kids," Tomas says, smiling in my direction. "And you've worked so hard on the structure. Don't you want to spend some time with the kids who'll be using the space?"

"I...I..."

"Excellent!" Tomas claps his hands together. "This way then. The kids will be very excited to hear all about your life in a pack." Tomas takes Jasper by the shoulder and leads him away. "You'll have to watch out for Benny though—he's teething and tends to bite."

"Have a good time," I call out, feeling a little sorry for Jasper, who looks back at me with true panic in his eyes.

"Grumpy Pants and a bunch of four-year-olds," Omar says, suddenly at my side. "Sounds like a recipe for disaster."

"I feel sort of bad leaving him here."

"He'll be fine," Omar says, slapping me on the back. "You ready to moonwalk, cuz?"

I take a breath.

"Just let me get my sequined glove."

THE MOONWALK

"It's mega hot," I say, wiping my brow. "How much farther to this sacred rock formation?"

Omar shoots me a sideways grin. I'm basically a water fountain with the amount I'm dripping sweat—he, on the other hand, has worked up a thin sheen of moisture, which only accentuates his tanned features. He was obviously made for this type of climate. We've been hiking for nearly four hours at this point. The midday sun has come and gone and now we're entering sweltering afternoon temperatures.

"Not far, cuz."

I trudge on, my trainers getting covered in even more dust.

"This moonwalk," I say. "Have you ever tried it?"

Omar squints into the distance. "Once."

"And did it work?"

He walks a few paces without replying, then nods. "Yeh, it worked."

"What was it like? What did you see?"

The muscles in his jaw are working overtime, like he's grinding his teeth, hard.

"Not much."

Either he's disappointed with his time on the lunar plane or he seriously doesn't want to talk about it.

We walk for another fifteen minutes or so in silence until I can't bear it anymore.

"So, uh, it looks like you've found a really great home at the Sanc."

"Definitely. The Sanc really saved my ass. I owe Yoki and Mal and everyone there a lot. You wouldn't believe how hard it can be out there as a rogue. You'd think packs these days would be more progressive, more welcoming. But they'd sooner spit on you and turn you away than consider letting you hang for one night." He glances at me quickly. "For the most part."

"I'm glad you found somewhere," I say earnestly.

We walk a little farther. Up ahead I can just about make out some rocks and I wonder if that's where we're heading.

"And uh...have you met any nice wolves since you got here?"

Omar eyes me sideways once more, only this time he's smirking.

"You have?!"

He shakes his head and is he...blushing?

"Okay, spill. Who's the lucky wolf?"

"Nah, cuz, it's not like that. I haven't..." He trails off, staring into the distance. "Let's just say I've got my eye on someone but that whole situation has about as much chance as growing moss in the desert."

"Come on, you're, like, totally smoldering—any wolf would be lucky to have you."

"I'm glad you think so."

Without warning he picks up his pace and we don't talk about much else until we finally arrive at the rock circle. Unlike the circle at the Rocky Pack, this one is much bigger, the stones are large and smooth, rounded by millennia of abrasive dust and wind. They encircle a bowl-like crater in the desert, at the center of which Yoki is sitting next to a small fire, cross-legged in a meditative state, surrounded by all manner of trippy accoutrements—bronze bowls, large crystals, a set of bongo drums, a flute made from bamboo, and a metal platter strewn with what look like old wolves' teeth.

We trudge slowly down the short incline until we're standing on the flat circle in the center of the basin. Yoki doesn't open their eyes, but their mouth tilts up in a corner.

"You've made it," they say. "Ready to walk with the moon gods, Blood Wolf?"

"Here, drink this," Yoki instructs, holding out a small stone cup.

They're sitting in front of me, the fire crackling between us. Omar is to my right. Above the ridge of the basin, the sun is setting, the sky between the rocks is all pastel, burning orange and violet and pink. Behind me the deep navy of night is creeping in. Somewhere the moon is about to rise.

I reach out and take the cup. In it is some new herbal tea.

"What is it?" I ask.

"It will help you access the lunar plane. Drink." Yoki nods and I glance at Omar for reassurance. He nods as well.

"Bottoms up," I say, then pour the tincture down my throat. It's sweeter than I imagined, almost like chamomile, but with the spice of cinnamon, and the herby-ness of nettles and basil. "Not bad. Does it come as a Frappuccino?"

"Now close your eyes," Yoki says.

I take in our surroundings one more time: a thin ripple of clouds is hovering overhead, a sprinkle of stars are shining beyond, the sunset is warm but the desert cools as the light diminishes, the boulders rise around me like teeth and I'm in the jaws of some massive beast, about to be swallowed whole.

I know that sounds dramatic, but that tea must already be going to work because my head feels lighter and the sandy banks rising on all sides are quivering, like a gazillion snakes are slithering under the surface.

One more deep breath and then I do as I'm told.

"Concentrate," Yoki says, exhaling as I close my eyes.

I breathe in through my nose and try to practice everything I've learned. I let my breath move slowly, filling my chest and expanding my stomach, although my lungs feel bottomless, like I could inhale forever and never stop, never stop needing more air. I try to tune my ears into the hum of nature—the wind, the dust, the faint chirp of crickets—and somehow everything is amplified. A mile away I can make out the scurrying feet of a desert mouse darting between yucca trees; under a rock another mile to the south a rattlesnake is contorting into a new twisted configuration. Somewhere a drop of water falls from the flower of a cactus and hits the earth, evaporating the second it touches the scorching soil.

"Good," Yoki says. "Let your mind expand. Let the walls surrounding your consciousness disappear. Let your wolf-self wander and explore."

As I've done in all our meditation sessions up until this point, I try to let my guard down, to access the part of me at the core that's pure wolf, but everything is different this evening, each action or thought is bigger than normal, and I'm scared of what's beyond those invisible walls.

To my right, Omar drags a mallet around the inside of a bowl, causing it to ring out like the extended ping of a bell. He does this again with a different bowl, one with a higher pitch. And again, until three chords are ringing in harmony.

Yoki hums, the sound coming out all nasal and reverberating in my ears.

The vibrations of Yoki's voice and the metal bowls wash over me like waves, tingling my muscles, enlivening every inch of my skin. Omar or maybe Yoki, one of the two, picks up another instrument, this tube filled with dried beans that sounds like rain when it's flipped. Almost, I feel as if I'm being rained on, the cool wetness of each drop refreshing and revitalizing me and my senses. Suddenly, the cry of a wolf pierces the melodic soundscape, and without thinking my eyes dart open. But when they do I find I'm no longer in the desert.

It's raining lightly in the forest. I'm standing in a clearing and I lift my face and let the cooling water drip onto my skin. It's night, the woods are dark and quiet, the only sound is the hoot of an owl somewhere in the branches arching overhead. Between trees the shadows are impossibly dark, I can't see beyond a few feet.

I turn in circles.

"What the...? Where am I?"

The air is cool and pine scented. Above, the patch of visible sky is heavy with low-hanging clouds from which the rain continues to tumble. Then all of a sudden the bank of clouds rolls back to reveal the moon—full, of course, and brilliantly white. I stare at her and it feels as if she's staring back.

Then that familiar howl, the one that's been calling to me for months, the one that always seems to interrupt when I'm trying to mind-link with Jasper or access the greater wolf consciousness. It's high and far away, but tears through the stillness like a razor blade.

A twig snaps nearby and I spin in the direction of the sound.

Nothing, but then movement, a pair of eyes glowing in the darkness. A wolf emerges from the tree line. My wolf.

His honey-colored fur looks extra golden in the moonlight, his eyes narrow and fierce, his shoulder blades roll with every step forward.

"Hey, buddy," I say, extending a hand palm down, a gesture of friendship you might extend to a neighbor's pet dog. "Did you hear that howl too?"

Have I done it? Managed to access the deepest, most animal part of myself? Is this clearing in the forest the depths of my soul?

My wolf and I stare at each other.

"Hey pal." I know this wolf is me, that we're the same, and also that my inner wolf is no domesticated puppy, but I can't help myself. "Are you going to take me to the crying wolf like a good boy?"

My wolf snaps his jaws at me, a thick strand of saliva flinging from his glistening jowls. I retract my hand, just barely avoiding the loss of a finger, as it turns and bounds away into the trees.

"That was not cool. Hey! Wait! What do I do? Am I supposed to follow you?"

I've heard people talk about spirit guides when they embark on this sort of journey. Is that what my wolf is?

I look around for some sign or other of what I'm supposed to do on this new plane, but find nothing. Yoki couldn't have given me some kind of instruction manual for once I got here?

So without any idea what else I'm supposed to do, I take off jogging after my wolf.

The forest floor is soft, mossy, littered with pine needles. The damp smell of petrichor and the tangy scent of sap fill my senses, so starkly different from the desert I've gotten used to. Somewhere nearby water is trickling, I must be running parallel to a river. I become aware of some other noises—yelps and howls, and then...laughter, people. There are people here.

A group runs by a few yards away, just visible between redwood trunks. I don't recognize any of the faces but they're smiling, waving each other on. I watch as they speed up and finally shift mid-step, their clothes ripping apart as they turn into wolves, landing gracefully on all fours and charging off into the forest.

Behind me a single set of running footsteps approaches. I turn just in time to see Jasper, in the workout gear he was wearing during capture the flag back at the Blue Moon Festival, as he runs past me.

"Hurry up, Bonehead," he says without slowing down. "Don't want to get left behind."

"Jasper?" He doesn't stop or turn around again. "Wait up!"

With no other option I speed up to try and catch Jasper. For some reason my superspeed isn't kicking in and I lose him just as quickly as he appeared. There's a break in the trees so I dart between two massive trunks and skid to a stop.

"Wait...what the...?"

I spin around again.

"This can't be. Is this...the same clearing?"

If I'm not standing in the exact same clearing as before, then this one looks remarkably similar. Off to my right is a tree with a gnarly scratch mark on it, three ragged lines scraped across the bark where someone, some wolf has dragged their claws.

"Was that there before?"

I make a mental note to remember that tree.

Again footsteps and then Jasper appears once more. He comes running right at me and I can barely brace myself before he slams into me and I go flying backward, hitting the soft earth with a thud.

"Ow, hey, watch it!"

When I look back up at Jasper he's no longer wearing his workout clothes. He's in a crisp white tee, a black blazer, fitted black pants, and combat boots.

"Watch where you're going, Bonehead," he says, his face screwed up in disdain.

"You ran into me!" I call back.

"You should be more careful."

Wait...this feels oddly familiar.

"Here." He extends a hand to help me up and the second I take it sparks ignite in my fingertips, fizzing up my arm and into my chest.

"Jasper?" I lean forward, trying to get a better look at his face, but he stares back like I'm a stranger. "What's going on?"

His expression twists like he's gone from staring at a stranger to his worst enemy.

"I don't know who you are, okay Bonehead? But stay away from me."

And with that he's off again, running out of the clearing.

I follow once more.

Back in the forest the rippling river runs at my side again. I run and run but can't catch Jasper, until once again I emerge into a clearing.

To my right is a tree with scratch marks.

"It is the same!"

A growl breaks the otherwise quiet night and all I can do is watch as a large and fearsome wolf leaps from the shadows into the moonlight. His midnight fur is sleek and shiny, blacker than black. His green eyes are vibrant and glow emerald. Jasper's wolf lands and digs its claws into the soil, skidding to a stop.

"Jasp?" I ask tentatively.

His lips curl, he huffs and backs away, growling the whole time. A warning.

Stay back.

"It's okay," I say. "It's me. It's…Max. Your mate."

He snaps his jaws, twisting his muzzle.

I risk a step forward, lifting a hand like I'm going to cradle his face. What do I need all these fingers for anyway?

"Jasper." I stare into his brilliant eyes. "Do you recognize me?"

Then to my surprise he whimpers and backs away.

"It's okay—"

Before I can reach out and touch his fur, Jasper turns and leaps again, penetrating the tree line and almost instantly vanishing, his fur and the shadows as dark as each other.

"What do I do now?" I ask no one in particular, maybe hoping my wolf is going to reappear and tell me what the hell I'm supposed to do. "If I chase after him I'll just end up back here again."

A weight slams into my back, knocking me forward. I hit the earth with an "Oomf!" and before I can gather my wits, whoever knocked me down flips me over onto my back and presses my shoulders into the earth. A stone digs into my ribs as I stare up at Jasper, his hair hanging over his eyes, his lips parted just enough to show his teeth, and his freckles…I'm always surprised by his freckles.

He presses his lips to mine, kissing me intensely with passion but also anger. This kiss tastes sour.

When he pulls back he eyes me darkly. "There," he says. "Is that what you wanted?"

The ground falls away from beneath me and somehow, even though I was pressed to the earth, I'm suddenly tumbling through the air, like I've fallen from a great height. Jasper doesn't come with me. He and the trees stay where they are, growing smaller every second I plummet away.

Mountains sprout below me, growing sideways as I flail my arms and legs through the air. Snow-covered peaks surround me, pointing to the now dusky sky, a reddish hue tinting the smattering of clouds. I open my mouth to scream but no sound comes out as the ground comes rushing toward me.

My fall is cushioned by a thick layer of snow. I hit the powder hard, but sink into it, and arrive back on land uninjured. Standing as icy wind whips at my face, I look around to catch my bearings.

It's snowing something ridiculous but through the blizzard I can make out the lights of a chalet at the top of the tallest mountain. It will be a long climb but at least if I head up there I can get out of this storm.

I begin my ascent, struggling to make much headway in the crazy deep snow. With each step forward I feel like I'm sinking back another three. Scrambling, I manage to claw my way to a level plateau and stop when I notice something, a word, scrawled in the snow in what looks like blood—the word *TRAITOR*.

It's the same handwriting as whoever graffitied my parents' garage door. But how did they get out here and where did they get enough blood to write the letters so big?

Somewhere behind me, in the depths of the valley below, comes the cry of the howling wolf. I turn and without thinking, I follow the sound.

The descent is easier, or at least faster, than climbing in the opposite direction. I manage to make my way with seeming ease and in no time I'm wandering along a stony path with more mountains rising on either side of me. A familiar-looking shelter comes into view—Agatha's cottage. When I reach the door I bang on it, hoping to find the wolf who's been calling to me, or Agatha or anyone who can let me in from the cold.

The door swings open and Omar steps into the doorway. Behind him it's daytime, and where the inside of the shack should be, the desert stretches out toward a hazy horizon.

"Hey cuz, thought you'd never make it."

"Omar, what is this? Are you—are you really here?"

"Here enough. Quick, this way. It's about to start."

"What's about to start?"

He nods at the nighttime sky behind me, and I peer through the continuing blizzard, so cold and inhospitable compared to the warmth and light of the desert. From behind the ridge of a mountain the blood moon rises, crimson red and so large it covers almost a third of the sky.

"Am I going to change?" I ask, half to Omar and half to myself, fearful of the last time I saw a blood moon, afraid my teeth are about to become fangs and my fingers claws.

"Change?" Omar says. "Change is inevitable."

He slips a solid hand into mine as a wind vortex spirals through the valley picking up snow and rocks in a tornado that's hurtling toward us, then he pulls me through the door.

Together we run through the desert, the sun hot on my back. Rocks whiz by, after a while replaced with tents until we've somehow arrived in the depths of the Sanc. We slow as we approach Yoki's tent, only something tells me to stop. The shelter is giving off a weird vibe. Dark smoke wisps from the entryway. Omar's hand slips from mine and he looks back in confusion.

"Come on," he says. "It's just through here."

"What's through there?"

He smiles. "The answer to your question. Come on."

With a gesture for me to follow he slips through the entrance. I take a step forward, then I hear a voice nearby.

"Psst, Max." Off to my right Jasper is leaning from the flap of a different yurt. "This way."

"Jasper, what's going on?"

"I've been looking everywhere for you. This way."

He takes my hands and tries to pull me inside but I resist.

"Jasp, something's not right. I'm supposed to be finding a wolf or...no, wait...I'm supposed to be figuring out how to use my blood-wolf abilities, or...how to mind-link with you. But I keep getting lost. I need help."

He wraps his arms around me and kisses the top of my head. "I'm here now."

"Thanks, I feel like I've been running all over the place."

"What do you want?" he asks, like that's an easy question.

I lean back so I can look up at him. "I want this." I touch his face and kiss him once, quickly. "And I want things to be—different. I want to make things better."

He smiles and brushes the hair from my face.

"Come with me."

We slip through the entrance and I stumble as I emerge at the edge of the packhouse's balcony.

Somehow it's night again and we're a hundred stories in the air, at the very top of a Manhattan skyscraper. I clutch the metal handrail atop the balustrade, all that's keeping me from a steep drop to the sidewalk below. Wind blows and messes my hair. Behind me the tent is gone and all that's left is an empty patio, the building is dark, no lights are on inside. Jasper is watching me.

"Why did you bring me here? What is this?"

Jasper steps forward to my side and stares out across New York.

"This is what we can build together."

I turn to look out across the city.

Fires…everywhere. The city is ablaze. Smoke rises in all directions, from too many buildings to count. Lights are out across whole blocks. The acrid stench of ash and destruction catches in my nostrils. Below, fire engines and ambulances whir by, sirens wailing. Desperate cries ring out into the night.

"This is…the city—it's destroyed. What happened?"

"War. The pack and the rogues tore the city apart."

I stare at the side of Jasper's face. He isn't blinking, he doesn't even seem concerned, when the world is on fire.

"Shouldn't we do something?" I ask. "Shouldn't we try to help?"

He turns to me with a sickening grin on his face. "Help? But Max, this is what you wanted."

"No." I shake my head. "I never wanted this. I never…"

"Where are you going?" he asks, a hand raised, as I back away. "You can't run from me. I'm your mate."

"You're not him. You can't be."

His grin stretches wider, his fangs on show.

"We're meant to be together," he says, and as he does fireworks shoot up right in front of the building, too close, too bright, and too loud.

"Stop this!" I shout, unsure if I'm talking about the fireworks or the weird look on Jasper's face.

"You can't escape fate, Max!"

"I won't let this happen. I can't!"

All of a sudden Jasper's expression changes, his eyes shoot open, and his hands clutch at his stomach. There under his touch a bloom of red blossoms, spreading and staining his pristine white button-down. I glance from the wound to his face and back again. His mouth falls open in pain and a trickle of blood runs from the corner of his mouth.

"How could you do this to me, Max?" He sounds like himself again, only weaker, panicked, like he knows the wound is fatal. "How could you?"

He holds out his bloodstained hands so I can see the red liquid marking his skin.

"No, Jasper, I didn't, I—"

"You'll pay for this." In an instant his expression has shifted again. Now he appears cold, deadly, his fangs grow and his claws extend. "You'll pay for what you've done to me."

"NO!"

I turn and run back toward the building. The balcony feels like it must extend for miles as I run and run, heading for the glass doors of the packhouse but never reaching them. Then suddenly the doors are somehow right in front of me, my reflection visible in the dark, silver surface of the glass. Only it isn't my reflection. It's me in my wolf form, hurtling toward the doors from the other side. As me and my wolf draw nearer, its form growing larger with each step, it leaps toward me.

From the opposite side of the glass I leap as well and at the same time my wolf self and I collide. I cross my arms over my face to shield them as the glass shatters, shards sent flying every which way.

THE CRYING WOLF

I should be falling, landing with a thud inside the packhouse. But instead my body becomes light, held aloft by some unseen force or maybe...a lack of gravity.

When I open my eyes I find I'm no longer in the packhouse, or Manhattan, or anywhere I'm able to recognize.

Darkness surrounds me, stretching on forever. The shards of glass from the shattered doors float around me, like dust particles in the sun. They drift outward until they grow small, reflecting some unseen source of light, twinkling in the pitch blackness of wherever the hell this is. Eventually they drift far enough from me that all I can make out are millions of glittering specks...like stars.

Gently, I come to land on an invisible floor, my toe sending ripples outward in concentric circles, almost like I'm standing on water. But there is no water here. There isn't anything. Just darkness and stars.

Staring at the ripples emanating from my feet, I spot another set of circular waves meeting mine and interrupting their pattern. The cause of these other ripples is my wolf, standing across the galaxy, watching me.

The anger and violence he evoked before are gone. Now he seems calm. His eyes are soft, subdued, almost…pleading.

We stand at the center of this shattered glass universe and for the first time during this whole trippy moonwalk thing, a sense of calm and purpose washes over me.

"I've made it," I say quietly.

Then my wolf lifts his muzzle into the air, opens his jaws, and howls.

My ears perk up, every hair on my body stands on end, a shiver runs right through me.

"I know that howl. That was you? That was…me?"

My wolf howls again, the crying howl that's been haunting me for months, the same howl that has sent splitting pain through my brain and interrupted my attempts to mind-link with Jasper. But how can that be? How can it have been me this whole time?

"He calls to you."

I freeze at the resonant sound of a woman's voice, echoing in the endless nothingness. I spin around to find my wolf and I have company. A tall, statuesque woman is hovering just above the nonvisible ground, her delicate silver toes drifting millimeters above the surface. She is wearing the most insanely gorgeous gown, a flowing silver dress made of this sheer, iridescent fabric my mind can't quite comprehend. It's almost as if it's emitting a sort of glow, like she's shining. Her face is long and narrow, her skin pale but not white—it's almost gray, but shimmering just like her outfit. Her long hair wafts in silver waves, held aloft like she's underwater. Her arms are long and her elegant hands float by her sides.

"Your wolf," she says, only her lips don't move. *"He has been waiting."*

Her voice moves through me like electricity, like she's speaking directly to my mind. "How are you doing that?"

"I am capable of many things. As are you."

"Is this what it feels like to mind-link?"

"That is an earthly term. I am not of the earth." Gently, she bows her head, smiling benevolently. *"Is that the most pressing question you have to ask me?"*

For some reason I'm not scared of her—even though I should be, because she's a floating freaking hallucination with a one-way communication channel to my brain. But I feel this strange sense of familiarity toward her. Like I know her, have known her, for...forever. Like she's always been there, watching, looking over and protecting me.

"Why does my wolf call me if he lives within me?" I ask, somehow finding the question at the tip of my tongue.

She lifts her hands as if telling a room full of people to stand, except we're the only ones here and we're already standing.

"You speak of your wolf as if it is apart from you. As if you and it are two separate beings."

"I only mean because, well, he's there"—I gesture to my wolf, who is still standing quietly behind me—"and I'm here."

"And yet you are one."

"Right. We are one."

"Your wolf spirit is able to appear on this plane because he is at home here."

"I was going to ask...where exactly is here?"

"The lunar plane," she mind-says.

"So I did reach it."

Once again she smiles, and a hint of color almost rises in her cheeks.

"The lunar plane is not a place you journey to or from. It exists in all of wolfkind, the domain of our lunar selves."

"Is that the same as our wolf selves?"

"Why do you run from that which is most inherently you?" she asks.

Okay, come through with the non sequitur, I think before realizing she can probably hear what I'm thinking and rein my sassy self in. I clear my throat and straighten my shoulders.

"I guess I'm afraid."

"Afraid of what?"

"That—if I let myself be…myself, that I won't like it. Or that other people…won't like it."

"You doubt your mate?"

"I doubt everyone and everything. I'm full of doubt. I have abundant doubt. And I want to be more sure. I want to know who I'm going to be and whether I'm making the right choices, but all the voices in my head are pulling me in so many different directions it's hard to make sense of what's even me anymore—of who I am or what I want. Like maybe I'm just doing what I think I'm supposed to or what's expected of me. Maybe I'm just chasing around a boy because that's all I know how to do. Maybe I'm not special, maybe this whole idea of community and belonging is bullshit and we're all just alone—less like one pack under the moon and more like a whole bunch of weirdo loners making shit up so that we feel better about ourselves, so that we feel less alone. Maybe there's no such thing as the blood wolf and it's a story I've made up, a fairy tale, to give myself some sense of meaning. I mean, come on, mind reading? Special powers? It's all a bit out there. And I know you're a floating spirit guide or hey, maybe you're actually the moon goddess Selene"—even though I'm mid rant I swear I catch her shrug in a knowing way—"you probably love all this woo-woo magical, moon energy stuff. But that was never my thing.

I just wanted to draw and hang out with my friends and now everything is so complicated. And how do I know I'm not just fucking things up? How do I know I'm not doing everything wrong? How do I know I'm not running into a burning building, or running in circles...or..."

I trail off, waiting for her to finish my sentence or answer one of the many, many questions I just spouted at her, but instead she waits for me to finish.

"How do I know I'm heading in the right direction?"

My chest heaves as I pant and catch my post-rant breath. I have no idea where all of that came from. Or why I chose the moment an actual moon spirit or whoever chose to reveal themself to me to offload all my emotional baggage. But standing before this ethereal woman, in this place, with my wolf behind me, I couldn't hold it all in any longer. And it's all true...I am filled with doubt. And I thought I needed to escape to clear my head and figure things out but that's just thrown more voices into the mix. More questions. I lift my eyebrows at the woman, basically begging her to give me some answers or at the very least a little reassurance.

"The truth is, Max—"

Wait, she knows my name? Holy smokes.

"People often ask the moon gods to light the way for them, but there is no one singular path. There is no preordained route you must take. The path is yours to forge. We are only here to light the way."

With that last sentence, her ethereal glow intensifies. I lift a hand to shield my eyes. Am I right in thinking...did she just say...she *IS* one of the moon gods.

"Are you Selene?" I ask, hot in the face.

"I am but the light in the darkness."

Okay, not a real answer.

"Now Max, you should go. He's still waiting." She lifts a long hand and gestures to the wolf behind me. *"Take my blessings as you forge your way."*

When I turn back, she's gone, the only trace she was ever here a smattering of pixie dust or space glitter or some other twinkling remnant of her majestic presence sparkling as it drifts slowly to the ground.

"Just you and me now, bud," I say, walking over to my wolf and crouching down in front of him. I take his furry head in my hands, one supporting his chin and the other nuzzling the fur behind his ear. "I'm sorry I tried to block you out. What's say we do this next part together?"

I wait for a response, half expecting him to open his mouth and speak, but instead he licks my cheek, a big wet slobbery dog kiss, and I wrap my arms around him, closing my eyes as I hold my wolf self, trying to show the comfort and love I've been too scared to give to myself.

"Hey, Squishface," Katie says.

Wait, Katie's here too?

I open my eyes and find myself kneeling on the carpet of my bedroom back at Stony Point, my arms wrapped around myself. My wolf is gone...no not gone, he's just not apart from me any longer.

"You're going to be late," Katie says from where she's sitting on my bed, "as usual."

Her back is against the headboard and one knee is pulled to her chest, and she looks younger than I remember, as if she's de-aged by about four years, back to when we were an inseparable duo, besties forever.

"Oh yeah. Late for what?" I ask.

"Oh you know," she says with a casual shrug. "Everything."

"How do I get back?"

She tilts her head in the direction of the door. "Through there."

"Thank you," I say and head for the door. "And Katie..."

"Yeah?"

"I miss you."

Young Katie smiles as I step through my bedroom door and suddenly the world is full of light.

I open my eyes and this time I'm back in the real world. Pale dawn light is creeping over the edge of the desert basin. The rocks that surround me look less like teeth now and more like mountains, a series of peaks between which run any number of valleys, each its own path.

Yoki and Omar aren't here. The accoutrements from the ritual sit in a circle around me, the plate of wolf teeth right in front, only now it's empty. Feeling strangely awake and nowhere near as sore as a person who slept sitting cross-legged on a patch of sand should, I stand and dust myself off.

Slowly, I make my way to the top of the ridge. The sun is just peeking over the horizon, a few stars remain visible, and to the west a pale outline of the moon hangs low. A short distance from the basin I spot Omar, asleep on his side, half in, half out of a sleeping bag, and a little farther beyond that Yoki is sitting upright, facing the moon, with their eyes closed and their hands palm up on their knees.

I approach cautiously, not wanting to disturb them.

"You're back," Yoki says before I've quite reached them, a knowing smile playing in the corner of their mouth.

"I am."

"I hope you found what you were looking for."

I rub the back of my neck, then catch myself doing it and stop.

"Yeah, I think I did."

I plop myself down next to Yoki and for a moment I study the moon, just barely visible but still there, always there, moving around and above, always shining.

"Shall we wake the sleeping beast?" Yoki asks, referring to Omar I assume.

"No, let him sleep a little longer. It's still early."

Yoki and I watch the moon until it's fully hidden behind the horizon and the sun is almost a quarter of the way through the sky. Behind us Omar sits up, yawning and stretching. Without speaking we stand in unison, dust off the sand, and prepare to head back.

A ROGUE CELEBRATION

"So what did you see?" Omar asks as we trek back to camp.

My mind is still reeling a little from the whole experience. As the day has heated up, my drifting, calm state of mind has turned into more of a haze and I think the lack of sleep may be affecting me. I keep yawning and my eyelids weigh a ton.

"A whole lot," I say.

"Did you at least get some clarity?"

I may be yawning and a little spaced out but when I stop to think about it, yes, I definitely have some clarity. In fact, I feel certain a demolition crew is on its way to break down the walls I'd built around my mind.

"Yeah, I think so."

"That's great. I'm happy for you, cuz."

"What about you?" I ask. "You never told me what happened when you did the moonwalk. What clarity did you find?"

Omar scrunches up his mouth and shoos an invisible fly from in front of his face.

"I didn't find much clarity," he says, his tone darker than before.

We walk the rest of the way in silence.

The first thing I want to do when we get back sometime in the early afternoon is find Jasper. After everything I saw last night, every version of Jasper, and the distinct feeling like he was always just a hair's breadth out of reach, I want to hug him and feel his solidity, to know that he's real.

"Thank you," I say to Yoki as we prepare to part ways. "For everything."

Yoki doesn't say anything. They smile wryly and bow a little before twirling and heading for their tent.

"I'm glad you found what you were looking for," Omar says a little gruffly, trailing a circle in the dirt with the toe of his sneaker.

"Thanks, and—Omar?"

He looks up.

"Thank you too, for helping me and coming along with me and, you know, being there."

"Anytime, cuz. I'll catch you later. Don't leave without saying goodbye."

Oh. I hadn't really thought about it, but I guess now that Yoki has done just about everything they can and I'm feeling good about my connection to my wolf self, Jasper and I should be getting back to the Elite Pack.

"Yeah, okay," I mumble. Omar turns and something in me tells me to call out. "I'll see you at dinner, right?"

His placid expression turns into a smile and he salutes with two fingers. "Be there or be, I dunno, human or something."

Omar leaves and I wait until he's out of sight. At least we'll have tonight, I think, trying to ward off the encroaching sense that I still don't quite want to leave this place. When he's gone I make my way to the new school tent.

"Oh my moon gods."

I stand at the edge of the lofty new school tent and can't quite believe the sight I'm greeted with. Jasper is standing in front of a rapt audience of kids sitting cross-legged on a large carpet, a book in one hand, performing a lively interpretation of whatever adventure story they're reading. He glances at the book, then hunches over, making his hands into witchy claws and giving the performance of his lifetime.

"I'll get you, my wolfies," he says in a creaky character voice. "You'll never escape my labyrinth, not in a million—"

He stops short when he glances up and his eyes catch on mine. Instantly, his face is beet red.

"Why did you stop?" one particularly precocious kid calls out.

"Keep reading, Mr. Jasper!" another shouts.

I gesture for him to keep going, to which he purses his lips and huffs but then clears his throat and continues on.

"You'll never escape my labyrinth, not in a million years, not until the moon can be seen in the daylight!"

I recognize the story suddenly. It's called *The Wayward Pup and the Pale Moon*. It's a children's story, derived from ancient werewolf lore. A pup strays from his pack and as he tries to get home he makes friends with a bunch of other animals: a raccoon, a bear, a rattlesnake, and a hawk. But eventually they're all captured by this evil witch—who I think is supposed to represent humanity—and in order to escape this giant maze they have to make the moon rise during the day. So the wayward pup recalls everything he learned about the moon gods from his parents and teaches the other animals and together they call on Selene and her family and she lets the moon stay in the sky even after the sun is up. It's supposed to be an origin story of sorts, to explain why you can sometimes see the moon during the day, what we call a Pup's Moon.

Jasper bursts into a maniacal evil laugh as the witch who's trapped her prey in her maze, and the kids explode with screams and shrieks.

As he continues reading, Jasper takes on the roles of the wayward pup and his friends with the same theatricality and commitment as the witch. Who knew my mate had this outstanding acting talent?

Somewhere toward the end of the story, as the pup and his friends call to the moon gods, Tomas appears at my side.

"He's an excellent teacher," Tomas says, watching Jasper attempting to play all five animal friends at the same time, resulting in him jumping from spot to spot, contorting his face in all sorts of disturbing ways. "There's more of his mother in him than even I imagined."

I glance at Tomas, who has this proud sort of look in his eye and just the first hint of moisture.

"You were close with her?" I ask, although I already know the answer.

He takes a breath and lets his head drop slightly. "She would have been very proud."

The crowd of pups erupts into applause and I assume the witch has been defeated. When I look back, Tomas is gone.

As the kids jump up, run to Jasper with their little arms outstretched, overwhelm him with their sheer number and the force of their excitement, and tackle him to the ground, I can't help but wonder if maybe Tomas knew Jasper had this in him all along. That maybe putting him to work at the school wasn't so much about Jasper learning about his mother, but more about Jasper learning how much of his mother lives on in him.

Finally, Jasper manages to extricate himself from the pile of wolf pups and makes his way to me, a wide smile on his face.

"Enjoy the show?" he asks.

"I didn't know you were classically trained," I joke.

"Stop," he says, a playful note of warning in his tone.

"Seriously, someone call the Academy! Get Scorsese on the phone!"

Jasper shakes his head and rubs his eyes. "You're never going to let me forget this, are you?"

"Forget! How could I forget the performance of a lifetime? Seriously, I'm changed. The depth! The range! The physicality!"

"Insufferable," Jasper mutters.

"Jasper?" a squeaky voice asks, and we both look down to find a kid has attached itself to Jasper's leg. "Will you read us another? You do the best voices."

He groans and rolls his eyes, his head flopping backward. But then he scoops the little girl up into his arms and says, "Just one more, okay?"

She nods emphatically.

He turns back to me. "Are you okay to wait a little longer?"

"Actually," I say, "I really need a shower and maybe a nap. Meet you back at the tent?"

"Okay," he says. "Great. Oh, how was your moon dance or walk or—you know?"

"It was..." I pause because it's not a thing you can quantify quite like a movie or a meal. "It was pretty special. Intense but special."

"You're okay?" he asks.

"I'm good. And you can't keep your audience waiting." I gesture over to the waiting pups, their expectant eyes on Jasper like a pack of meerkats.

"I won't be long. Oh and there's this party tonight, to celebrate the completion of the new school. It'll probably be lame." He shakes his head dismissively but I know he wants to go. "But I was thinking we could go?"

"I'd love to."

"Okay."

The girl in his arms is squirming but Jasper just stares at me.

"Okay," I say.

"Great."

He keeps staring and smiling and then I'm smiling as well and we must look like two lovesick teens who don't know how to act around each other.

"Yeah, great," I say. "Shouldn't you...?"

It's like he realizes he's holding an actual child at that moment.

"Oh, right! Yes. Okay, see you in a bit."

"See you in a bit."

He turns to head back into the school tent but spins around super quick to add one more thing.

"You look different," he says, "good still, but different."

For another beat he smiles at me like he's lost his goddamn mind.

"Go!" I say and finally he nods and returns to his adoring fans.

As Jasper launches into a new story, all the energy I have left in me seems to flood out the bottoms of my feet and I know I need to find somewhere to lie down immediately.

I wake from a long nap to find Jasper's arms wrapped around me.

"Hey," he says as I hum and roll over to face him.

"Hey," I say, noticing just how groggy I sound. "Have you been here long?"

"Just a few minutes."

"How was the rest of the show?"

"The kids had a few notes, but they liked my Big Bad Wolf impression."

"Mmm, I always thought the Big Bad Wolf was misunderstood. Wait, you read them that human propaganda?"

"We did the alternate version where Little Red and Big Bad team up to defeat the evil woodsman."

"Ah! I see."

"How are you feeling?"

"Sleepy but good."

"How was the moonwalk? You didn't tell me much before."

"Well, you were busy giving the performance of a lifetime."

He punches my arm softly.

"Stop. Tell me about your experience."

"It was...I saw a lot of things. You were there."

"I was?"

"Uh-huh. Actually you were kind of everywhere. Except the lunar plane, that was just me and...I think I met Selene."

He pulls back, sitting up just a little.

"You met…Selene? *The* Selene?"

"I think so."

"Wow." He lies back down, wrapping his arm tighter around me. "What's she like?"

I give a casual little shrug. "She was nice."

Jasper cups my face and runs a thumb over my cheek.

"You do look different," he says, reiterating his point from earlier.

"In what way?"

"I don't know." His eyes dart about my face, taking in my features, and I imagine him running them through his mind, comparing them to what he remembers from before I left yesterday. "You seem older."

I throw my head back sarcastically. "Oh great! Thanks!"

He pulls me closer. "Not in a bad way. You just look more like you."

"So…good change."

He licks his bottom lip and nods. "Good change."

I breathe a breath of relief and Jasper nuzzles his face into the crook of my neck.

"I feel different," I say, sitting up slightly. "It's like all this time there's been something blocking my connection to my wolf-self and now…now that blockage is gone, and I feel…"

"What?" he says, his eyes wide in genuine excitement.

"I feel connected to everything, every wolf, and—I feel powerful."

Jasper tilts his head back to take another look at me, gently moving a strand of hair from my face.

"What?" I ask when he doesn't say anything, just stares with this amused sort of smile.

"It suits you."

He kisses me once then holds me close.

"I missed you," he says, and I love the way his breath feels on my skin.

"I missed you too."

He lifts his lips from my neck to my mouth and kisses me again. We stay like that for a long time, and after everything that's been going on these past few days, it feels so good—like kissing for the first time, or like we've unlocked some new level of kissing, the big boss of kissing.

When we come up for air I run a hand through Jasper's hair.

"I think we should try again," I say.

"Okay." Immediately Jasper tries to kiss me but I dodge his lips.

"I meant the mind-link," I say, laughing. "We should try to mind-link again."

"You think it'll work this time?"

"I'm not a hundred percent sure. But with this new access to my blood wolf abilities, I think I'm closer than before."

"Okay," he says and kisses me once more.

This time I don't avoid him.

A short while and a whole lot of making out later, Jasper and I are washed and dressed and ready to attend the school-opening celebration.

"You look…like, super fresh," I say, eyeing Jasper, whose hair is still wet from the shower.

He's wearing a loose, cream-colored linen shirt and a pair of khaki shorts. He's really made an effort. The moon gods only know how he's managed to keep a set of smart clothes clean this whole time.

"Thanks. You look pretty great too."

I roll my eyes. "Whatever." I'm in the cleanest T-shirt I could find, which isn't saying much—although I do like the scent of this earthy handmade soap they have in the showers here.

"Ready?" Jasper seems eager to get to the party, which is very cute.

"Sure."

"So when can I hear more about your moonwalk?" Jasper asks as we make our way through the Sanc.

"Woof, maybe in like ten years' time?"

He eyes me sideways with a smug grin. "I'll hold you to that."

"And what about you? You seemed to be having fun earlier. Helping out with the rogue school wasn't so bad in the end?"

Jasper keeps his eyes forward as we move through the tents.

"I think perhaps I understand now—why my mother cared so much about these people." A couple of kids run by us, one kicking a ball and one waving a ribbon. Jasper turns as they pass. "There is no difference between a rogue pup and one from a pack." After the kids are gone he turns back to me. "Except the privilege they were born into. We should do more," he says, nodding gently. "To help. The packs should do more."

"I bet that's what your mom would have said."

He stops suddenly, the hint of a smile cracking his pensive expression.

"I think you're right. And..." He takes my hand and gives it a squeeze. "I am glad we came here. I'm glad I got to see this place she cared so much about."

"You feel closer to her than before?"

"I do. Thank you." He pulls me in for a soft, meaningful kiss, and while we have our eyes closed music begins to play nearby, an upbeat song heavy on the drums and the horns.

"Sounds like the party is underway," I say. "Shall we?"

The party is in full swing when Jasper and I arrive. Under the new school tent and all around the surrounding area wolves are gathered. Balloons and ribbons have been strung up on every tentpole. Off to the right, one of the large industrial barbecues has been set up and Miss Sammy is the grill-meister. She's flipping ribs, stacking cheese on top of burgers, and piling sausages high on a platter, bellowing for people to come and get it. Music is blaring from a number of speakers set up around the edge of the tent, and as I glance around I spot some familiar faces in the crowd.

Mal is sitting in a foldout chair with Kairos next to her by a campfire just outside the tent. Tomas is talking with some of the rogue teachers we saw the first day we were here, pointing out areas of the floor space, I assume discussing how best to use the space once the kids start attending classes. Yoki is swirling a long rope on a couple of sticks on the far side of the tent, making giant bubbles out of soapy water, while kids jump and dance around them. The other council members are knocking about as well, as are a few of the rogues who apprehended us at our campsite. The only person missing is Omar.

I squint harder to try and find him but come up short.

"Let's get a drink," Jasper says, keeping my hand in his and leading me over to a table with a very full punch bowl.

As Jasper pours and hands me a solo cup of pink, sweet-smelling liquid I take a closer look at the inside of the tent.

"Looks pretty sturdy," I say. "Must be well constructed."

"It'll stand." Jasper turns to face into the tent, looking proud of his accomplishment, which makes my chest all warm and fuzzy. Then his attention catches on something and a growl rolls in his throat.

I follow his eyeline to where George Peng has just entered the tent.

Jasper takes a small step forward and instinctively I put a hand on his arm to stop him.

"What's he doing here?" Jasper asks.

"I'm sure he just wanted to help celebrate."

Mr. Peng wanders farther into the tent, seemingly lost or looking for someone. When he spots us, his and Jasper's eyes lock. I can just about hear Jasper grinding his teeth, which I'm pretty sure are fangs by now. Then to my astonishment George steps in our direction. Is he...? He can't be seriously coming over here? Can he?

"Keep calm," I say. "Remember this is a school."

George stops a couple of meters short, probably being careful not to get too close. Then he drops to his knees.

"Mr. Apollo," he begins, speaking to the dusty ground. "I submit myself to you and beg for your forgiveness. I have had a lot of time to think during my time in exile and I know now what I did was wrong—the actions of a deranged man driven crazy by the hierarchies of the society he was born into."

Jasper edges forward and I squeeze his arm tighter.

"And I don't mean to make excuses. I did what I did of my own volition. But it has cost me everything. My life and my daughter. Please, accept my apologies. I do not expect forgiveness, but..."

"But?" Jasper rasps, incredulous.

"But I would ask one thing of you."

Jasper's teeth are the most clenched teeth I've seen. "And what would that be?"

"Eleanor, my daughter. I have no way of knowing if she's healthy, or—alive. Could you please, tell me...is she okay?"

For a minute I remain terrified Jasper is about to shift and tear this poor guy's throat out. Yeah, he did almost have me killed and he kidnapped Aisha, and he nearly toppled the whole Apollo dynasty, but looking at him now, he seems so small, frail. His hands are digging into the soil, tears wet his wrinkled face. I shift my gaze from him to Jasper and realize that Jasper's jaws are no longer snapped tight, his face is loose, his expression somewhat bemused.

From the corner of my vision I spot Mal watching us and Tomas as well. They're both waiting to see how Jasper will react. In fact, more and more eyes turn to watch the spectacle as Mr. Peng waits to see if Jasper will rip him to shreds or...is it possible he'll offer forgiveness?

"For the things you have done," Jasper says, sounding every bit the young alpha, "I can offer no forgiveness. You tried to destroy my family and taint our legacy."

Tomas takes the smallest step forward and Mal sends him a warning glance, telling him to stay back, just a moment longer.

"But I understand the pressure that could lead a man such as you to drastic measures, and I too understand the power of the link between a parent and their child. As far as I know Eleanor is behind bars, but she is alive, healthy, and provided for. She is serving out her sentence in peace."

"Thank you," Mr. Peng says, bowing even lower. "You are very kind to tell me this. Your words soothe the ache of a broken man."

"I do not wish to soothe," Jasper continues. "Only to prevent more unnecessary suffering."

"Thank you," Mr. Peng says again, and again, and again, until finally Mal stands and whispers into the ear of a nearby wolf.

He and a friend move to either side of Mr. Peng and lift him from the dirt, helping him to walk away.

We watch until he's gone, and the party closes ranks, the vibe shifting from a tense, somber one back to one of joyous celebration.

"That was—really nice of you," I say, rubbing Jasper's arm.

"It's more than he deserves," he spits to the side.

"Maybe, but also now we can maybe move on. That's what you deserve."

The girl from earlier, the one desperate for Mr. Jasper to read her yet another story, appears next to us.

"Jasper," she says a little quietly, swaying from side to side. "Will you come and dance with us?"

He glances at me, as if I'm about to give him some sort of escape route, when in fact, there's no way I would give up the chance to see him dancing with a gaggle of preschoolers. Besides, maybe it's the tension release he needs. Instead of making excuses on his behalf I shrug, as if to say *I've got nothing*.

"Sure, Janie, I'd love to."

She reaches up her little hand, which Jasper takes, and he's immediately pulled across the floor.

Once he's fully entrenched in a circle of four-year-olds I look around again, wondering where Omar could have gotten to and if everything is okay. But that concern vanishes when I look back over to find Jasper fully breaking it down, doing some cross between swing dance and the twist. A circle of kids is jumping around him, swishing their hips, meanwhile he's spinning Janie under his arm and dancing up a storm.

He glances over, red-faced but smiling, and I lift my cup to him. Who would have thought my moody, rogue-averse mate would end up the belle of the preschool ball?

"Your mate is full of surprises," Mal says, appearing beside me.

"Yeah, he is."

"Maybe there is hope for the packs after all."

She's studying Jasper intently, as if she's thinking something through.

"Of course," she continues, "I have a feeling you will be instrumental in bringing about the necessary change."

"I—uh—I..."

"One thing I may not have made clear just yet..." She sips her drink and moves her bottom lip in a weird half circle. "The rogues have always been a friend to the blood wolf." She eyes me sideways. "And the blood wolf has always been a friend to the rogues."

What is she trying to say?

"I hope this is a relationship that will continue to be fruitful."

I turn to her and say as earnestly as possible, "I hope so too."

"And I hope you found everything you needed during your stay here."

"Yes, thank you. I think I did."

"You'd be welcome to stay longer. I'm sure Yoki and yourself have made excellent progress these last few days but there is always more to learn, Blood Wolf."

"Thanks for the offer." I glance back over at Jasper, who is smiling like a complete goon and dancing like Fred Astaire. "But I have to go back with Jasper."

Mal nods like she's had something confirmed. "So I thought. Just know you are welcome here anytime."

"I do. Thank you, ma'am."

"Call me Mal," she says, now with a cheeky smile and wink. "All my friends do."

She pats my shoulder a couple of times and then moves off back to Kairos and her waiting chair.

For a moment I watch the party and feel like I'm floating just outside my body. I know there is more to learn about my blood-wolf powers, but I also feel ready to take that journey on my own—to explore what it means to be connected to wolfkind like this without guardrails, to fully dive in. And I feel ready to head home and tackle what's waiting there, too. The friendships, the attention, the pressure, the people who would rather I wasn't preternaturally linked to their future leader.

While Jasper continues to dance, I glance around in search of Omar once more. I would really like to speak with him before we leave. Then a sharp pang slices through the back of my consciousness. I double over, wincing in pain. And before I can try to figure out where it came from, a woman screams and chaos breaks loose.

THE INVASION OF SANCTUARY

The Sanctuary erupts into chaos. Screams tear through the music still pumping from the speakers, although one is swiftly knocked over by the rushing crowds. Wolves are running in every direction, swooping up kids, and gathering their families. The stampede kicks up dirt and makes it hard to see.

"Jasper?" I call across the tent because I can't spot him any longer.

Where is he? I spin around and try to assess what's happening. A loud crash pulls me from the tent and I stare into the sky where a large plume of smoke has erupted and is spiraling into the clouds. Did someone set fire to the Sanc?

The crunch of bones snaps in my ears as around me a handful of rogues shift, leaping into action in their wolf forms. Off to one side Mal is shouting to the shifting wolves, pointing in the direction of the fire, directing them toward the heart of whatever this conflict is. Tomas is ushering folks away from the explosion and hopefully to safety. I spin around again. Still no sign of Jasper.

Miss Sammy runs by, hurrying two kids across the open space between tents to where Tomas is directing the younglings.

"What's happening?" I ask.

"I don't know," she says, shaking her large mane of hair. "We must be under attack. The Sanctuary has been invaded."

I don't hold her up any longer, instead letting her shield the children she's with as they run from the tent.

I need to know what's going on and I need to find Jasper, so I try to steady my breathing, close my eyes, and focus.

At first it's hard to make anything much out. There are so many wolves, all of their thoughts and emotions heightened, making them loud and hard to ignore. But I expand my consciousness, looking specifically for Jasper's familiar figure plus anything out of the ordinary.

"Yes!" I shout when I find him, but my celebration is short-lived because he's standing in an open space between tents, surrounded by wolves who are snapping their jaws and emanating a furiously angry energy. And to top it off he's not alone. Janie is with him, shielded behind his back, clutching onto his leg, terror flying off her in panicked waves.

There's something about the invaders, these snarling wolves, that's familiar, but for some reason I won't let myself believe what I'm sensing. They can't be...are they...Elite Pack wolves?

There's no time to stand around while Jasper is potentially in danger from his own people, so I take off running.

Chaos reigns as I sprint through the rogue settlement. People are running, darting into tents, shifting, and there are pack wolves too, all in wolf form, tearing doors off tents, knocking over chairs, and digging up gardens. They're sniffing around inside people's homes, backing innocent people, children even, into corners.

And I don't need my blood-wolf senses to confirm what I already knew. These are Elite Pack wolves—soldiers, gammas in the alpha's security forces. Their scent alone gives them away, I'd recognize it anywhere. But what are Elite Pack soldiers doing here? Why are they treating these people like criminals?

Luckily, Jasper isn't too far from the school. He must have run with Janie but then became trapped when the explosion happened, before the Elite Pack wolves surrounded him.

"Stand down," he bellows.

And while they don't come any closer, the circle of Elite soldiers doesn't follow his orders, either. Instead, they remain en garde, their lips pulled back to show their teeth.

"I am Jasper Apollo," he continues red-faced, one arm behind him, holding Janie to his leg, keeping her safe. "The son of your alpha. I command you to stand down."

"Jasper!" I call out. A couple of wolves turn to watch me as I dart between them, sniffing the air to assess my threat level, but they let me pass. "What is this?"

"I don't know."

"Why do you ignore a direct order from your superior?" he asks again, his voice loud, commanding, strong. "These are innocent people. Stand down!"

Then a voice cuts through the chaos. "They won't follow your orders because they are following mine."

Beta Castillo emerges from behind a nearby tent and saunters all too casually into the circle of wolves—*his* wolves.

"I outrank you," Jasper growls.

"Yes, but you don't outrank the alpha, from whom my orders were given."

The circle of soldiers isn't lessening their intense energy, they still look about ready to pounce and flay us.

"When my father hears what you've done here, Salazar—"

Another explosion erupts somewhere across the settlement, more screams rising with the smoke from the fires, plural, now burning in all directions.

"Your father has charged me with rescuing you. I'm simply ensuring your captors are sufficiently brought to heel."

"Stop this!" Jasper spits desperately. "We weren't in any danger. These people have done nothing wrong."

"You disappeared," Salazar continues. "When you didn't return to your father's property, your security detail contacted me. We assumed the worst. When we discovered this encampment of rogue reprobates we assumed you'd been kidnapped."

"Well, I'm telling you we're fine, these people are not our captors. We chose to stay here. Tell your wolves to stand down."

"Unfortunately, we can't do that. Now that we're here it's important we ensure this rogue faction is subdued."

"Since when did Beta Castillo go all cartoon villain?" I whisper to Jasp.

His eyes flick to me but he doesn't let his guard down. My curiosity gets the better of me, so while the standoff continues I try to reach out and see if I can glean anything from Salazar. I probe his mind with my senses and have to clutch my chest at the pain I feel radiating off him.

"He's hurting," I say. "Great loss and anger."

"Salazar, these people have given us their hospitality," Jasper says. "This is an affront to them and their community. Stop what you're doing, call off your wolves. Now."

Salazar pauses, he levels a half-confused, half-accusatory stare at Jasper. Would he really challenge Jasper's authority like this? What has driven him to such extreme actions?

"How dare you!" a new voice cries. Mal arrives in the square, flanked by Tomas and Akari in human form, along with Kairos and a wolf I assume is Buck in their animal states, plus a host of rogue wolves. "How dare you invade our sanctuary!"

"You must be the leader of this pocket rebellion," Salazar says, his voice void of any emotion.

Mal steps forward, the rest of the council right behind her. "This land is protected. Pack warfare has no place here. I demand you call back your forces and leave this place at once."

Salazar rubs his chin with two knuckles. "I'm afraid I can't do that."

"We are peaceful," she says, her voice wavering just slightly. "Your actions here are a violation of the rights of wolves regardless of pack status."

"Peaceful?" Salazar sneers. "Then tell me, why do you harbor violent criminals?"

Mal sucks in a breath, expanding her cheeks. "We do no such thing."

My mind flicks to Mr. Peng. Have they found him? Could that be who they mean?

Salazar begins to pace a little, looking like he's enjoying this too much. "You're telling me you aren't housing dangerous terrorists? Perpetrators of crimes against my alpha and my pack?"

"We do not ask why people come here," Mal says. "But we trust that everyone here will abide by our governing principles of peace and communion with the wolf spirits. Any crimes our people may have committed, as long as they do not prevent the wolf in question from participating in our society, are forgotten when they step foot on our land."

Salazar stops pacing and eyes Mal with a dangerous gleam in his eye. "Ah, but sadly, we in the pack system are not in the business of forgiving crimes without first doling out punishment."

"You have ransacked our town." Mal throws out her arms. "Harassed our people. Terrorized the innocent. The only criminals I acknowledge here are you and your soldiers."

Now Salazar smiles, and for the first time, he truly terrifies me.

"Is that so?" He turns to one of his wolves. "Bring him out."

I expect George Peng to be dragged from the shadows but instead my jaw drops when two Elite Pack soldiers in human form appear from behind the side of a nearby tent, holding Omar by his arms and dragging him into the light.

"Omar!" I call out, stepping to him, but Jasper holds a hand out to stop me.

Omar's head lolls on his shoulders like he can barely hold it up. His face is bruised and swollen, one eye almost entirely closed shut, blood running from his busted brow and lip. One of his legs hangs limp and he's barely able to put weight on the other. The Elite Pack soldiers keep hold of him as they display him like a battered trophy.

"What is the meaning of this?" Mal asks. "Release him immediately!"

"This rogue has been charged with the unlawful entry of the private residence of Jericho Apollo, acts of terrorism, and the violent battery of numerous innocent citizens of the Elite Pack."

"What? That's impossible," I say, pressing against Jasper's hand, which continues to hold me in place. "He wouldn't do that."

"When did these crimes occur?" Jasper asks.

Salazar turns to Jasper, a look of triumph on his face. "The night of the harvest moon, one year ago."

That's the night Jasper almost rejected me and became mates with Olivia, Salazar's daughter—the night the rogues invaded Jericho's house in the Hamptons and disrupted the party, the night we were kidnapped and almost killed by Eleanor.

I stare at Omar, unwilling to believe that he could have taken part in that, unwilling to believe that he was one of the rogues who was there, who helped Eleanor to knock me out, drag me to that yacht and nearly...

His gaze catches mine and I plead with my expression, with every fiber of my being, for him to shake his head or say something to deny these charges, anything to let me know Salazar is lying or that he's made a mistake. But instead Omar simply stares back, his eyes dark, glassy with tears, solemn with admission.

"No," I say, raising a hand to my mouth and shaking my head. "No."

Jasper's jaw is clenched again, his shoulders vibrating with anger.

Neither of us move or say anything.

Mal steps forward once more, her features wide with desperation. "Whatever crimes this boy has committed in the past, he is here under our protection. You cannot take him from here. You cannot—"

"The packs do not recognize the authority of rogues," Salazar says matter-of-factly.

Mal's chin is quivering, and I've never seen her look so small, so defeated. Buck moves forward, snarling. But one raised eyebrow from Salazar and Mal knows to tell him to withdraw, a simple hand gesture that has Buck whimpering and scratching the earth, but staying back nonetheless.

"You are a sad excuse for a wolf," Mal says, tears falling down her weathered cheeks.

"I am simply following orders," Salazar replies, unbothered. "However, now that we have what we came for I see no reason to continue on here. We will leave your people to their business."

Mal's mind must be whirring, trying to think of a way to save Omar, but coming up short. She knows there's a trade-off being made—Omar for the rest of the Sanc— and Mal isn't willing to risk the safety of her entire encampment.

"Do something," I whisper to Jasper, but he remains stoic. "Jasper?"

"He was there, Max. He should return with us to face the consequences of his actions."

He turns and kneels in front of Janie, who has kept quiet this whole time. "You're okay," he says. "No one will hurt you. Go with the others."

He pats her arm and turns her in the direction of Mal and the council. A gentle push and Janie runs to them, Akari and Tomas kneeling to meet her and ushering her away from the drama.

"We will take our leave," Salazar says. "Mind your wolves allow us safe passage back across the desert or we will return with greater numbers and raze this camp to the ground."

Mal presses her lips together until they're purple, but nods to accept Salazar's conditions. The beta turns to his wolves.

"Take him and the alpha's wayward son," he says, gesturing to Omar and Jasper. "We wouldn't want him running off again, would we."

Two of Salazar's gamma wolves approach and flank Jasper, and without argument, he lets them lead him from the camp.

As the rest of the Elite soldiers turn and stalk off between tents I turn to look back once more.

The Sanc is no longer in chaos. The screams have stopped, so have most of the fires. Smoke hangs over the quiet settlement still, a brutal reminder that nowhere is safe, that the destructive might of the packs is ever present. I know these people are resilient. They've been through so much already. They will shake this off too. They will rebuild, recover, and continue to live in peace as long as the packs let them.

But what I'm leaving behind right now is a row of disappointed and angry faces.

Mal looks shaken. Kairos is rubbing at her leg with his muzzle. She returns my gaze and her last words flicker in my mind. *The blood wolf has always been a friend to the rogues.* I grit my teeth and bow my head, hoping she knows that that's exactly what I plan to be from now on: a friend to rogues and to any wolf who doesn't fit in, who deserves more than what they've ended up with, who is looked down upon by those with more.

"Max?" Jasper says, having stopped to look back. His wolf escorts won't let him linger for long.

"Coming," I say, and with a heavy heart and tears in my

eyes, I turn away from Mal, the council, and the Sanc, promising I will do everything in my power to make this right.

THE PRODIGAL WOLVES

"Do you think he did it?" Katie asks from her lawn chair.

We're sitting on the patio out the back of my house, a couple of ice teas on the wooden slats next to our chairs, the sun high and hot over the forest.

"I..." I start but falter.

I've been home for two days. After we were escorted from the Sanc, the Elite gamma wolves marched us back across the desert to Jasper's mom's cottage. We weren't even allowed to grab our stuff before we left, which means my sketchbook and clothes are still at the Sanc. We were shoved into cars and driven straight to a private airfield where we were flown home on one of Jericho's private jets.

After a long and quiet flight, Jasper dropped me off at home, and while I basically begged for him to make sure Omar was taken care of, to do everything he could to ensure Omar was released, Jasper remained quiet. Though it pains me, I understand. If Omar really was one of the rogues who invaded Jericho's house in the Hamptons, then maybe he should be held accountable for his crimes—or at least, I can see why Jasper might think that. His dad nearly died that night, and because of that intrusion the pack's security has been under scrutiny.

That one attack has opened us up to all manner of other attempts on our territory.

But after spending so much time with Omar, getting to know him, learning how much he's gotten into the spiritual side of being a wolf and what he's been through, I can't help but think he doesn't deserve to be locked up. He should be out in the desert still, learning from Yoki and continuing to figure out how to be the best wolf he can be. The things he'll be able to accomplish, the good he could do for wolfkind, have to outweigh his crimes. Right?!

"I don't know," I say finally. "But I don't know if it matters. I just wish—I wish I knew why he might have done it. Because I'm sure there's a reason."

"What does Jasper have to say about it all?" she asks, sipping from her metal straw.

"He hasn't said much. Not in a we're-not-speaking sort of way, just in a whenever-I-bring-it-up-he-changes-the-subject kind of way. I've only managed to speak to him properly once since we got back. He's been a little busy."

"Right, pack drama."

"Understatement of the century."

It seems while we were away things have gotten even more tense at Elite Pack central. Olivia and Mia have disappeared—a fact I learned from Mason via text when my cell finally caught some service on the way out of the desert.

"MIA'S GONE AWOL!!!" he texted me, followed by a slew of other messages, each as hyperbolic as the one before it.

It wasn't till I got home that I learned Olivia was gone as well. Which explains why Salazar was being a complete asshat. He's pissed and terrified and hurt because his daughter has literally run away from home. And to top it off, instead of being out looking for her he was ordered to hunt down Jasper. Then when he found us, we were cavorting with the supposed enemy. No wonder he was being such a dick—not that that gives him any right to terrorize innocent rogues.

Their disappearance has caused the fracture between the Elite and Rocky Packs to spread even farther and now it appears Morven is courting favor with the very packs Jasper has spent the better part of this year trying to win over to our side. If he manages to convince them to join him, we'll be sitting ducks, one pack cornered by a slew of others.

"From what I hear," Katie says, "things are tense even in the inner circle."

"Oh yeah?"

"Simon's mom said that some of the upper-ranked wolves were pissed Jasper had run off right when they needed him to fortify our position with the packs. Some are saying Jericho has lost control of the pack. And now the beta's daughter has jumped ship. I bet Jasper is going through it at home."

"Yeah," I say, wishing I could do more for him, be there for him somehow. It seems our plans of trying to mind-link again are on the back burner until Jasper is able to help calm things down in the packhouse.

Katie eyes me and must spot my furrowed brow because she shrugs and immediately changes the subject.

"Soooooo, I know everything here is a bit of a mess but I'm dying to know…" She puffs out her cheeks and leans across the arm of her chair. "How was your *alone* time with Jasper?"

I roll my eyes but can't help smiling, even in the face of all this turmoil. "It was...pretty amazing. Right up until it wasn't."

"And did you...you know?"

"Katie! A gentlewolf doesn't kiss and tell."

She squeals and almost jumps to her feet. "You did! Ah! Oh my moon gods. You did it!"

My head lolls about on my shoulders as my cheeks heat up super fast.

"You did it with the alpha's son!" she continues. "How was it?"

I take a breath and lean back in my chair, my eyes drifting across the treetops on the horizon.

"I—I couldn't have imagined it any other way. It was—perfect."

Katie leans even farther, until I'm worried her chair is going to tip over, and tries to give me an awkward hug.

"I'm so happy for you, Max!"

"Thanks," I say into her hair, which has fallen all across my face, choking me with its strawberry shampoo scent.

"I can't believe how grown-up we are," she says as she falls back into her seat.

"Me neither." I grab my drink and take a long sip.

"And how do you feel now?" she asks, her eyes glinting.

"Well..." It's such a loaded question. How *do* I feel? Like things with Jasper and me have reached a whole new level? That we've never been this close? But that we still haven't managed to mind-link and I'm scared we never will? And scared of what it means if we don't? That things were perfect while we were away in the desert by ourselves but now that we're back things are exactly the same as they were before? That all this pack drama is a big wedge between us and now there's the Omar situation which I can already tell we're not on the same page about? That I'm terrified we were living in some escapist fantasy and that things could never be as good in the real world?

"Max?" Katie asks, and I realize I've taken about a decade to answer her.

"I think we just need to talk," I say. "And…"

"Come on, I know you're holding something back."

"I guess it's about Omar."

"Oh?"

"It wasn't just Jasper I got closer to in the desert. Omar is a really great guy and I'm worried about him."

"Do you *like* him?"

Instinctively, I lift a hand to my chest, where my muscles have gone all tense.

"I'm scared Jasper is going to want to punish him," I say, knowing that's not an answer, or maybe it is, sort of. "And if he does that I'll…"

"You'll have to choose between them?" She finishes my sentence for me.

For a moment I close my eyes and press my head back against the solid wood of the chair.

"I need to speak to Omar and find out why he was part of the attack," I say. "And then I can decide what to say to Jasper. But I don't know how to get to him without Jasper's help."

She reaches over, calmly this time, and places her hand on mine. "If he sees what this means to you, I know he'll understand."

I hope Katie is right, but she didn't see Jasper's face when they pulled Omar from behind those tents.

"Guess there's only one way to find out."

"Where do you think you're going?" Mom asks from the living room as I head for the door.

After much messaging and long waits between replies last night, Jasper agreed to let me visit Omar. I stop in the arched doorway and rub my neck.

"Uhhh, to Jasper's place...in the city."

Mom slams the remote on the armrest of the sofa and it falls to the floor. "Uh-uh, no way, kiddo."

"What?"

"You disappeared!" she says, eyes blazing. "Again!"

I roll my eyes and drop my shoulders. I'm so sick of this. "We were safe. I told you everything that happened."

She shakes her head like she's having too many thoughts and can't decide which to shout at me first.

"You've been back three days and you're already taking off again."

"I'm not taking off. I'm going to speak with Jasper about Omar. You know this is important."

"More important than your safety?"

"Yes!" I don't mean for it to, but the word explodes out of me.

Mom sits back in her chair like the force of my yell has collided with her and thrown her into the cushions.

"Sorry," I say, less harsh this time. "I don't mean to yell but yes, this is more important than my safety. There are so many things that are more important than me. Omar needs me. He needs my help. He doesn't have all the things I have. He doesn't have amazing parents like you, who are accepting and who actually give a shit. He doesn't have a pack. He's all alone in some prison cell and I'm all he has." I pause briefly, expecting Mom to jump in, but she doesn't, she sits and lets me continue.

"I've seen a vision, I spoke with Selene, the moon goddess! I'm the blood wolf, Mom, that means I have a gift. It means I'm connected to a greater purpose, to all of wolfkind. There are people out there who need me, who need my help. And I'm sorry but that means I can't avoid every single dangerous thing that could be out there. I'm going to be put in more danger, that's just the truth. The world is dangerous and we can't avoid that."

"But you don't have to go running into danger," she says quietly, tears brimming in her eyes.

I take a step toward her. "Maybe I do. Maybe when no one else is willing to...I do."

Her eyes are shiny with unshed tears, but she doesn't look sad, instead she has this sort of impressed half smile going on.

"When did you get so brave?" she asks, followed by a strange grunt of a laugh that could also be a sob.

"I dunno. I don't think I am brave. I just—care, is all."

Mom wipes away her tears before they can streak her face.

"Are you going to ground me?" I ask. "Because I sort of know how to sneak out anyway."

For a second I'm terrified she won't get the joke, but relief floods me as she smiles and laughs.

"There's no holding you back," she says, sniffing. "I know that. I think I've always known that." She stretches out a hand for me to take, which I do. "I just wish I could protect you always."

"I know."

"It's so weird." She shakes her head gently.

"What is?"

"I have no idea when you got so mature. You've grown up, Maxie. Guess I can't call you *kiddo* anymore, hey?"

"Yes you can, Mom."

She gives my hand a tight squeeze and leans forward, her eyes blazing into mine. "You do what you've got to do," she says. "But be safe."

"I'll try."

For a moment she doesn't let go and I wonder if she ever will.

"Uh, kind of need my hand back, Mom."

"Oh right," she says and lets go. "Try and be home before midnight."

"Sure." I head for the door but turn back one more time when I reach it. "Love you, Mom."

"Love you, Blood Wolf," she says.

The elevator door opens with a ping and I step out into the sparse living room of Jasper's Manhattan apartment.

Jasper is leaning on the back of a white sofa, waiting for me.

"Hey" he says, moving off the sofa and wrapping his arms around me.

"Hey," I say back, thinking this was going to be a quick *hello* hug, but Jasper keeps me held against him.

"I missed you," he says, his breath warm on my neck.

"You too. Is everything all right?"

He finally pulls back and is about to answer when a door opens down the hallway. We both turn to look as the muffled sound of voices travels across the wide living room.

"Let's talk in my room," Jasper says, taking my hand and pulling me away from the approaching voices.

We're almost out of the living room when three men step out of the adjacent hallway.

"I don't see why we should have to spend this much just to assuage some rogue-supporting…" Walter Bridgers, leading the charge, trails off when he spots us. He's accompanied by Jericho and Salazar. The trifecta. The holy trinity! The three most powerful wolves in the Elite Pack. "Oh, it's you."

Only Jericho looks even mildly pleased to see me.

Salazar remains stoic, his eyes cold and distant. I don't need to read his mind to know that he resents us for distracting him while his daughter is missing. I wouldn't be surprised if he blames us for Olivia running off, too. After all, we set the precedent for queer wolf pairings, we ran off as well. Not to mention I'm the reason Olivia and Jasper weren't forced into an arranged mateship. If it weren't for me, she'd be the future luna of the pack and safe at home now.

Walter isn't as good at containing his emotions. His eyes travel from my head to my feet and back again, a disdainful sneer on his lips.

Jericho steps forward, his hand outstretched. "It's good to see you, Max." I shake his hand, doing my best not to squeal at his vicelike grip. "Jasper and I are counting on you during these unsettling times."

"Yes, sir," I say automatically, the ever-obedient pup.

"We were just finishing up our discussion," Jericho says, referencing his surly companions. "Jasper, I need to speak with you about the outreach program."

"Yes, Father."

"I'll see these men out and then we'll talk." Jericho turns to me. "I'm sorry but this will need to be a brief visit, Max. I know you understand."

As a ripple runs down my spine, my shoulders instinctively pull back. What exactly am I supposed to be understanding? That the pack comes first, even over

Jasper and my relationship? Even over the travesties that took place back in California? I glance at Jasper, who is bowing his head ever so slightly, a sign of submission.

"Gentlemen, let me walk you out." Jericho ushers his visitors toward the elevator, and as he engages Salazar in one last piece of business, Walter glances over at us, his beady eyes dark and penetrating, a smug grin playing in the corner of his mouth.

What the hell, I think, and I reach out with my mind. I want to know what's going on in that privileged head of his. We meet eyes and I extend my consciousness until it rams into his. He resists at first, visibly straining, but I'm able to pierce his protective barrier and catch a few glimpses.

Walter is standing in a dark corner of an empty parking lot, glancing furtively to the sides. A man approaches in a black leather jacket, with a greasy ponytail, his hands shoved into the pockets of his jeans. When he reaches Walter, he unzips his jacket and holds one side open. In the vision I can't see what it is he's showing Walter, just that Walter nods, satisfied, then produces a manilla envelope stuffed with a rectangular-shaped block. Is that cash? Lots and lots and lots of cash? Walter hands the man with the ponytail the envelope, then turns and walks away.

As I leave the vision, I'm left with a sense of satisfaction, a crumb of what Walter must have been feeling in that moment—the sort of satisfaction that comes when the pieces of a well-laid plan fall into place.

Walter and I are still staring at each other, his eyes tight and his jaw tense, but he relaxes as I withdraw my consciousness and stop probing at his mind. He gives me one last dark look, a cautious, questioning sort of look, but also a warning. *Don't test me.*

What did I just see and what is he planning?

"Max?" Jasper says, already halfway down the hall to his room. "You coming?"

"Yeah."

Walter slips into the elevator behind Salazar, and I wait until the doors close, not wanting to turn my back on him for even a second.

I follow Jasper into his room. He stands for a moment between the door and his bed, not looking at me, running a hand through his hair.

"Are you okay?" I ask.

He doesn't turn to face me, just looks back over his shoulder.

"Things are bad, Max. I don't know how they got this bad. After everything I did, I don't get how they could have fallen apart so easily."

I step to him and put my hands on his shoulders, rubbing his back with my thumbs.

"You're talking like we're about to go to war or something. Is it that bad?"

"Maybe."

Finally, he turns to face me.

"Just because of Olivia and Mia?"

"No, there's something else going on," he says, his eyes pointing to a spot on the rug. "It's not just Morven. More and more packs are turning on us. Alphas who I spent time with, who promised me they were aligned with us, are defecting."

"Who's changing their minds? Morven?"

"Not from what I can tell. Morven hasn't sent anyone south of DC. Either the packs are turning on their own or there's something else."

"Your dad has to have some idea."

"Maybe." He shrugs and huffs. "Or maybe he's too blind to see it."

I pull my head back, super confused. "See what?"

"Someone within our pack has turned on us. Someone on the inside has been in touch with the southern packs. It's the only reason I can think of."

"Who do you think?" Immediately, one name comes to mind, but it's not the one that comes out of Jasper's mouth.

"Salazar, maybe. You saw how he acted at the Rogue Sanctuary. I've never seen him like this. What if he's turned on us? On my father?"

"Do you really think he would betray your dad like that?"

Jasper turns again, pulling away from me and holding his forehead in both palms. "I don't know! I don't know what to think. But I can't help feeling I'm the one who has to fix things. It's all on me to make things right, and before things get any worse, before anyone gets hurt—anyone *else*."

I wrap my arms around his waist and squeeze gently, just enough so he knows I'm there for him.

"It's not all on you," I say. "It's not. You're not the alpha yet, your dad is in charge. He knows what to do. And even if he doesn't, you have me. I won't let you go through this alone."

Jasper spins around and returns my embrace, his eyes lit up with some notion.

"I have you," he says.

"Yeah, you do."

"Do you think...? Are you able to reach out and see what might be affecting the other alphas?"

"What do you mean?"

"Like use your blood-wolf powers to see what they're thinking?"

I pause for a while, staring into Jasper's face. He looks so hopeful, like he's found the solution he's been looking for.

"I don't know," I say. "I'm not sure I'm that good at using my powers yet, even after my moonwalk, and besides...I...I don't know if that's what they're for."

"What do you mean?" He pulls away and puts a couple of steps between us.

"I mean, I'm not a spy, Jasper. I haven't been given this gift so I can sneak around surveilling foreign alphas."

"I'm not asking you to become a spy. But we could stop a war, Max. Isn't that a good thing?"

For a moment I don't know how to answer. I rub the back of my neck and scrunch up my face.

"Isn't it?" Jasper presses.

"Yeah, of course. I don't want there to be a war but—"

"But what?"

"But my powers are supposed to help bring people together, not give one pack the upper hand over another."

"It's not just some pack," he says, and I notice the dark circles under his eyes for the first time. "It's *your* pack."

I don't say anything. Instead, I shoot him a look to let him know that he's on the edge, one step away from crossing a boundary.

Finally, he drops onto the side of his bed, letting his head hang low. "I'm sorry," he says. "I didn't mean to imply...I didn't mean anything."

"It's okay," I say hesitantly.

"No, I shouldn't have asked you to use your powers like that. I'm sorry. I'm just so..."

"Stressed?"

He looks up finally and huffs a sad little laugh. "Yeah." He holds out a hand, which I take as I come to sit next to him on the mattress. "Everything seemed so simple when it was just us." He kisses the back of my hand. "Now that we're back, everything just seems so—fucked. And I miss you. I miss us. Why can't it be like the desert all the time?"

I wrap my free hand around our interlaced fingers, making a little cocoon for his hand.

"Because that would be too simple," I say. "And if I've learned anything in the last year it's that being a werewolf in love is anything but simple."

"What should I do?" he asks, and for a second he looks twelve, like a kid who needs some direction.

"We do what we can to help," I say. "One wolf at a time."

"Where do we start?"

I chew on my lip, bracing for Jasper's reaction to what I have to say next.

"Omar," I say. "We need to speak with him and find out why he did what he did."

"Does it matter?" Jasper seems genuinely curious, like maybe it does.

"He's a good wolf," I say. "He deserves our help."

Jasper looks skeptical.

"If he did a bad thing he must have had a reason," I continue. "Maybe he can help us understand how the rogues were able to invade the packhouse so easily? It might help us with our situation now."

"I don't know if I can get him released," Jasper says, preempting what he knows I'm going to ask for.

But relief washes over me because he's not fighting me on this, instead he's worried he won't be able to do everything he can to help me.

"That's okay. Let's just talk to him and we'll see what happens then."

Jasper watches me for a second, and I can't help wondering if I'm the one crossing some boundary, if asking him to help Omar is the thing that will finally pull us apart.

"Okay," he says.

BENEATH THE PACKHOUSE

It's dark out by the time Jasper has finished speaking with his father and we're able to slip out of the apartment. Of course, it's never actually dark in Manhattan—the streetlights, the gleam of office windows and storefronts, illuminate everything. There's not a star to be seen overhead, just the moon, waning and low on the horizon. I glance at it as we make our way around the back of the packhouse to the prison's separate entrance. Is Selene up there now? Is she watching me? Does she think we're doing the right thing?

"Come on," Jasper says, a few feet ahead of me, waving me on. "The entrance to the prison levels is this way."

"Seems a little weird to me that we'd keep all our most dangerous criminals right under the hub of pack activity," I say as we approach a rolling garage door.

"We don't," Jasper says. "Our major prison facility is upstate at a secret location. My father only told me where exactly last year. This is more like a holding facility, a halfway house, where we keep prisoners before they're officially sentenced."

When we reach the entrance to what looks like an underground parking garage, Jasper waves a fob over a spot on the wall and a door I hadn't even noticed opens up, a piece of the metal wall sliding away to reveal a dimly lit, concrete box.

"So Omar hasn't been sentenced yet?"

Before we step inside, Jasper turns and places a hand on my arm. "Not officially, but Max…"

"What? What is it?"

"Earlier today he confessed."

"Why would he do that?"

"He was probably told the judge would be more lenient if he fessed up. It's a tactic they use to avoid lengthy trials."

"So they won't be lenient? It was a trick?"

He sighs and drops his gaze. "He attacked the alpha's family in their home. There is no leniency for traitors."

I flinch at that word.

"I wish there was more we could do," he says, and I almost believe he means it.

We step into the concrete chamber and the door slides shut behind us. No defining features distinguish one wall from another, apart from the glass square in the center of the wall to my right. The light in here is weirdly yellow, casting a sickly glow across the single window, and there's a strong industrial smell, like metal and dirt, and strangely I can't sense the presence of any other wolves above or below me.

Jasper steps to the window, which I see now is not a portal to the outside but rather a partition between this and a small room on the other side. A gamma wolf in uniform sits behind the glass reading a magazine and chewing gum.

"Jasper Apollo, son of Alpha Jericho," Jasper says to the man in the window. "I request access to the prisoner Omar Martinez."

The guard looks up, unimpressed. "Reason for the visit?"

"The alpha wishes me to interrogate the rogue, for personal reasons."

When Jasper drops Jericho's name like a hot tamale, the guard stiffens up in his chair. "ID?"

"I'm the alpha's son," Jasper says, a little pouty.

"It's just a precaution, sir. Even the alpha himself has to show ID."

"Fine." Jasper pulls out the same fob he used to open the door and swipes it over a black pad in the bottom right corner of the window. The guard turns to a screen, casting a blue light on his pale face.

"Very good, sir." He glances behind Jasper at me. "And this is?"

"Maximilian Remus," Jasper says proudly in a way that makes my stomach do a little flip. "My mate."

"He got any ID?"

Jasper glances at me hopefully, and frantically I pat myself down, searching for the wallet I know is in my left jeans pocket. I pull out my school ID and hold it up for the guard to see.

"It's all I have," I say. "Will this do?"

"That's fine," the guard says. I exhale with relief. "Prisoner 18157215 is in cell D-17 on floor minus-four. Take the elevator straight down. Your visitation time is thirty minutes, you will be notified when that time is up. You'll need to return here and register your IDs again to leave. Understood?"

"How is he?" I ask, before Jasper can say anything. "Is he being treated well?"

The guard gives me a bored look, like he couldn't give two shits. "The prisoners are treated equally and within the precautions set out under the Prisoners' Rights Act of '87."

"What does that mean?" I ask, stepping closer to the glass, a hint of danger in my voice.

"It means he gets fed three times a day and fresh sheets every seven days. Other than that, I really don't care."

"You're a real hero," I spit.

"Your visitation time has begun. Return here in thirty minutes or we will have you escorted out." The guard shifts his attention to Jasper. "And that goes for your whole party."

Jasper moves to step forward to hand this guy his ass, but before he can the guard smashes down on an unseen button and the wall to our right slides open, the concrete making an earsplitting scraping sound as it drags across the floor. Behind it is the inside of an elevator, all metal and chrome. The guard has already turned back to his magazine, so deciding it's not worth it, I take Jasper's arm and pull him inside. The elevator door slides shut behind us and we are swiftly lowered into the depths of the packhouse's basement.

The elevator clanks to a stop and the door behind us grinds open. The temperature down here is hotter than outside—the air no longer has the sterile scent of the entry room, instead it's thick with wolf sweat. All the layers of concrete must be to block out the wolf energy that's pulsing through the walls down here.

It's darker than I imagined. I thought the packhouse prison would be well lit, with decent ventilation and guards prowling everywhere. But instead I feel like I'm in the industrial basement of a warehouse somewhere on the outskirts of the city. The walls are plain cinder-block brick, with patches of damp where water is leaking from the pipes that run overhead. The lights must be super low watt, and only dot the long corridor that stretches out ahead of us every few feet.

"This is a prison?" I ask Jasper, who is staring down the hall with an unpleasant look on his face. Clearly he doesn't come down here all that much either.

"You thought it would be cheerier?"

"No, I...I just didn't think it would look like this. They really keep people here?"

"I guess so," Jasper says and takes his first step down the hall. "For what it's worth, I wasn't expecting this either."

A few feet away is a large panel of black glass that reaches from the floor to the ceiling, and next to it the number D-1, spray-painted on the brick with a stencil.

"Is that a cell?" I ask.

We both stare into the shadows before us and I can just make out more of the glass panels. They must be the cells. Picking up our pace, we make our way to the one that corresponds with Omar's cell number, D-17. We stop in front of the glass panel and a red light, from a black box on the ceiling, blinks to green. The color of the glass slowly changes, the black fading, until the glass is transparent.

"It's automated," I say to Jasper, who seems just as bewildered as me.

Behind the glass is a small gray room, complete with a low-hanging bed attached to the wall with a couple of chains, a chair and a metal desk on the opposite side, and in the back corner what I assume is a toilet. Omar is sitting on the bed, his back pressed against the wall, his knees to his chest. As the glass finally finishes transforming he looks up, anger and fear twisting his bruised and swollen features.

I step forward and place a hand on the glass.

"Oh my moon gods. What did they do to you?"

"Cuz," he says, his voice hoarse, "what are you doing here?"

"Your face," I say, unable to ignore the crusted blood under his lip, the purple and yellow protrusion around his eye.

He lifts a couple fingers and touches the bruise gingerly. "Oh this. It's nothing."

"It's not nothing."

"You're right." He nods into his knees. "They busted me up pretty good. Just the price of doing business I suppose."

"That's not okay."

"Oh yeah, what's he got to say about it?" He lifts his head at Jasper, who has remained a couple of steps behind me, lingering in the shadows.

"He didn't know, otherwise we wouldn't have let them do this to you." I turn and gesture for Jasper to step forward. "Right?"

He doesn't move, but the look on his face says it all. He's horrified.

"This is unacceptable," he says, or chokes is more like it. "I will make sure the wolves who did this are suitably reprimanded."

Omar lifts his brow. "Sure, sure." He returns his gaze to me. "What are you doing here anyhow?"

"I wanted to—to see you and make sure you're okay and..." Suddenly, in the face of Omar's brutalization and this rank excuse for a holding facility, the idea of asking Omar to explain himself seems ridiculous. No one, especially him, deserves to be treated this way.

"And to see why I did it?" he finishes the thought for me.

I press my other hand on the glass, wishing there wasn't this barrier between us.

"If you tell us we might be able to help you. Right, Jasp?"

He crosses his arms, but nods.

Omar scoffs. "I told your hounds everything, already. Then they did this. What's telling you going to help?"

"I don't know, it just—it has to. Please, let us try?"

His head flops backward onto the wall like he's thinking about it, then he turns and looks at me, studying my face. I try to convey just how serious I am, how badly I want to see him freed from this cell.

"Fine," he huffs. Omar stands and comes to the glass. Up close his wounds look even worse. And there are more, on his arms and neck, I couldn't see before. He's wearing a white tank top and where the tattoo on his shoulder is exposed is a deep, nasty-looking gash, like someone slashed him with a blade. "What do you want to know?"

"Just start from the beginning," I say. "Try to be detailed."

Omar takes a deep breath. "Okay. It all started when my pack threw me out and my mate rejected me to stay. I was homeless, more or less, with no way to make money or to buy food. I spent a long time traveling, a long time. It's easy to keep walking when you don't know where you're heading. I spent some time hunting on the prairies down south, living wild, you know? I thought maybe I could make a life like that but eventually food became too scarce and hard to find, and something, I don't know if it was boredom or loneliness, made me leave. I went in search of other wolves."

I glance at Jasper. Even rogues need to know they're not alone.

Omar continues, his voice tired and catching, but he pushes through. "Eventually I found this group of rogues."

"In Pittsburgh?" I ask. "Rogue City?"

"Yeah I guess. They all had this tattoo and I knew they were no good. Rough types mostly, the dregs of society. But they offered me a corner to sleep in and food if I hung out. I didn't realize their kindness came at a cost."

"Like what?"

"Small stuff at first. They gave me tasks, assignments. We'd rob some random gas station way out nowhere, scare campers away from their vehicles then take what we could. It was mostly food, small amounts of cash, just enough to get by. But things got more intense pretty quickly. The jobs got bigger. We'd terrorize towns on the outskirts of packs, raid their stores and homes. I didn't want to do any of it. But after spending all that time alone I didn't know where to go. And as long as we were only taking a little something, from wolves with too much anyway, it didn't seem so bad."

"Did you ever think of leaving?"

He puffs out some air. "Yeah, all the time. But where was I supposed to go? And besides, I saw what happened to wolves who tried to leave."

"What?" I press closer to the glass.

"They were beaten, left for dead."

"Right, of course you couldn't leave." I glance at Jasper once more. He seems unmoved, or maybe he's just trying to process all this new information.

"Eventually, after a couple of wolves tried to escape they gathered all of us in this shed." My mind goes back to the grain silo in Rogue City where Aisha was held—I wonder if that's the same place Omar is talking about. "They gave us this big dumb speech about how we owe them and how if we're ungrateful and try to leave they'll straight-up kill us. That's when they decided to mark each of us."

He reaches up to his tattoo, wincing where some pack wolf has torn through his skin.

"Once we'd been branded we were told we could never escape."

"So what about the attack at the packhouse? That seems like another escalation even for these guys."

"I remember the day it happened, I was sitting out on these stairs with a bucket trying to get my one set of jeans clean when this fancy car showed up and a man from the city got out."

Again I flash back to my time in Pittsburgh, that time we were there and we saw the car with the blackout windows. At the time I'd wrongly assumed Jericho was inside. Now the pieces start coming together.

"Mr. Peng," I say. "He came to hire the rogues to abduct Aisha."

"Huh?" Omar looks genuinely confused.

"You know, George? He was at the Sanc. He paid the rogues to kidnap Aisha when he thought she was Jasper's mate, then he hired them to attack us in the Hamptons."

"George never came to Rogue City."

My head feels like it's about to spin off my body. Jasper steps forward now, a perturbed look on his face.

"What do you mean George never came to Rogue City?" he asks, a deep rumble tumbling in his chest.

"We saw him," I say. "Or at least we saw his car."

Omar shakes his head.

"George may have been involved—I know he suggested we replace you Max, with his daughter. But he wasn't the one in charge."

"What do you mean?"

"You think a chauffeur could afford to pay off enough rogue mercenaries to infiltrate the alpha's house?" Omar's eyes dart from me to Jasper. "Don't tell me you all are that dopey."

Jasper and I are both dumbstruck. What is he talking about?

"George was just as much a pawn in this as me. The real wolf responsible is someone much more powerful."

THE PUPPET MASTER AND THE ROGUE ON THE STAIRS

Omar has just dropped a bombshell.

All this time we assumed George Peng was responsible for everything that happened to us last summer. He arranged with the rogues to kidnap Aisha, then he hired them to attack Jericho at his house and forced Eleanor to threaten Jasper into becoming her mate.

But now Omar is saying there was another person, a third party, who was responsible for all of it. Someone else who was pulling the strings all along.

"But who?" I ask. "If someone was controlling George then who?"

Omar's face drops. "I—I don't know his name. I only ever saw him."

"The rogues in charge didn't say anything? They never mentioned what his position was in the pack?"

Jasper is conspicuously quiet at my side. From the stern look of concentration on his face I can tell he's running the numbers, trying to compute this new information and make it make sense, trying to figure out who this mystery puppet master is.

"No," Omar says. "But I can remember what he looks like. I'll never forget that face as long as I live."

"Can you describe him?" Jasper asks.

Omar glances at Jasper then back at me and I see a sort of strange determination in his eyes, a spark that's been missing this whole conversation.

"No, but I can show you. Max, use your gift, find the memory."

"You want me to go looking around inside your head?"

"It's the easiest way."

I'm not sure about this, especially about doing something so intimate with Omar in front of Jasper, but I give him a questioning look and he nods.

"Okay," I say. I press a palm flat against the glass and Omar lifts his hand to meet mine. I close my eyes and try to concentrate.

Like a rocket I shoot through the darkness toward the red veins of consciousness, and faster than ever before I'm able to identify which belongs to Omar, like he's calling out to be found, signaling so I can find him. I reach out and grab it, and all of a sudden I'm pulled into a memory.

I'm sitting on a set of metal stairs. It's hot and dusty, the scent of petrol and wolf musk fills my senses. Below me is a bucket of warm, soapy water, in which I'm holding a pair of blue jeans. Suds cover my wrists as I rub to get them clean. Damn grease never gets out. Just then a black town car arrives, a trail of dirt and dust pluming out behind it. I recognize the car as belonging to Alpha Jericho, but Omar doesn't have the same recognition. I drop the jeans in the water and stand, wrapping my wet hands around the iron railing of the stairs. A driver wearing a gray uniform and dark sunglasses steps out of the driver's seat. It's not George, it's some other chauffeur I don't recognize. He opens the back door and finally a wolf I do recognize steps out.

His gray hair is swept back where it sprouts like waves on the sides, the remnants of what was once a thick head of blond. His blue suit is expensive and immaculately tailored. Sunlight reflects off his polished cuff links and patent leather shoes.

Walter Bridgers surveys the industrial site before him as his lips curl downward in an unpleasant snarl. He glances my way and my instinct is to duck, to hide, to not let him see me. But of course, I'm not here, this isn't happening now. It's Omar's memory and in it he doesn't move, just watches as the fancy pack wolf in the designer clothes turns to glare in his direction. His eyes lock with mine, with Omar's, and I want desperately to turn away, but Omar doesn't have the same impulse. He stares Walter down. From his expression, it's clear Walter has no idea who the random rogue on the stairs is. His sneer turns to a grin as he and Omar continue their staring contest, the grin of a hunter having laid eyes on his prey.

The roar of a large metal door rolling back breaks the tension in the air and Walter turns, ending their moment. Two familiar-looking rogues exit the nearby warehouse. One with a long scar on his face, the other in a denim jacket with the sleeves chopped off and the mark of his gang tattooed on his bicep. Two of the wolves who kidnapped Aisha. They shake Walter's hand and lead him inside.

As he goes the vision fades and I leave Omar's memories, my senses flooding back into my own body, and my eyes snap open.

"Max?" Jasper asks. "Are you—?"

"We have to get Omar out of here," I say.

Omar squints at me, concern wrinkling his forehead.

"Why? What did you see?" Jasper asks.

"Walter. He's behind all of this. He's the one who paid the rogues to attack us. He must have used George and Eleanor as a way to cover his tracks. He must be the one who's turning the other packs against us too."

"Why would he do that? He has too much invested in the pack, his whole family history is rooted in the Elite Pack. Why would he—?"

"Because he wants power," I say. "I don't need to read his mind to know that, it's clear as day on his face. Who do you think taught Clayton he was entitled to the whole world? Maybe he's convincing the other packs to align against us to oust your dad."

"But why try and mate me off to Eleanor?"

"It was never about that," I say. "Don't you see? He just wanted to show that we were weak. He wanted to show the other packs that we were vulnerable."

"Hey, uh, cuz," Omar jumps in. "I'm glad you all are figuring this out but what was that you were saying about getting me the heck out of here?"

"Right." I think back on the flashes of a vision I was able to sneak from Walter this afternoon. "I saw something."

"When?" Jasper asks.

"Earlier today, upstairs in your apartment. I snuck a look at Walter's memories and saw him making a deal with a super shifty-looking wolf. He gave him this big wad of cash. Like he was paying him for a job. He was being all sneaky and underhanded. Definitely up to no good."

"Come on, cuz, what's that got to do with me?"

"He saw you," I say. "The day you watched him arrive at Rogue City, he looked up and he saw you. He knows you know it was him."

"And you think—"

"He may have been paying that guy to take care of—"

"Loose ends," Jasper says, finishing the thought for all of us.

We each exchange glances. Then when it feels like we're all too scared and caught up in the moment to do anything, I can't hold back any longer.

"He's going to have Omar killed."

A moment passes between Jasper and me and I wish more than anything in the world right now I could know what he's thinking—if he's willing to go along with me and save Omar, even if that means stepping out of line and breaking the pack rules, or if he'll back away. I wait for an answer.

"Then we need to get Omar to safety," Jasper says finally, and both me and Omar release a long-held breath.

"Great," Omar says, looking around at his seemingly impenetrable cell. "How you gonna do that?"

Just then a beep sounds, reverberating down the hallway, and the little light on the black box overhead turns red.

"Oh no," I say. "Our time is up."

"Wait, what—?" Before Omar can finish speaking, the glass turns back to black and whatever technology was allowing us to hear him shuts off.

It's just Jasper and me left in a dark corridor.

"What do we do?" I ask.

Jasper looks up and down the hall, trying to think of a solution.

"Jasper Apollo and Maximilian Remus," the voice of the guard from earlier echoes from a speaker attached to the ceiling a few feet away. "Your visitation time is up. Please return to the entrance and log out."

He clicks his microphone off and Jasper and I meet eyes. Something tells me we're thinking the same thing.

"He said they'd escort us out," Jasper says.

"Which means there are more guards here somewhere," I add.

"And they might have access to the cells," Jasper concludes.

"It's a risk."

He takes my hand and gives it a squeeze. "It'll be worth it. All we have to do is stay right where we are."

"And let them come to us."

We nod in agreement and adrenaline rushes through my body.

The guard's microphone clicks on again, the rattle of static breaking the silence.

"Report back to the main office now!" the guard bellows.

Jasper smiles at me then turns to the speaker and a small camera he's spotted next to it.

"Come and get us!" he shouts.

And like clockwork the elevator doors at the end of the hall clank open. Two guards emerge in uniforms, with clear visors covering their faces. *They're wearing riot gear for Selene's sake!*

"Uh, Jasp," I say, my fingers grazing his elbow. "Maybe we didn't think this through. How do we get the keys off them?"

The guards growl as they approach ever so slowly. One of them whips out a baton, blue electricity fizzing at one end.

"Can you, ah, do your mind thing?" he asks. "Like with Clayton? Pull up some painful memory or...something?"

"Uh, let me see, I need to concentrate."

I snap my eyes shut and try to find peace to clear my mind and reach out for theirs but it doesn't come. I peek through one eye and the guards are nearly at us, their fangs fully extended.

"I'll give you some time," Jasper says, and steps forward, leaping into a run.

Before I know it he's barged into the guard on the left. The guard tumbles backward but Jasper somehow remains upright. The other, the one with the baton, swings his weapon back but Jasper manages to block the blow with his forearm. Meanwhile the tackled guard has gotten to his feet. Jasper engages them both at the same time, trying to keep them distracted while avoiding the zap of the electric baton.

"Anytime, Max," he says while dodging a punch.

Knowing there's no time left to gawk at my action hero boyfriend, I close my eyes again and reach out, and just like before, I whiz through the sea of wolf consciousnesses and zero in on the guards. I grasp onto their threads simultaneously and search frantically for anything I can use to bring them down—a death in the family, a rejection from a mate, anything painful that will render them useless. But there's nothing. These guys have either led very lucky or very uneventful lives. Then I notice something: they're both mated. And I wonder...

I pull a moment from both of their lives to the forefront, letting the emotion wash over me, pulling it into myself until it's amplified and fizzing. It's warm and comforting and makes me want to stay with it, bathe in their shared elation, but I know I can't—I throw it back into them.

My eyes dart open as they both stagger backward, away from Jasper, who stands hunched and huffing. Then one after the other the guards drop to their knees crying tears of joy.

"What did you do?" Jasper asks.

"I found the moment they met their mates and made them feel all that gooey goodness at once."

"You overcame them with…happiness?" Jasper asks, a little bemused but also sort of impressed. He rolls his eyes affectionately. "Of course you did."

"You can stop gushing now," I say. "We need the keys."

"Right."

Jasper is on the crying men in an instant. One even reaches out to him with a giddy smile on his tear-streaked face, laughing and spluttering like a big emotional mess. For a moment Jasper searches his body, trying to push his hands away, until finally he finds something. It's a fob similar to the one he used to enter the building.

"This might work," he says.

Next to Omar's cell panel is a small censor. Jasper swipes the fob over the censor and we wait with bated breath as the light on top blinks red, then orange, then…green!

The glass turns from black to clear and then rises in an instant into the ceiling. Omar is waiting, a wild, panicked look in his eyes. He surveys the scene around him.

"What's up with them?" he asks.

"Overcome with happiness," I say.

Omar smirks. "Cool, should we?"

"Yes," Jasper says, his voice suddenly low and serious. "They'll be locking this place down any second."

And with impeccable timing, like they can hear us or something, an alarm blares, the lights flash red, and the elevator begins to slide slowly shut.

"Move, now!" Jasper orders.

We sprint for the closing elevator, knowing if we don't make it we're stuck down here. But that's not an option. Accessing my superspeed, I take the lead and reach the elevator just before the door closes. I slide between it and the wall and hold it open. It takes all the strength in my lanky arms to keep the thing from closing and crushing me but I manage to just long enough for Omar and Jasper to dive through. The door slams shut with a bang.

For a second we stand in the elevator not knowing what to do.

"Won't they just stop the elevator from working so they can trap us here?" Omar says.

"Maybe," Jasper says, running a thinking hand through his hair. "But if this fob was able to unlock a cell maybe it can override the elevator too?"

He swipes at another panel but it doesn't do anything. The light blinks red, time after time.

"Don't you have some alpha authority or something?" Omar asks, leaning against the back wall. "Can't you override the system?"

"It doesn't work like that," Jasper says.

"Man, sucks to be you."

Jasper turns in a circle looking for some way to get this dumb elevator to move but there doesn't seem to be anything he can do.

"Nothing?" I ask.

He shakes his head. "This place will be flooding with gammas. There's no way we can get past that many wolves."

Omar lets his head flop against the wall. "Great plan, boyos."

"Wait," I say. "You said this place will be flooded with wolves, right?"

"Any second now," Jasper responds.

"When we were upstairs I couldn't sense anything, like the walls were built to block out any wolf energy. But down here it was different. If there are more wolves up there now though the energy will be stronger—maybe if I can latch on to it I can do something."

"Do you think you're up to that?" Jasper says.

No, no I really do not. "There's no other option."

"We can help," Omar says. "Use our energy to amplify your own."

"I can do that?"

"That's how you were able to access the lunar plane. Yoki and I transferred some of our energy to you."

"Is that why you fell asleep?"

"Nah." He shrugs. "You were out for so long and I was mad tired."

"Well," I say, glancing between them both, "if you think it will help."

"It will," Omar says and holds out his hand.

I glance at Jasper, swallow, and then take Omar's hand. I reach out for Jasper on my other side and he takes a breath before returning the gesture. Then Omar holds out his free hand, nodding at Jasper to take it. Jasper stares at it like it's a dead fish.

"Come on, dude. We need to complete the circle."

Jasper presses his lips together, settles his face, and takes Omar's hand.

"Good," Omar says calmly. "Now try and gather the energy in your core, channel your inner wolf, and when you have it centered, send it to Max. Max, you'll know when the time is right. And uh"—he looks at Jasper once more—"it helps if you close your eyes."

Jasper gives a subtle roll of his eyes first, but does what he's told. Next Omar gives me a reassuring nod and closes his. Then I close mine.

At first nothing happens. I compare the feel of Omar's rougher hand and Jasper's more slender hand and how they feel in mine. I notice Jasper twitching and give him a calming squeeze to let him know I'm here. My fingers begin to tingle, then my palms and wrists, and then suddenly, pulsing energy rushes up through my arms, flooding my torso and running down to my legs. Their energies wash over me, until they flow inside me like blood. Each has its own distinctive feel, but as they mingle and mix, I stop keeping track of whose is whose, and as their energy settles with my own, I begin to lose all sense of where I end and where Omar and Jasper begin. Our energies have become one.

That's when I know to reach out.

I expand my consciousness up and out like a mushroom cloud, searching in all directions for other wolves. As I reach the ground floor I'm suddenly hit with a wall of energy. That must be the entrance chamber. It's now filled with at least thirty strong wolves, waiting with tense muscles and set jaws. I don't attack them, instead I delve into their subconsciousness, I speak with their inner wolves, I pat their heads and whisper calmly to them, until one by one they fall asleep.

The guard behind the glass is the only one I leave awake. Him I coax into pressing the necessary buttons to activate the elevator and bring us back to ground level.

I open my eyes as we arrive and the doors slide open. Sleepily Omar and Jasper open their eyes as well. Jasper looks especially groggy, his eyes red and droopy, and Omar looks a little drunk, like one side of his face is too tired to move.

"Did we do it?" Jasper asks.

"Almost," I say.

Feeling strong, galvanized even, I step from the elevator and make my way through the carpet of sleeping guards.

"They look sort of cute," Omar says, following behind.

"You!" the guard in the window shouts. "You can't do this! When the alpha hears about this you'll be—"

"*Silence*," Jasper commands in his alpha voice, stepping forward. He's given an order and the guard has no choice but to submit. "*Open the door.*"

The muscles in the guard's face twitch as his cheeks turn pink. Clearly, he's struggling against the direct order from his future alpha. But the part of him that's a wolf, that's part of this pack, knows not to disobey his superior. He hits whatever buttons he needs to to open the door, and before Jasper can lose control or any of the other guards wake up, we hightail it out of there.

"Where will you go?" I ask Omar as the crowds of Grand Central rush like rapids around us. We ran straight here from the packhouse, knowing we needed to get Omar as far from the city, from Walter and his assassin for hire, as possible. "Back to the Sanc?"

"No," Omar says. "I'll only bring trouble with me. They don't need any more upheaval."

"Then where?"

Omar glances at the departures board as some passing commuter knocks into me.

"I'll head north," he says. "Maybe cross the border into Canada, see what it's like for rogues up there."

"I—I don't know when I'll see you again," I say, noticing the way Jasper clears his throat subtly.

Omar places one of his sturdy hands on my shoulder. "You can always find me, cuz." With the same hand he taps one finger against his forehead. "We're all connected, right?"

"Right."

"Jasp." Omar turns to my mate, who has been hanging out a couple steps away. "You're a decent guy. Maybe with you as a leader this pack has a chance of not sucking."

Jasper's voice catches a little in his throat. "Thanks."

"You take care of him."

"I will."

"Cuz. It's been real. Keep up the meditation. Stay true to your inner wolf. Don't let those walls get in your way. You're going to do amazing things."

I can't help the tears welling in my eyes. "Be safe," I tell Omar, then I give him a super tight hug.

He winces and I let him go.

"Sorry, I forgot about the bruises."

"Nothing a bit of time won't fix."

For a second we stand under the starry ceiling, letting the crowds drift by, not quite ready to leave just yet. Then Jasper clears his throat.

"You should probably get going," he says. "It's not safe."

"You're right," Omar says. He steps away then looks back one last time. "You're a cute couple. I hope there's someone like that out there for me."

"There is," I say. "I promise."

"I'll hold you to that."

And with two steps Omar is gone, disappeared behind the streams of travelers making their way to their destinations. Jasper gives me a second before coming to stand by my side.

"He'll be okay," he says.

I try to wipe an errant tear away and pass it off as if I'm scratching my face with the back of my hand. "I know."

"We should get moving too," he says. "I need to figure out how to explain all this to my dad."

"Right."

From Grand Central we walk across town back to the packhouse and Jasper's apartment. For most of the journey we walk in silence. I know Jasper must be trying to figure out the exact way to tell his dad that one of his closest advisers has betrayed him, not to mention that we broke a confessed criminal out of the packhouse's holding facility and knocked out a whole battalion of wolf guards. But I'm also worried about what he suspects Omar might mean to me.

When we approach his block I can't take the suspense anymore.

"Hey, I just want you to know what you did back there—I really appreciate it. And just so you know, with Omar, I—I do care about him, but it's not like what I have with you—it's not like—"

Jasper stops walking, a small smile threatening to turn into a bigger one on his lips.

"You don't have to explain," he says. "I trust you. And I trust your judgment. Omar is a good man. And you're allowed to care about other people."

"So you're okay?"

"I'm fine. In fact, I've never felt more certain about things—things I've been torn up about for a long, long time. That's because of you." He slides his hands into mine. "And back there, I felt connected to you in a way I never had before. Nothing can take that away."

"Good," I say. "Because I feel the same, I feel like we were really a team."

"An amazing team."

"Yeah we actually sort of kicked butt."

"We slayed."

I can't help but laugh. Did Jasper just say *slay*?

"Okay, slay," I tease. He laughs and blushes something stupid. "You're very cute when you're embarrassed, did you know that?"

"No I didn't."

"Well, you are. Like, incredibly."

"You're cute all the time."

"Well." I shrug like I just can't help it.

We walk a little farther.

"Jasper, I want you to know I'm ready now, to be a part of your life and everything that entails, but also I want to do more, I want to use the gifts I have to help people. No more running away. I want to stay and be in it, really in it."

"Me too," he says, stopping once more to lean in and kiss me.

"I love you, Max," he says as he pulls away.

"I love—"

Something catches my attention and I stop mid-sentence. A shadow darts across the windows of a closed store across the road and before I can do anything, the man in the leather coat with the greasy ponytail appears in the street. He rushes at us, pulling something from inside his jacket. My heart explodes when I see the gun.

"Jasper, watch out!"

As the gunshot rings out I shove Jasper away from me and he stumbles into the street. The gunman remains holding the smoking firearm in front of him. He sneers at me and my stomach roils, then he dashes off, vanishing around a corner.

I reach down and feel my stomach, my torso, expecting to find a bullet wound, but I'm fine. I breathe a sigh of relief.

"Jasper, are you...?"

In the middle of the street, Jasper is standing looking down at where his hands are clutching his stomach. A red blossom is blooming outward, staining his shirt. He lifts his head, panicked and confused, and our eyes lock.

"Jasper? Jasp?"
He crumbles, falling to the street, and I run to him.
"JASPER!"

WAILING TO THE MOON

Jasper's blood covers my hands. There's so much of it, pouring out of him, staining my shirt, my jeans. His body is heavy in my lap. I hold him tightly, trying to support his head, which he can no longer hold up on his own. His eyes are halfway shut, his mouth open in a silent scream of pain. His breaths are short and shallow. His face is ghostly pale.

"Jasper, hold on," I say. "The ambulance is on its way."

I don't know how I managed to speak calmly enough to the emergency services operator to get an ambulance here but somehow, maybe before the shock set in, I was able to. My phone lies beside me now, the screen smeared in red.

"Please, don't die," I whisper into Jasper's hair as I clutch his head to my chest. "Do you hear me? You're not allowed to die."

In my arms Jasper tenses, he struggles to keep his eyes open, looking around like he's having trouble focusing. Then finally his gaze lands on my face and he almost smiles...almost. With a shaking hand he tries to touch my face, like he needs confirmation I'm really here.

"M-Ma..."

He starts to say my name but can't get it out before he convulses in pain. His eyes slam shut. His body judders, tenses then relaxes, and he drops limply. His head falls back and his eyes close.

"Jasper?" I try to shake him gently, just enough to keep him here, awake—alive. "Jasper, no! Jasper, please!"

The hand he reached for my face with falls sideways, hitting the road. I rake my fingers over his cheeks.

"Jasp, wake up. You have to wake up."

He doesn't respond.

"No."

There's so much blood. It's in his hair, slicking the strands of midnight black together. It's on his perfect, pale-freckled cheeks. It's drenched his clothes and stained the pavement.

"NO!"

As all hope seems to drain from me, I hear the faint wail of sirens. Eventually the street becomes lit in flashing red and blue.

I barely notice as the paramedics haul me to my feet and go to work on Jasper.

All I can think about is the blood that's seeped into my clothes.

So much blood.

So much...

Someone should have been here by now.

I sit alone on one of the cold plastic chairs lining the hospital corridor. Nurses and doctors whoosh past, off to save lives.

Have they saved his yet?

Where is everyone?

The sterile smell of disinfectant cloaks all manner of human maladies. But not well enough that I can't distinguish the stink of illness and death.

A woman wheels an old man in a plaid dressing gown by in a wheelchair, he's hooked up to an IV that drags along beside him. The doors at the end of the corridor are thrown open, slamming as they hit the walls, and a gurney is pushed through carrying another patient. The white hospital sheets are stained pink.

I look down at my hands. Jasper's blood has dried and is beginning to crack.

I should go get cleaned up.

They told me he could be in surgery for a while.

I should get cleaned up, I don't want to be a mess when he wakes up.

If he…

Where is everyone? Why hasn't anyone else come yet?

I called his dad. I called Aisha and Melissa. I called my parents.

Someone should have been here by now.

"Max?"

From some far-off place I hear my name.

"Max?"

I hear it again and am able to pull my attention to the blurred figure in front of me. My tired eyes take a moment to adjust and then all of a sudden the world comes rushing back. The beeps of heart monitors, the wheels of gurneys, the doors, the nurses at their station, the clunk of a can hitting the drawer of a vending machine. I haven't moved since they plonked me on a chair in this hallway.

Blood still stains my clothes, only now it's hard and sticky. In front of me is a large dark figure, slowly coming into focus.

"Max, are you okay?"

The resonant boom of the alpha's voice pulls me back to reality.

"Jericho?" I ask, sounding like I haven't spoken in a thousand years.

"Yes, son. It's me." Jericho's face looms too large in my vision, his voice is loud and stings my eardrums. "I'm sorry I wasn't here sooner, I came as fast as I could. Are you okay?"

I pick at a piece of dried blood, watching as it flakes away and falls to the ground.

"Yes—I—I'm sorry, I should have gotten cleaned up—I..." It suddenly occurs to me I have no idea what time it is. "What's happening?" I ask, eyes suddenly wide, struggling to my feet despite my aching, numb limbs. "Is he out yet? Is he...?"

Jericho steadies me with his large hands and holds me in place. "I just spoke with the nurses. He's still in surgery. The internal bleeding is bad and there is damage to his organs. They're doing everything they can."

"He's not—they're still—" I can't seem to finish a sentence or form a complete thought. "Is he—?"

"I'm sorry you had to go through this," Jericho says. "And I know you're shaken but I need to ask you some questions."

"Questions?" I shake my bewildered head.

"Yes, Max. We need to know what happened. But"—Jericho glances in both directions—"not here. Can you walk?"

I have no idea but I nod anyway. "Uh-huh."

Jericho keeps his sturdy arm around me as he leads me to an empty room, flicks on the light, and closes the door behind us. A hospital bed sits unmade in the center, the monitors to the side switched off, the wires hanging loose, not attached to anything. I wonder whether or not the last person to use that bed got better.

"Max?" Jericho asks, coming to face me.

"Whose room is this?"

A confused flash crosses Jericho's face. "I need you to concentrate," he says, once again placing a firm hand on my shoulder. "Tell me everything you remember."

The gunman appears in my vision, darting from the shadows, the sound of the shot reverberates in my ears, my heart breaks at Jasper's face as he falls into the road. I clutch my chest and stumble backward. Jericho catches me.

"Max, I know it's hard. But it's important we catch the person responsible for this."

"Responsible?"

The word is familiar but my addled brain can't quite compute. Is the gunman responsible? Walter? Or is it Omar for what he did? Jasper for helping me break him out of jail? Or is it me? Did I do this to Jasper? Is that why he's left me? Why he's...

"Max, who did this? Who shot Jasper?"

My eyes shoot to Jericho's and suddenly I feel a sense of clarity dawning. There is only one person responsible for this and I want to see him ended.

"Walter," I say. "Walter Bridgers did this. He hired someone to shoot Jasper. We thought he was planning to kill Omar because he knew what Walter did, because he was the one who hired the rogues to attack the packhouse, but we were wrong. He wanted to kill Jasper because he wants to take your place."

My sudden verboseness must shock Jericho because he takes his hands away from me and studies my face carefully.

"That is a grave accusation, Max. Are you sure?"

"I'm sure," I say as firmly as I can despite my shaking right leg and trembling hands. "He hired a rogue to shoot Jasper. He's been going behind your back and corrupting the aligned packs against you."

"If this is true then we may be in bigger trouble than I thought." He pulls out his phone and hits some buttons. "Salazar, we need to speak. Meet me at the packhouse as soon as you get this."

He pockets his phone and eyes the door.

"You're leaving?" I ask. "What's wrong with you? Your son is dying and you're still wrapped up thinking about the pack? How can you care about any of that now? How could you?"

Jericho levels me with an intense stare. "I understand your concern, Max. But if I don't act now we could be ruined. If there's one thing I can do for Jasper, it's to make damn sure there's still a pack for him to return to when he wakes up."

"*If* he wakes up!"

He grits his teeth as if he's fighting the same doubts as me but is too scared to let it show.

"My son is an Apollo," Jericho says. "It will take more than a single gunshot to take him down. I've instructed the nurses to notify me when Jasper's condition changes. Until then I need to see to business."

He moves to step past me as my lip quivers uncontrollably.

"Thank you," he says when he reaches my side. He won't look at me and I won't look at him. "For what you've done for my son. I'm sorry you have to go through this. Is there…do you have anyone coming to keep you company?"

"Just go," I say. "I'll be fine."

His hand lands on my shoulder one more time and I don't sluff it off, I let it lie there, futile, pointless, until he leaves.

When Jericho is gone I stagger back to the corridor. Some kid is sitting in my seat reading a book, swinging his feet that don't reach the floor. His dad is next to him clicking away on his phone.

While I'm staring at this guy my phone buzzes in my pocket. I pull it out and see Aisha is FaceTiming me.

"Hey," she says, puffing like she's out of breath, the city bouncing behind her as she walks. "How is he?"

"I don't know, he's—he's still in surgery."

"Shit. Look, I'm on my way. The subway is a mess though, delays and weekend closures, and…ah!" Aisha turns to call after the moron who bumped into her. "Watch it!" She turns back to the camera, shaking her head. "Some people. Anyway, whatever, I jumped off the train but I'm still downtown. I'm trying to get a cab but it's a ghost town out here tonight."

Hearing this is almost too much for me to bear. I lean, basically fall, onto the wall behind me, rubbing my stinging eyes.

"I'll be there as soon as I can, okay, kid? Can you hold on for me?"

"We thought we could just run away and avoid all this," I say, unable to hold back the torrent of tears.

"I know, sweety."

"I thought things were going to get better when we came back. I thought it would be different."

"I know. I know. It's going to be all right though. He's tough. He'll pull through."

I stare into my phone screen, letting the tears drip off my chin. "We were just...after everything...we were just figuring things out, you know?"

"Yeah? That's great."

"We were finally on the same page and now..."

"What, sweety?"

"What if he's...? What if he...?"

"He won't."

"I don't want to lose him."

My knees give out and I slide down the wall until I'm bundled on the floor. People pass but I ignore them and their pitying glances.

"You're strong, Maxie. You're so strong. Whatever..." She pauses, whips a stray braid out of her face, and takes a breath. "Whatever happens...you're going to be fine. You have me and Katie and your parents. And you're strong, Maxie. But just...try to stay positive okay? Don't count him out just yet."

"There was so much blood."

"I know."

I wipe my face, which is all scrunched up and hot. Tears and snot come away with my hand.

"I just wish I could talk to him."

"What would you say...?" she asks, but I can barely hear her over the static as the call starts breaking up. "Max—Maxie, what wo—would—you—ay?"

The calls drops out.

"Aisha?"

For a moment I stare at the blank screen wondering where she went, where she is. It's well after midnight and I can't quite seem to figure out where the time has gone. I'm not even sure when I arrived at the hospital in the ambulance, my hand clutching onto Jasper's.

Over on the seats the kid has curled up in a ball with his head on his dad's knee. Little guy must be tired. I don't know what to do but I know Aisha was right, I shouldn't give up just yet. I need to be strong.

Slowly, I press against the wall and straighten my legs until I'm back standing.

I don't know where to go but I can't just sit here any longer.

Behind the nurses' station is the nurse I spoke to earlier. She's flipping through some papers on a clipboard and marking them with a pen when I approach.

"Hi," I say, sniffing to clear my blocked nose. "I was just wondering if there was any news about Jasper Apollo?"

She looks up with kind eyes, her head tilted to the side like an apology.

"I'm so sorry," she says, and my heart freezes, I hold my breath. "He's still in surgery." I exhale as my blood starts pumping once more. "It could be awhile. I'll let you know the second I have some news. Are you here by yourself? Do you need me to call anyone?"

"No, that's fine," I say, turning away. There's only one person I want to speak to anyway. "Thanks."

Without knowing where I'm going, I take off walking.

The moon is hanging low in the sky, almost like it's in mourning. But that's ridiculous and a little preemptive, I try to remind myself.

Somehow, I've ended up on the roof of the hospital. My aimless wandering led me to a set of stairs and now this. Manhattan stretches out on all sides, strangely quiet. I guess maybe the city does sleep sometimes.

It might just be me, maybe my eyes are tired and blurred from crying and staring, but the moon seems like it has a reddish hue at the edges.

"Are you watching?!" I cry at the waning crescent. "Did you know this was going to happen? Huh?"

The moon is silent. If Selene is up there watching, she's not talking back. Not this time.

"Why didn't you stop this?! You could have stopped this!"

The blinking lights of a plane pass by, the passengers unaware of the teen werewolf hollering at the moon.

"You can save him, right?" I continue pointlessly. "Please!" Nothing. "*PLEASE*! Save him!"

It's not like I'm expecting the moon to talk or for Jasper to suddenly show up, magicked here out of thin air. But I can't help thinking, *What are the moon gods for if not to help us in times like these?*

I wait anxiously, the cool evening helping to calm my anxious muscles, even though I know nothing is going to happen. Nothing is ever going to happen.

"Aren't you listening?! Don't you listen?"

I'm reminded of my own howl, piercing through my subconscious, trying to talk to me. My own wolf wailing in pain and how I ignored him for so long—how I didn't even know he was calling until I was face-to-face with him.

I haven't heard that howl since my moonwalk. Is that because we're properly attuned now? One being moving through this plane and the next?

Or maybe I've been ignoring him still. If I were to access the lunar plane now, what would he say?

Then it hits me. I've been wandering around this hospital waiting for Jasper to wake up and reach out to me. I've been hoping for someone to come and save me, to bolster me up and keep me aloft. But I don't need to wait for a call to answer. I am the call. And the response. And I have everything I need.

On the hard concrete roof I sit cross-legged with my hands resting on my knees, palms to the sky. Jasper and I haven't managed to mind-link yet, but that was before, before everything we've been through, before everything we experienced at the Sanc, before we were seeing things eye to eye.

And maybe we aren't quite there yet. Maybe we still have a ways to go. After all we're different people, with different experiences and traumas and ideas and opinions. But if there's any hope...

I close my eyes and reach out into the lunar consciousness, hoping and reaching and letting my guard down.

Concentrate. Connect.

Suddenly, I sense a presence, so calm and comforting and familiar.

I turn to him, and he speaks:

"Max?"

ACKNOWLEDGMENTS

I could never have imagined when Max and Jasper first entered my imagination that this cute little love story would turn into what it's become today. Drawing from my experience as a ghost writer in the shifter/werewolf space, I wanted to take familiar tropes and use them in a queer way to examine how they worked as a queer narrative. Which is why the first book in this series is perhaps more familiar in structure to some other romance novels.

In the sequel and now in this book I have been able to stretch my literary muscles to use the romantic foundations of the first book and examine what it means to be a queer young person and to define oneself within relationships, —which can be incredibly rewarding but also traumatic— as an individual, and as part of a wider queer community.

For me being a part of the queer community has given me great joy and strength and helped me to figure out who I am, apart from my beloved partner, and within this crazy, messed up, and sometimes terrifying world. In this way Max's journey is similar to mine and all of ours. Max is learning that there are people out there he can relate to, who are full of love, and who need him, a person of privilege, to stand up for them.

And so I have dedicated this book to the rogues, the mystics, and the warriors because this is a book and a series that is written with the queer community in mind, and as this is the third book (and I'm running out of individual names to mention) in these acknowledgements I want to thank the queer community, for keeping me afloat, for giving me spirit, and gifting me with purpose.

I also want to thank those who have found and championed these books, who have reached out with kind words, shared their art with me (always wild to see my characters through the lens of other people's art!), and for whom these books have become a part of their queer experience.

I hope they are strengthening and enlivening, romantic and joyful, and cathartic.

Your support and enthusiasm are what makes this process so worthwhile. And keeps me at my computer figuring out how to continue Max and Jasper's story.

I would be remiss not to mention the folks at Tiny Ghost Press, who are the best collaborators and who have helped guide me and these books in the right direction and who have shown all the care in the world for these characters and this story. So thank you Joshua Dean Perry, Reuben Davies-Hoare, and Thomas Shah.

Huge thanks also to Dana Keller, the most amazing copy editor, for polishing and making this book shine. Your care and attention to detail always has me floored.

And of course, to Kayleigh Fine who, in my humble opinion, is the greatest living artist today. You continue to bring Max and Jasper to life in new and stunning ways. I think you've truly outdone yourself with this cover. It might be my fave of them all...so far ;). Thank you!

And finally, to swing back to the queer community I want to thank the readers once more, thank you for staying with me and this story, I'm sorry for all the cliff hangers, but you'll be pleased to know there is (at least) one more chapter to go in this story, and I so appreciate you going on this ride with me. I hope you'll be there with me to see how it ends.

Don't forget to commune with your wolf selves and thanks for howling with me.

MORE BOOKS FROM TINY GHOST PR

AVAILABLE NOW WHEREVER BOOKS ARE SO

FOR MORE SPOOKY QUEER STORIES SIGN UP FOR OU
NEWSLETTER AND FOLLOW US ON SOCIAL MEDIA

WWW.TINYGHOSTPRESS.COM

@TINYGHOSTPRESS

www.ingramcontent.com/pod-product-compliance
Lightning Source LLC
Chambersburg PA
CBHW021216220726

48287CB00015B/1420